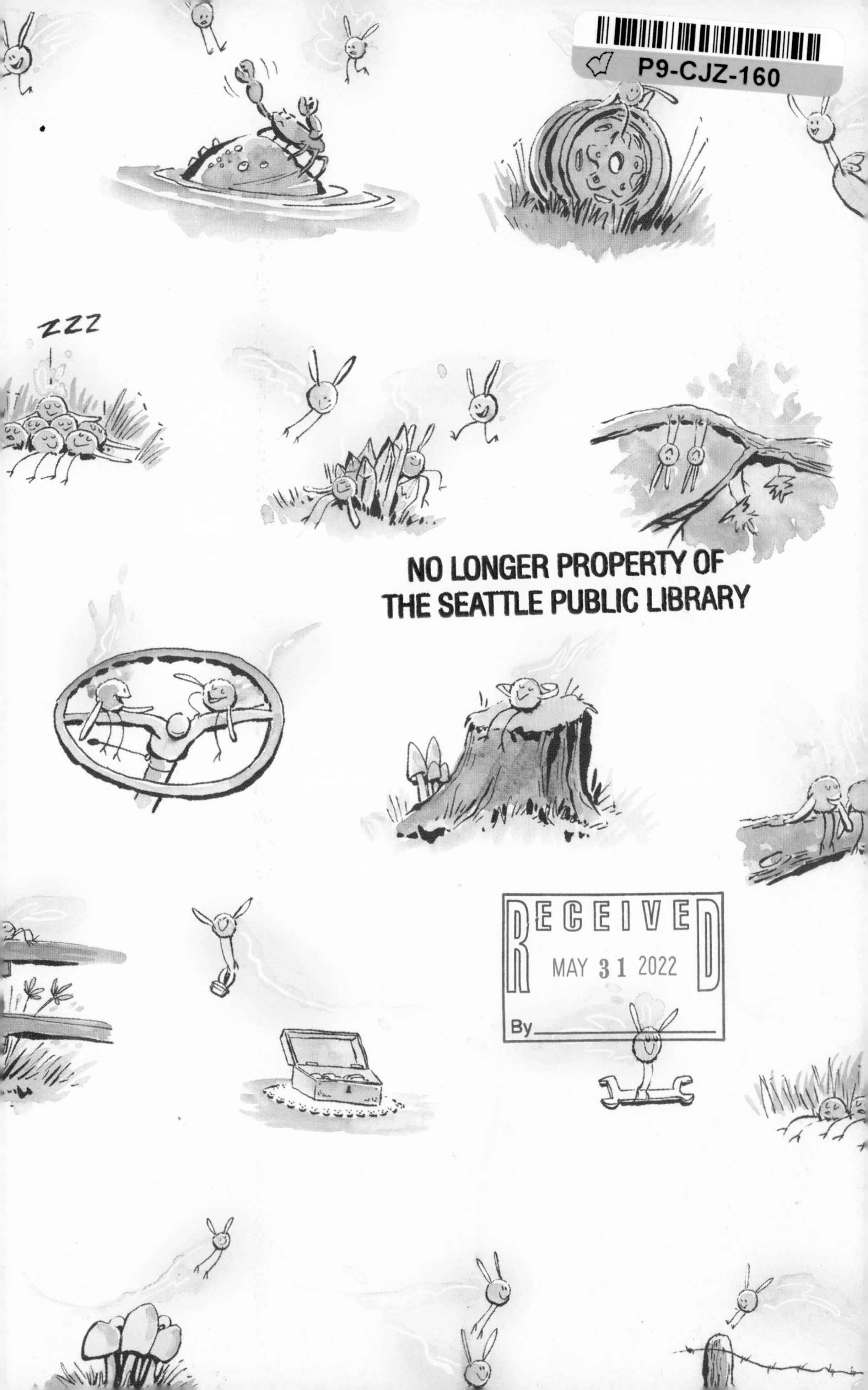
ZZZ

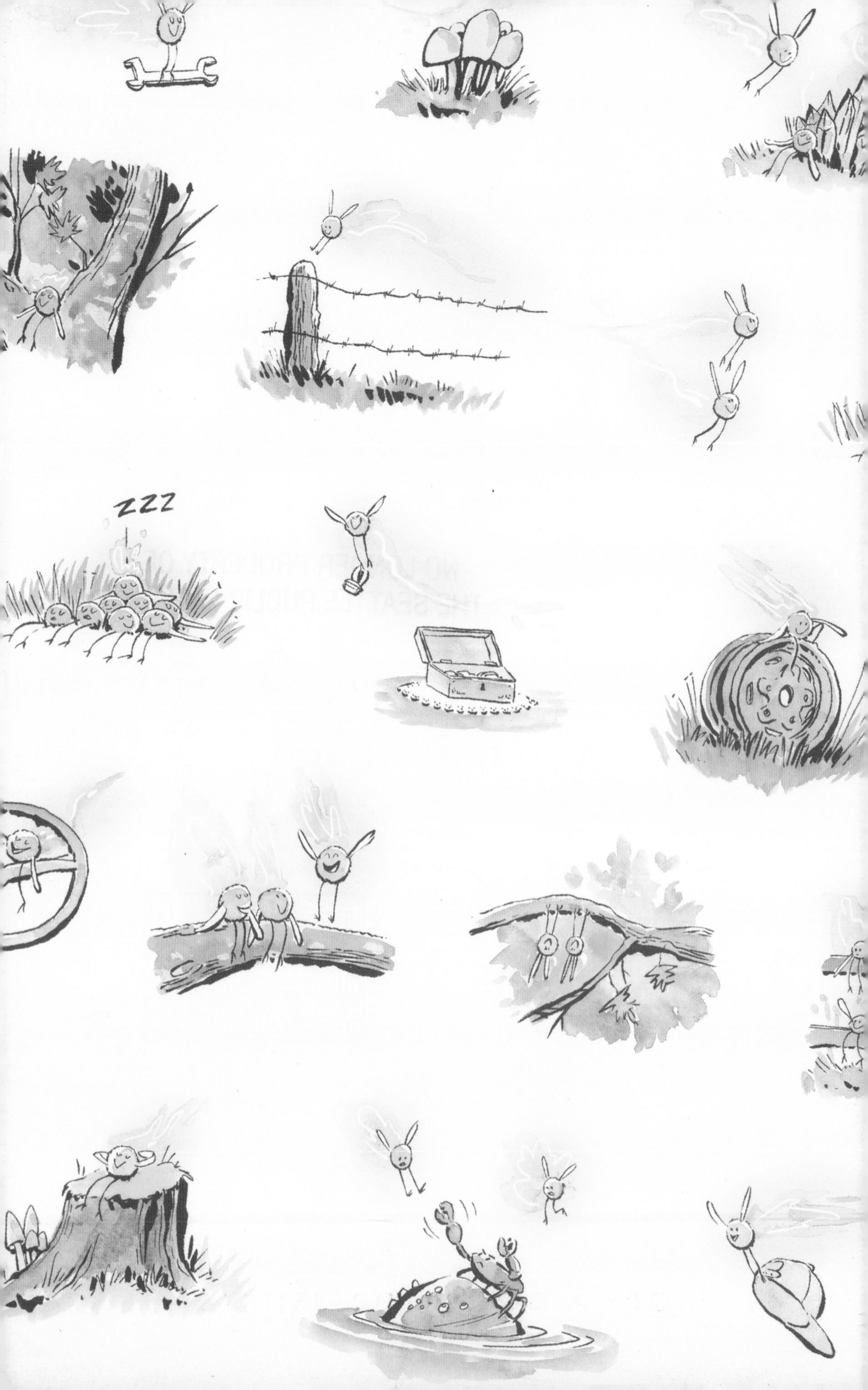
ZZZ

Hermit Hill

SUEÑO BAY ADVENTURES  3

MIKE DEAS AND NANCY DEAS

ORCA BOOK PUBLISHERS

Published in Canada and the United States in 2022 by Orca Book Publishers.
orcabook.com

Library and Archives Canada Cataloguing in Publication
Title: Hermit Hill / Mike Deas and Nancy Deas.
Names: Deas, Mike, 1982– author, illustrator. | Deas, Nancy, author.
Series: Deas, Mike, 1982– Sueño Bay adventures ; 3.
Description: Series statement: Sueño Bay adventures ; 3
Identifiers: Canadiana (print) 20210247398 | Canadiana (ebook) 2021024741x |
ISBN 9781459831490 (softcover) | ISBN 9781459831506 (PDF)
Subjects: LCGFT: Graphic novels. | LCGFT: Action and adventure comics. |
LCGFT: Comics (Graphic works)
Classification: LCC PN6733.D43 H47 2022 | DDC j741.5/971—dc23

Library of Congress Control Number: 2021941165

Summary: In this graphic novel for early middle readers, the youngest
member of a ragtag crew of kids feels left out of a big project and finds
himself a group of magical Moon Creatures to lord over.

Orca Book Publishers is committed to reducing the consumption of nonrenewable resources in
the making of our books. We make every effort to use materials that support a sustainable future.

Orca Book Publishers gratefully acknowledges the support for its publishing programs provided
by the following agencies: the Government of Canada, the Canada Council for the Arts and the
Province of British Columbia through the BC Arts Council and the Book Publishing Tax Credit.

Cover and interior illustrations by Mike Deas

Design by Jenn Playford
Layout by Dahlia Yuen
Edited by Liz Kemp
Photos of Mike Deas and Nancy Deas by Billie Woods

Printed and bound in South Korea.

25 24 23 22 • 1 2 3 4

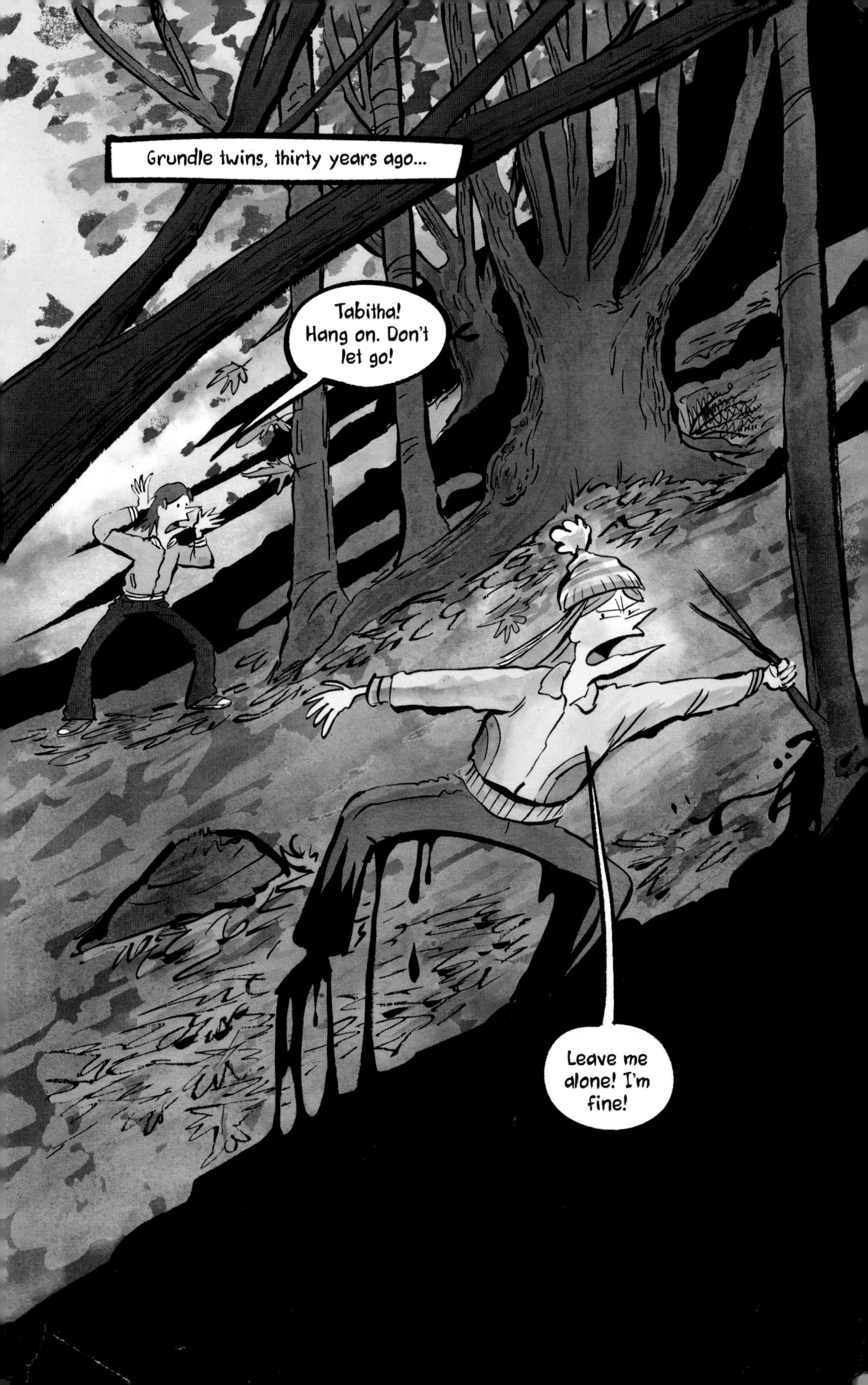
Grundle twins, thirty years ago...
Tabitha! Hang on. Don't let go!
Leave me alone! I'm fine!

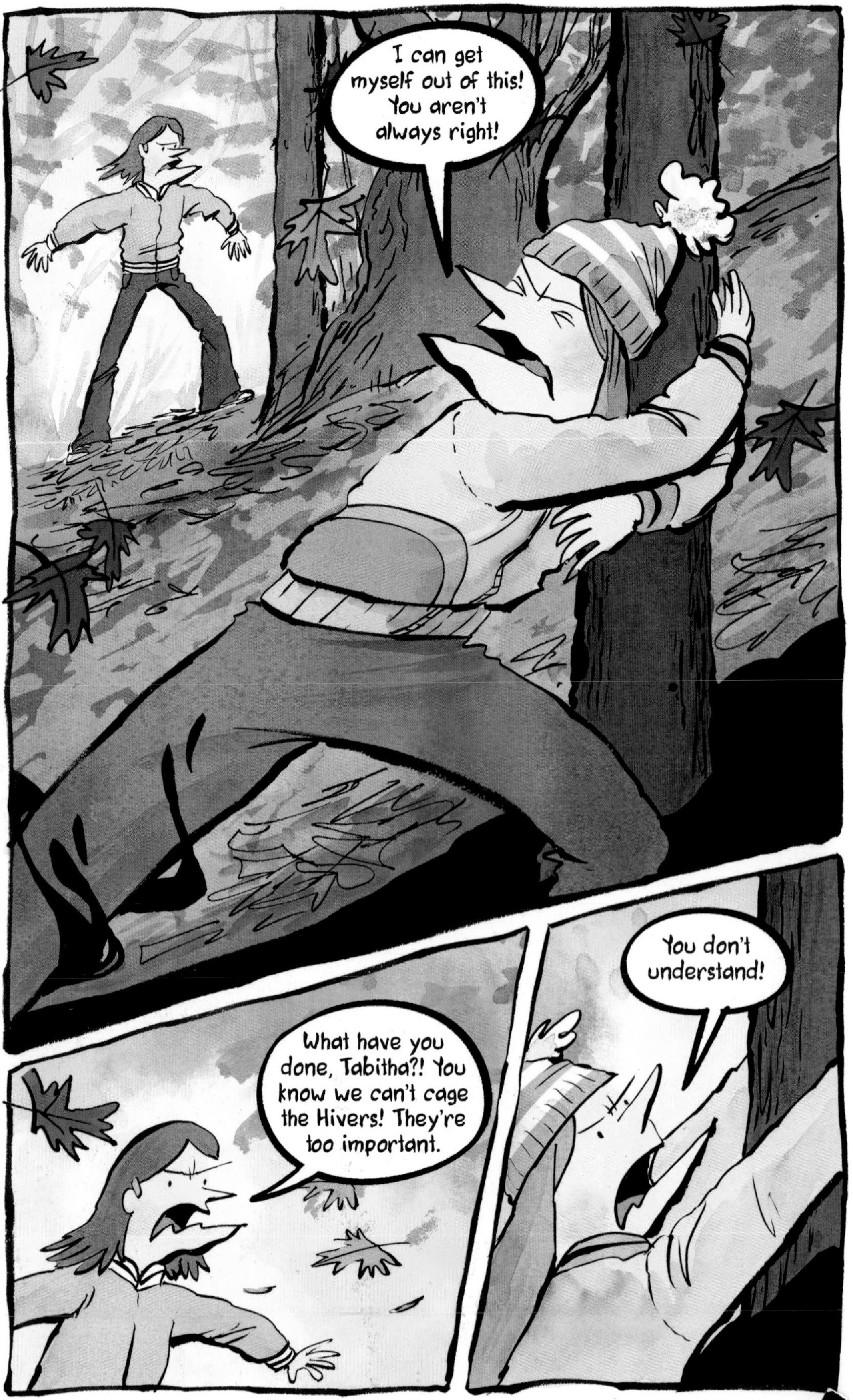
I can get myself out of this! You aren't always right!
What have you done, Tabitha?! You know we can't cage the Hivers! They're too important.
You don't understand!

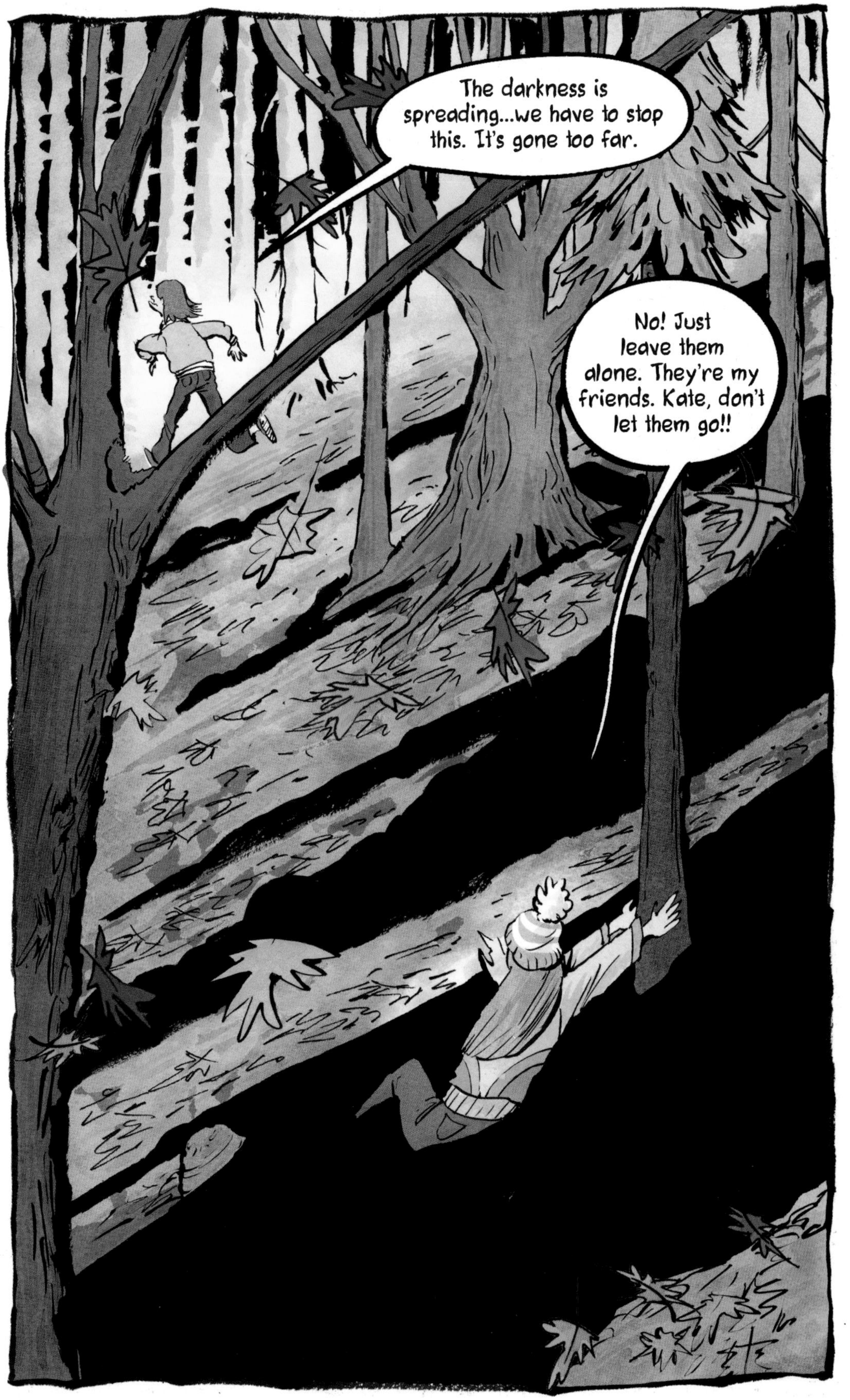
The darkness is spreading...we have to stop this. It's gone too far.
No! Just leave them alone. They're my friends. Kate, don't let them go!!

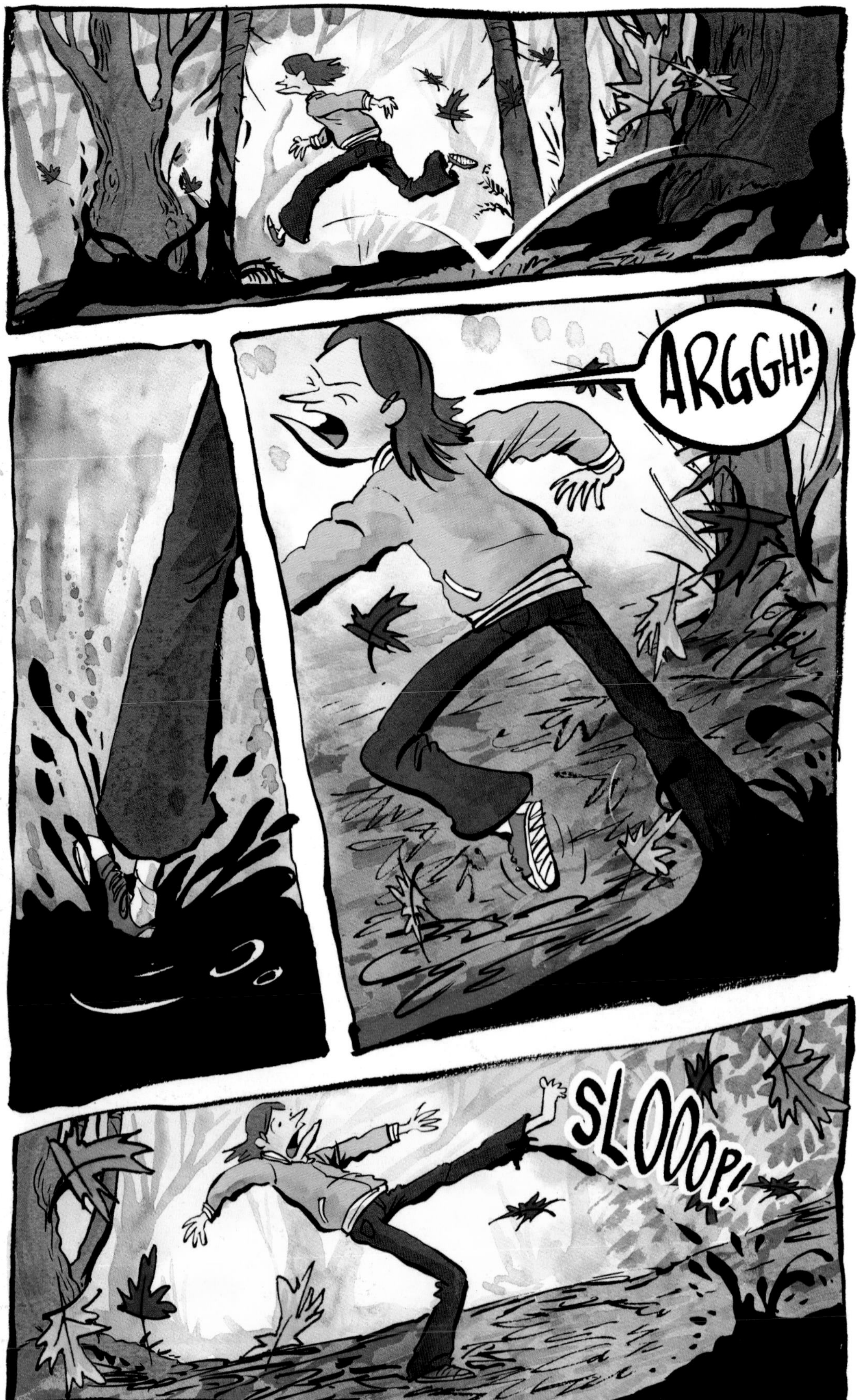
ARGGH!
SLOOOP!

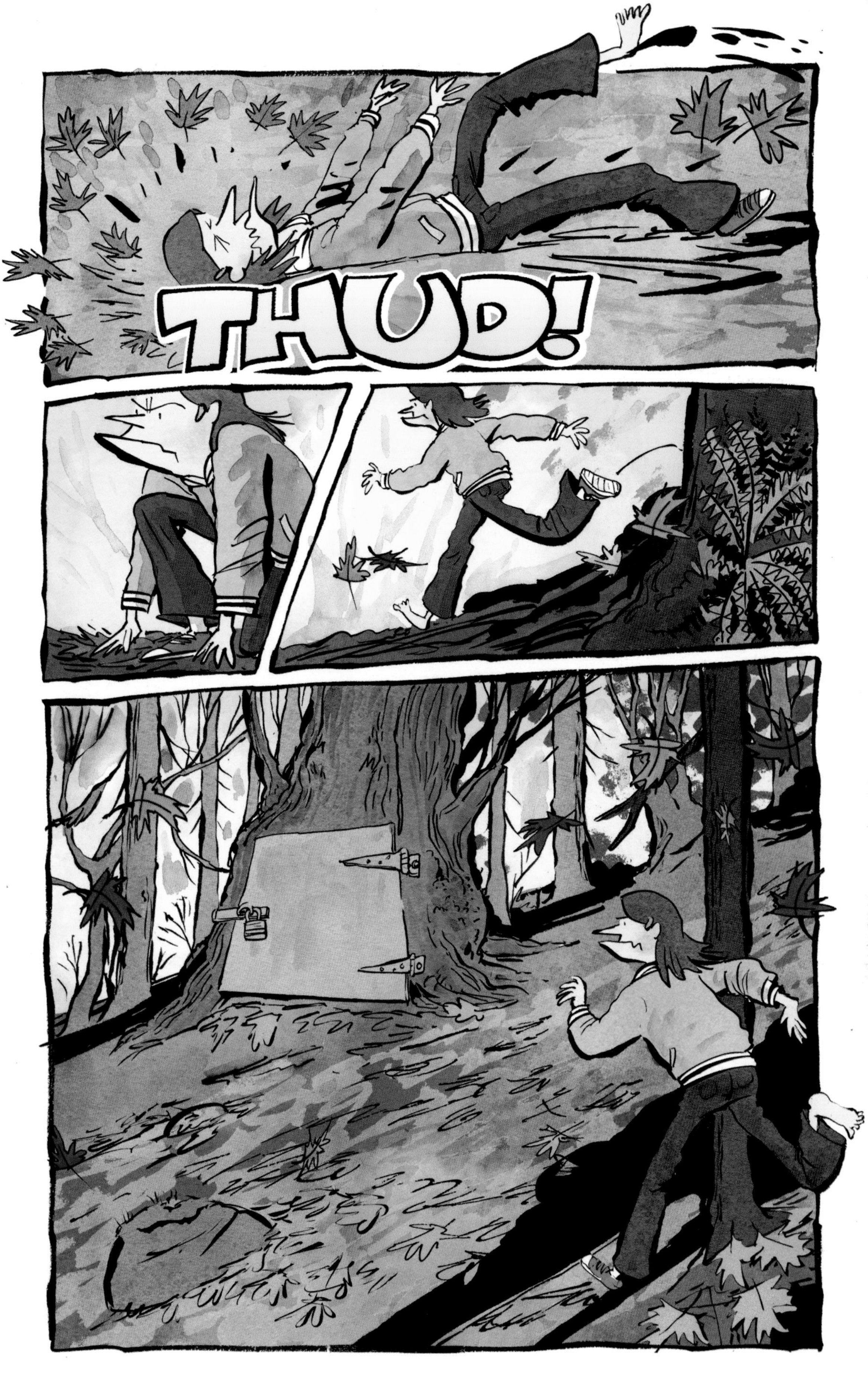
THUD!

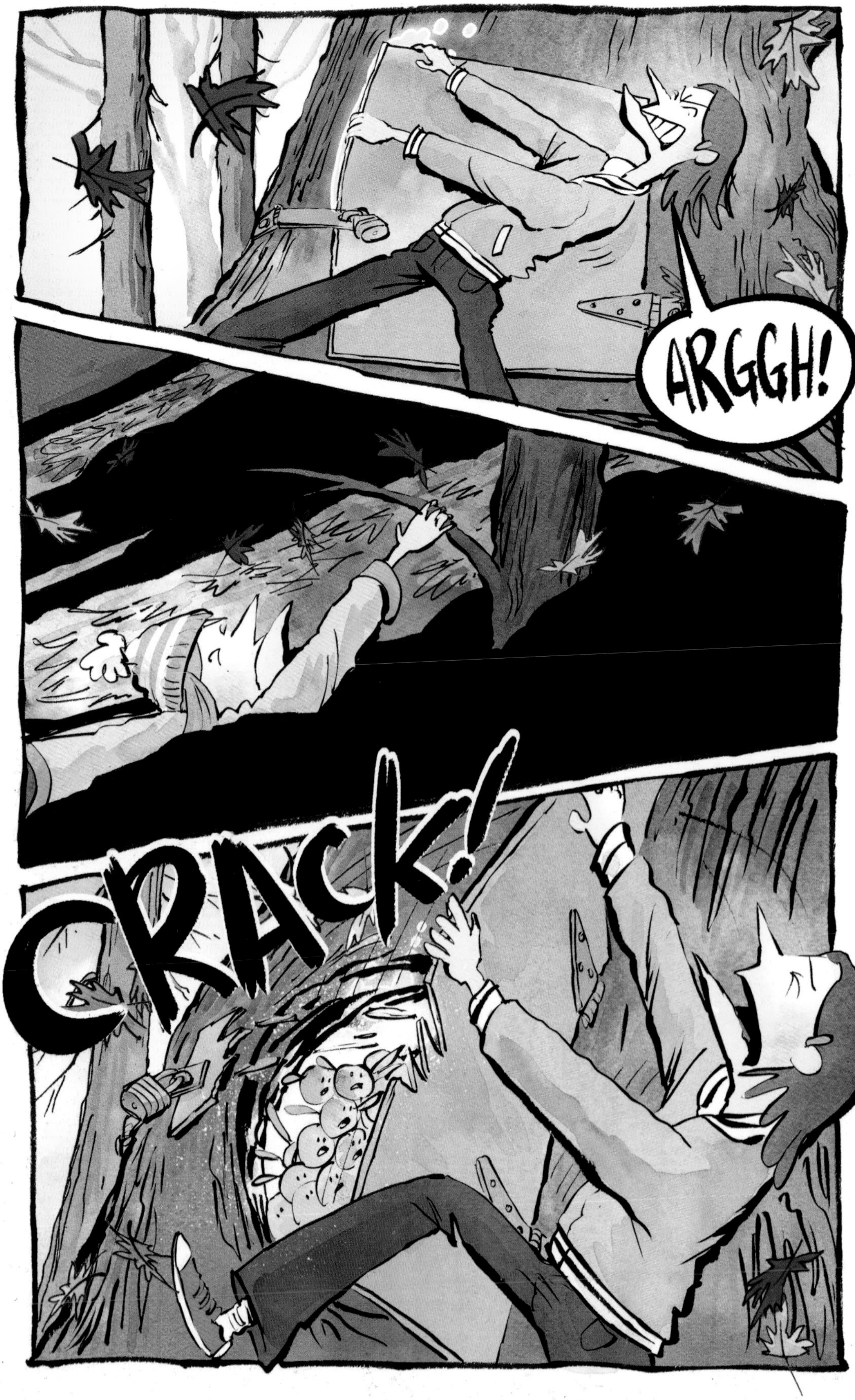
ARGGH!
CRACK!

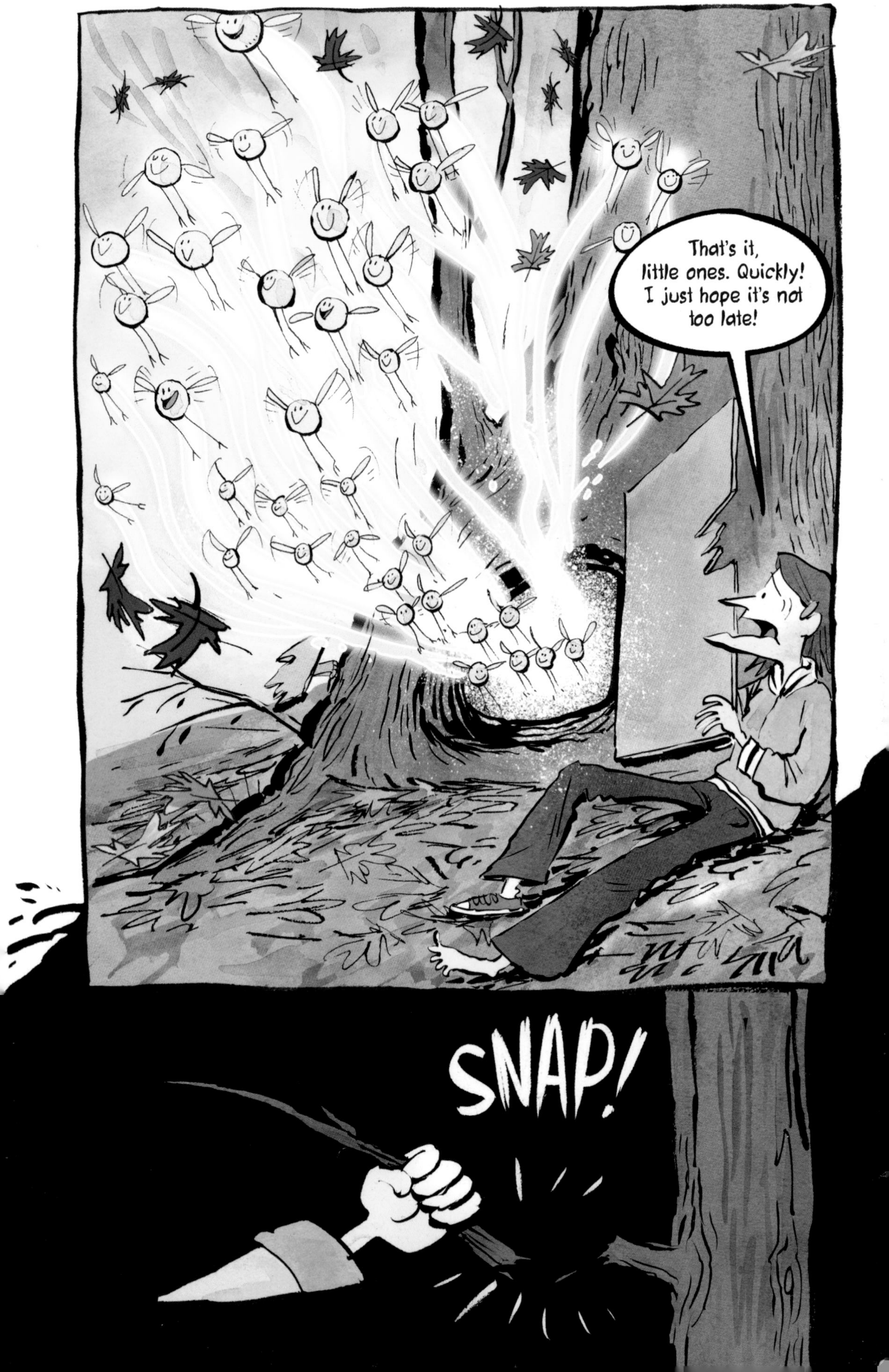
That's it, little ones. Quickly! I just hope it's not too late!
SNAP!

CHAPTER ONE

What Is This Place?

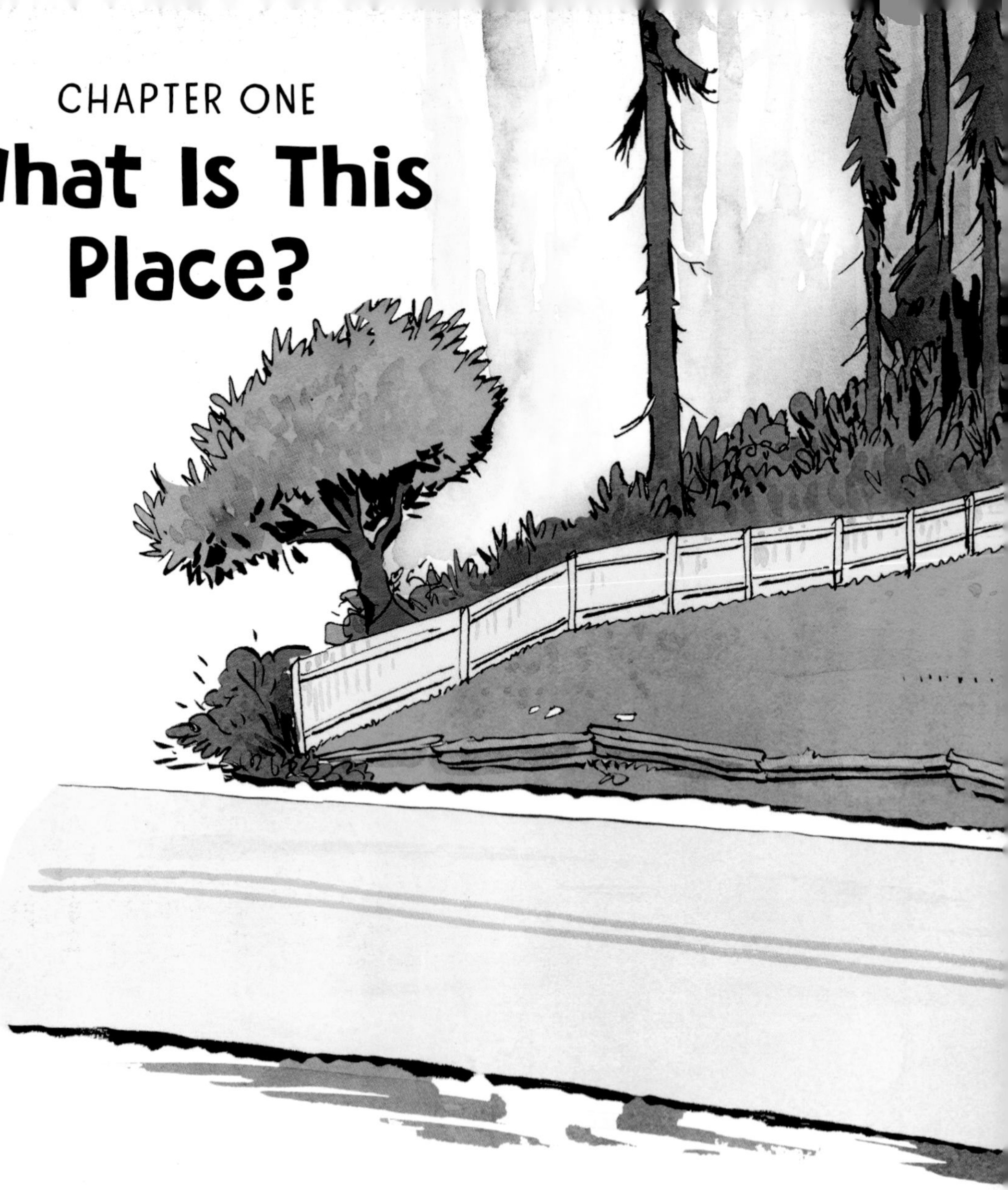

My dad is finally coming home. Just in time to see me in the fall fair talent show. We always do a ton of cool stuff together. I can't wait to go fishing with him and get away from my know-it-all sister. She thinks she's the boss of me.

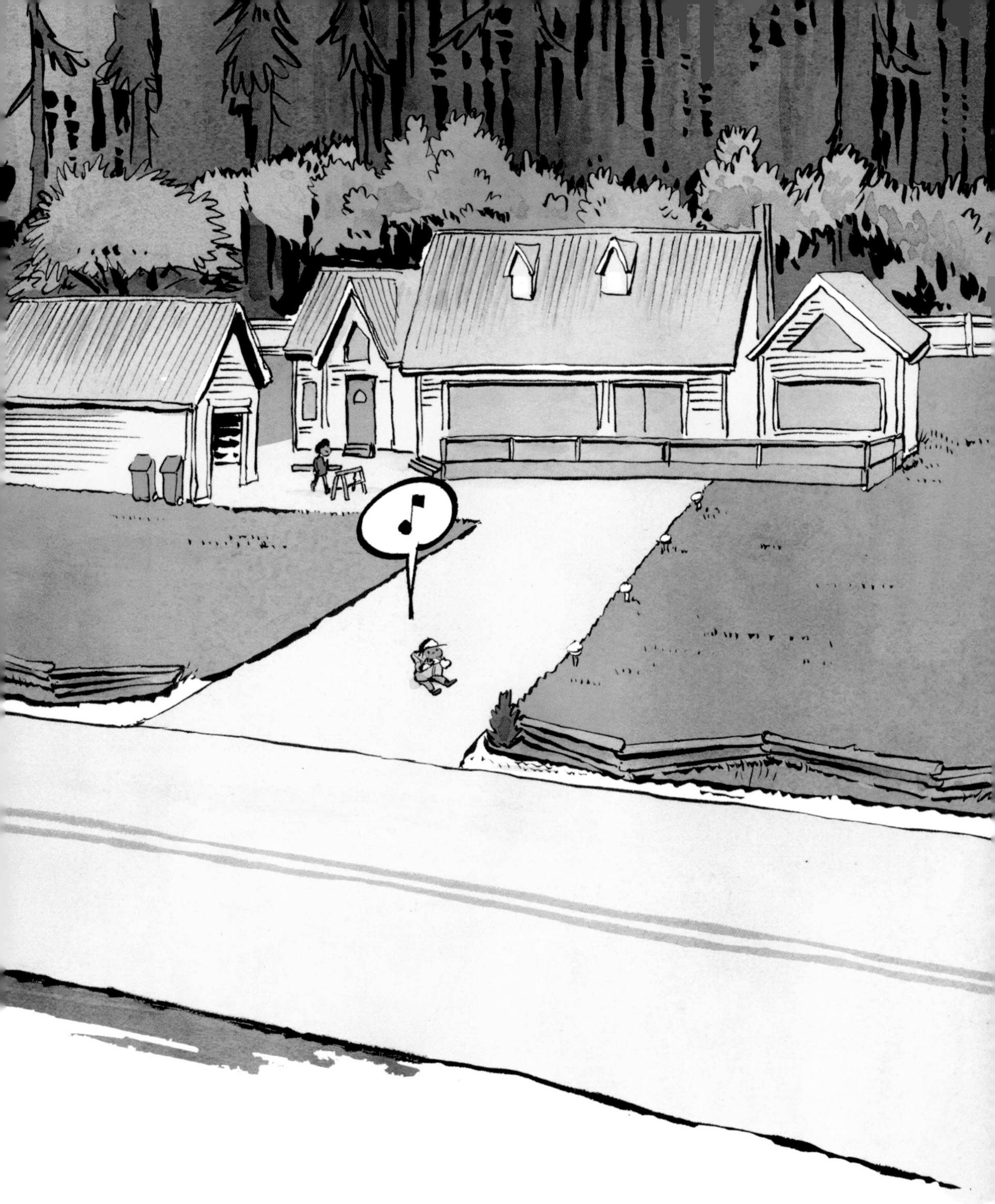

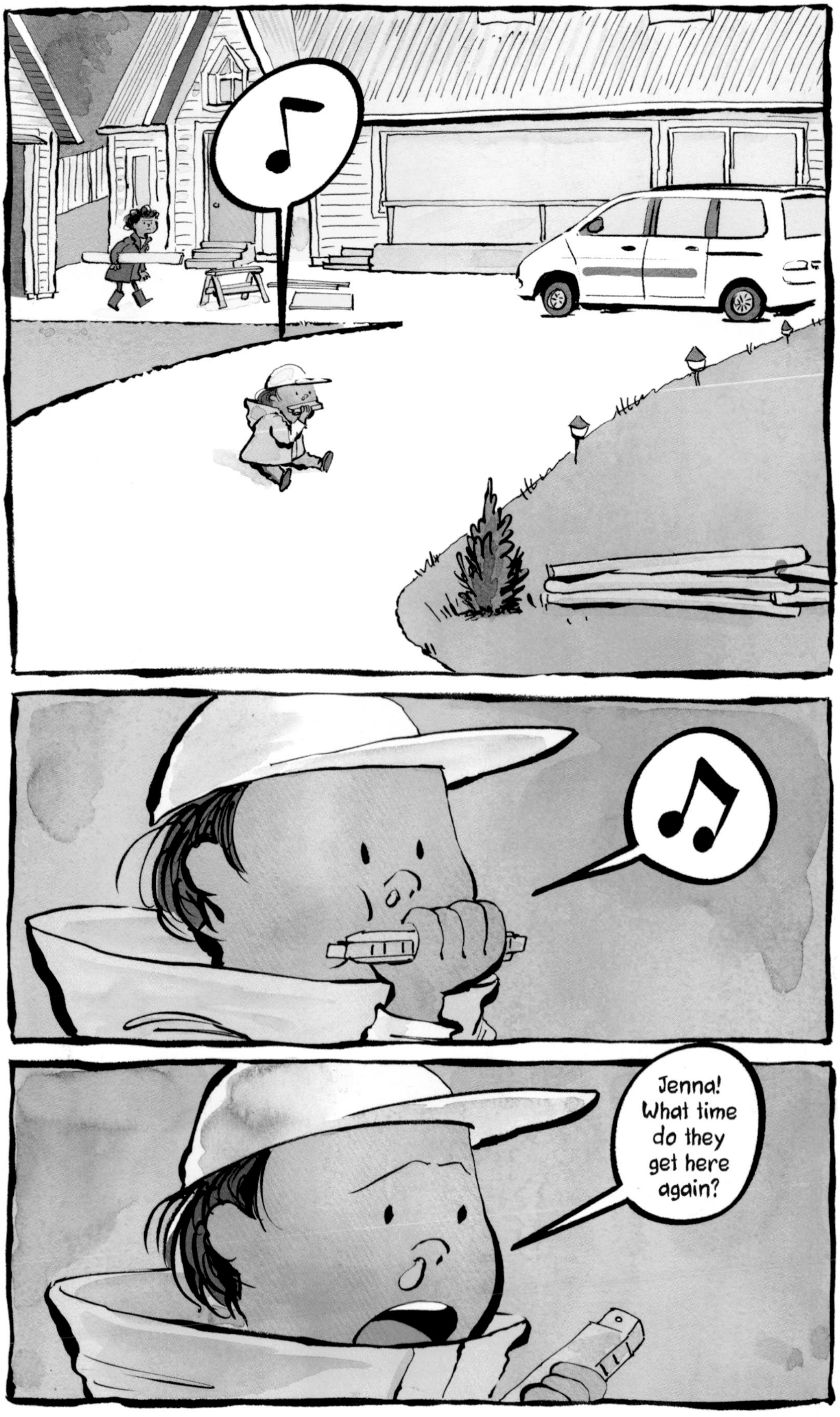
Jenna! What time do they get here again?

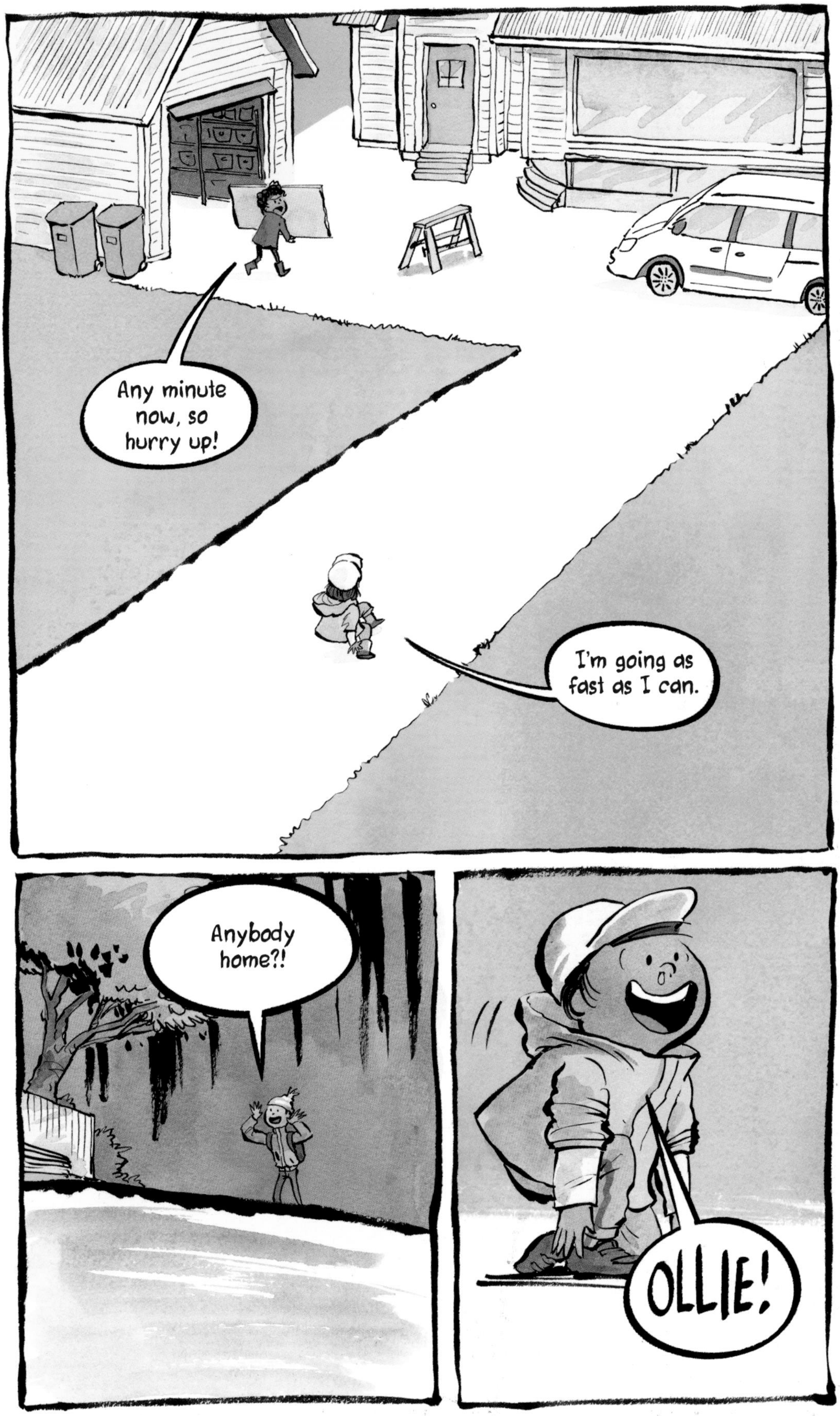
Any minute now, so hurry up!
I'm going as fast as I can.
Anybody home?!
OLLIE!

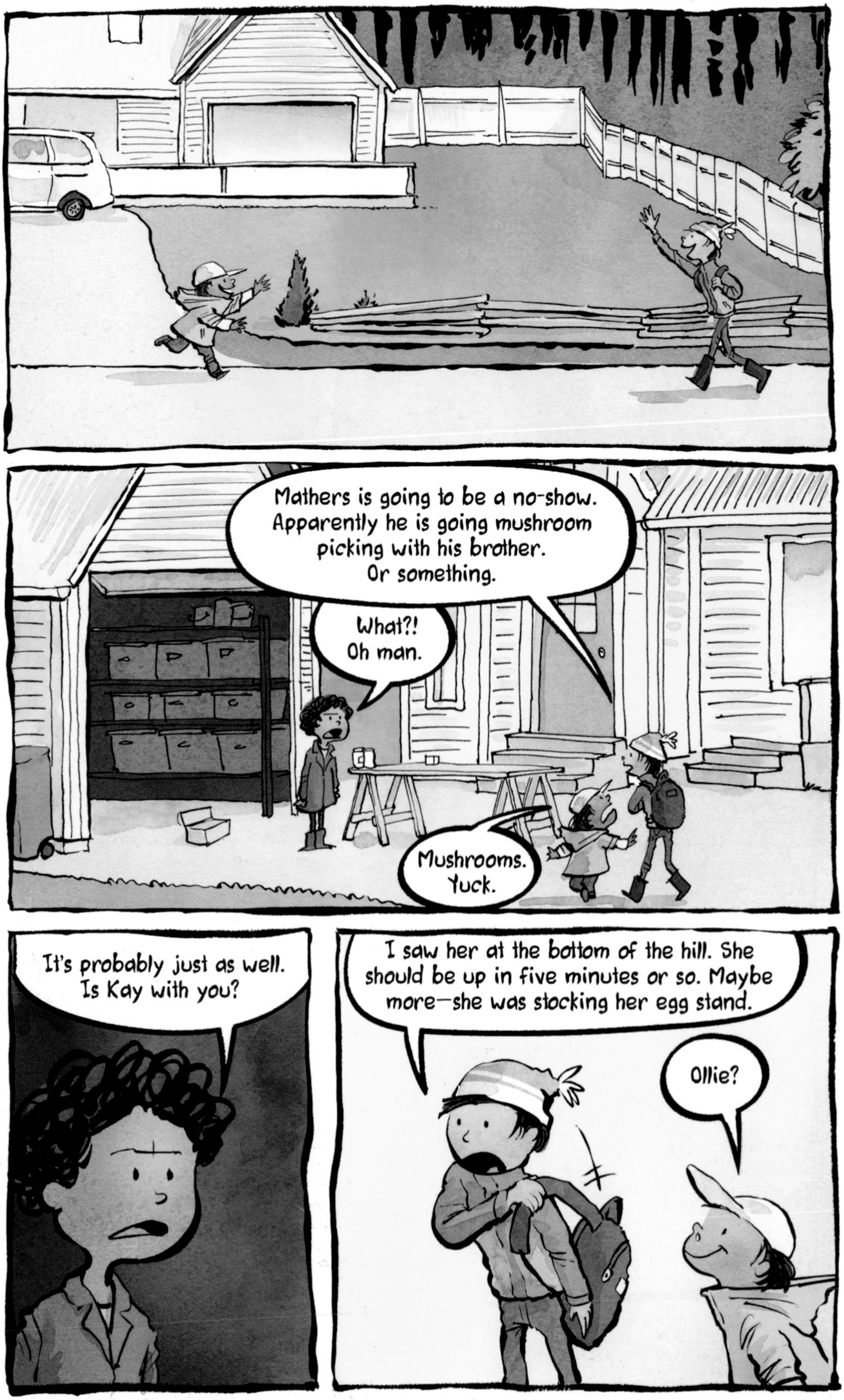
Mathers is going to be a no-show. Apparently he is going mushroom picking with his brother. Or something.
What?! Oh man.
Mushrooms. Yuck.
It's probably just as well. Is Kay with you?
I saw her at the bottom of the hill. She should be up in five minutes or so. Maybe more—she was stocking her egg stand.
Ollie?

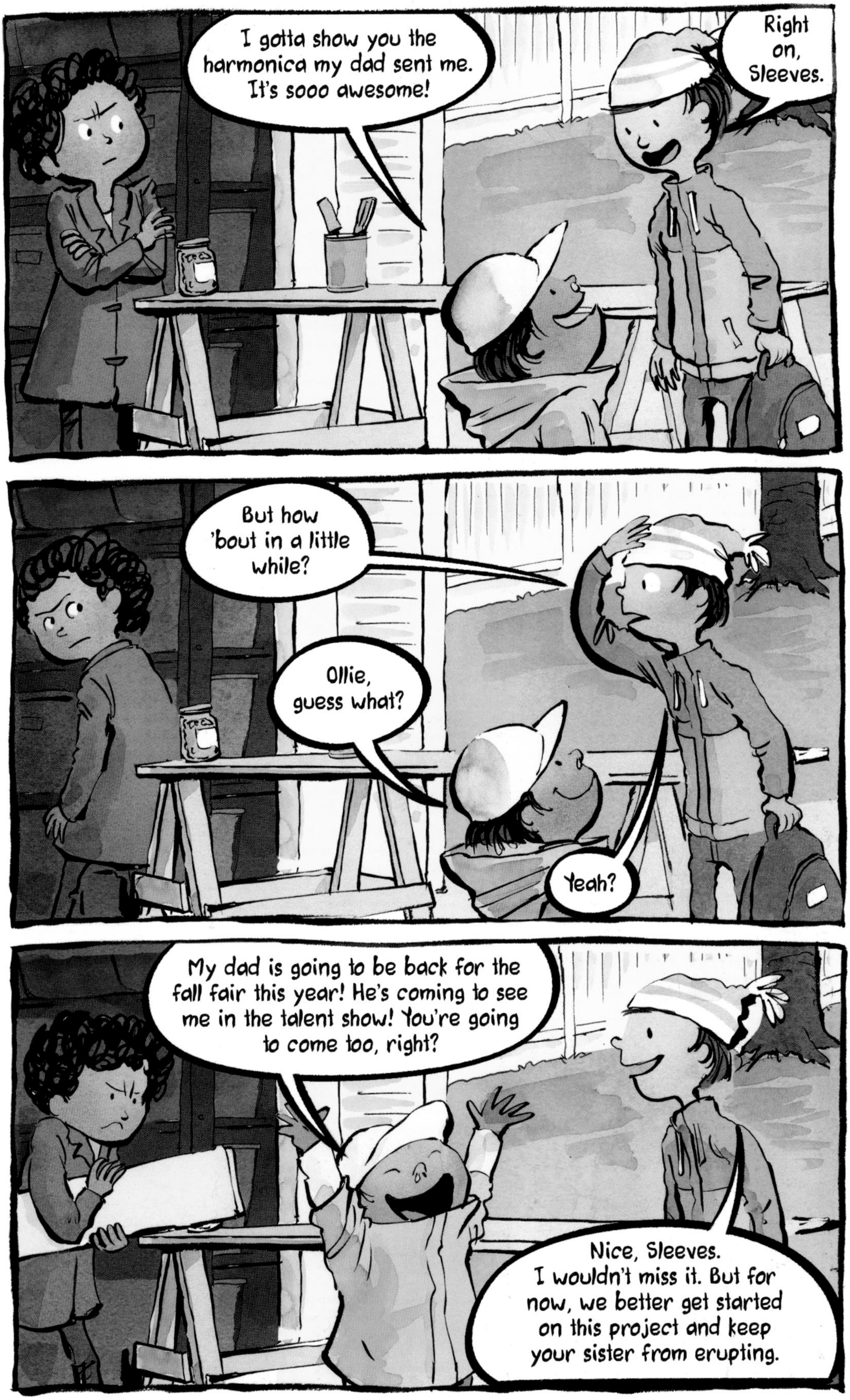
I gotta show you the harmonica my dad sent me. It's sooo awesome!
Right on, Sleeves.
But how 'bout in a little while?
Ollie, guess what?
Yeah?
My dad is going to be back for the fall fair this year! He's coming to see me in the talent show! You're going to come too, right?
Nice, Sleeves. I wouldn't miss it. But for now, we better get started on this project and keep your sister from erupting.

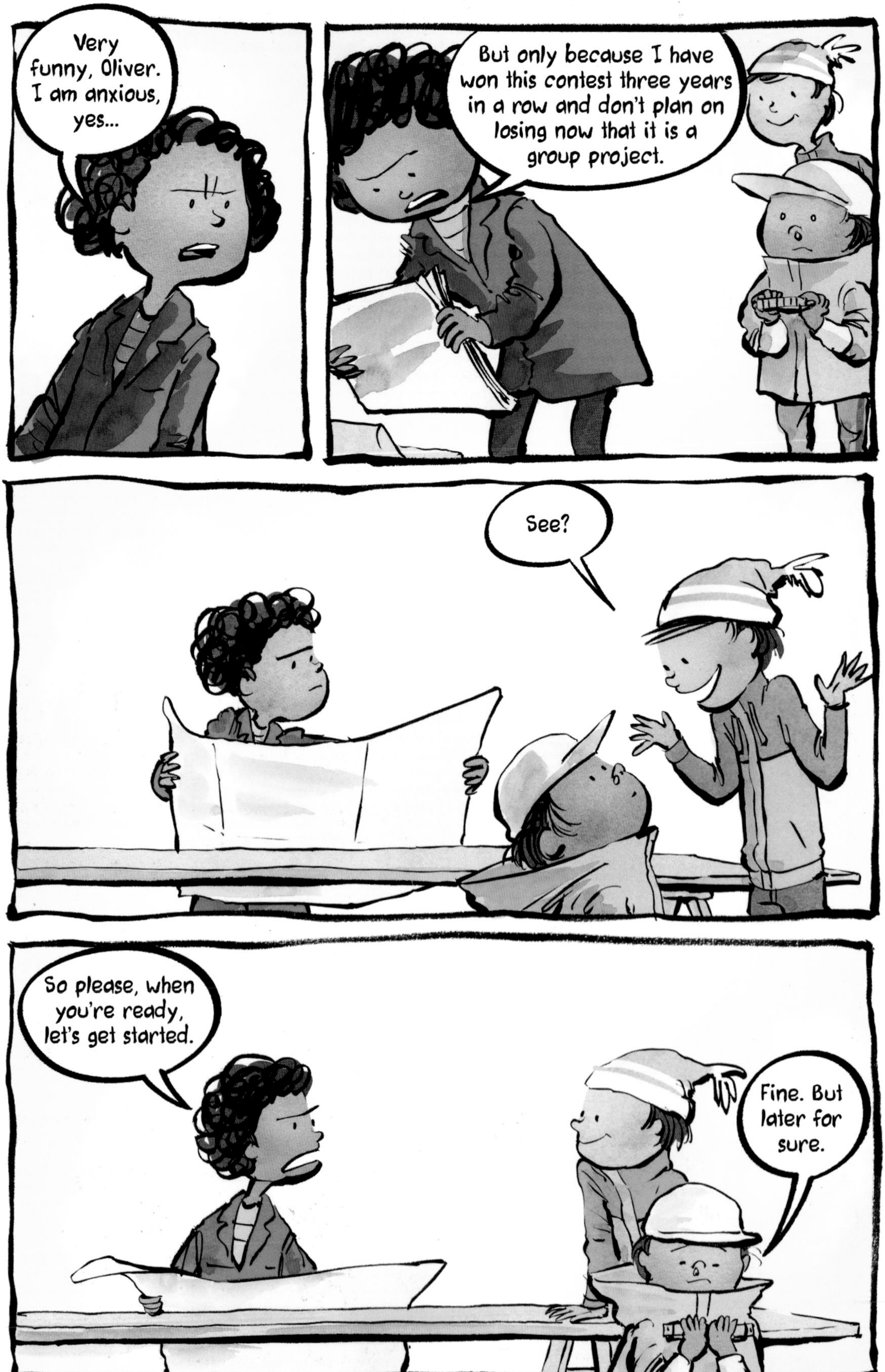
Very funny, Oliver. I am anxious, yes...
But only because I have won this contest three years in a row and don't plan on losing now that it is a group project.
See?
So please, when you're ready, let's get started.
Fine. But later for sure.

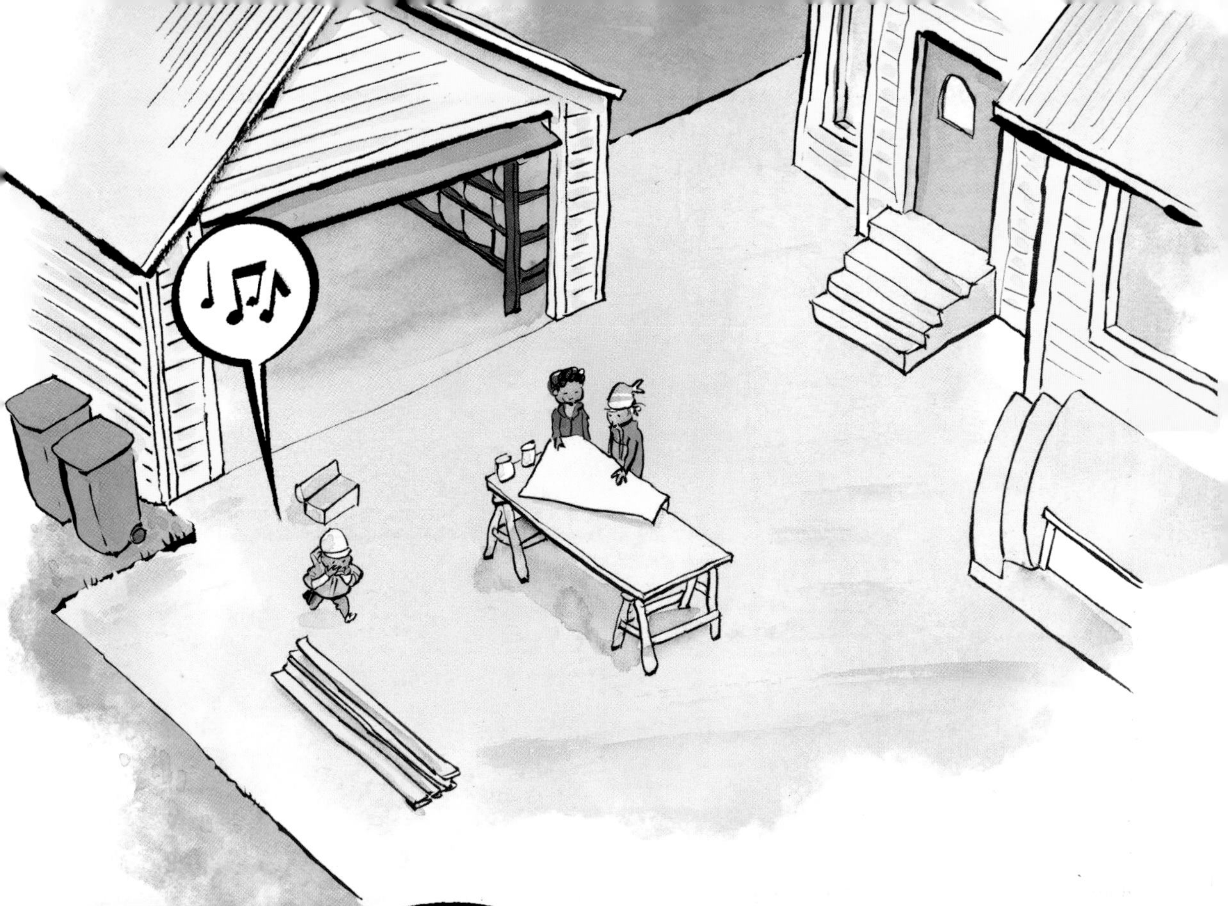

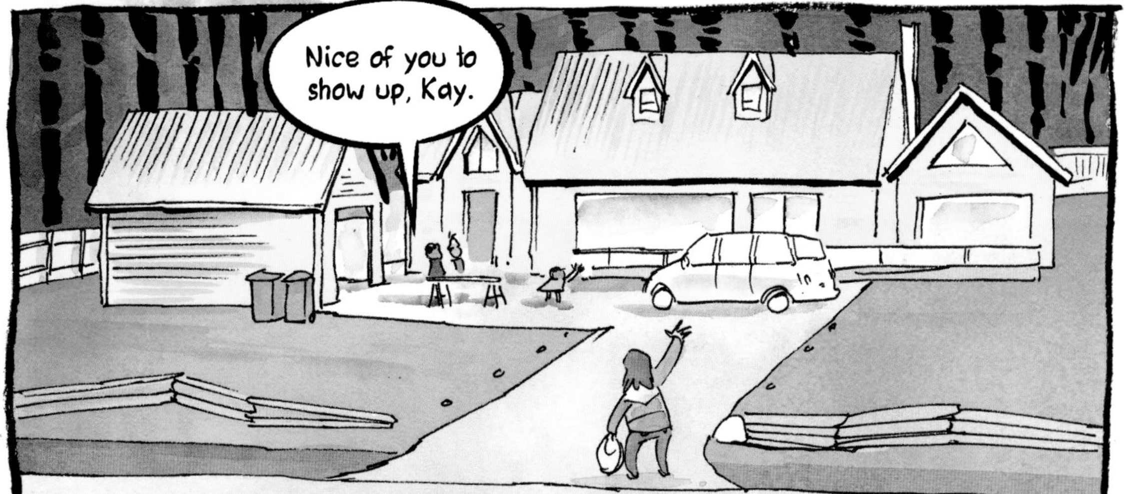
Nice of you to show up, Kay.

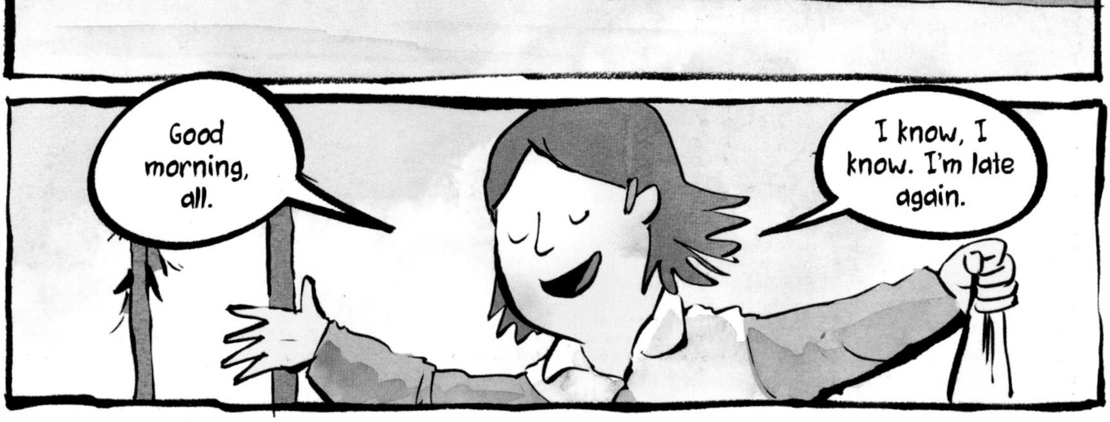
Good morning, all.
I know, I know. I'm late again.

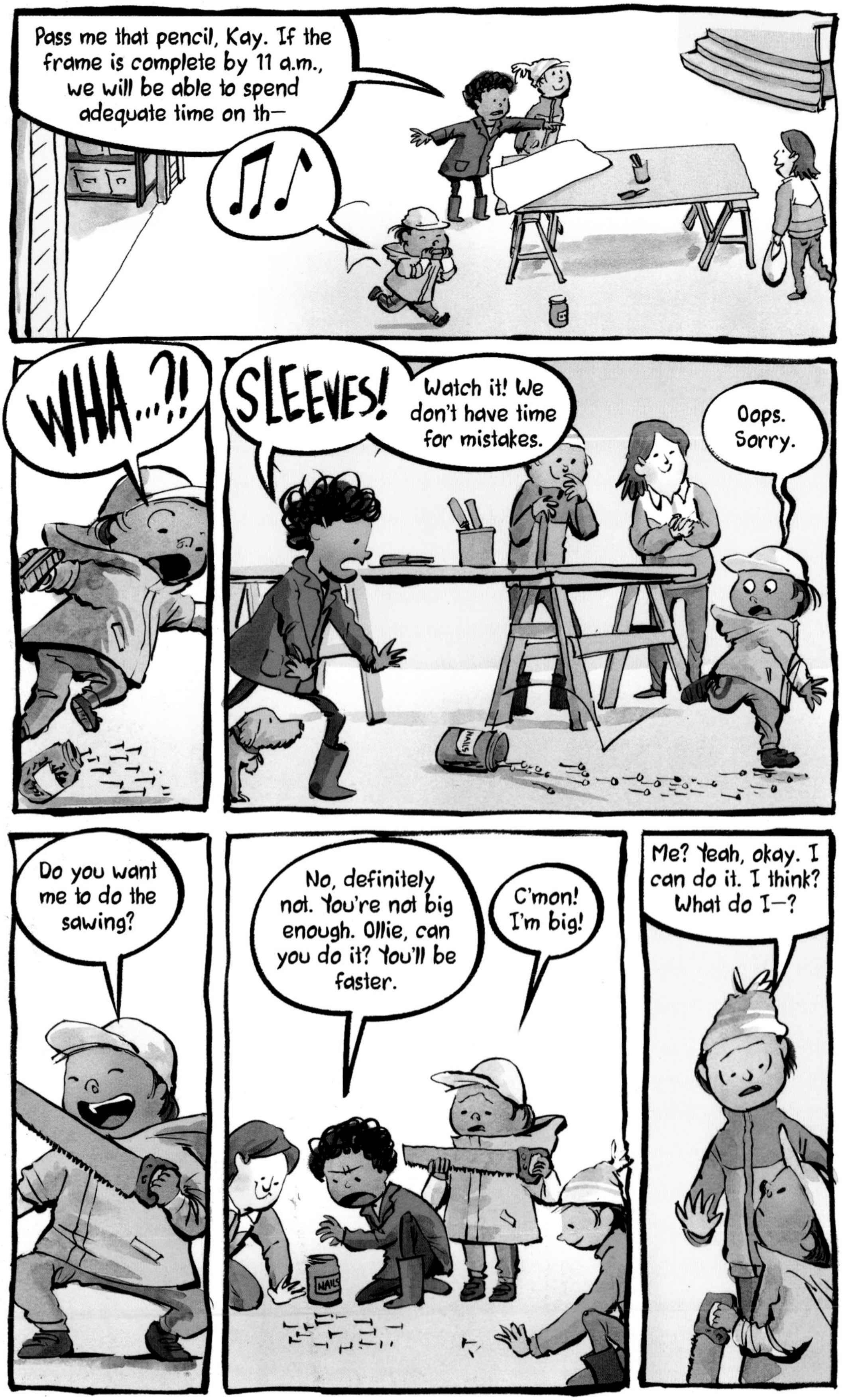
Pass me that pencil, Kay. If the frame is complete by 11 a.m., we will be able to spend adequate time on th—
♫♪
WHA...?!
SLEEVES!
Watch it! We don't have time for mistakes.
Oops. Sorry.
NAILS
Do you want me to do the sawing?
No, definitely not. You're not big enough. Ollie, can you do it? You'll be faster.
C'mon! I'm big!
NAILS
Me? Yeah, okay. I can do it. I think? What do I—?

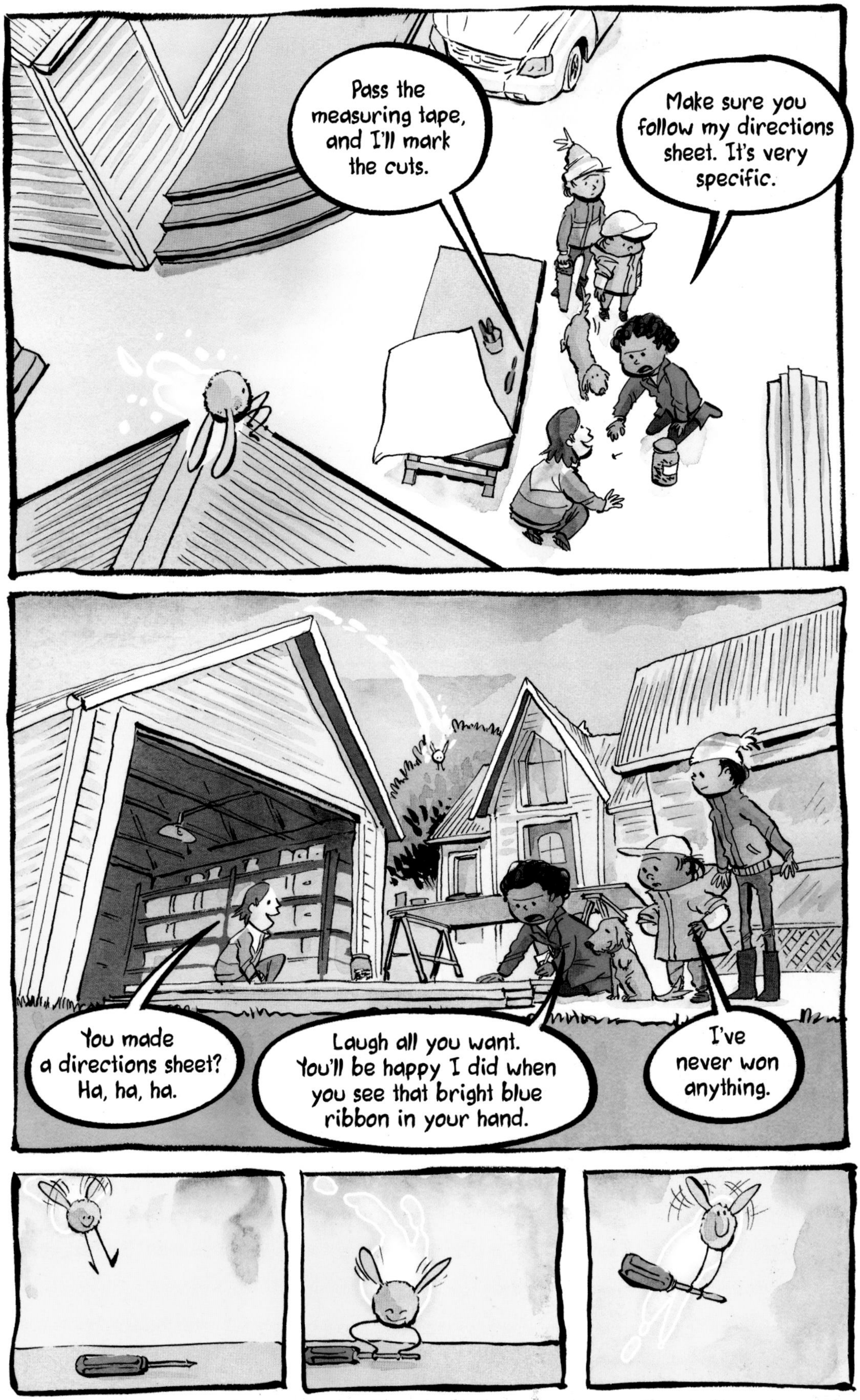
Pass the measuring tape, and I'll mark the cuts.
Make sure you follow my directions sheet. It's very specific.
You made a directions sheet? Ha, ha, ha.
Laugh all you want. You'll be happy I did when you see that bright blue ribbon in your hand.
I've never won anything.

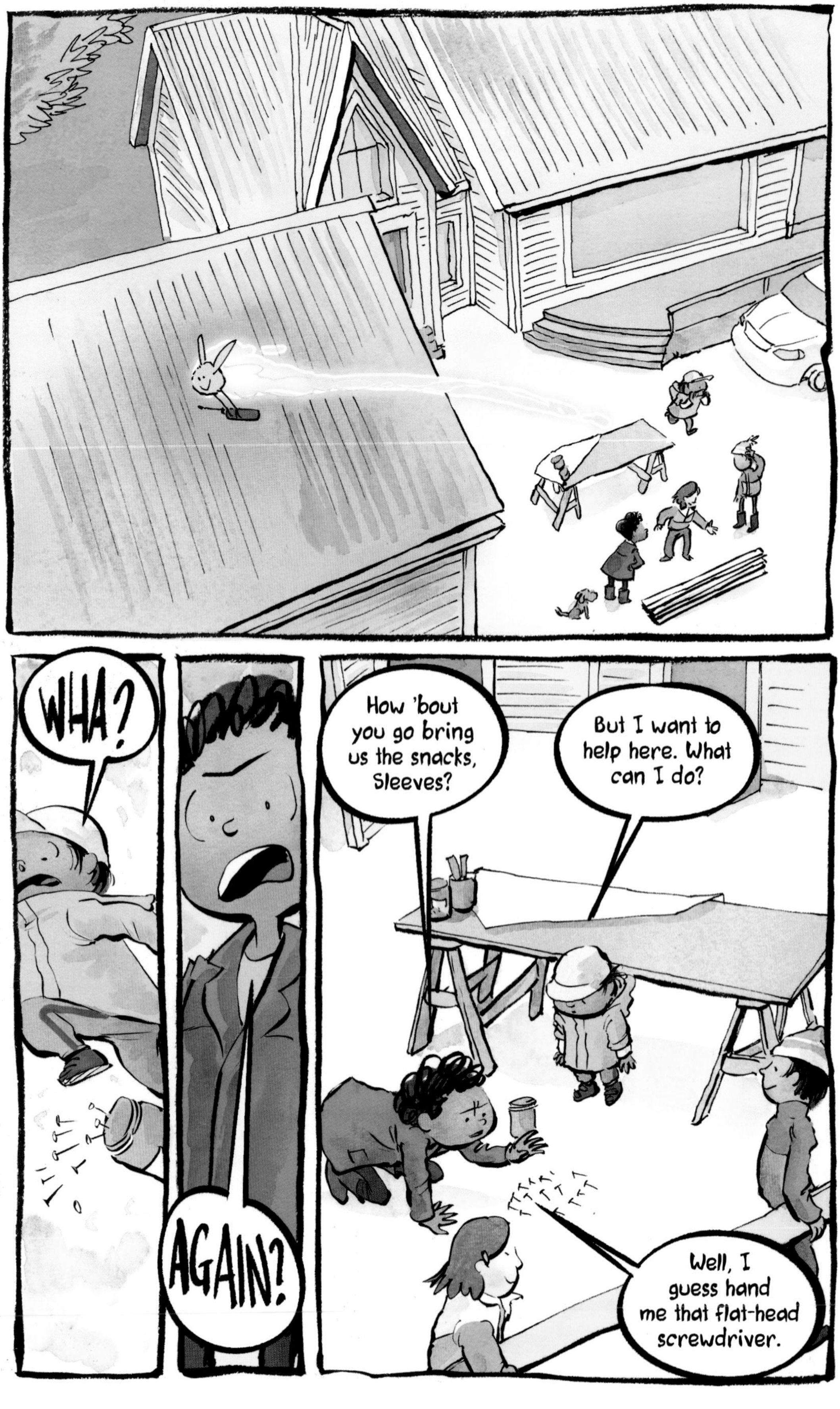
WHA?
AGAIN?
How 'bout you go bring us the snacks, Sleeves?
But I want to help here. What can I do?
Well, I guess hand me that flat-head screwdriver.

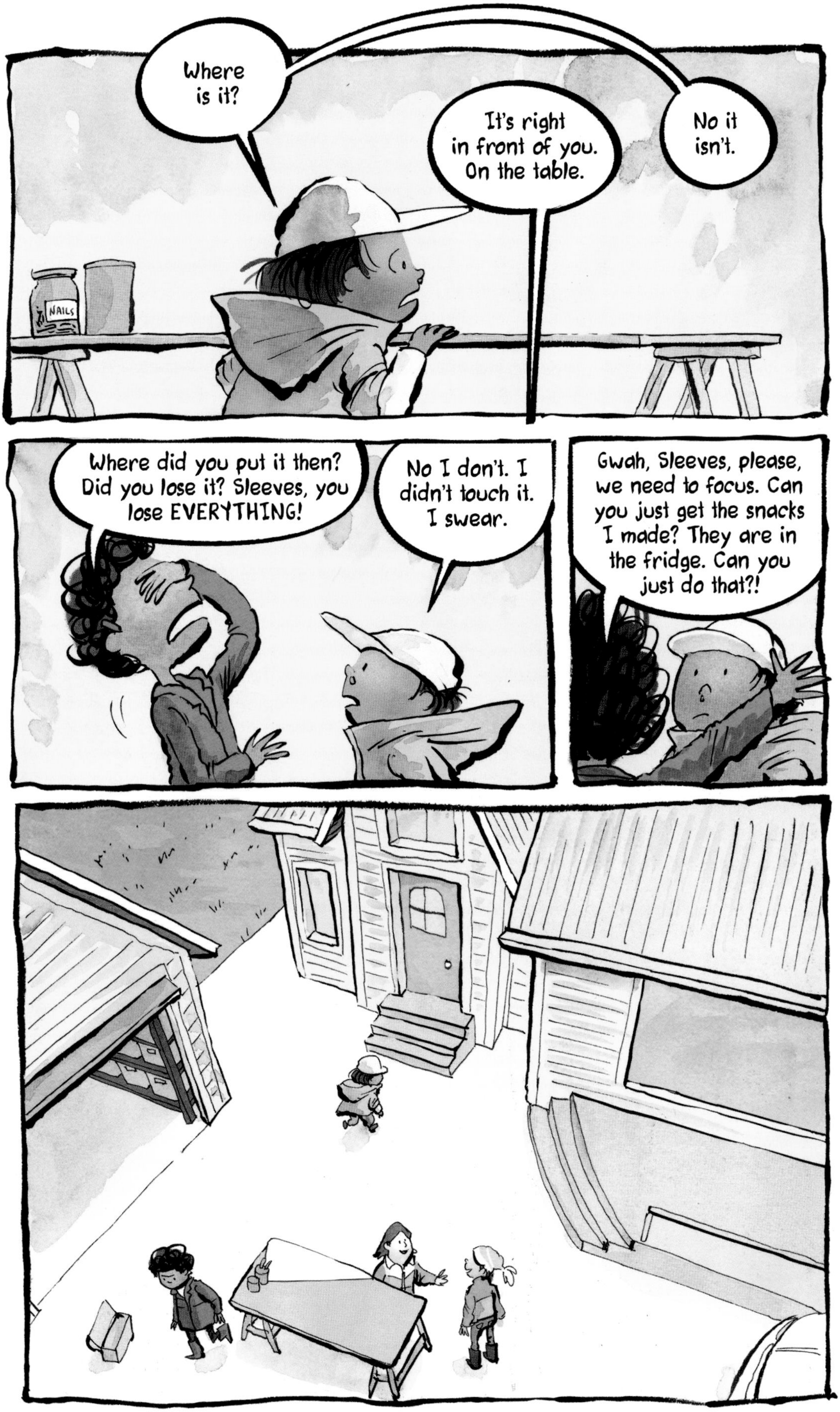
Where is it?
It's right in front of you. On the table.
No it isn't.
NAILS
Where did you put it then? Did you lose it? Sleeves, you lose EVERYTHING!
No I don't. I didn't touch it. I swear.
Gwah, Sleeves, please, we need to focus. Can you just get the snacks I made? They are in the fridge. Can you just do that?!

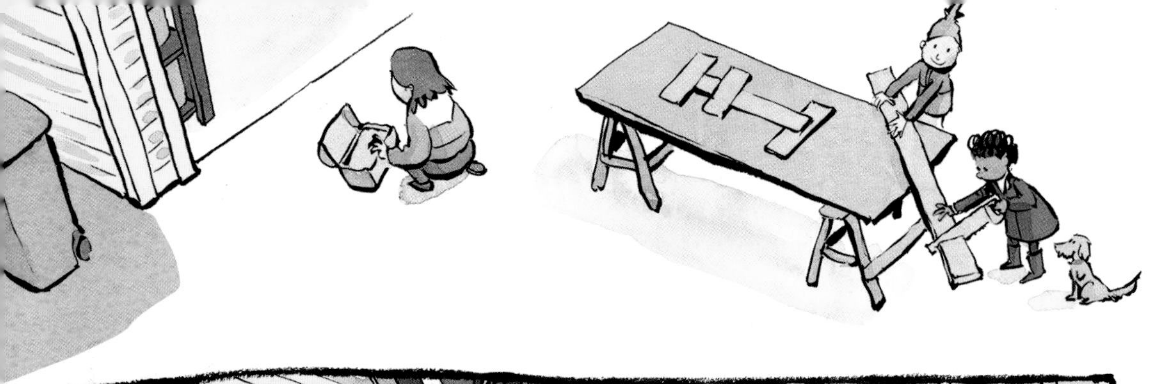

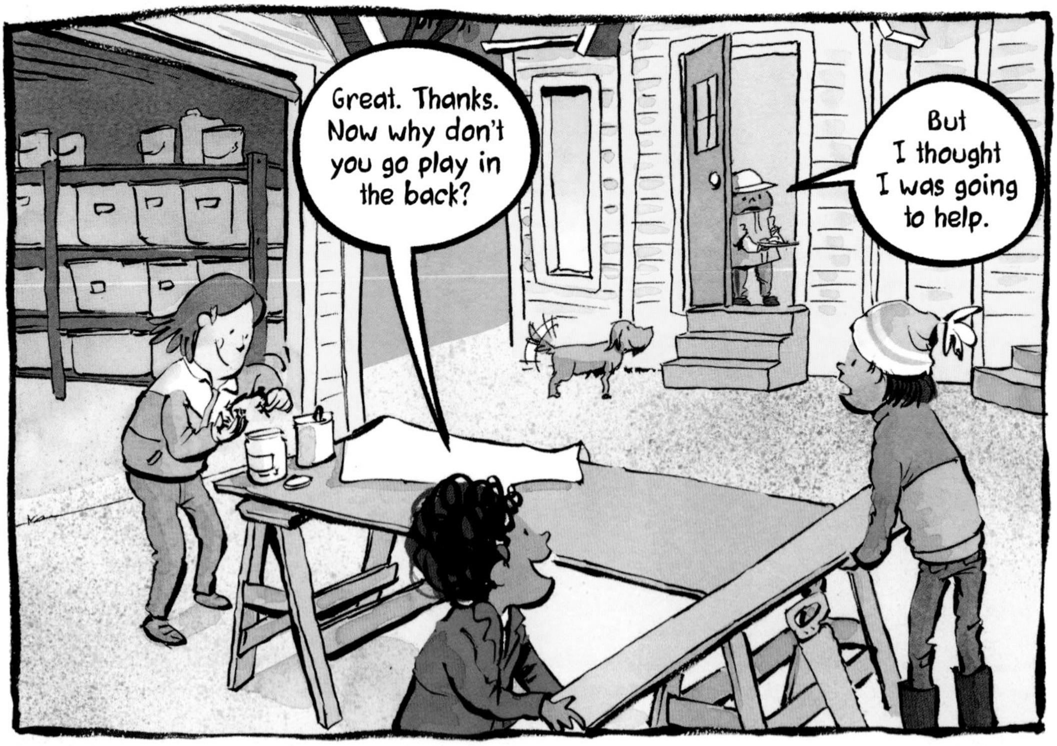
Great. Thanks. Now why don't you go play in the back?
But I thought I was going to help.

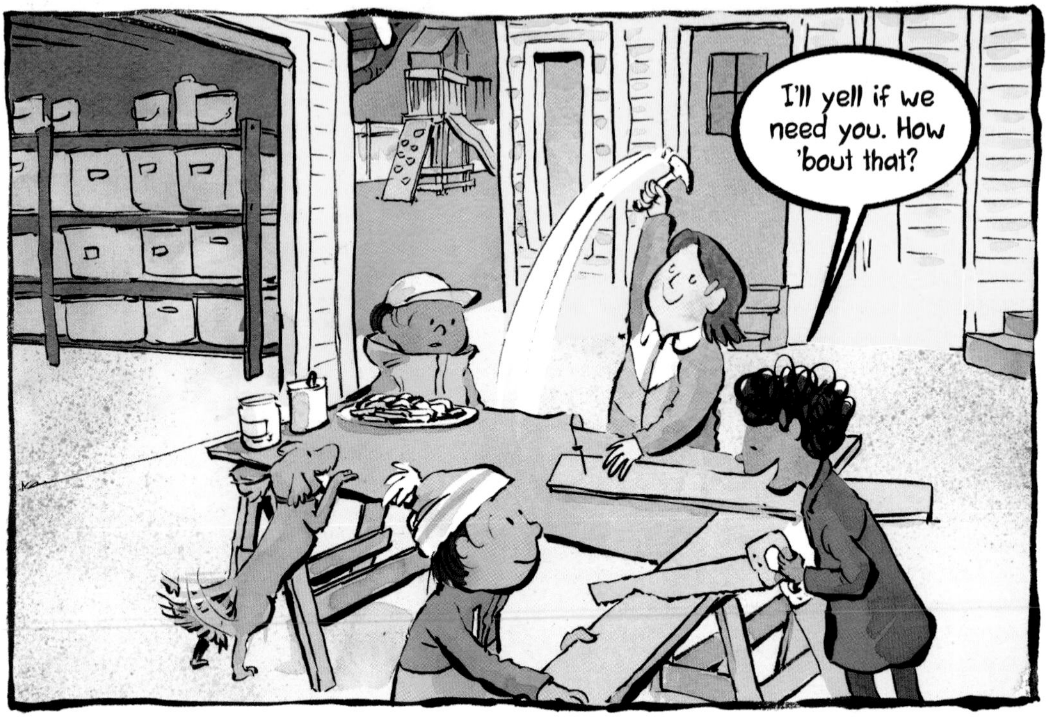
I'll yell if we need you. How 'bout that?

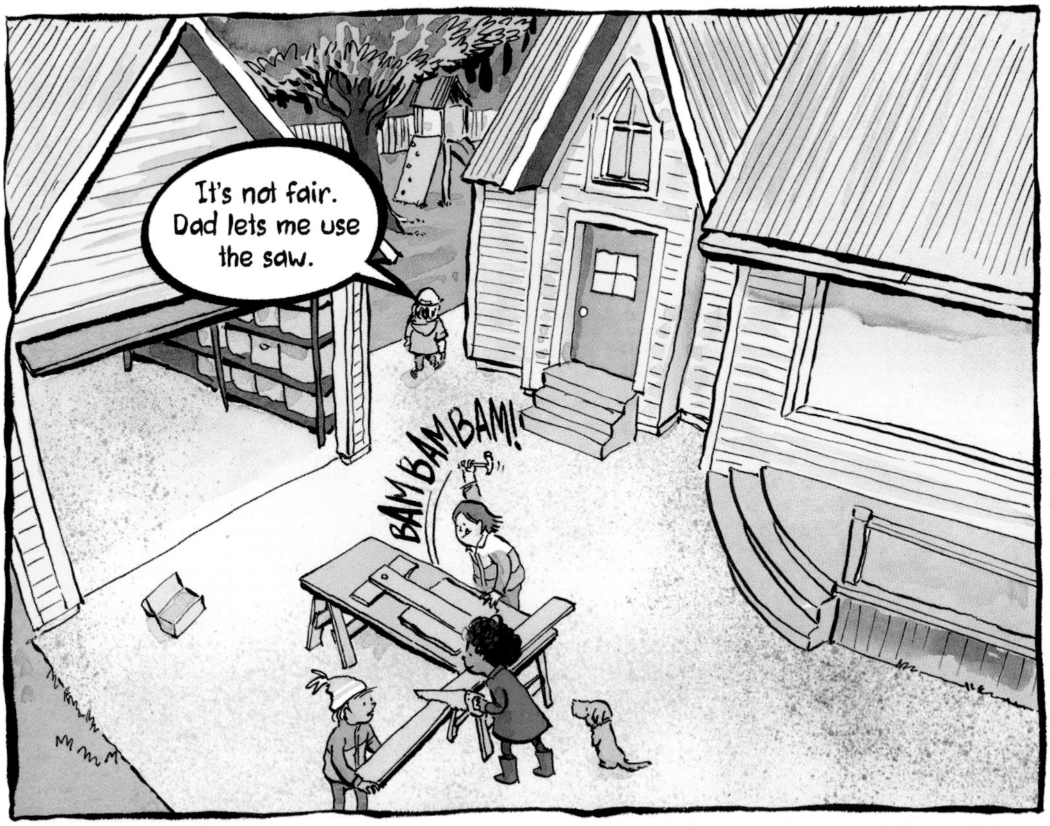
It's not fair. Dad lets me use the saw.
BAM BAM BAM!

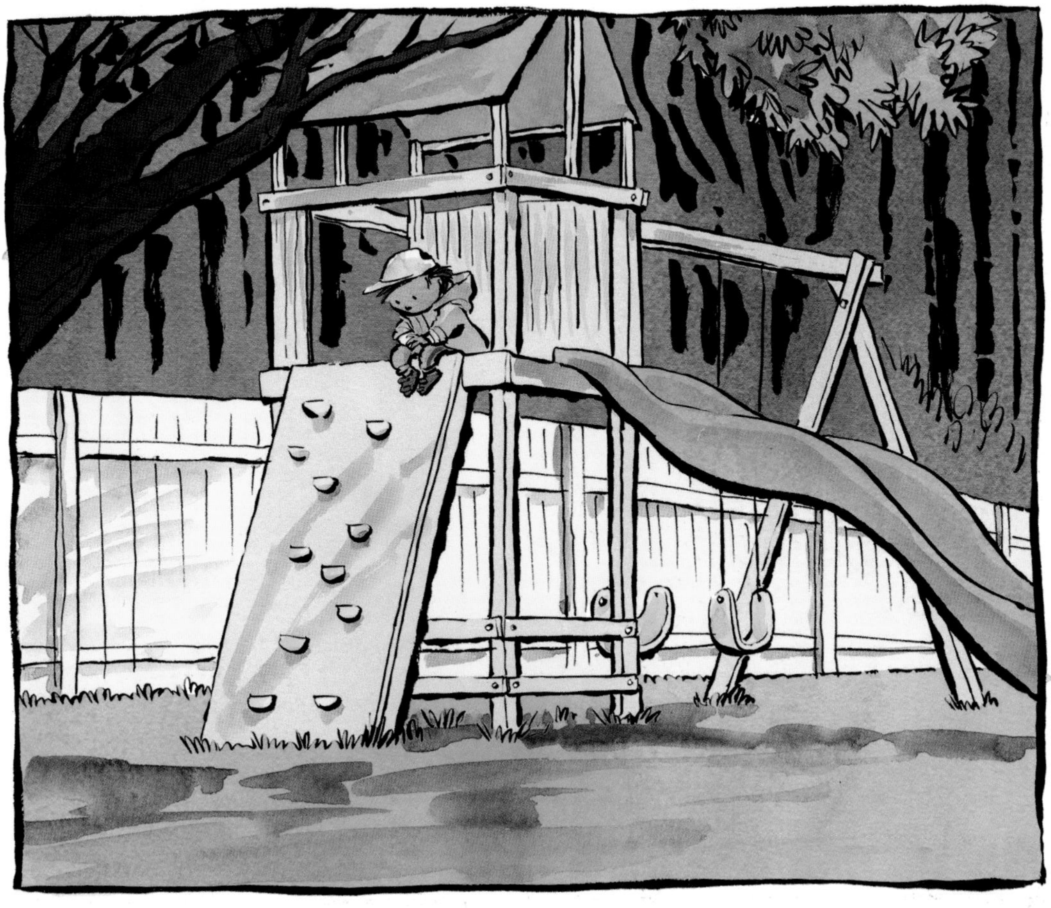

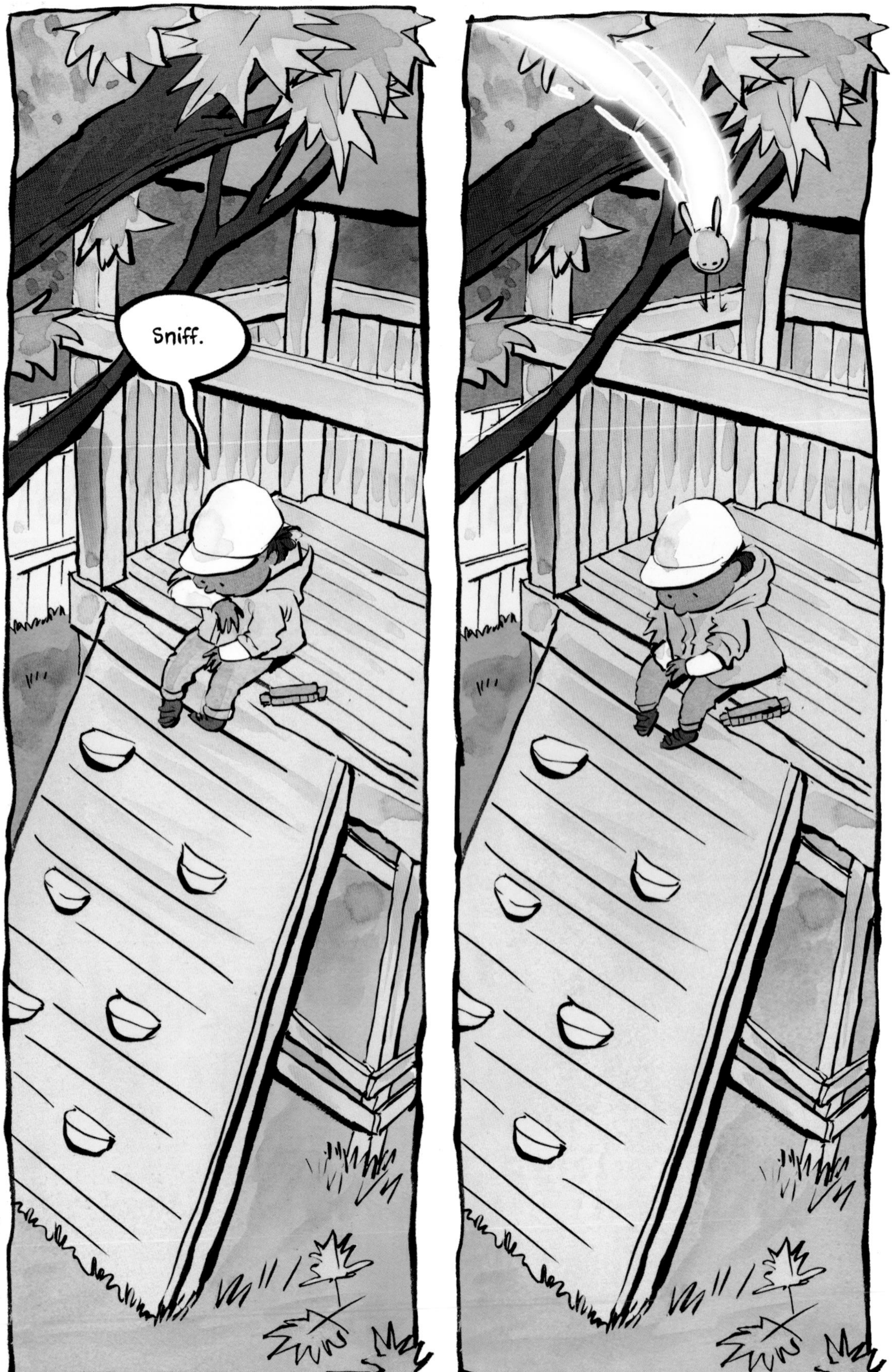
Sniff.

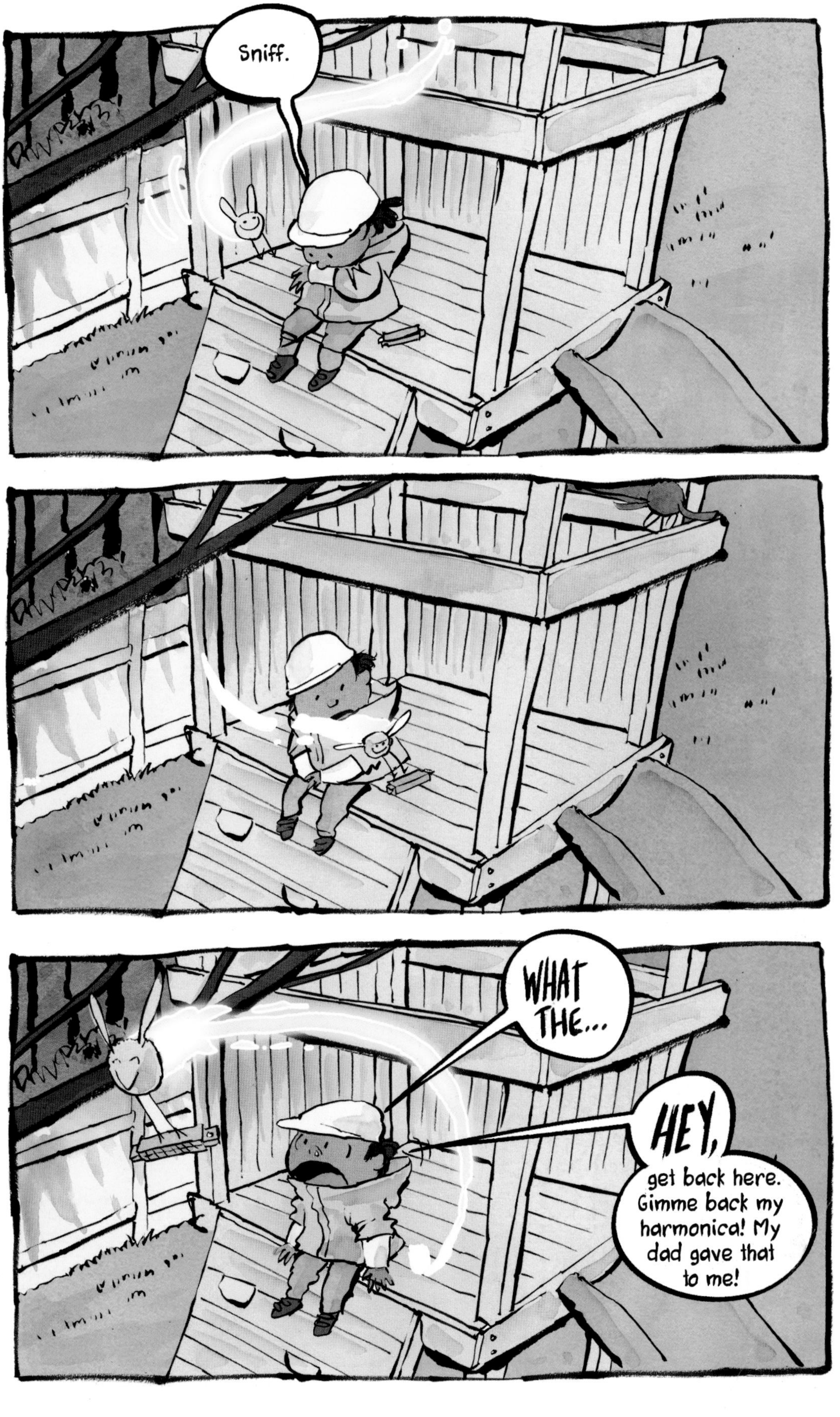
Sniff.
WHAT THE...
HEY,
get back here. Gimme back my harmonica! My dad gave that to me!

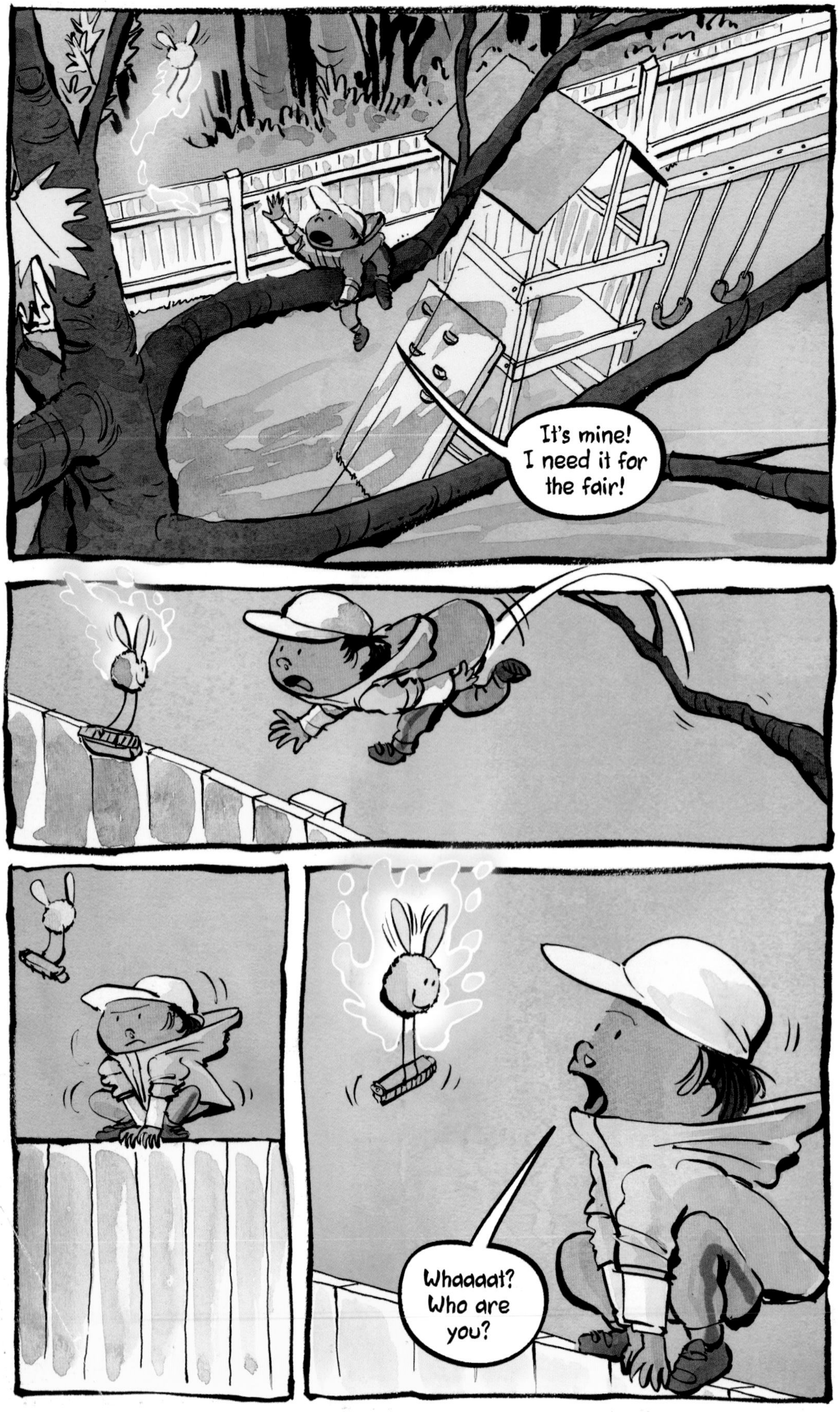
It's mine! I need it for the fair!
Whaaaat? Who are you?

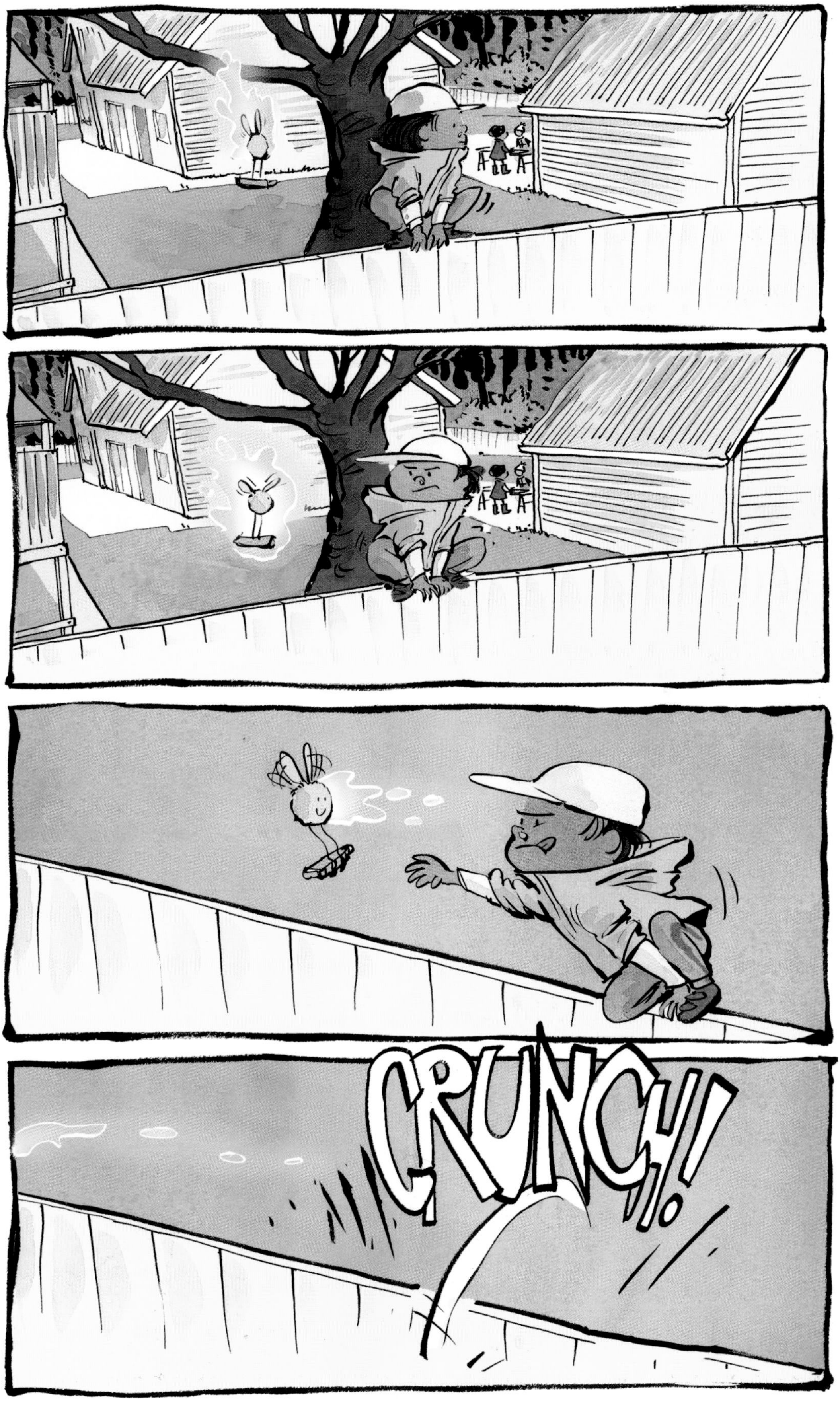
CRUNCH!

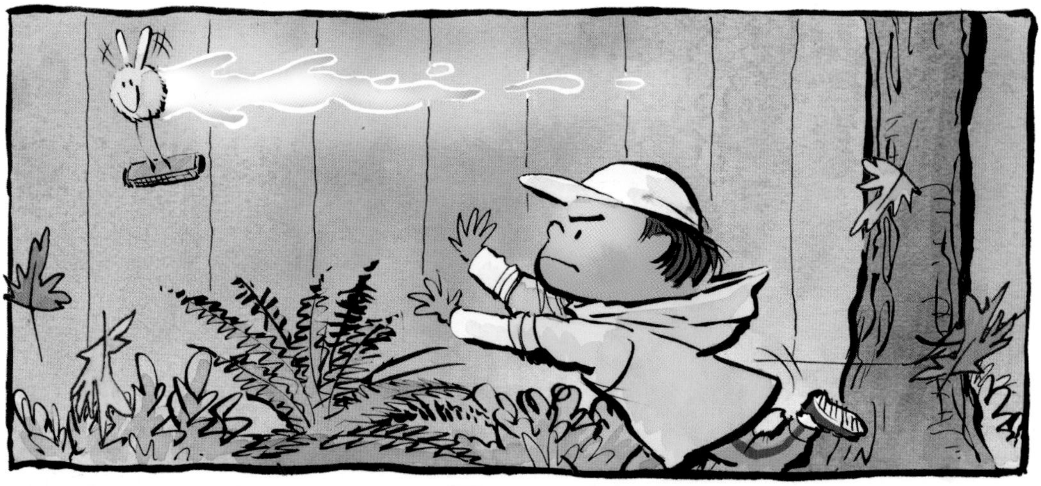

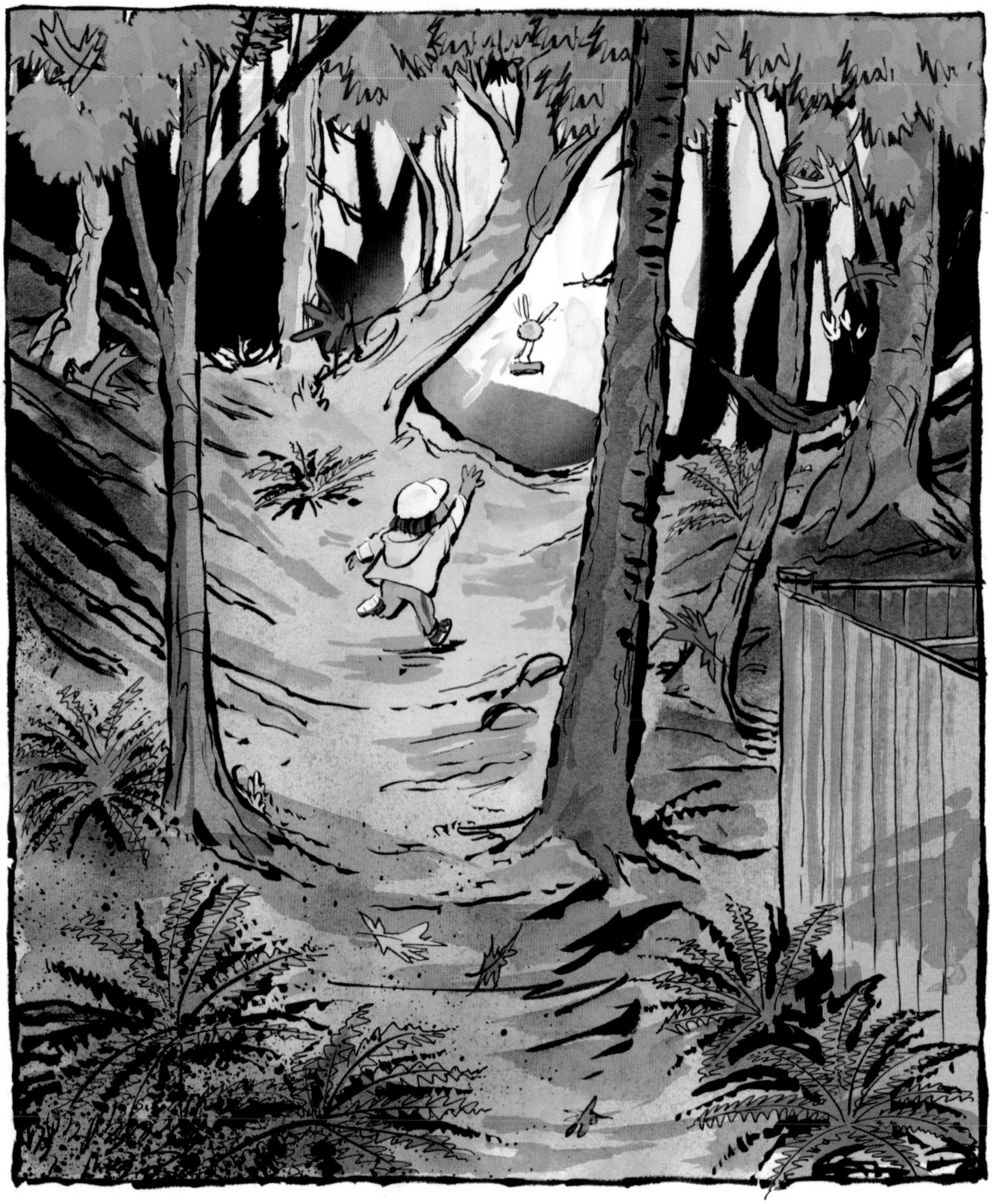

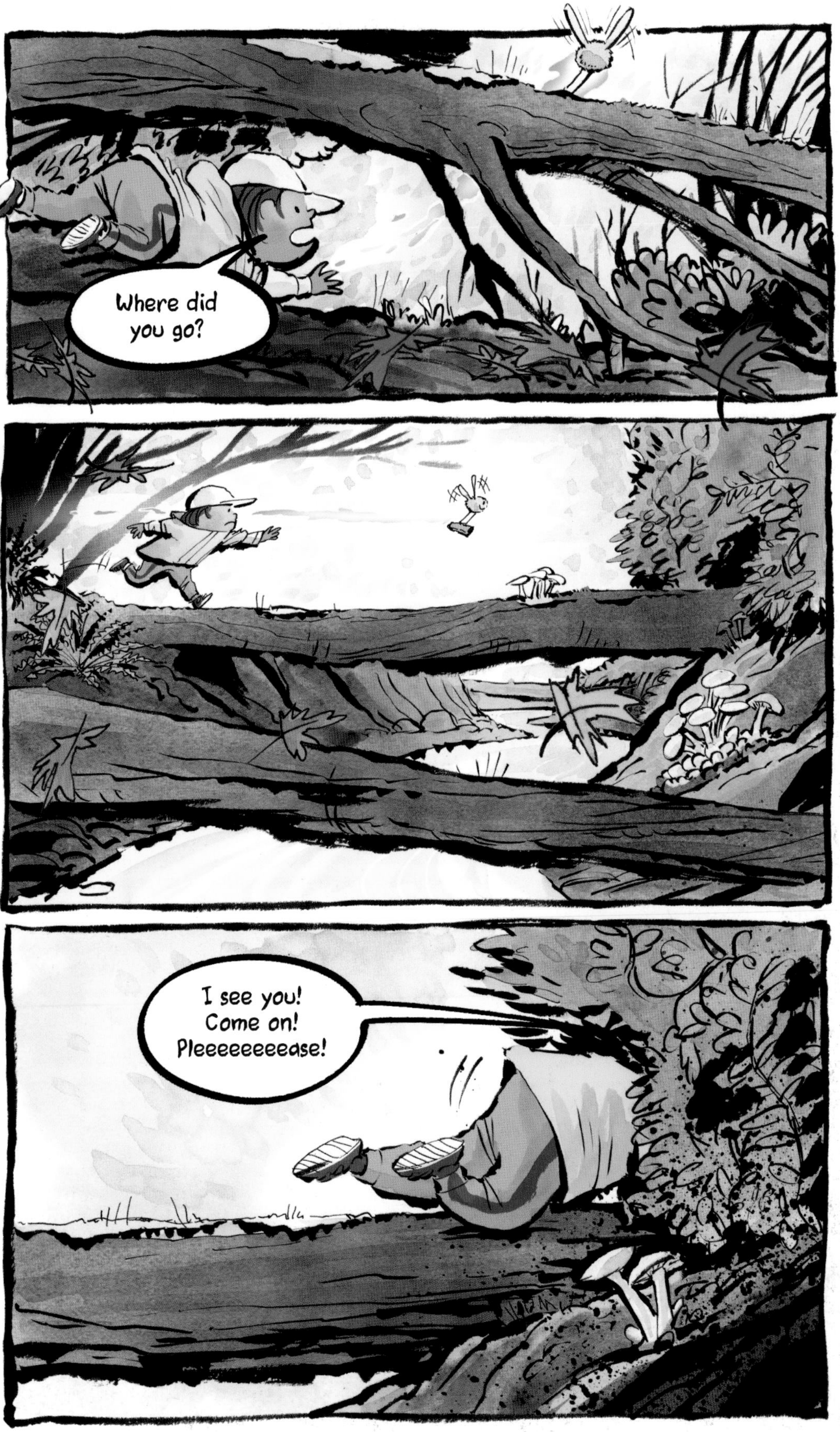
Where did you go?
I see you! Come on! Pleeeeeeeease!

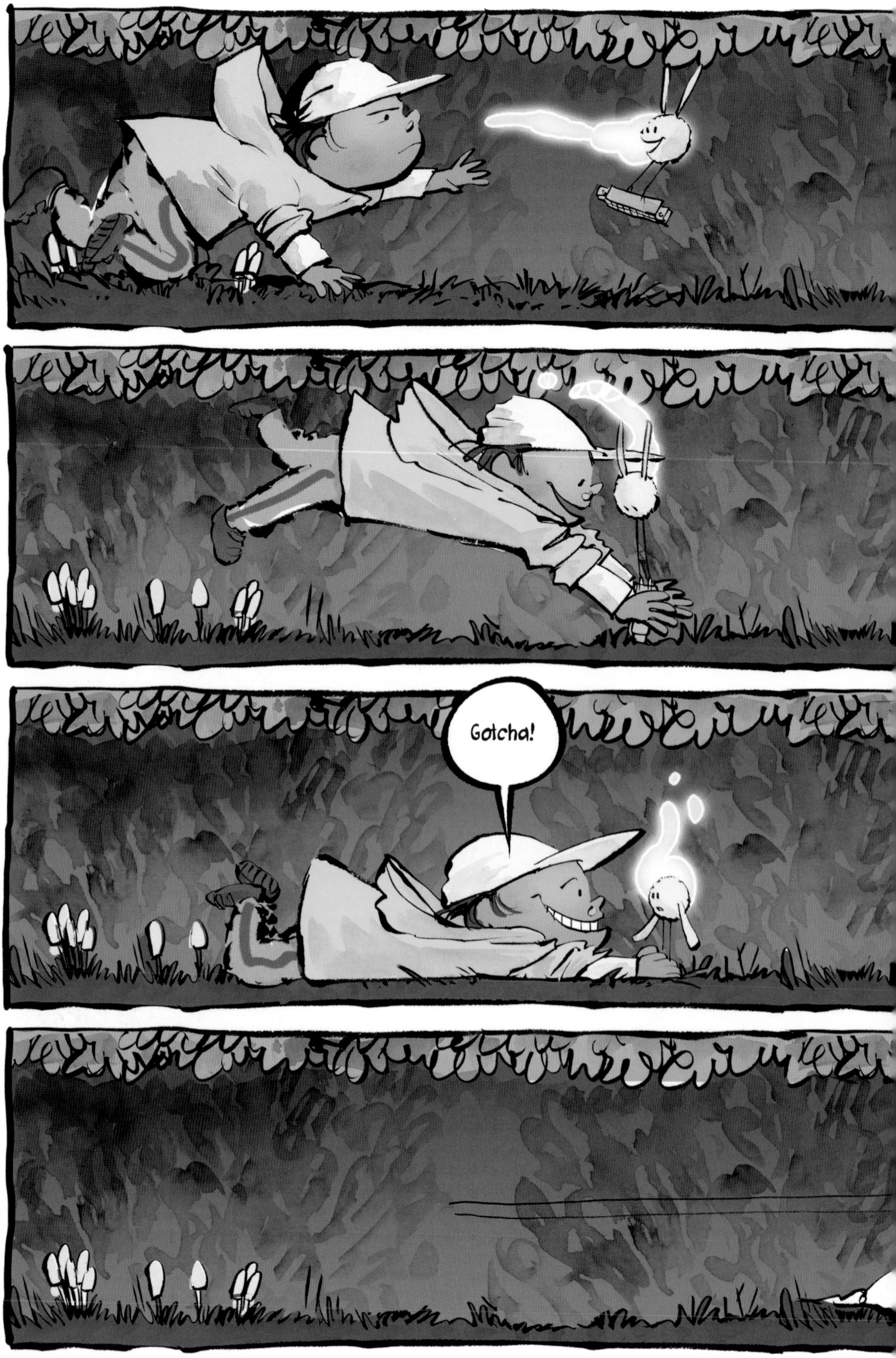
Gotcha!

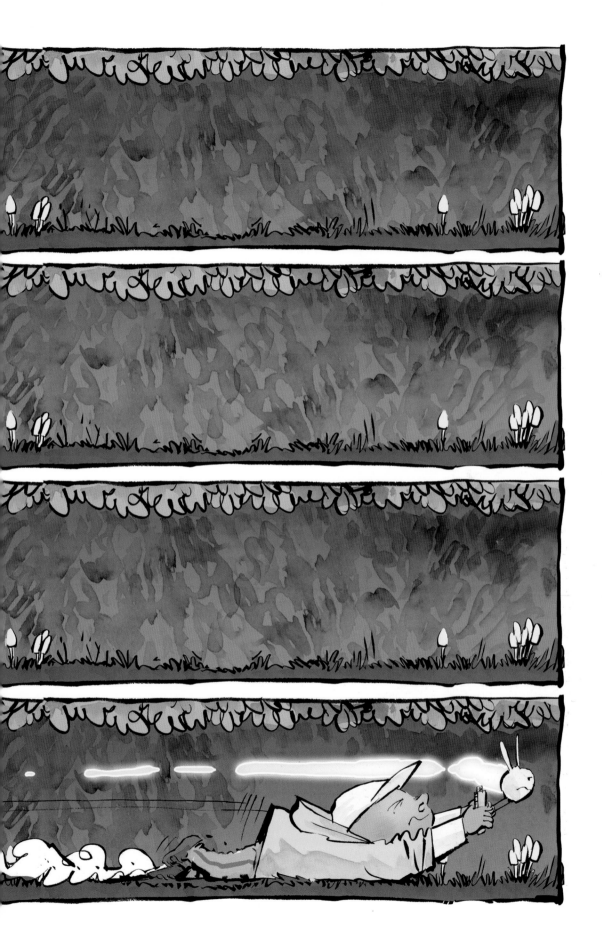

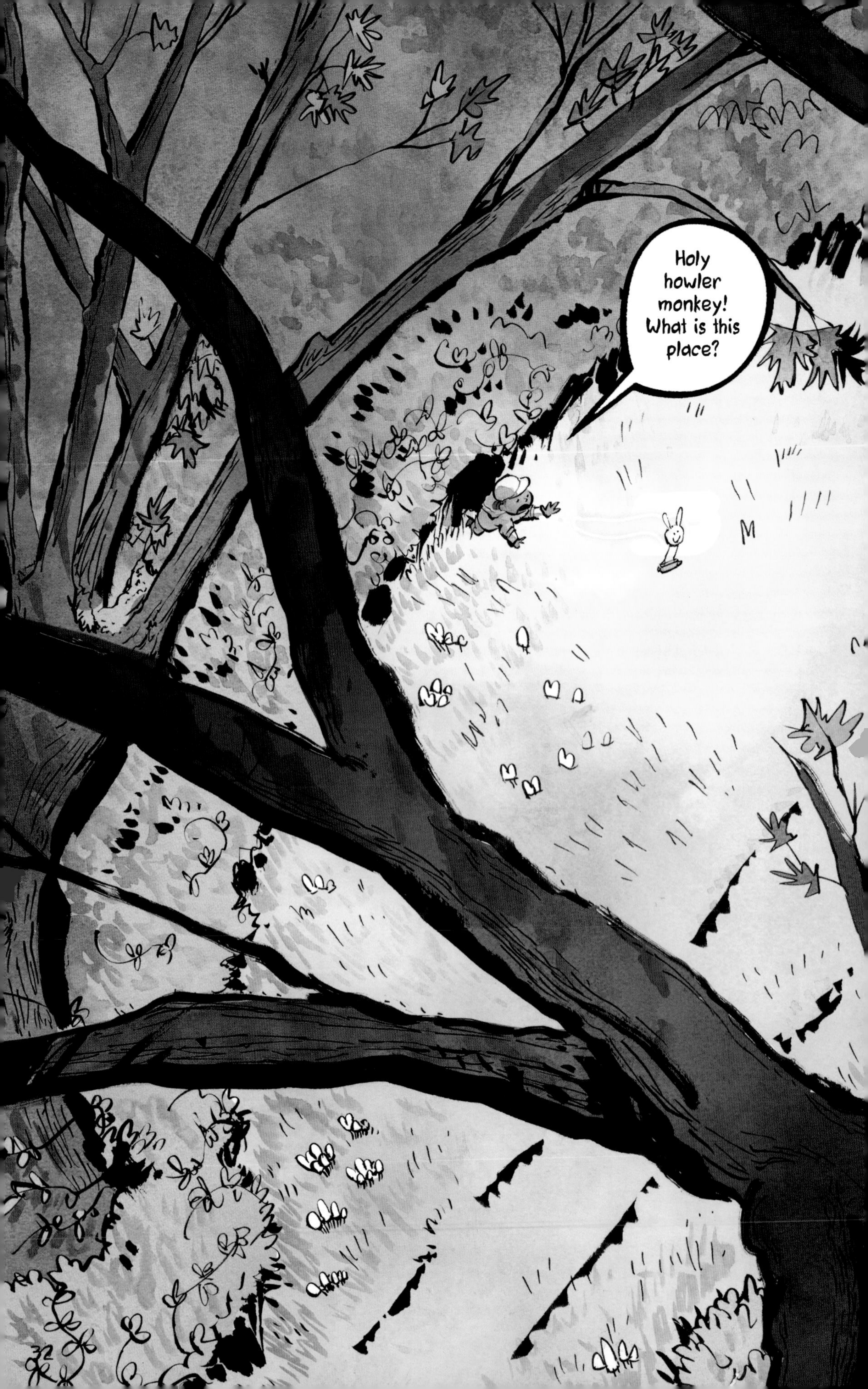
Holy howler monkey! What is this place?

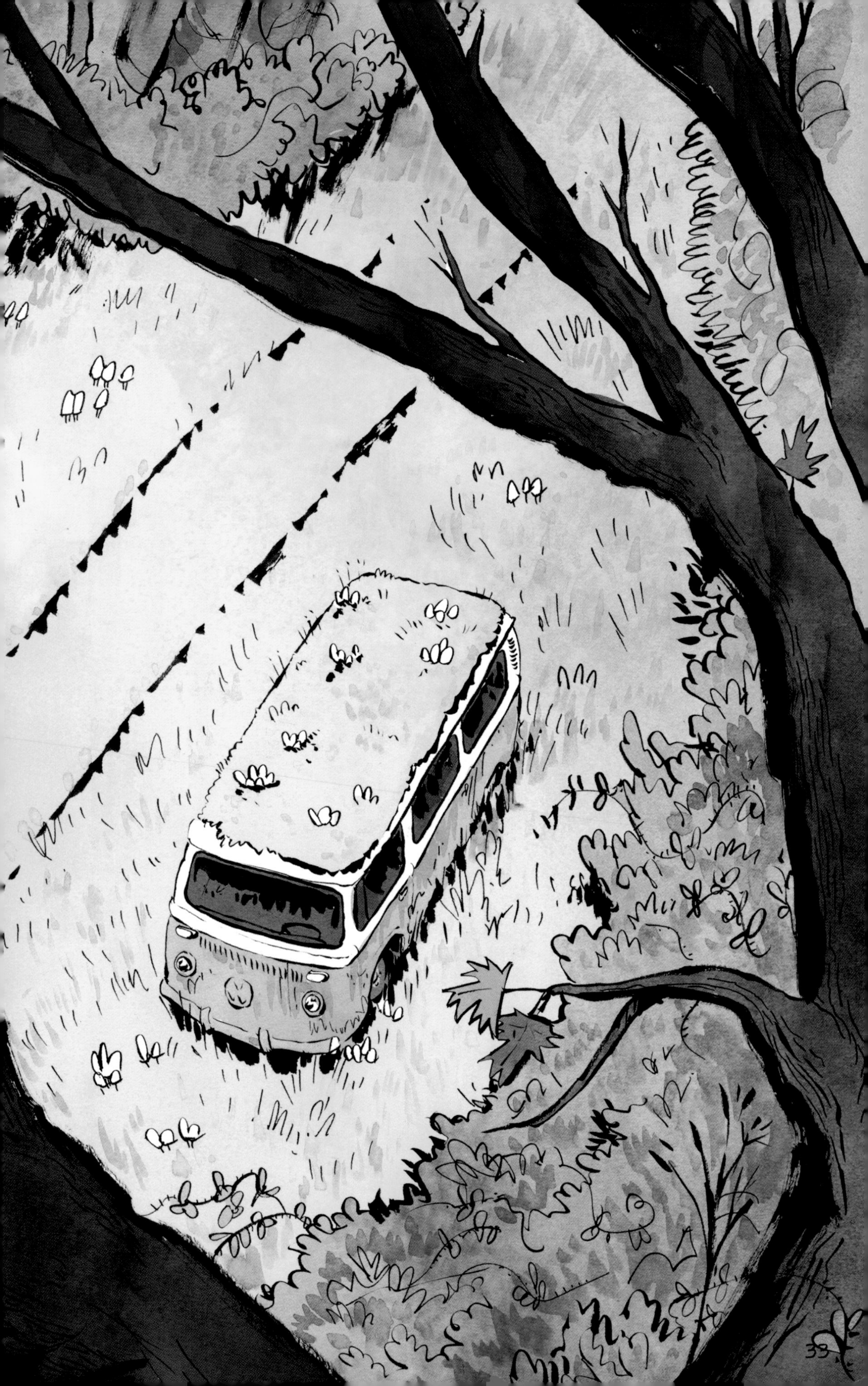

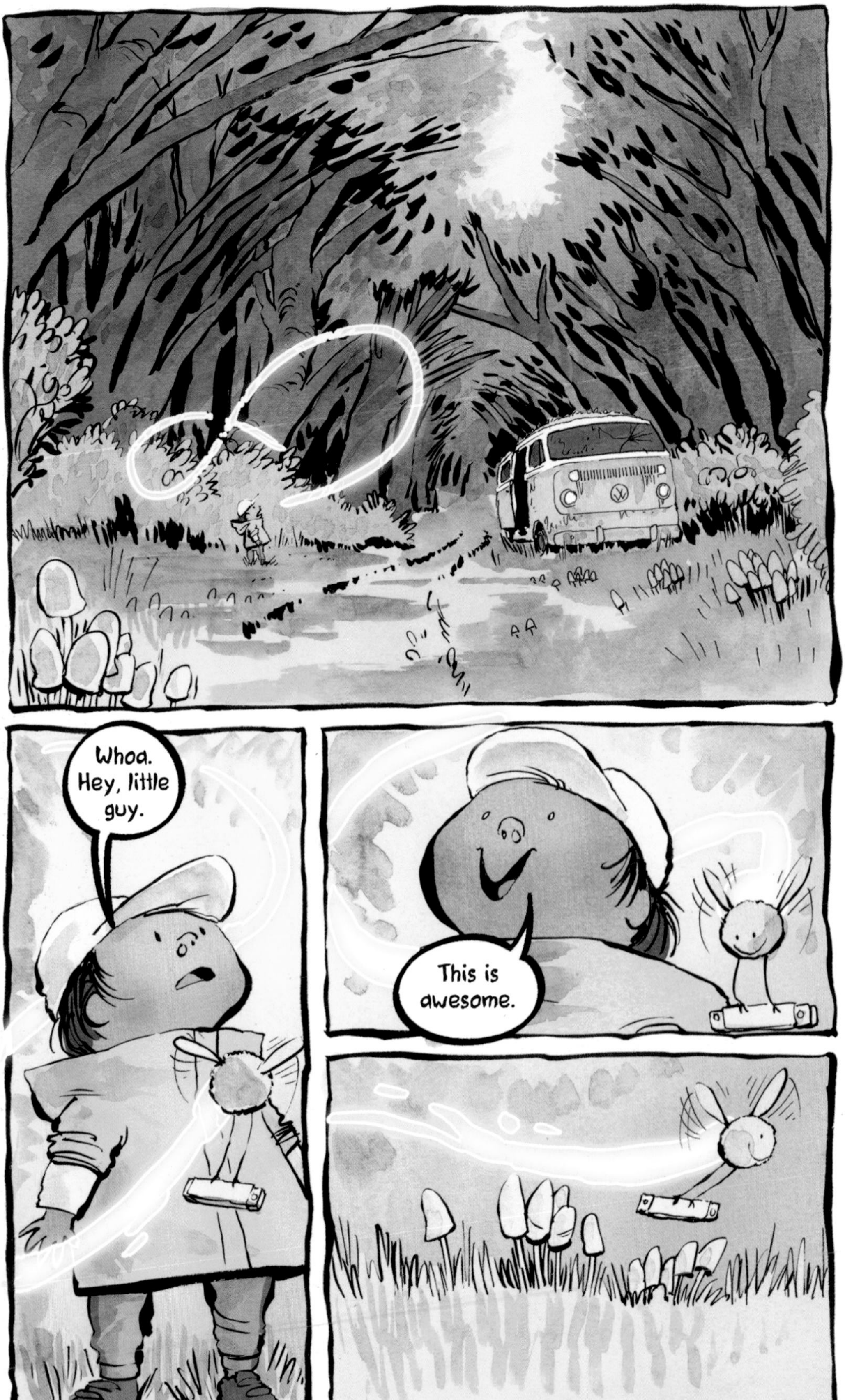
Whoa. Hey, little guy.
This is awesome.

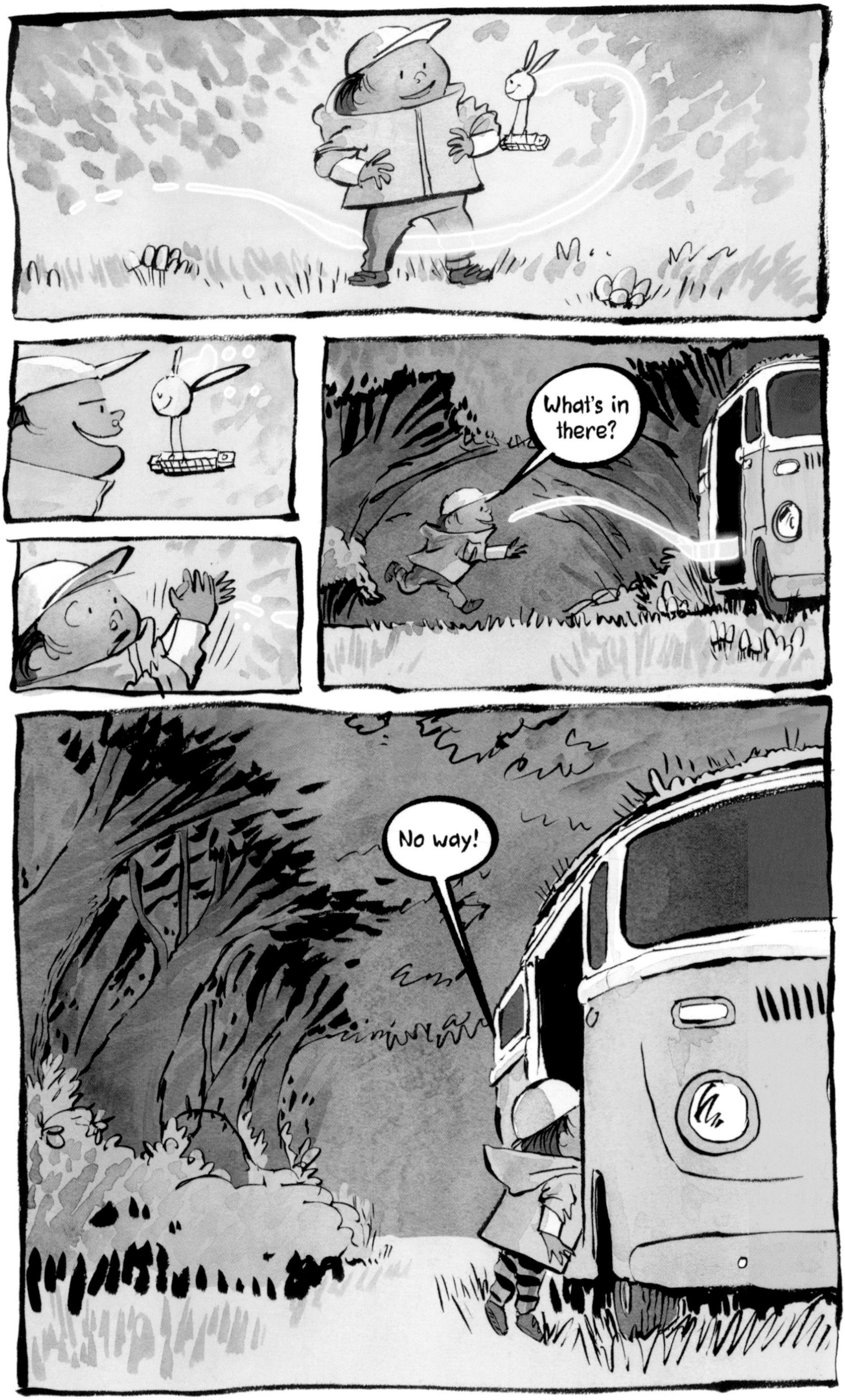
What's in there?
No way!

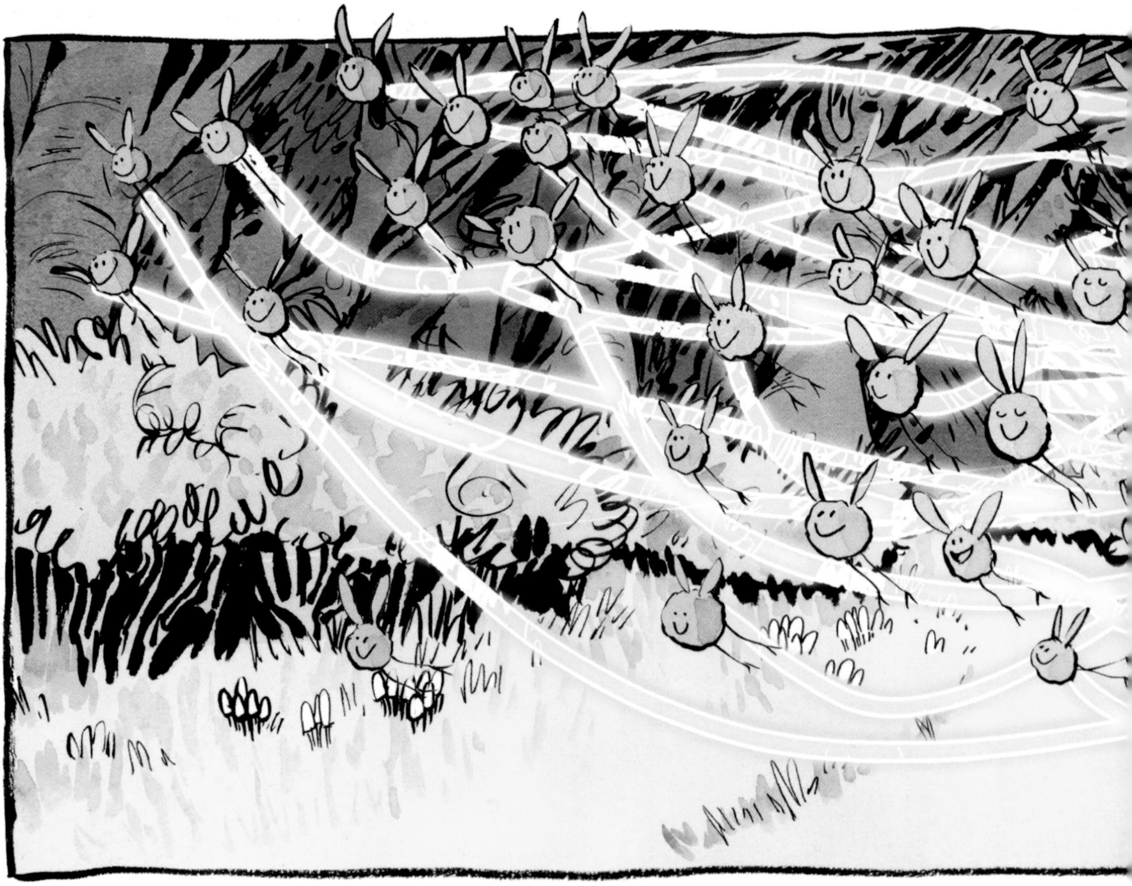

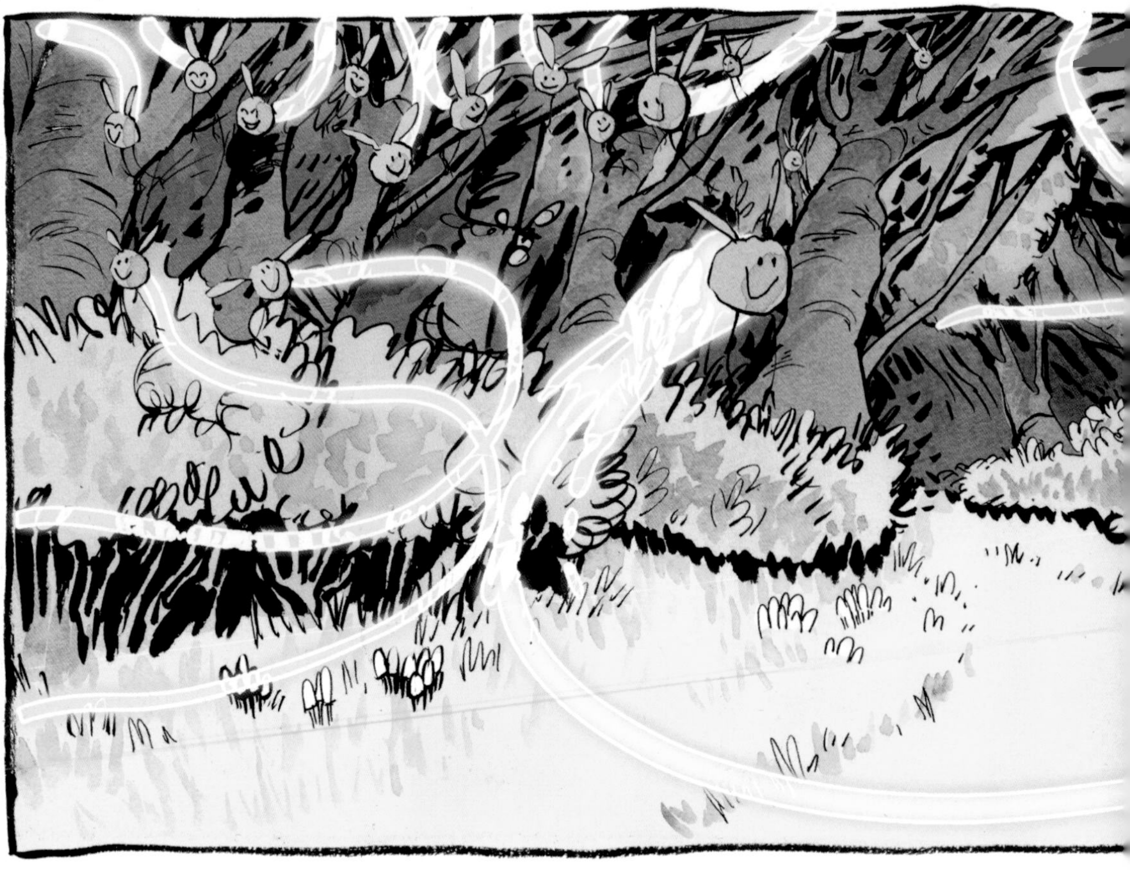

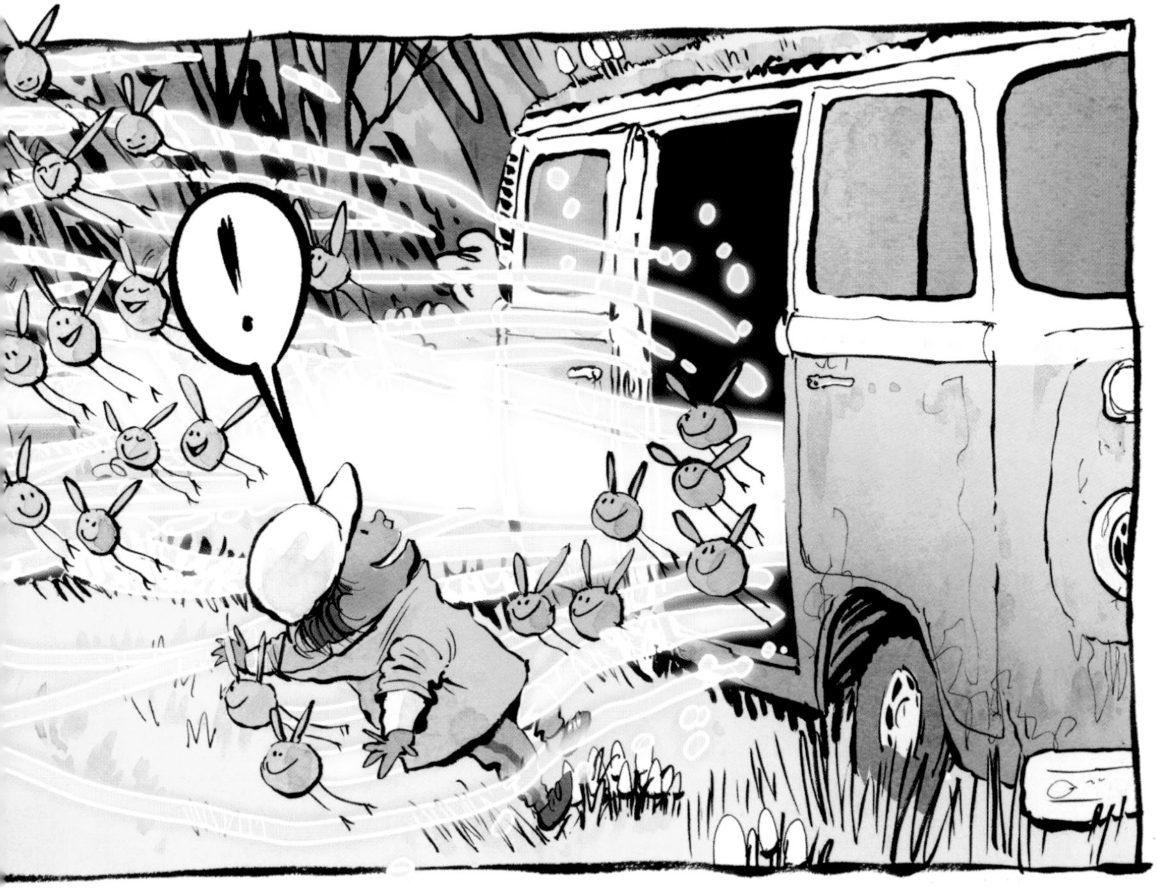
!

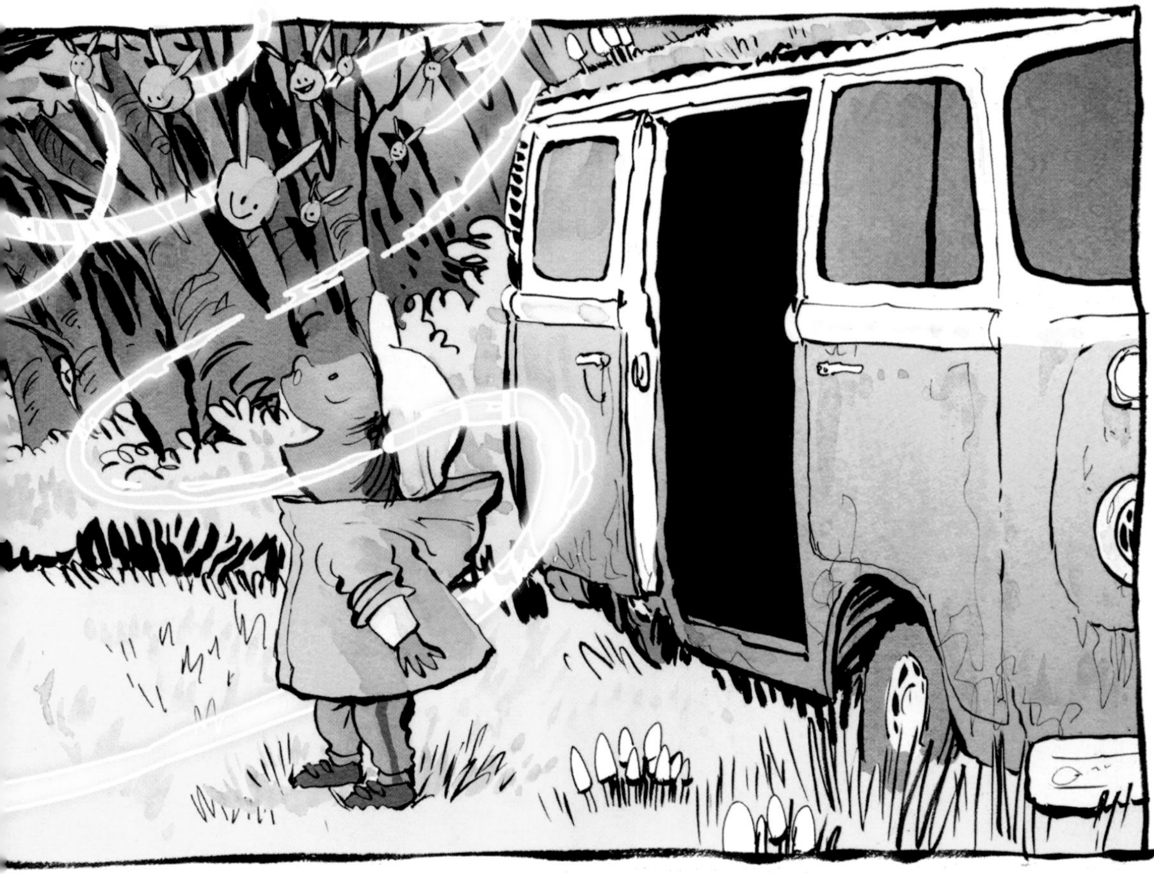

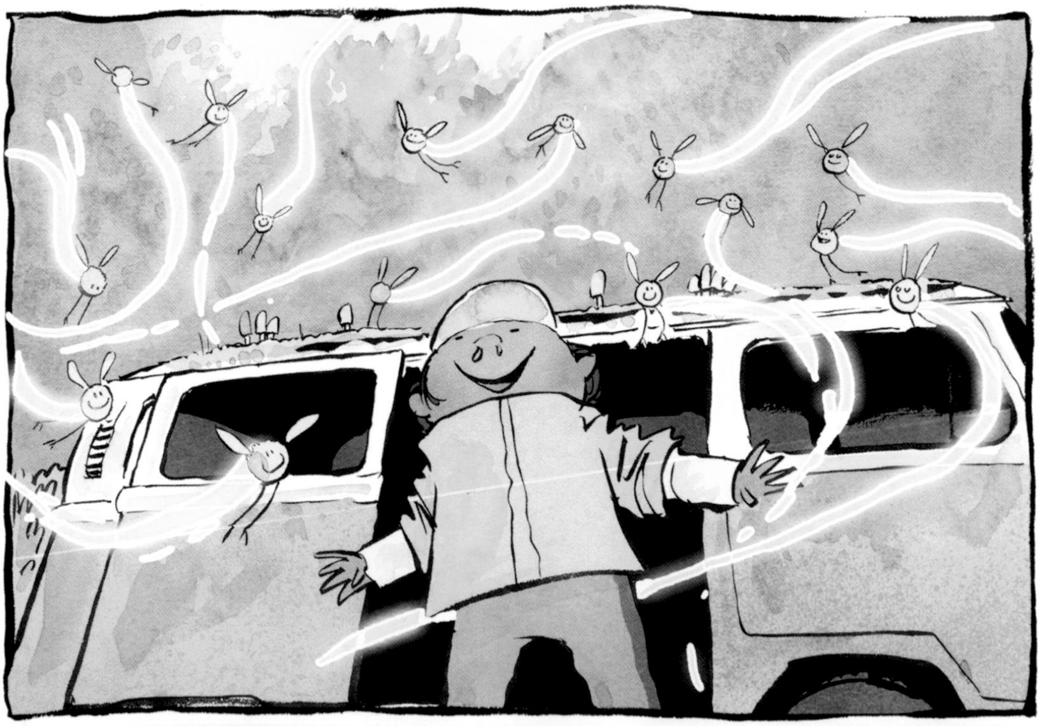

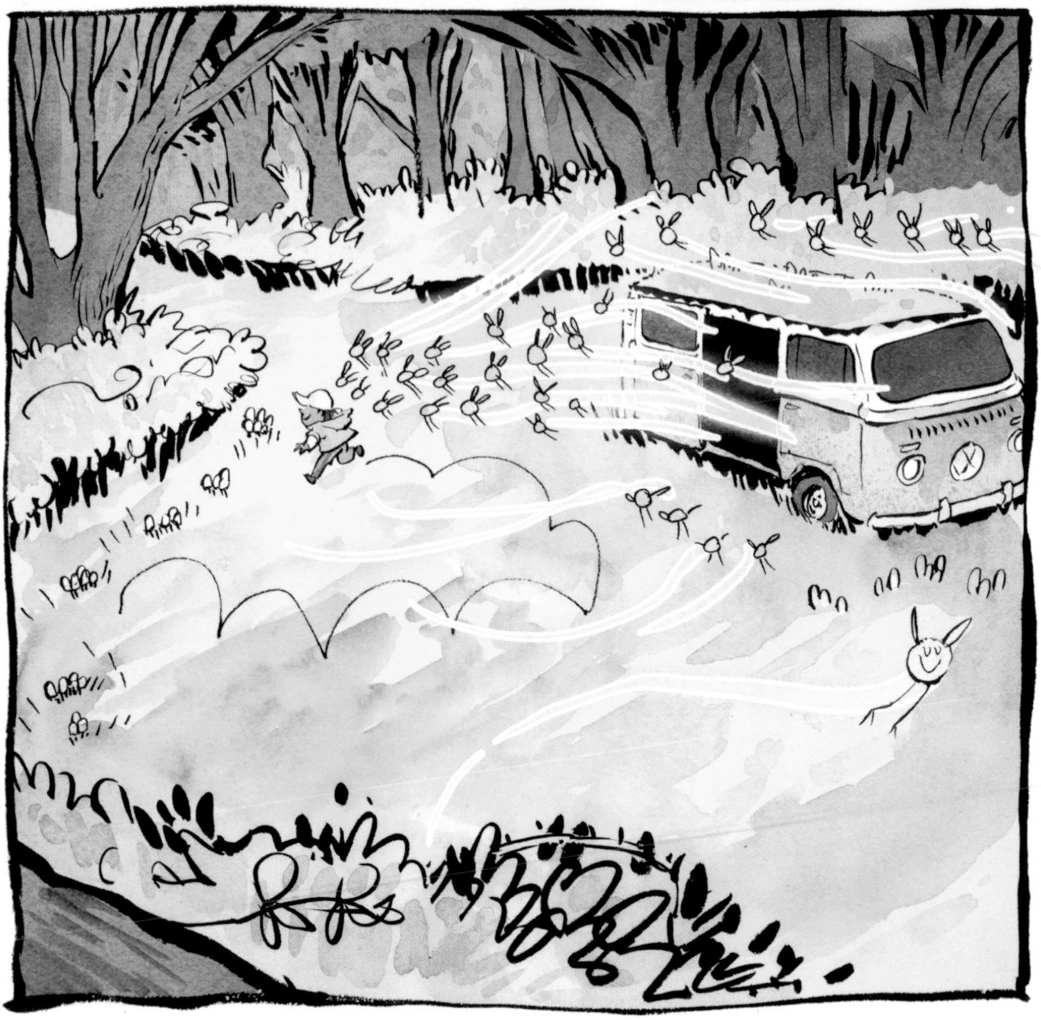

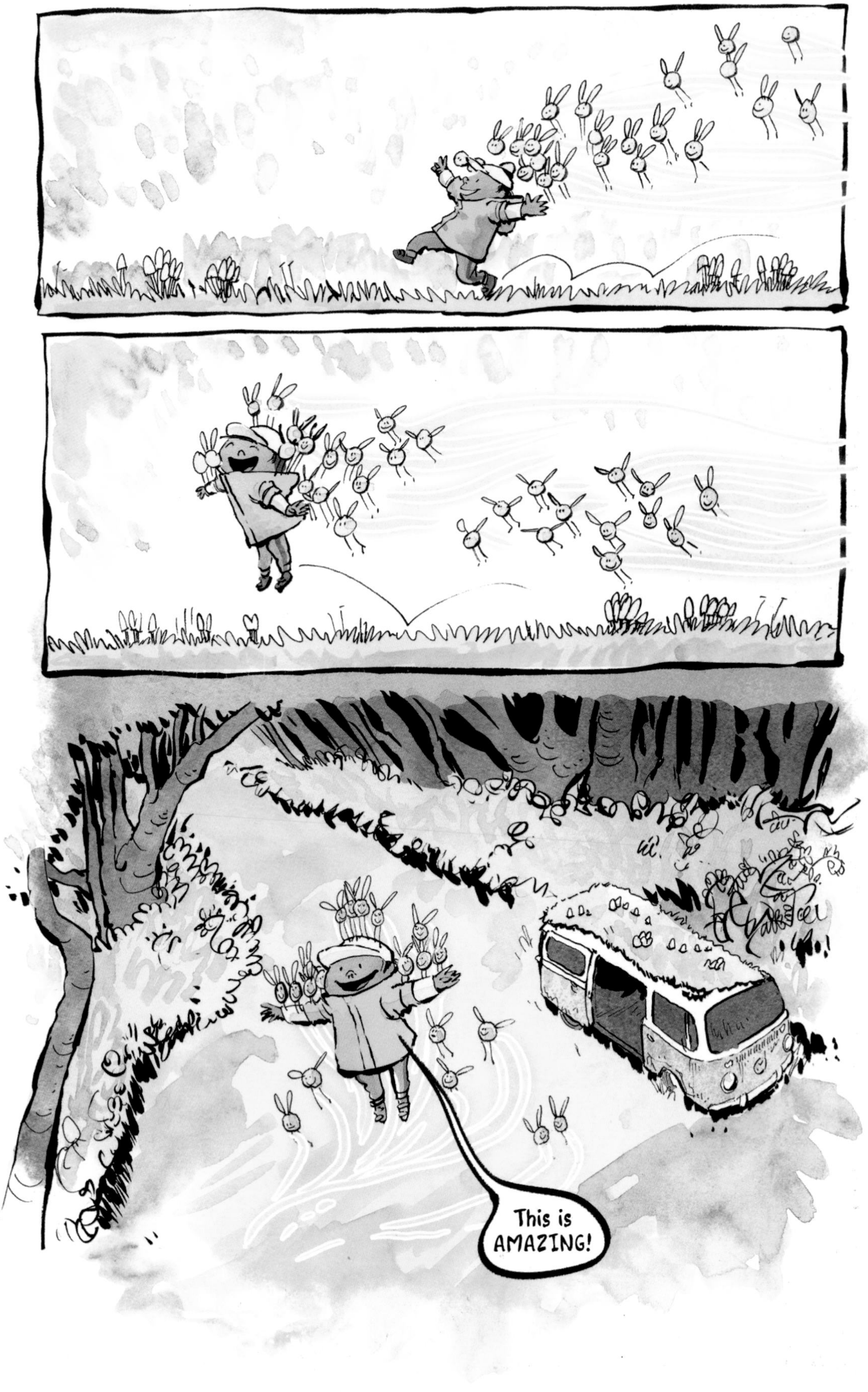
This is AMAZING!

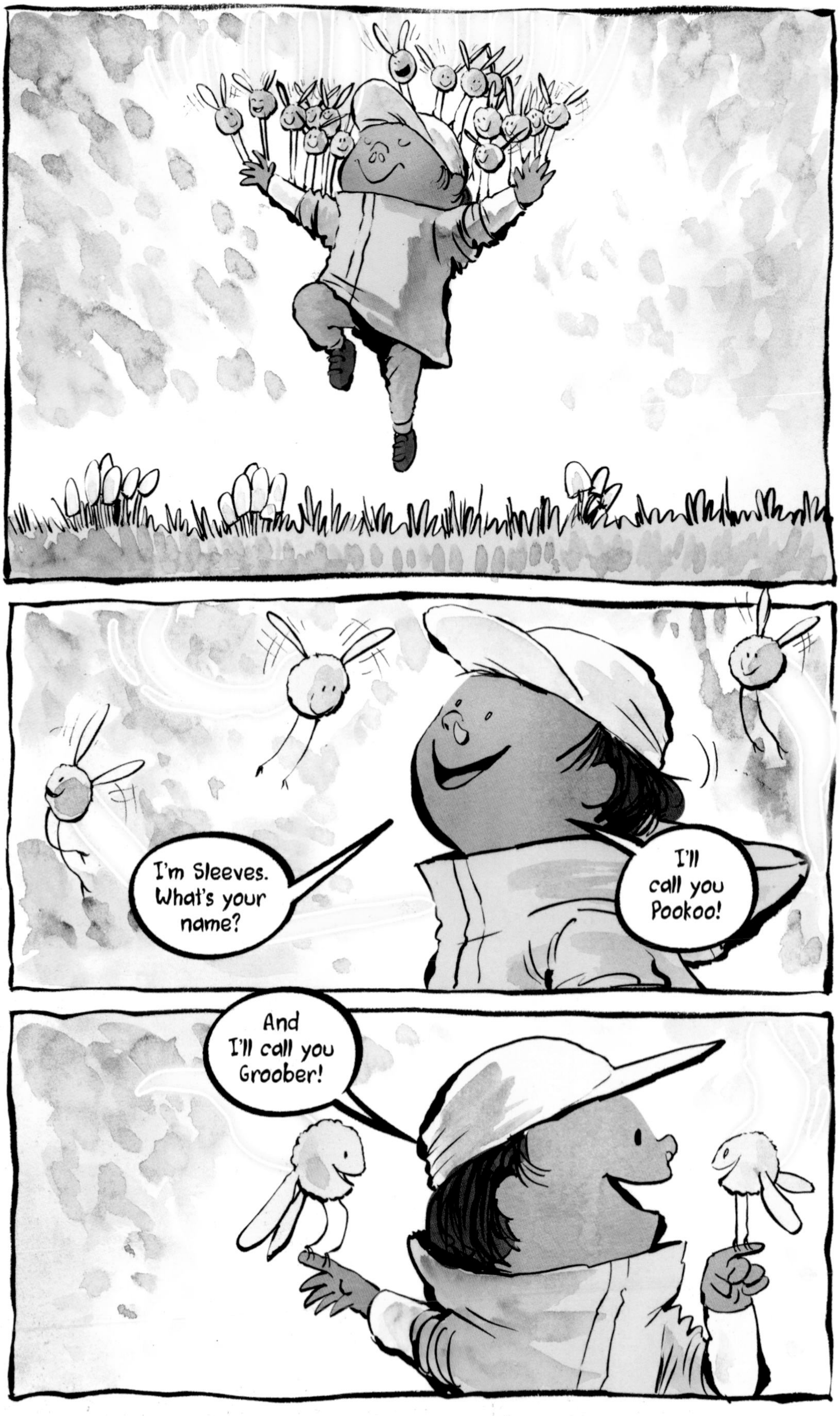
I'm Sleeves. What's your name?
I'll call you Pookoo!
And I'll call you Groober!

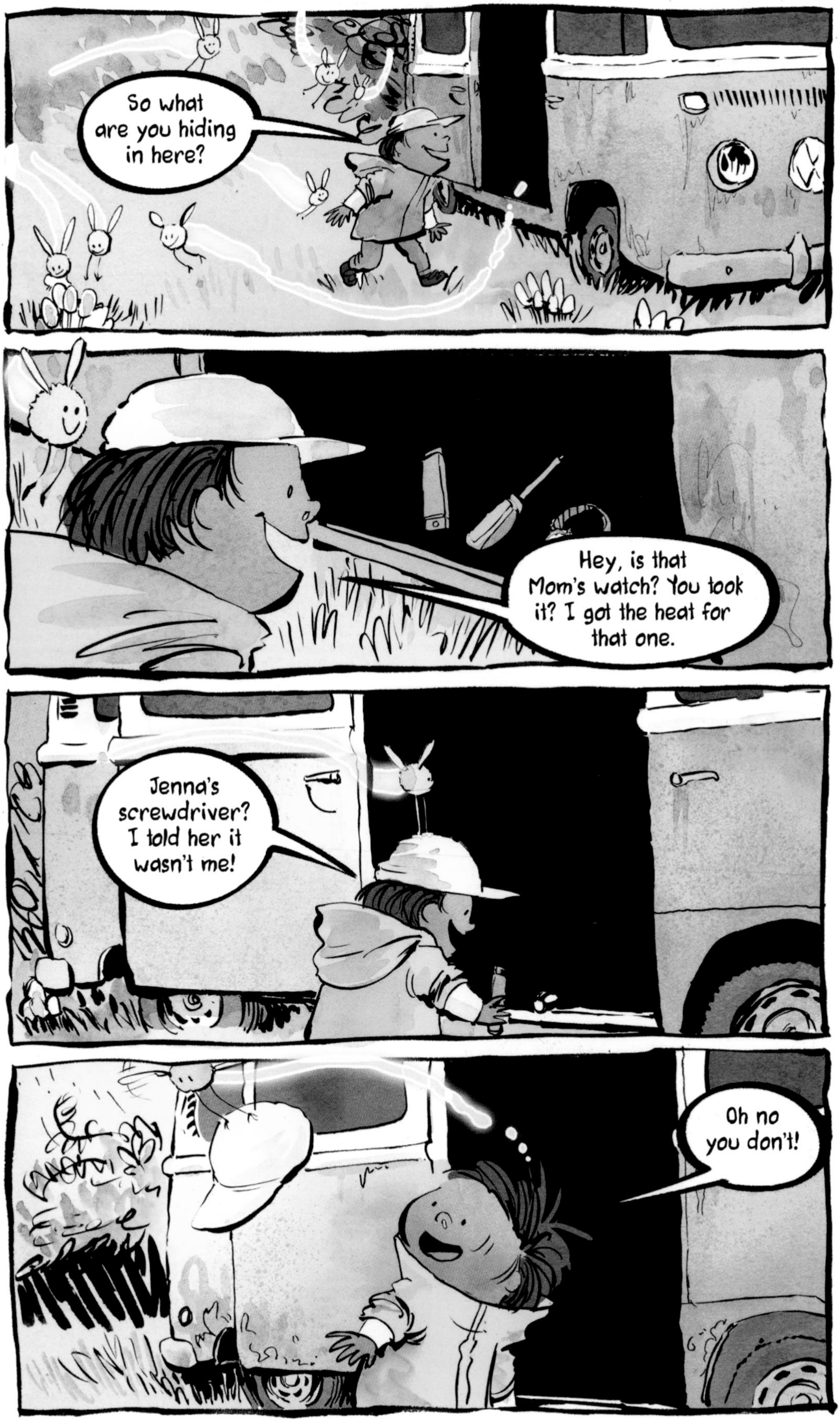
So what are you hiding in here?
Hey, is that Mom's watch? You took it? I got the heat for that one.
Jenna's screwdriver? I told her it wasn't me!
Oh no you don't!

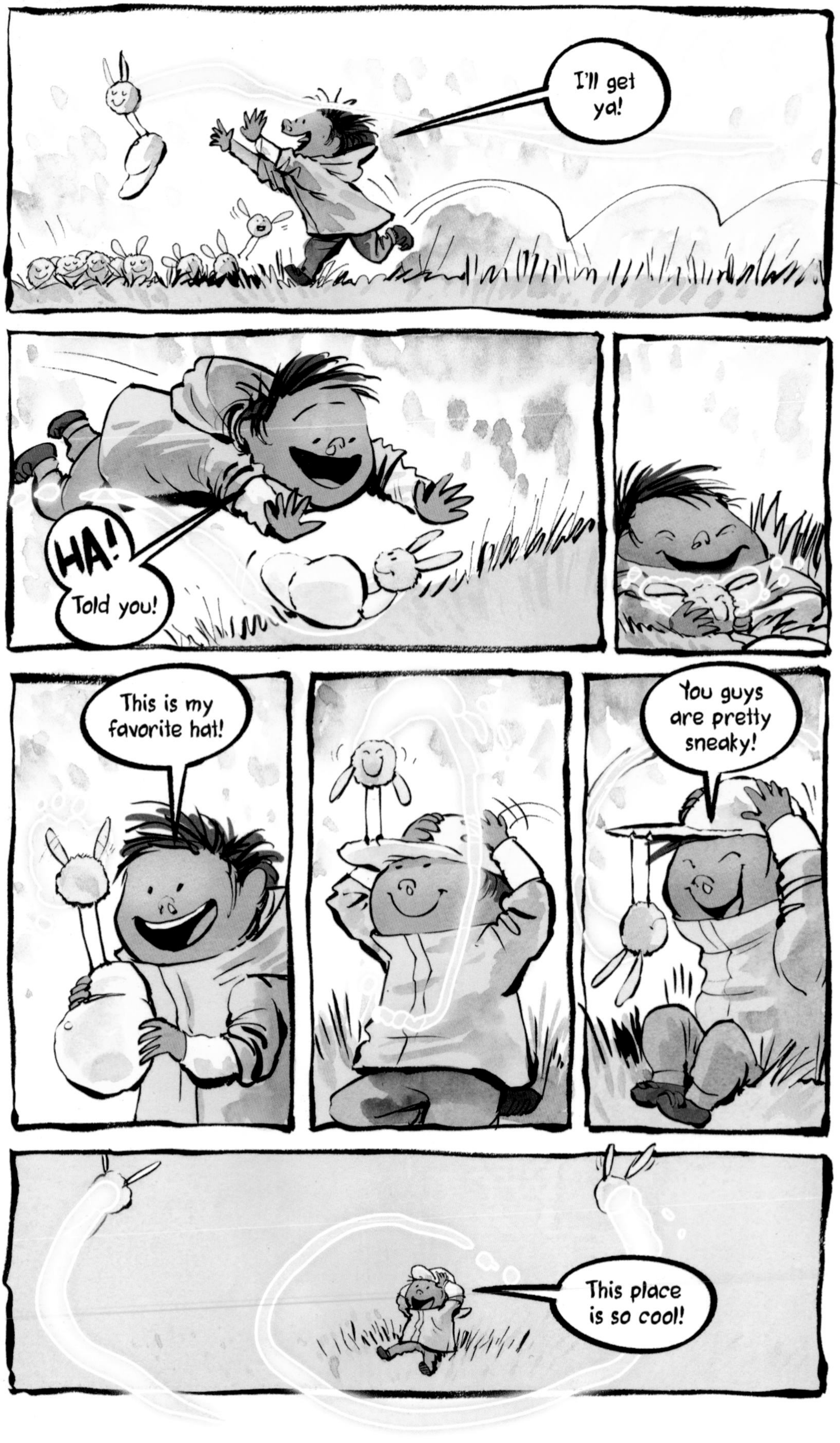
I'll get ya!
HA! Told you!
This is my favorite hat!
You guys are pretty sneaky!
This place is so cool!

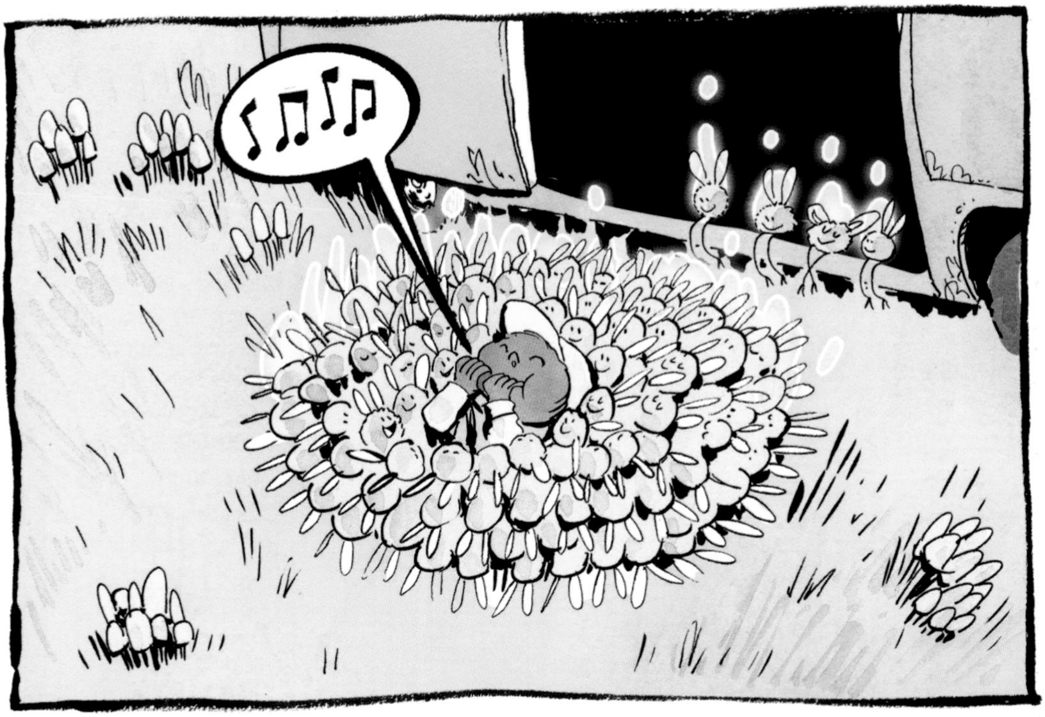

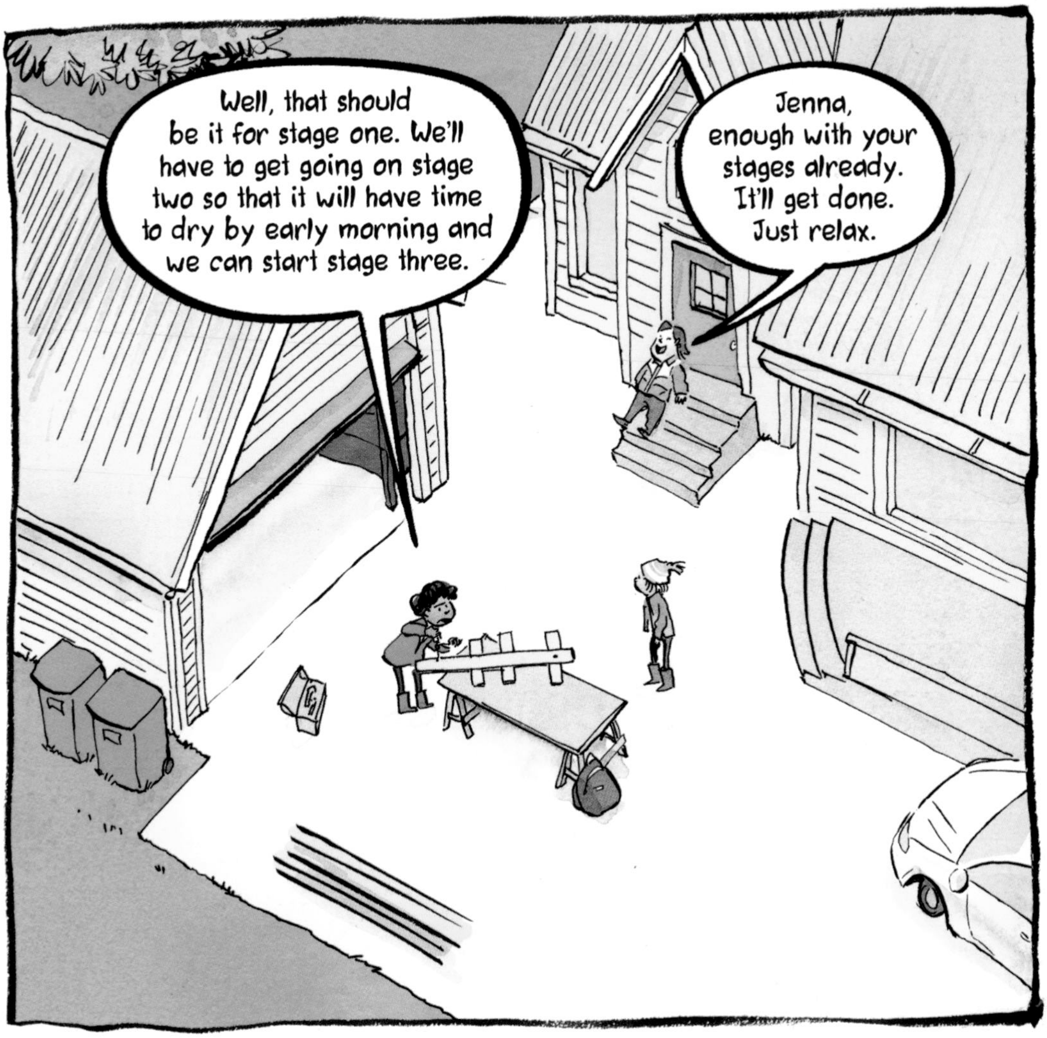
Well, that should be it for stage one. We'll have to get going on stage two so that it will have time to dry by early morning and we can start stage three.
Jenna, enough with your stages already. It'll get done. Just relax.

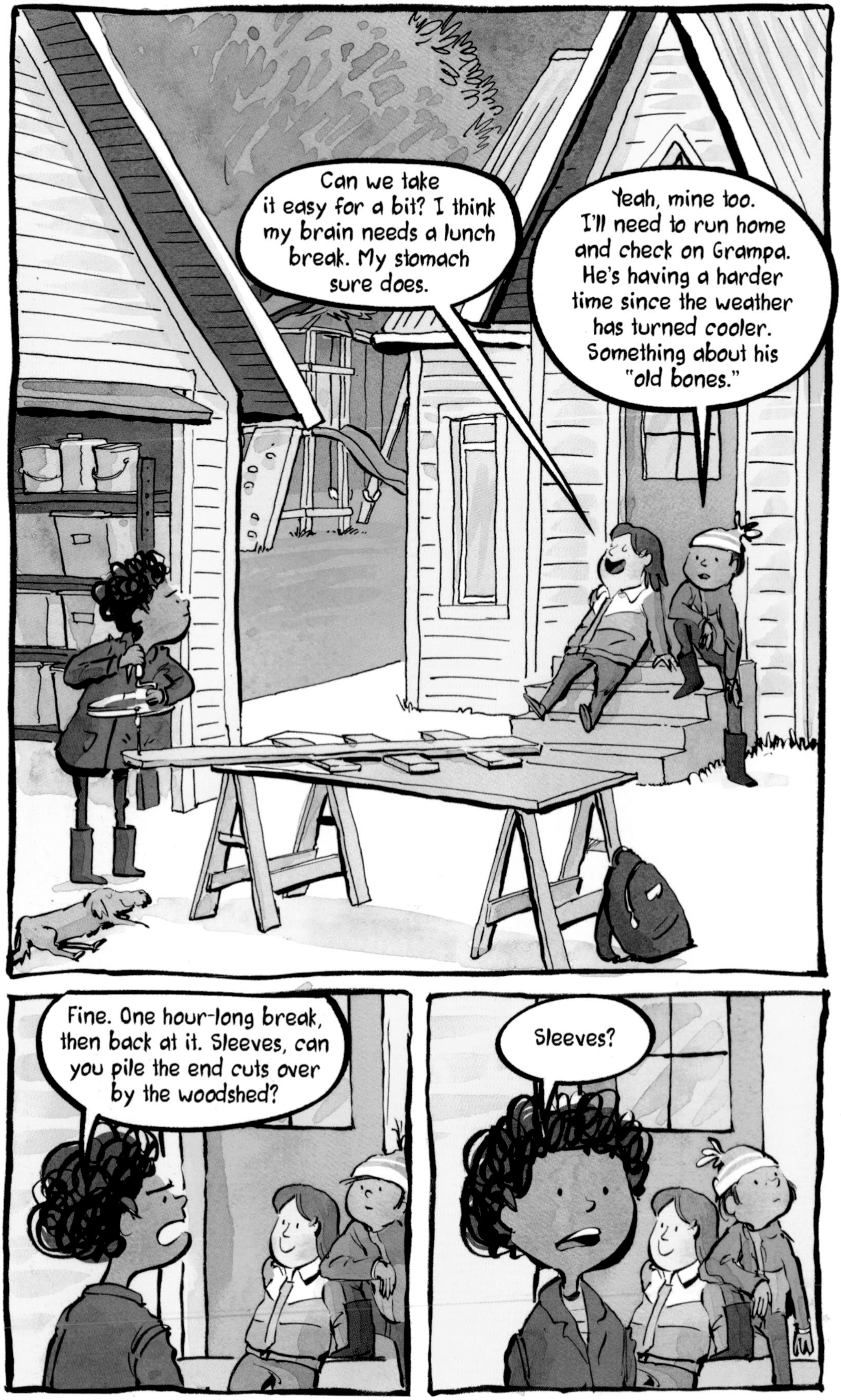
Can we take it easy for a bit? I think my brain needs a lunch break. My stomach sure does.
Yeah, mine too. I'll need to run home and check on Grampa. He's having a harder time since the weather has turned cooler. Something about his "old bones."
Fine. One hour-long break, then back at it. Sleeves, can you pile the end cuts over by the woodshed?
Sleeves?

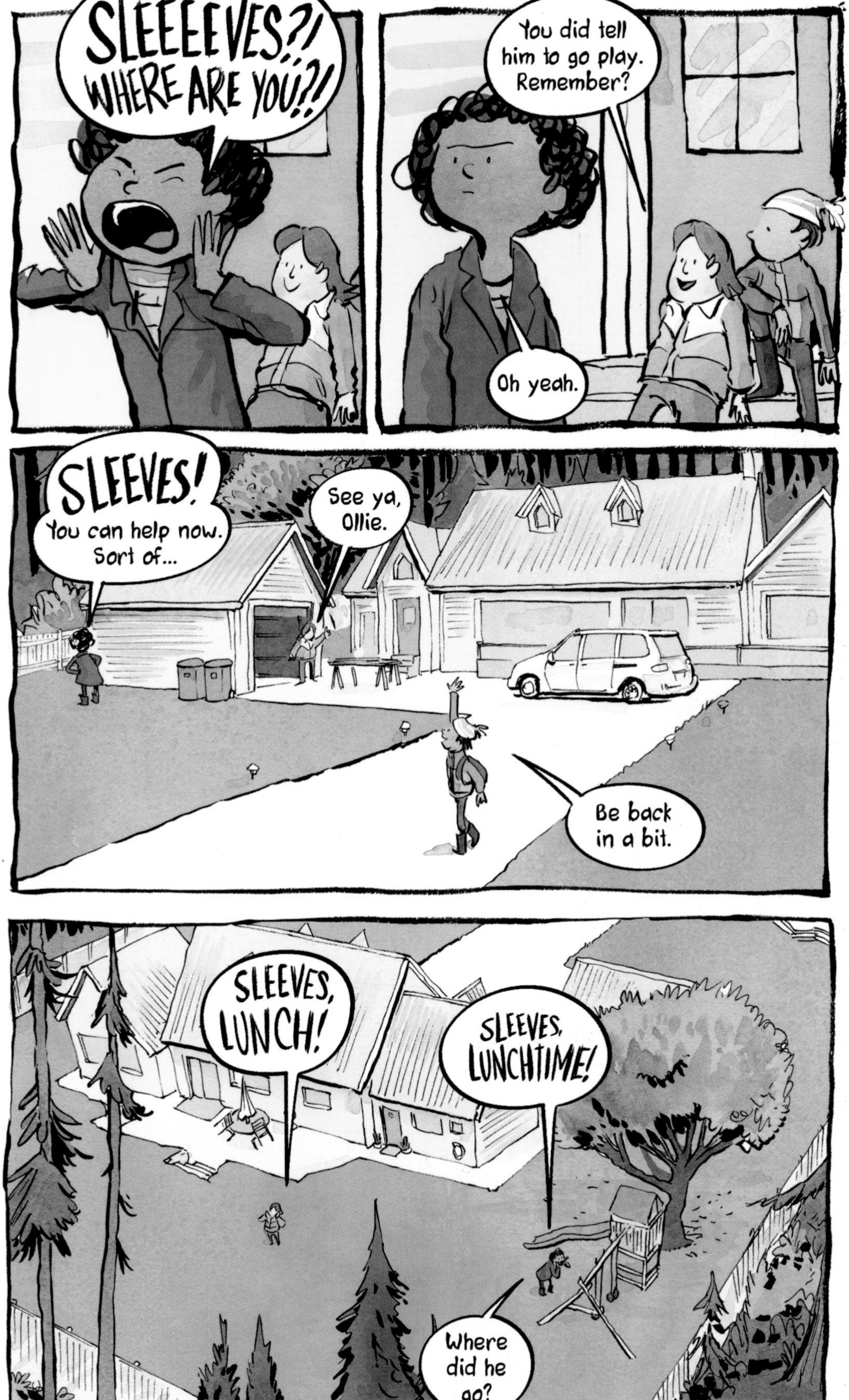
SLEEEEVES?! WHERE ARE YOU?!
You did tell him to go play. Remember?
Oh yeah.
SLEEVES! You can help now. Sort of...
See ya, Ollie.
Be back in a bit.
SLEEVES, LUNCH!
SLEEVES, LUNCHTIME!
Where did he go?

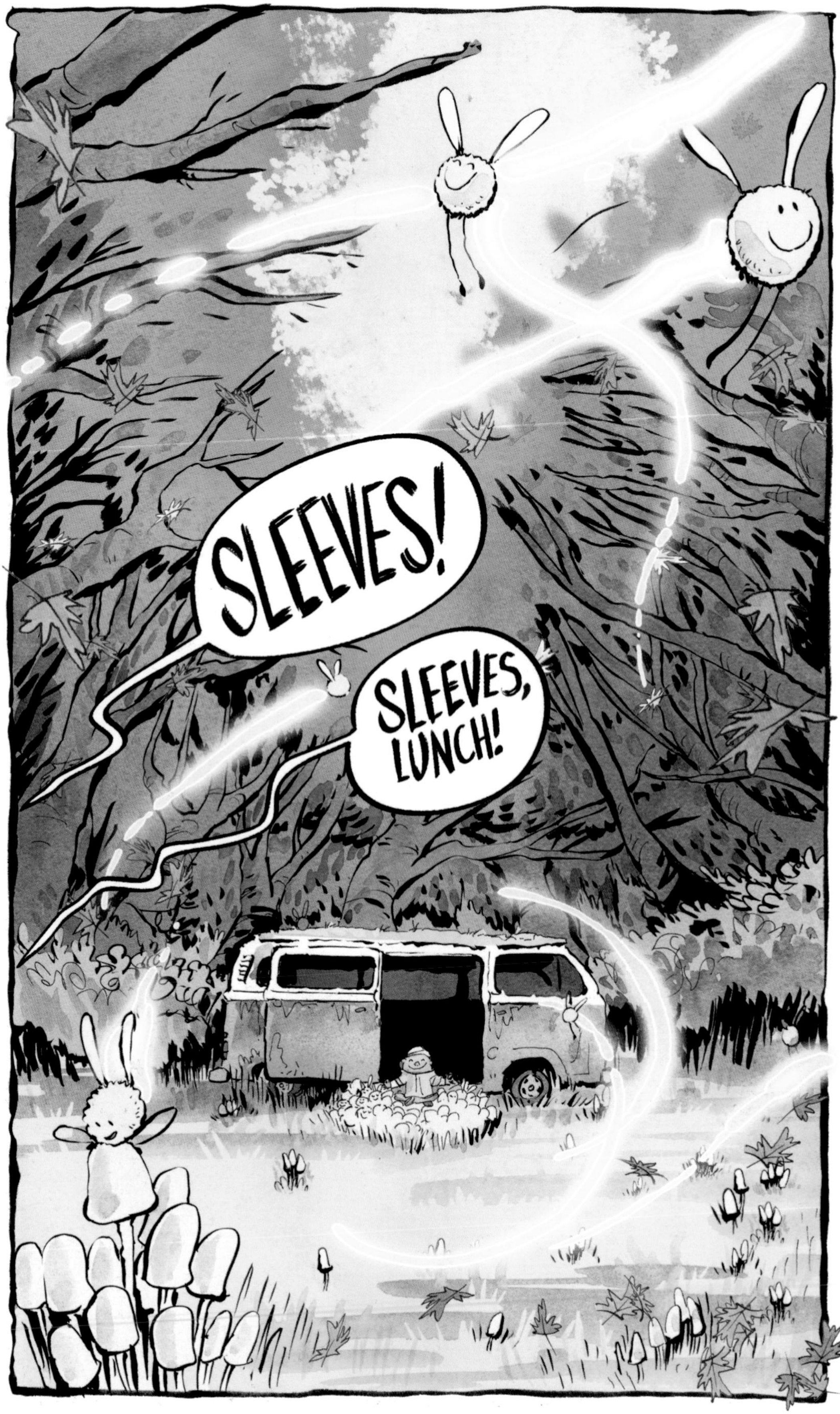
SLEEVES!
SLEEVES, LUNCH!

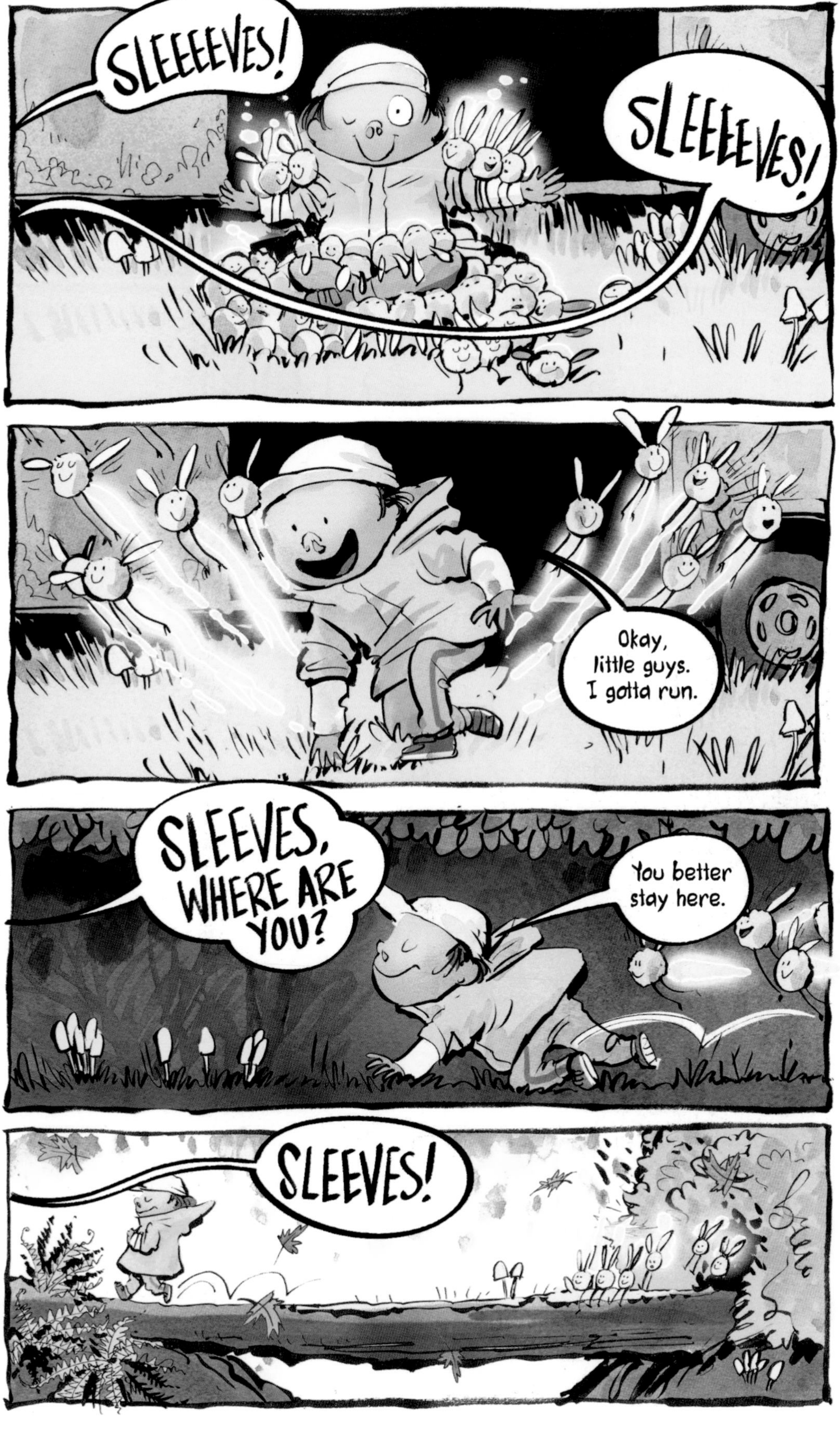
SLEEEEVES!
SLEEEEVES!
Okay, little guys. I gotta run.
SLEEVES, WHERE ARE YOU?
You better stay here.
SLEEVES!

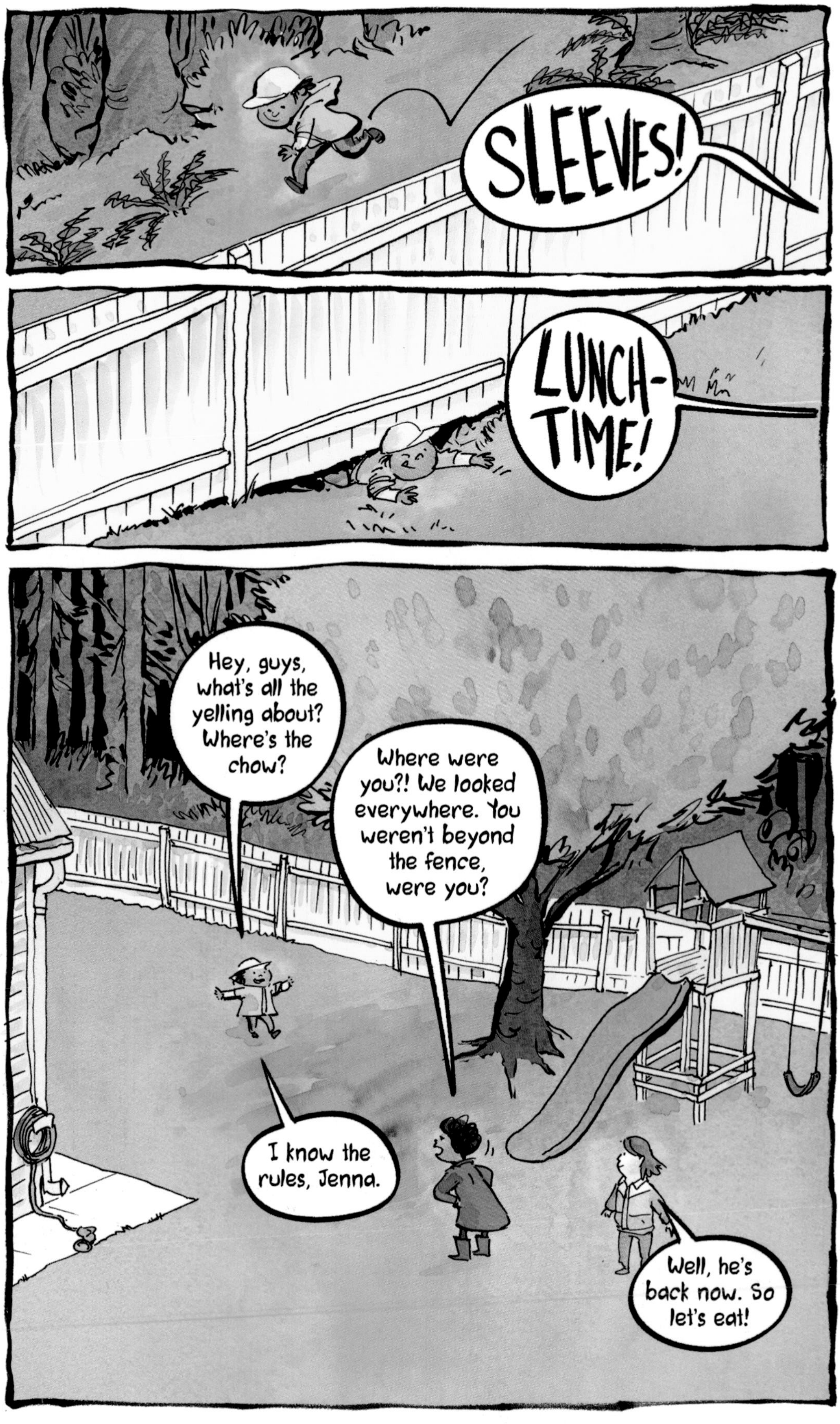
SLEEVES!
LUNCH-TIME!
Hey, guys, what's all the yelling about? Where's the chow?
Where were you?! We looked everywhere. You weren't beyond the fence, were you?
I know the rules, Jenna.
Well, he's back now. So let's eat!

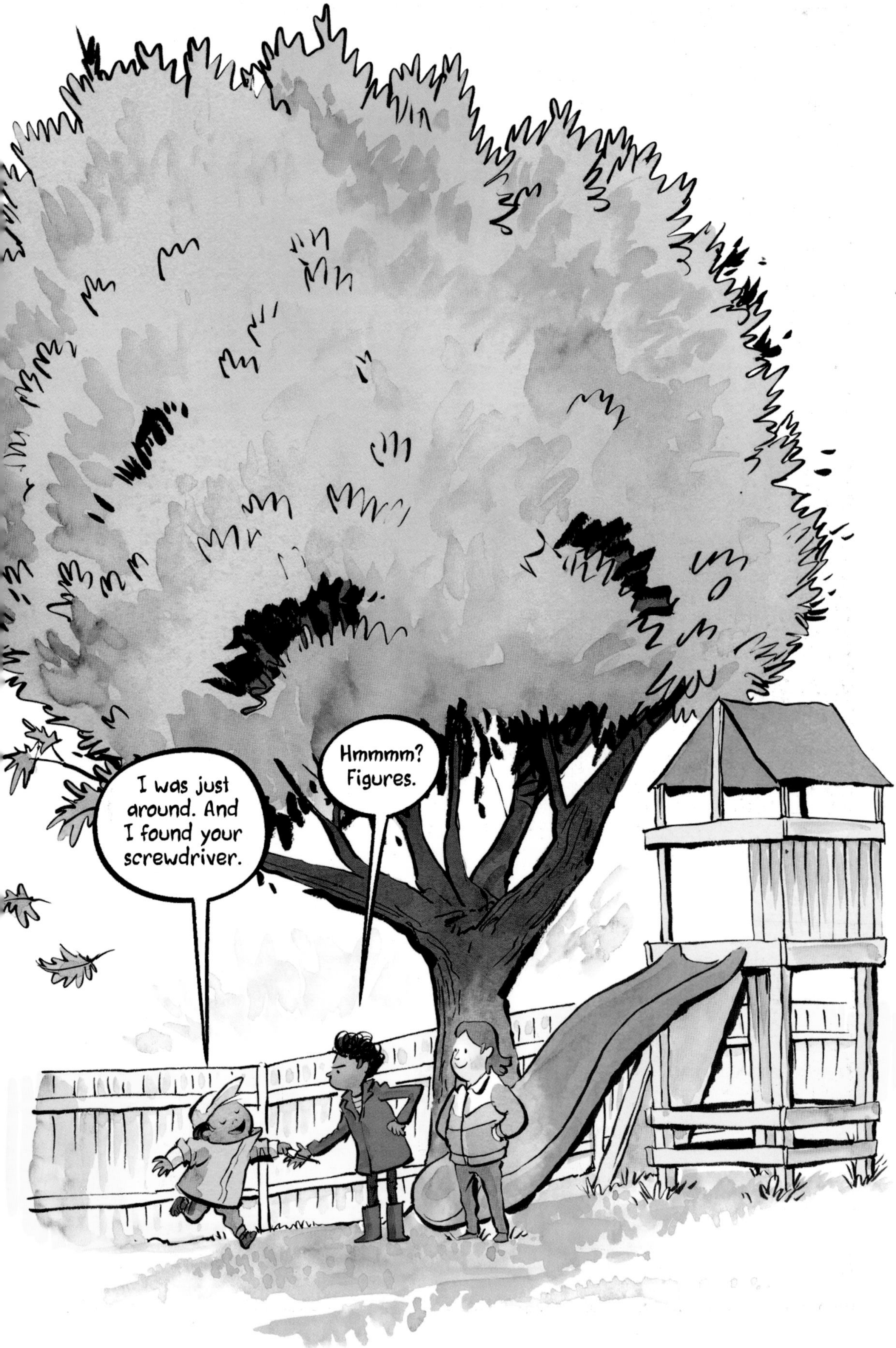
I was just around. And I found your screwdriver.
Hmmmm? Figures.

CHAPTER TWO

The Curse of the Hivers

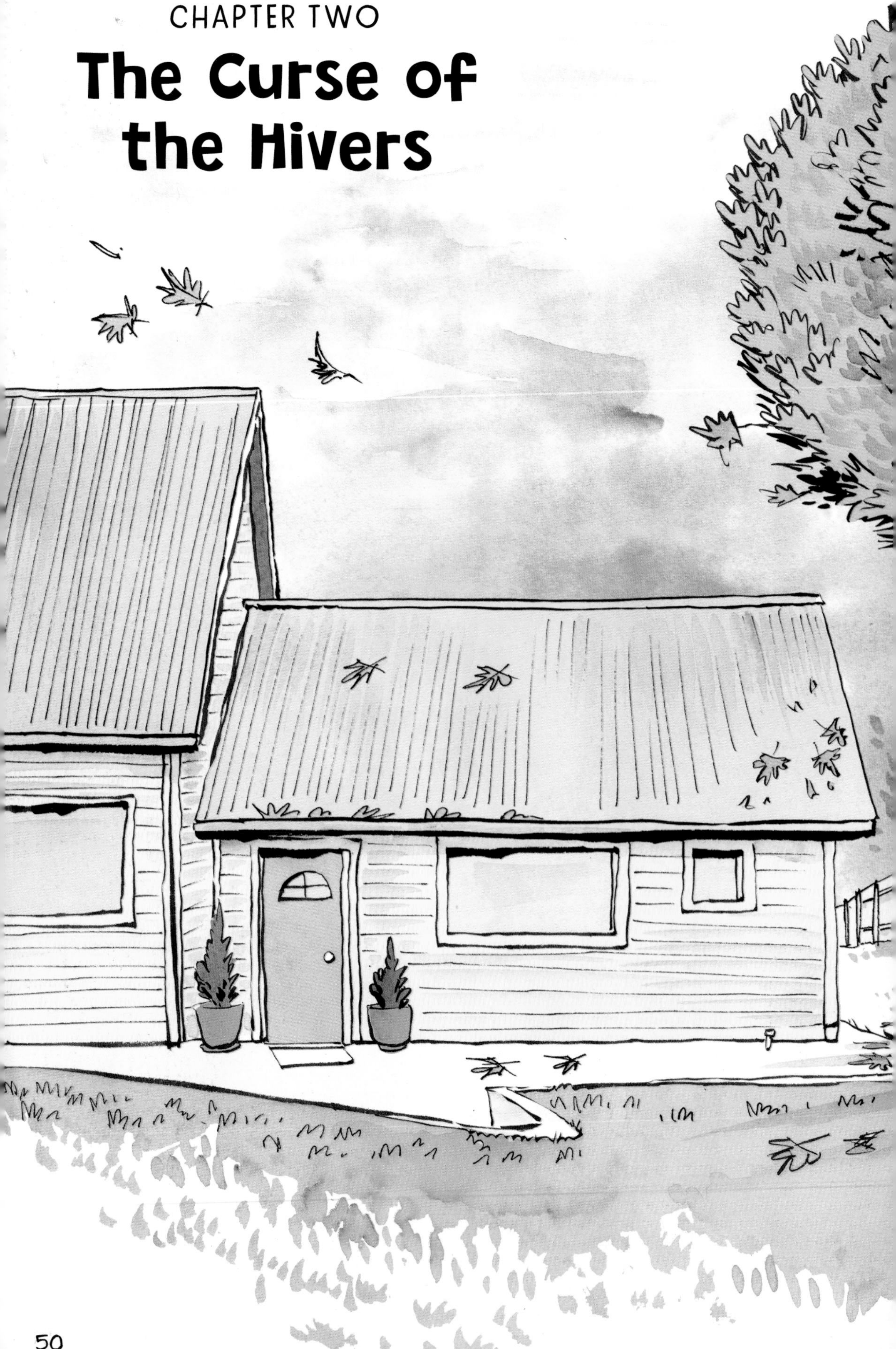

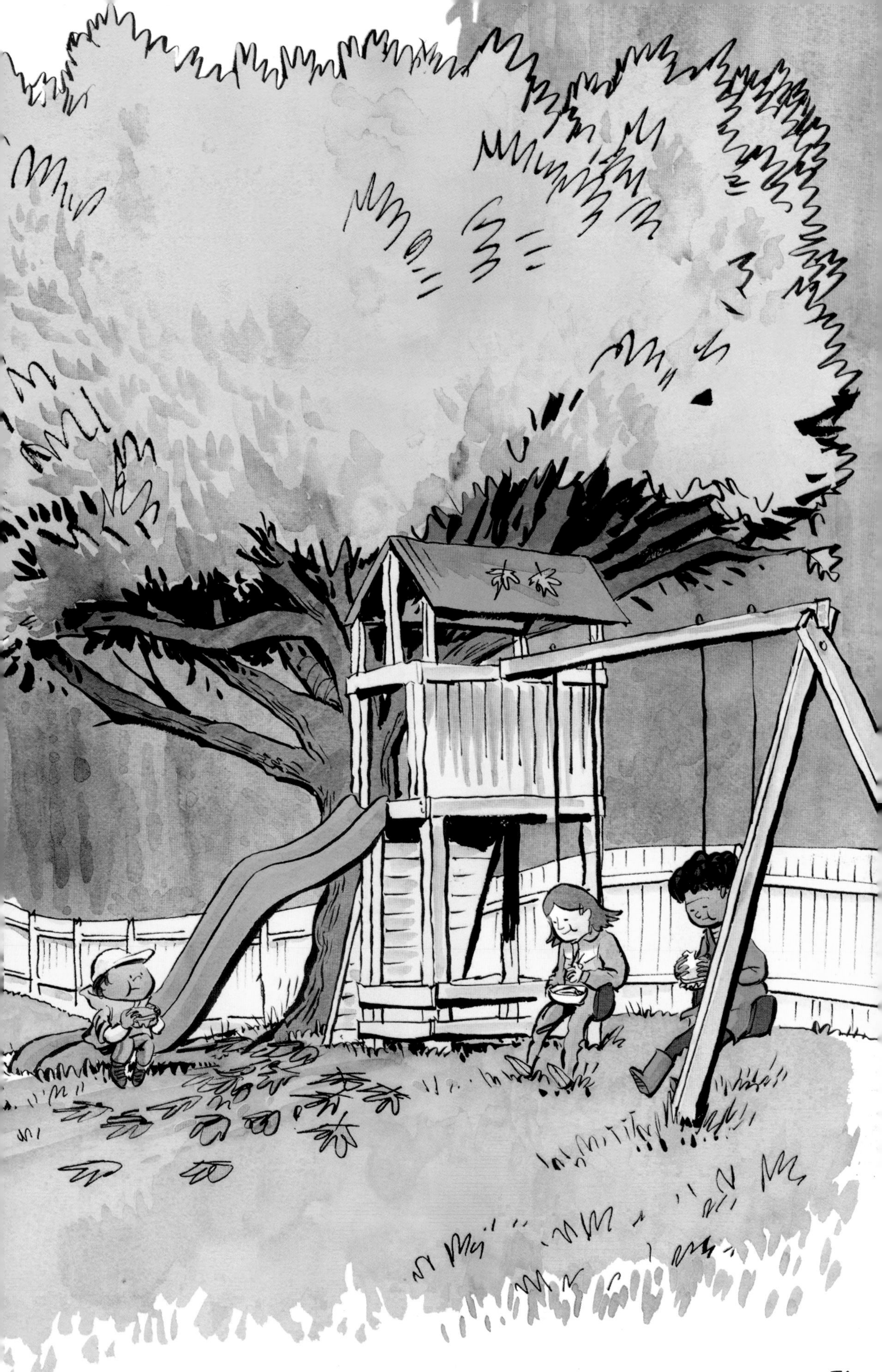

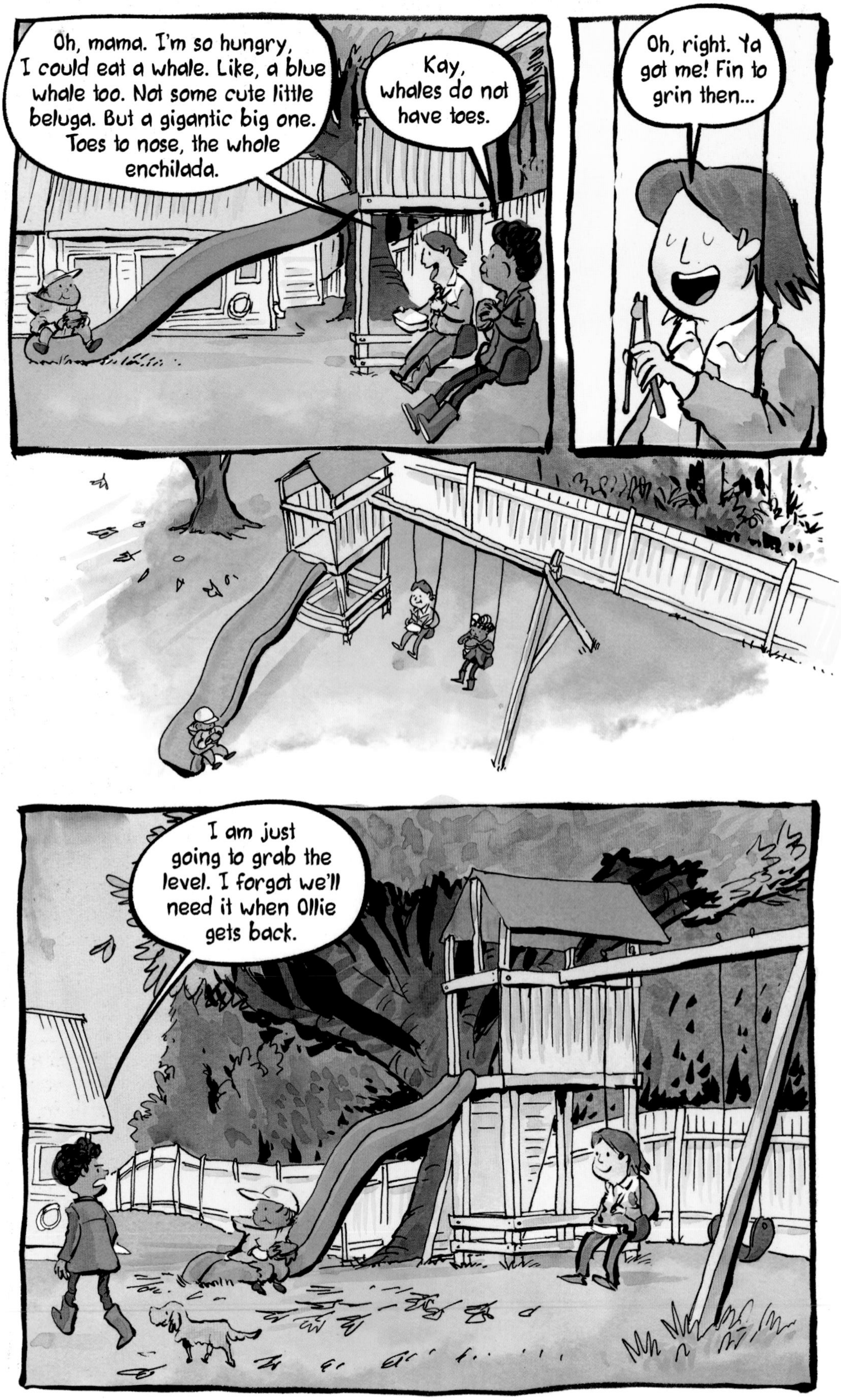
Oh, mama. I'm so hungry, I could eat a whale. Like, a blue whale too. Not some cute little beluga. But a gigantic big one. Toes to nose, the whole enchilada.
Kay, whales do not have toes.
Oh, right. Ya got me! Fin to grin then...
I am just going to grab the level. I forgot we'll need it when Ollie gets back.

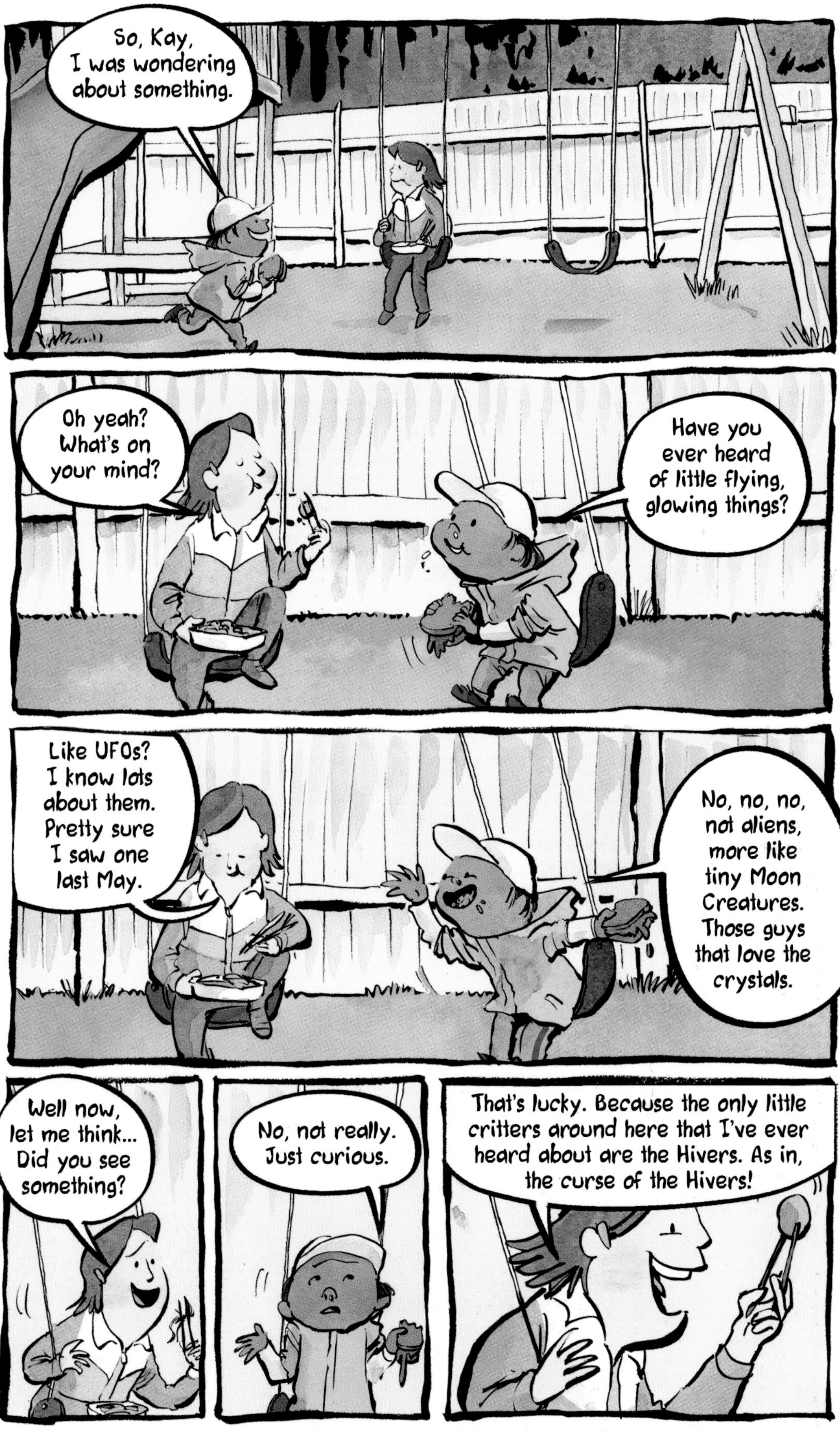
So, Kay, I was wondering about something.
Oh yeah? What's on your mind?
Have you ever heard of little flying, glowing things?
Like UFOs? I know lots about them. Pretty sure I saw one last May.
No, no, no, not aliens, more like tiny Moon Creatures. Those guys that love the crystals.
Well now, let me think... Did you see something?
No, not really. Just curious.
That's lucky. Because the only little critters around here that I've ever heard about are the Hivers. As in, the curse of the Hivers!

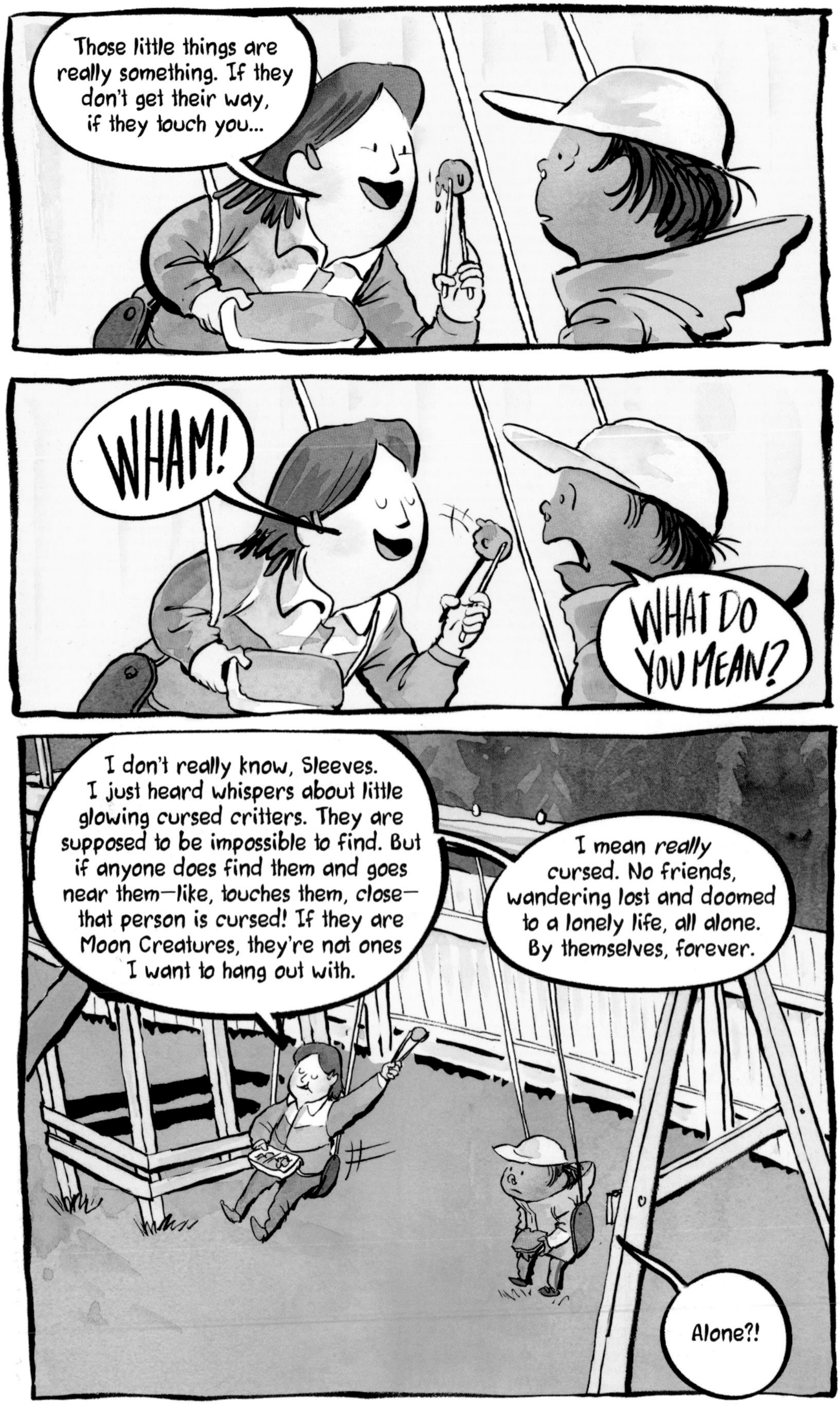
Those little things are really something. If they don't get their way, if they touch you...
WHAM!
WHAT DO YOU MEAN?
I don't really know, Sleeves. I just heard whispers about little glowing cursed critters. They are supposed to be impossible to find. But if anyone does find them and goes near them—like, touches them, close—that person is cursed! If they are Moon Creatures, they're not ones I want to hang out with.
I mean *really* cursed. No friends, wandering lost and doomed to a lonely life, all alone. By themselves, forever.
Alone?!

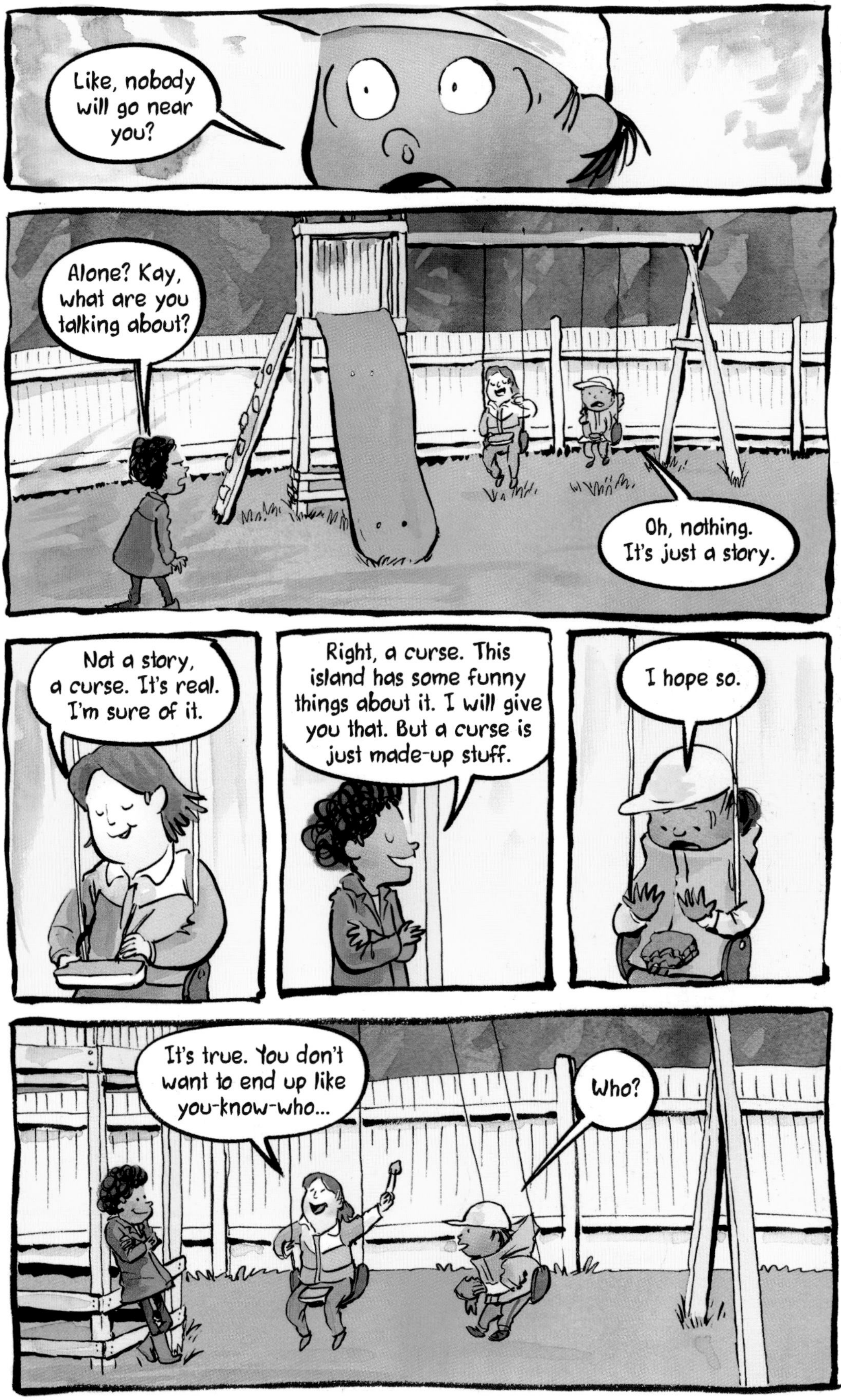
Like, nobody will go near you?
Alone? Kay, what are you talking about?
Oh, nothing. It's just a story.
Not a story, a curse. It's real. I'm sure of it.
Right, a curse. This island has some funny things about it. I will give you that. But a curse is just made-up stuff.
I hope so.
It's true. You don't want to end up like you-know-who...
Who?

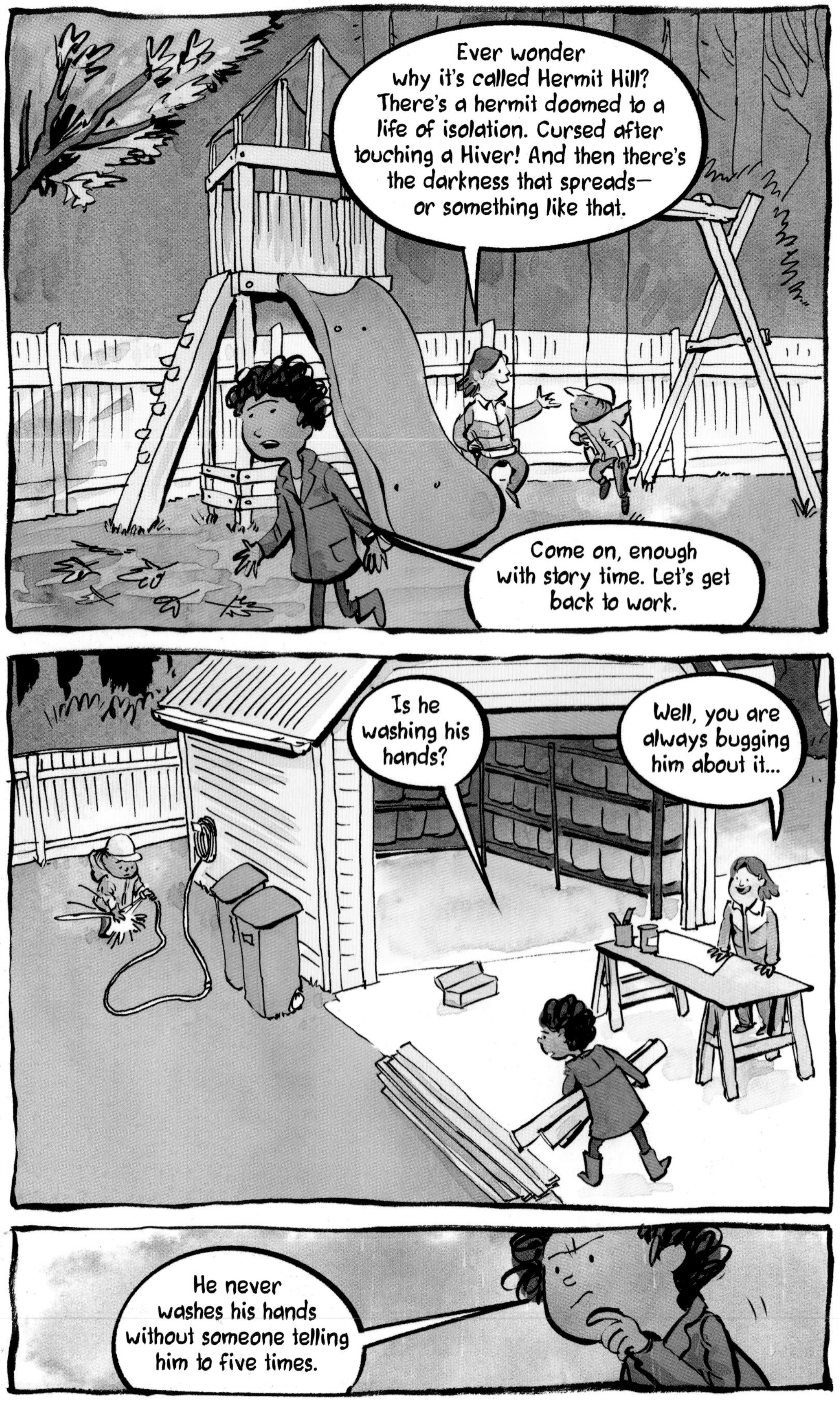
Ever wonder why it's called Hermit Hill? There's a hermit doomed to a life of isolation. Cursed after touching a Hiver! And then there's the darkness that spreads— or something like that.
Come on, enough with story time. Let's get back to work.
Is he washing his hands?
Well, you are always bugging him about it...
He never washes his hands without someone telling him to five times.

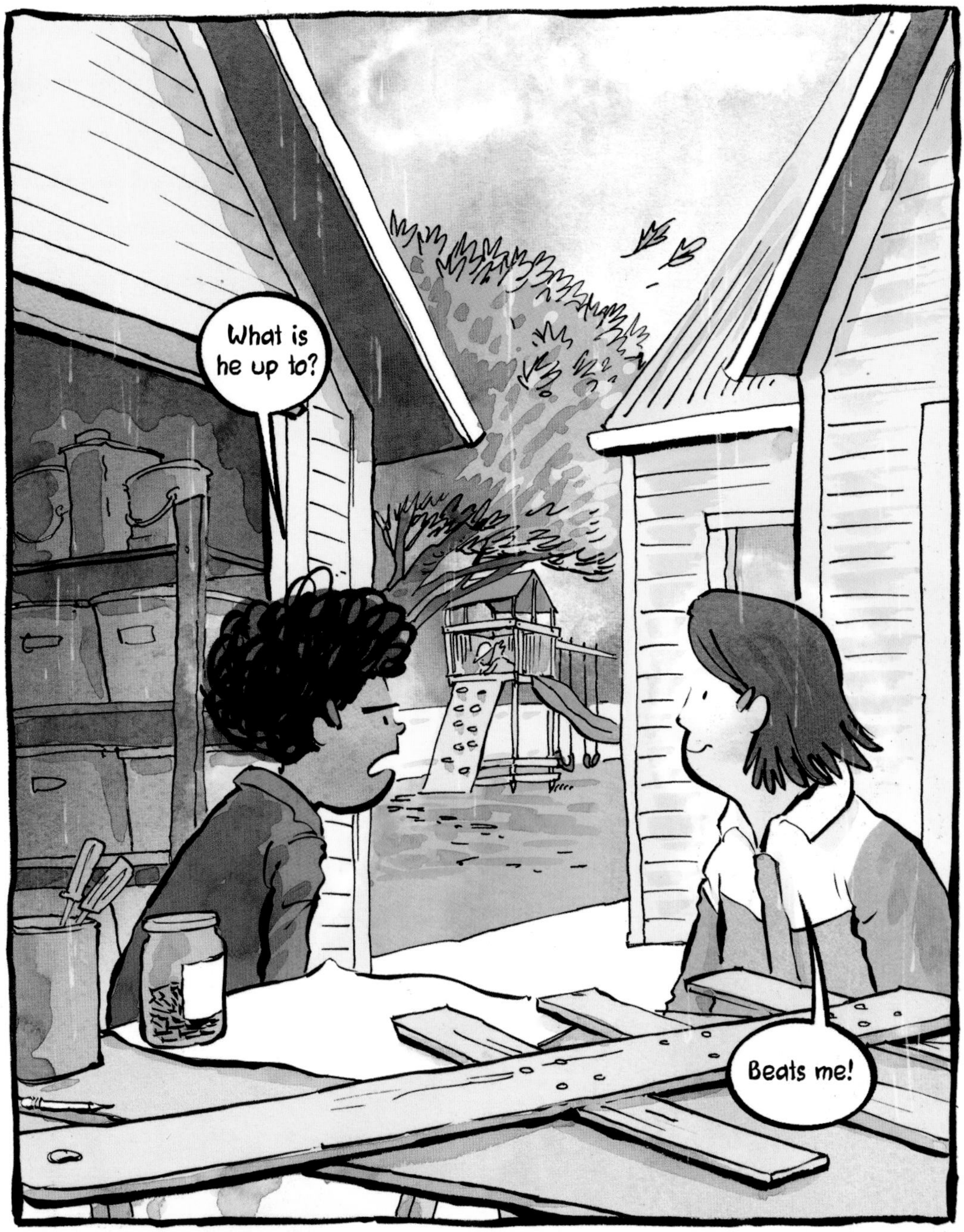
What is he up to?
Beats me!

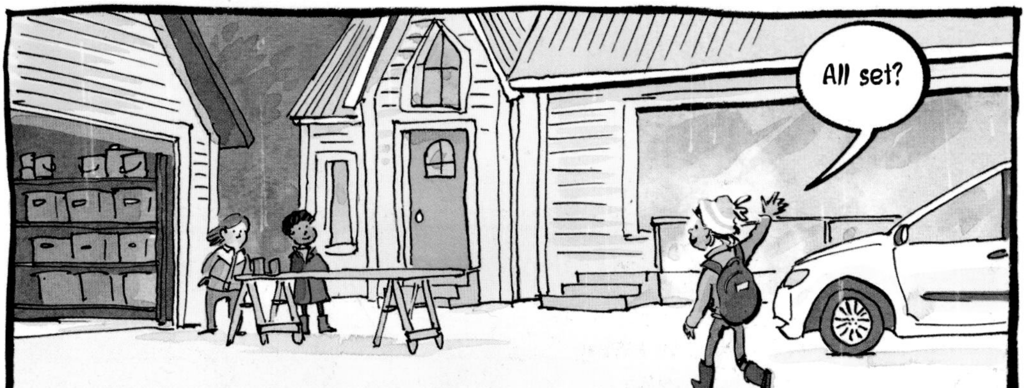
All set?

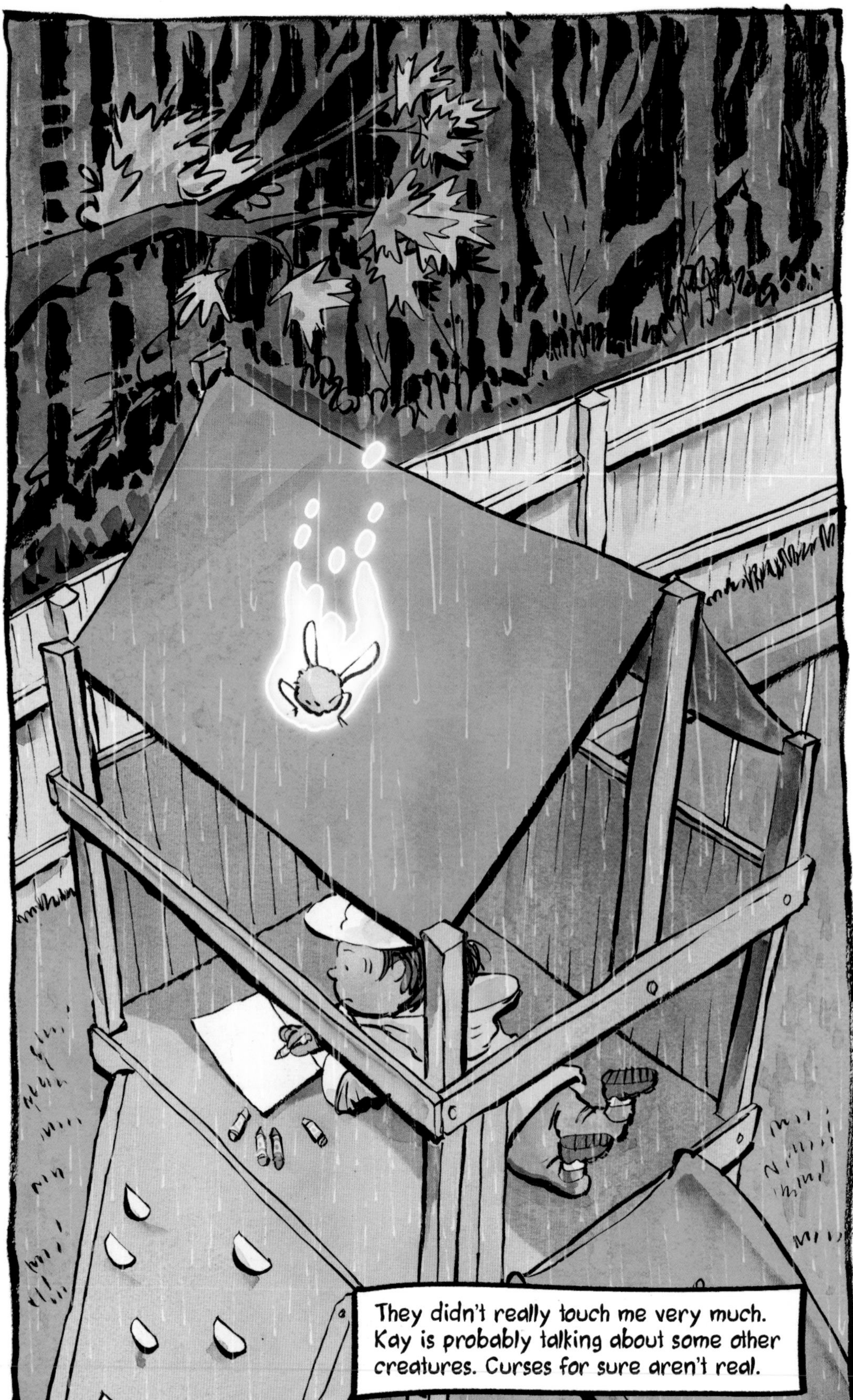
They didn't really touch me very much. Kay is probably talking about some other creatures. Curses for sure aren't real.

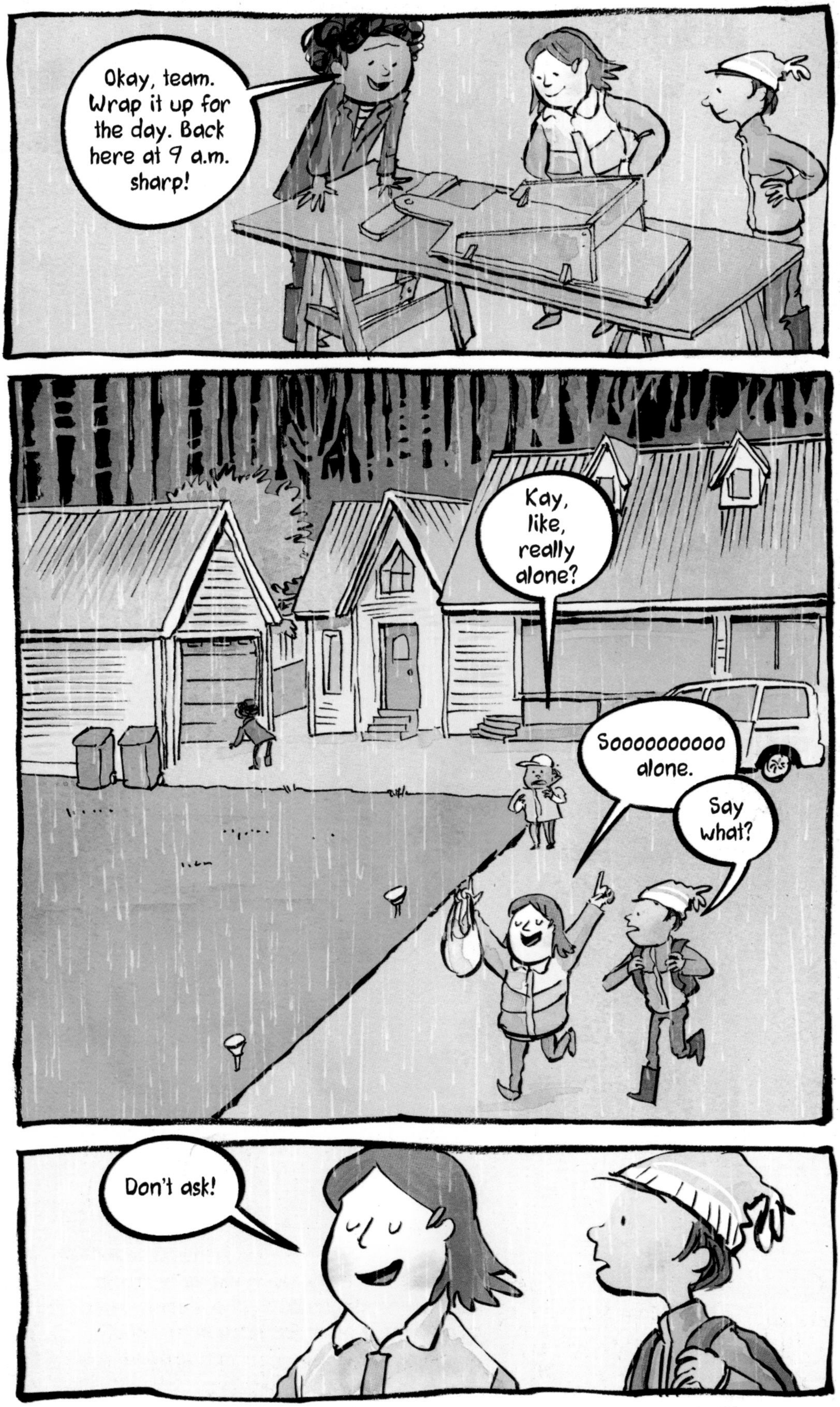
Okay, team. Wrap it up for the day. Back here at 9 a.m. sharp!
Kay, like, really alone?
Sooooooooooo alone.
Say what?
Don't ask!

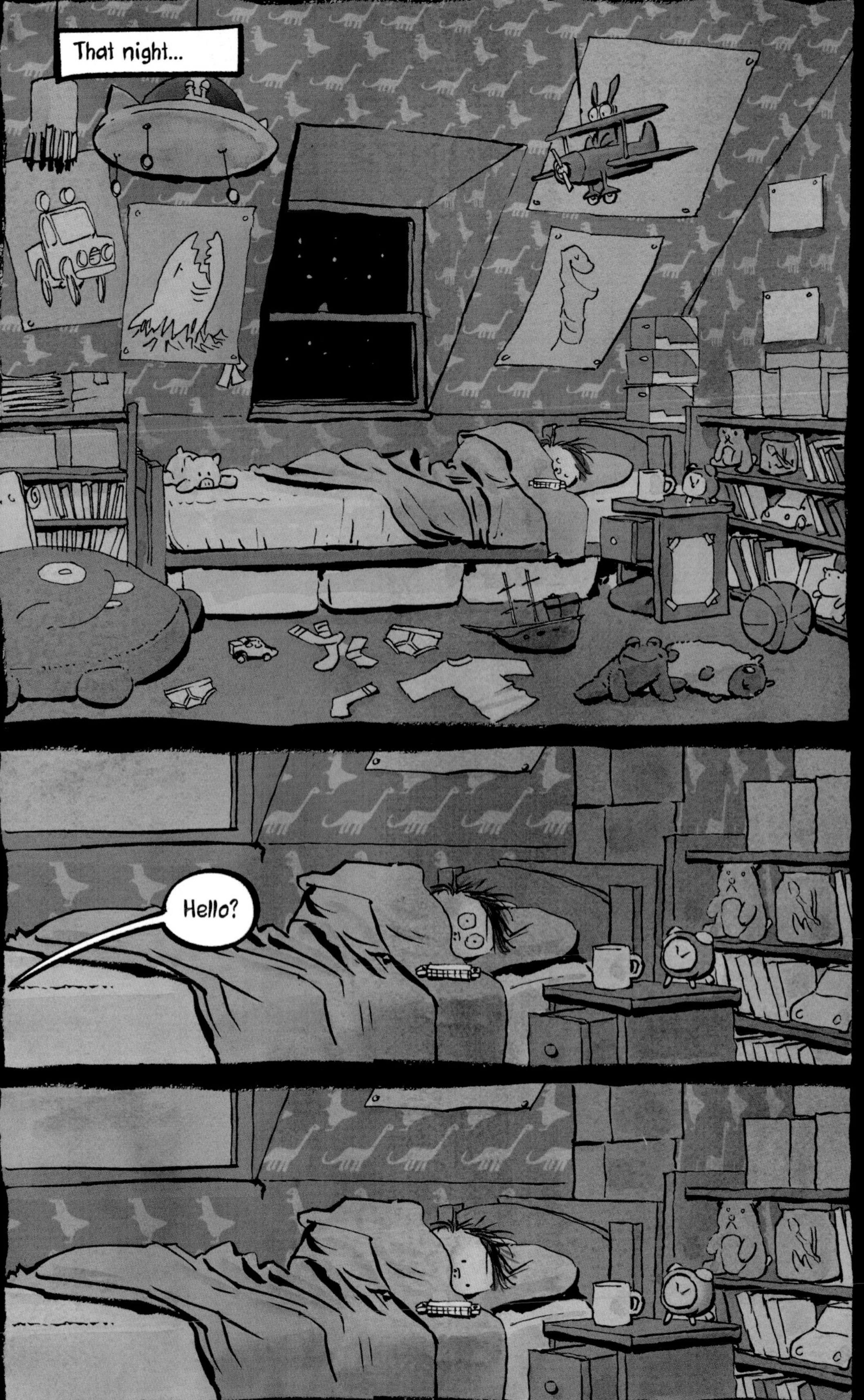
That night...
Hello?

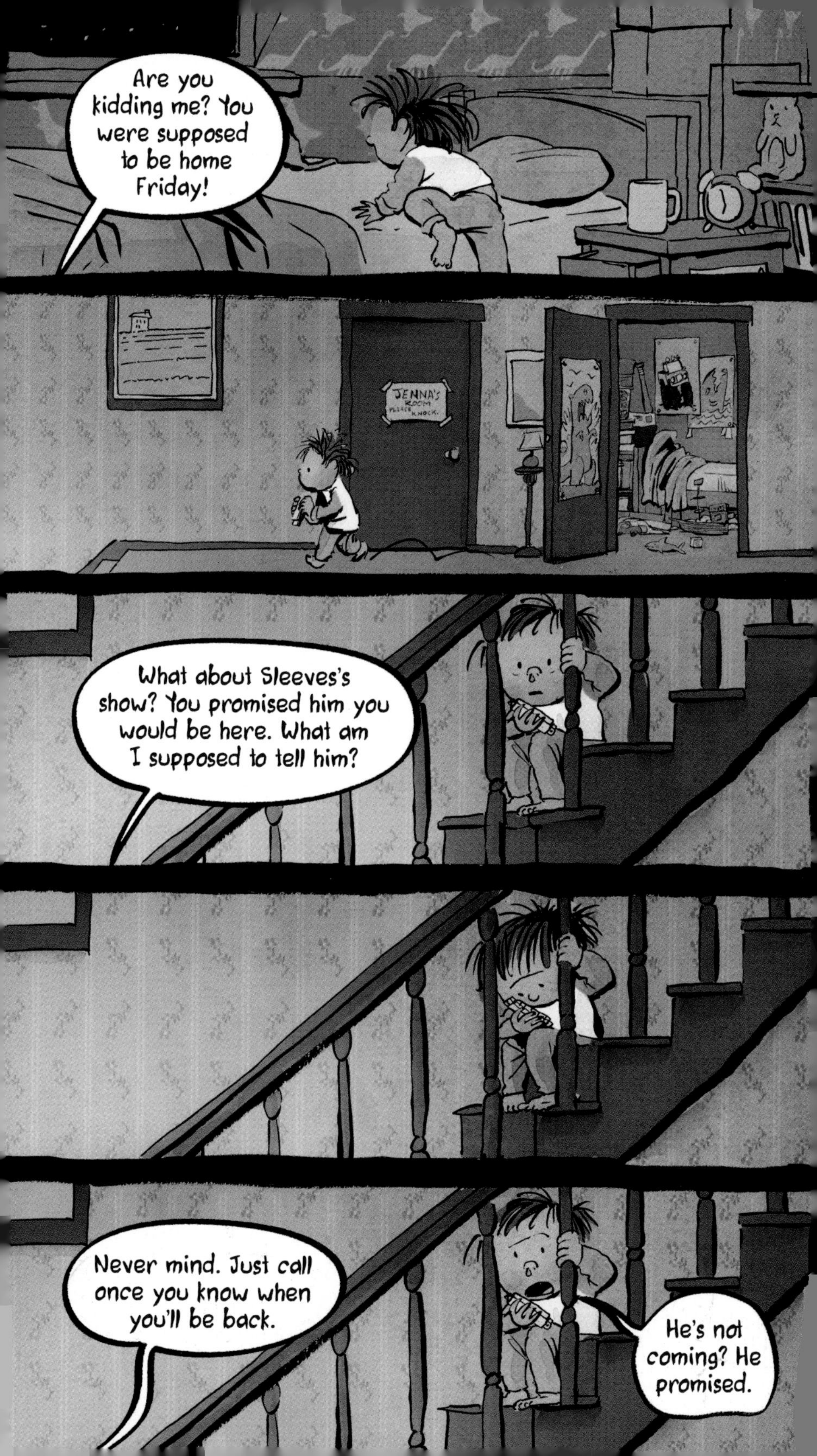
Are you kidding me? You were supposed to be home Friday!
JENNA'S ROOM PLEASE KNOCK.
What about Sleeves's show? You promised him you would be here. What am I supposed to tell him?
Never mind. Just call once you know when you'll be back.
He's not coming? He promised.

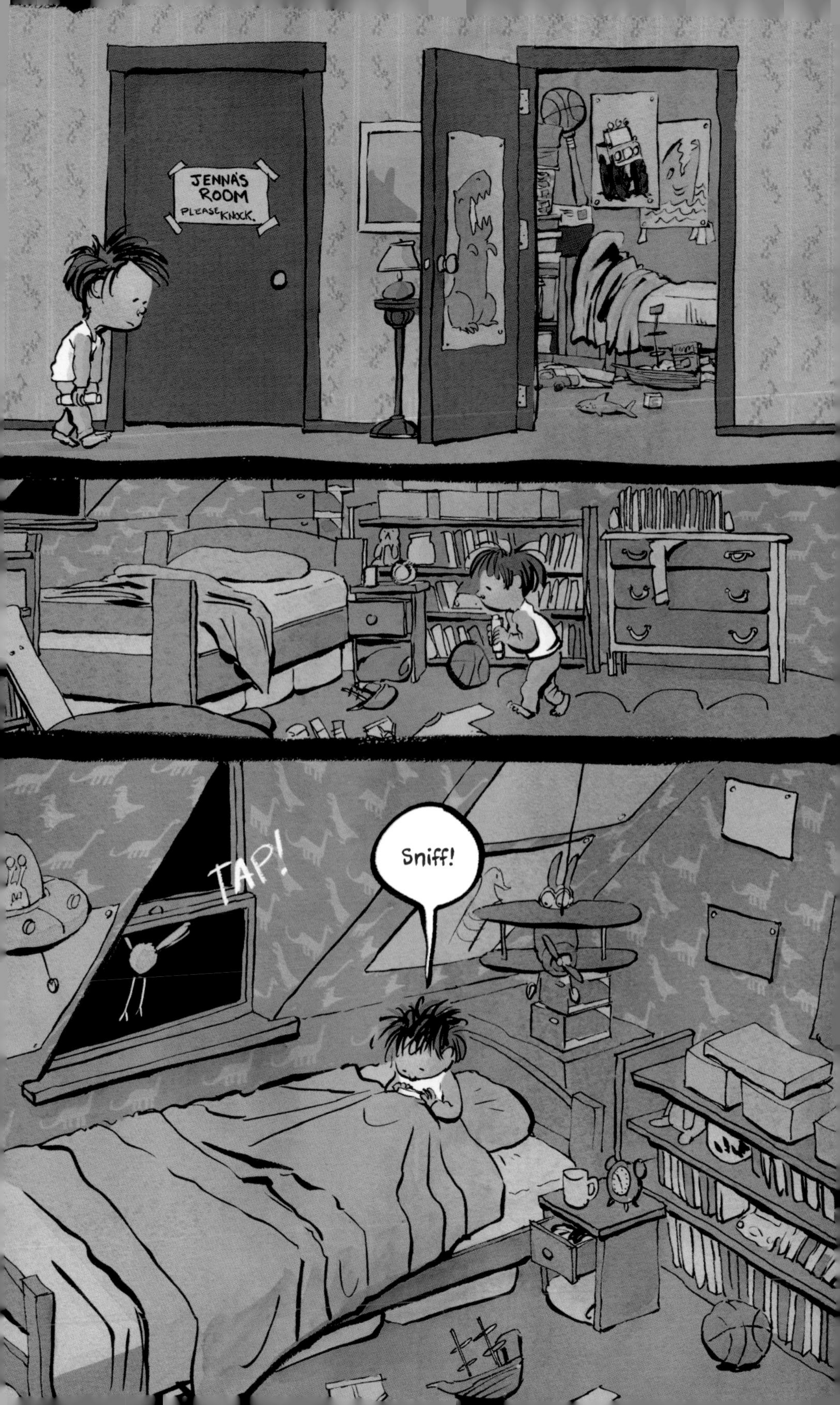

JENNA'S ROOM PLEASE KNOCK.
TAP!
Sniff!

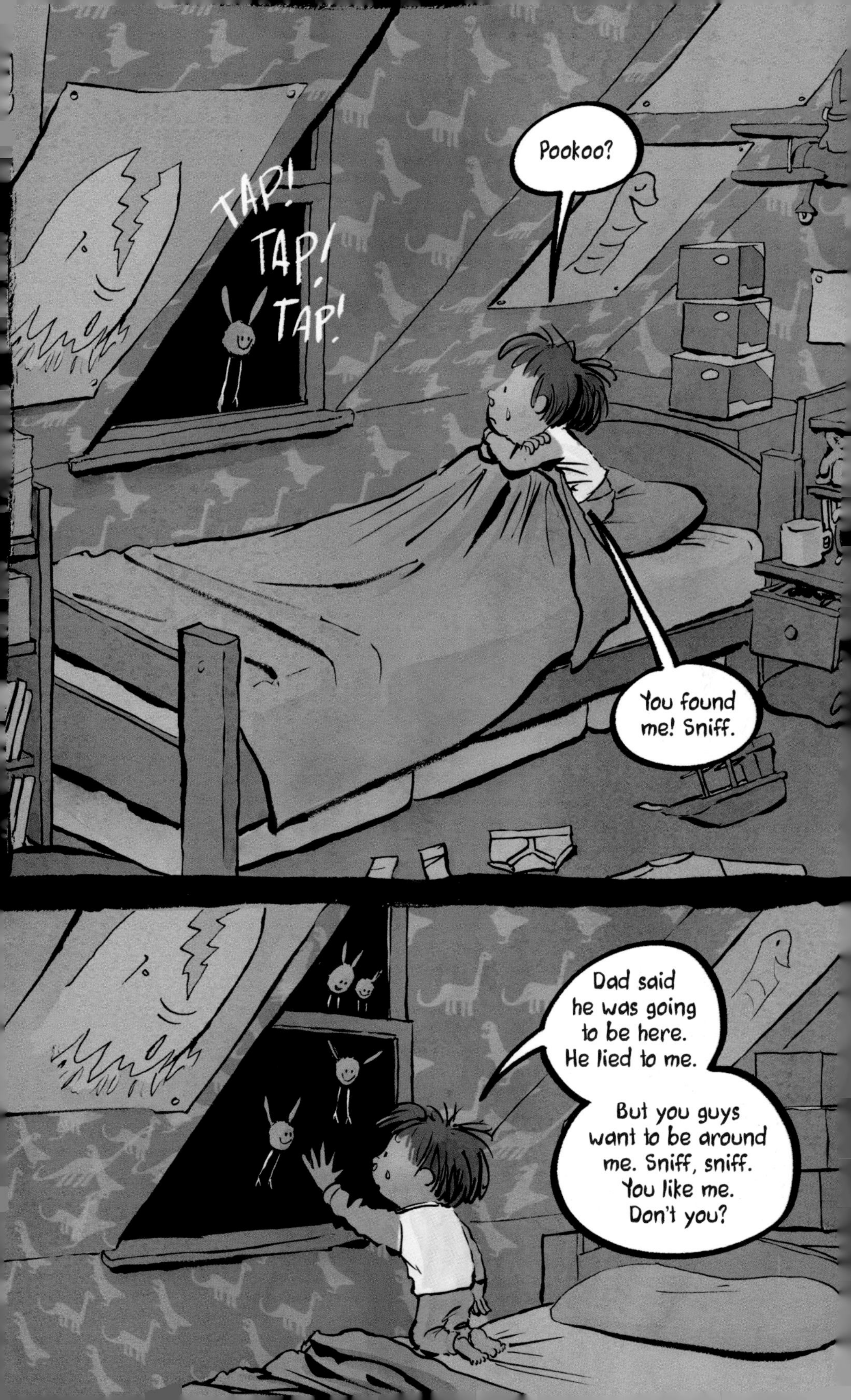
TAP! TAP! TAP!
Pookoo?
You found me! Sniff.
Dad said he was going to be here. He lied to me.
But you guys want to be around me. Sniff, sniff. You like me. Don't you?

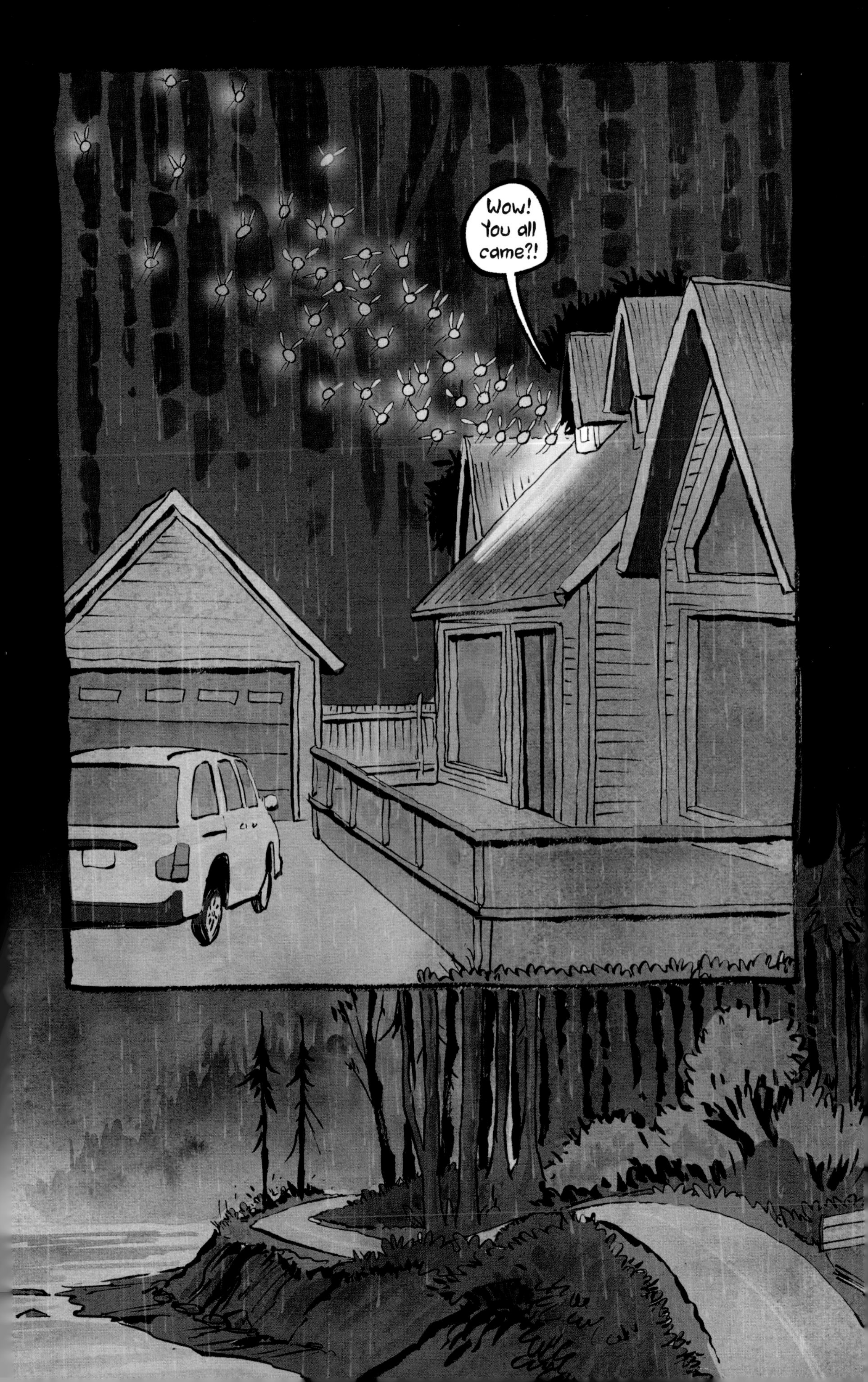
Wow! You all came?!

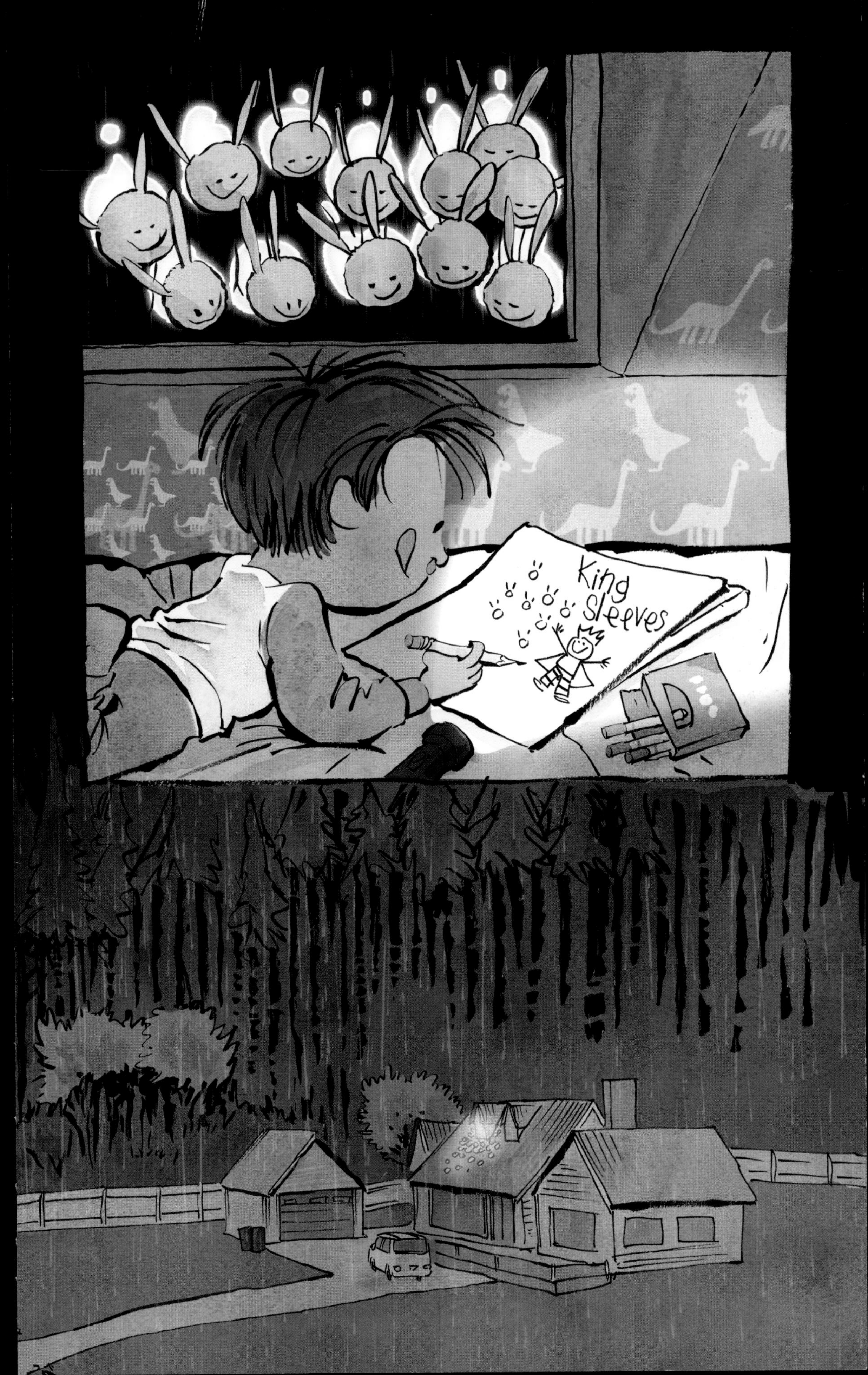
King Sleeves

CHAPTER THREE

King for a Day

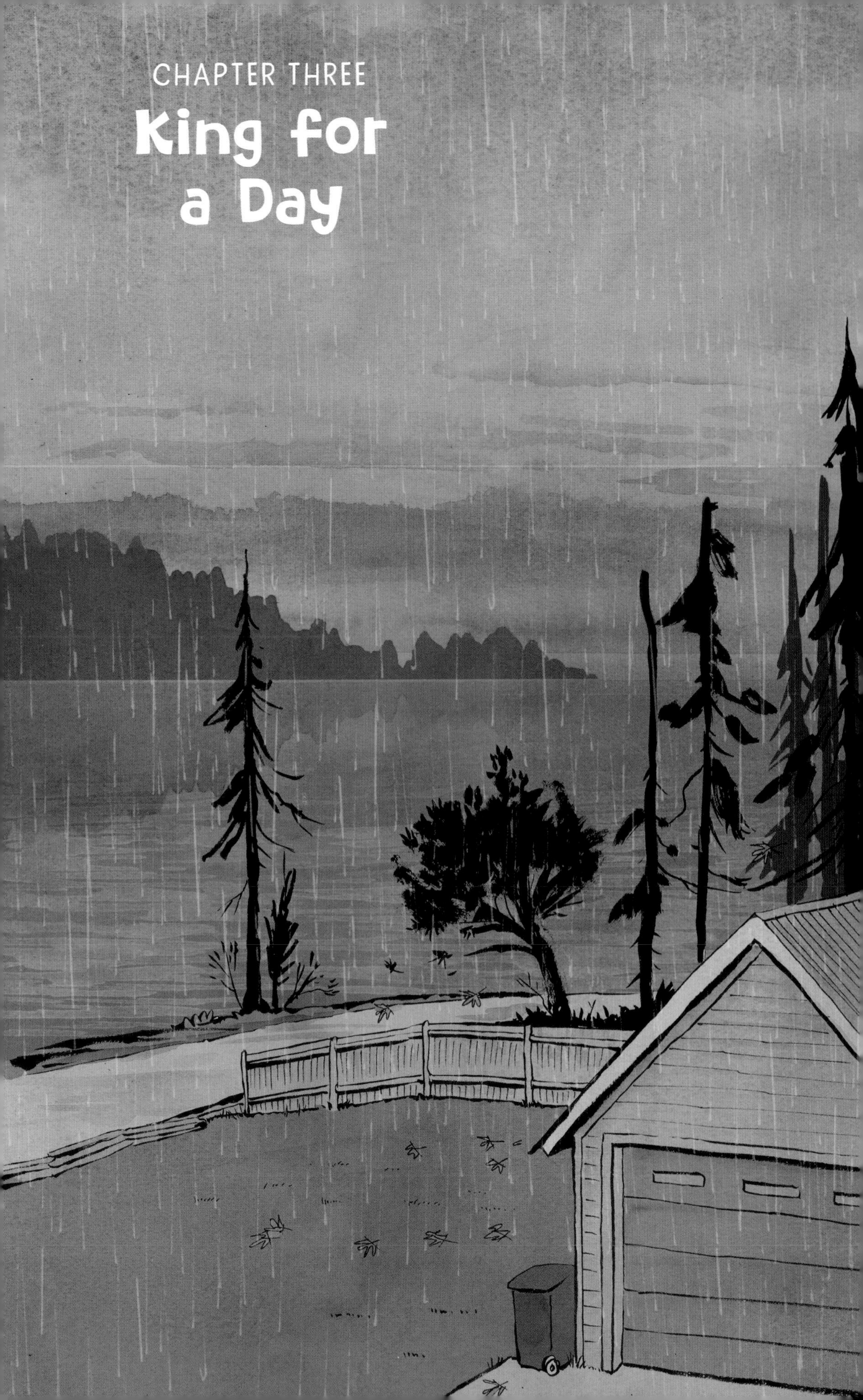

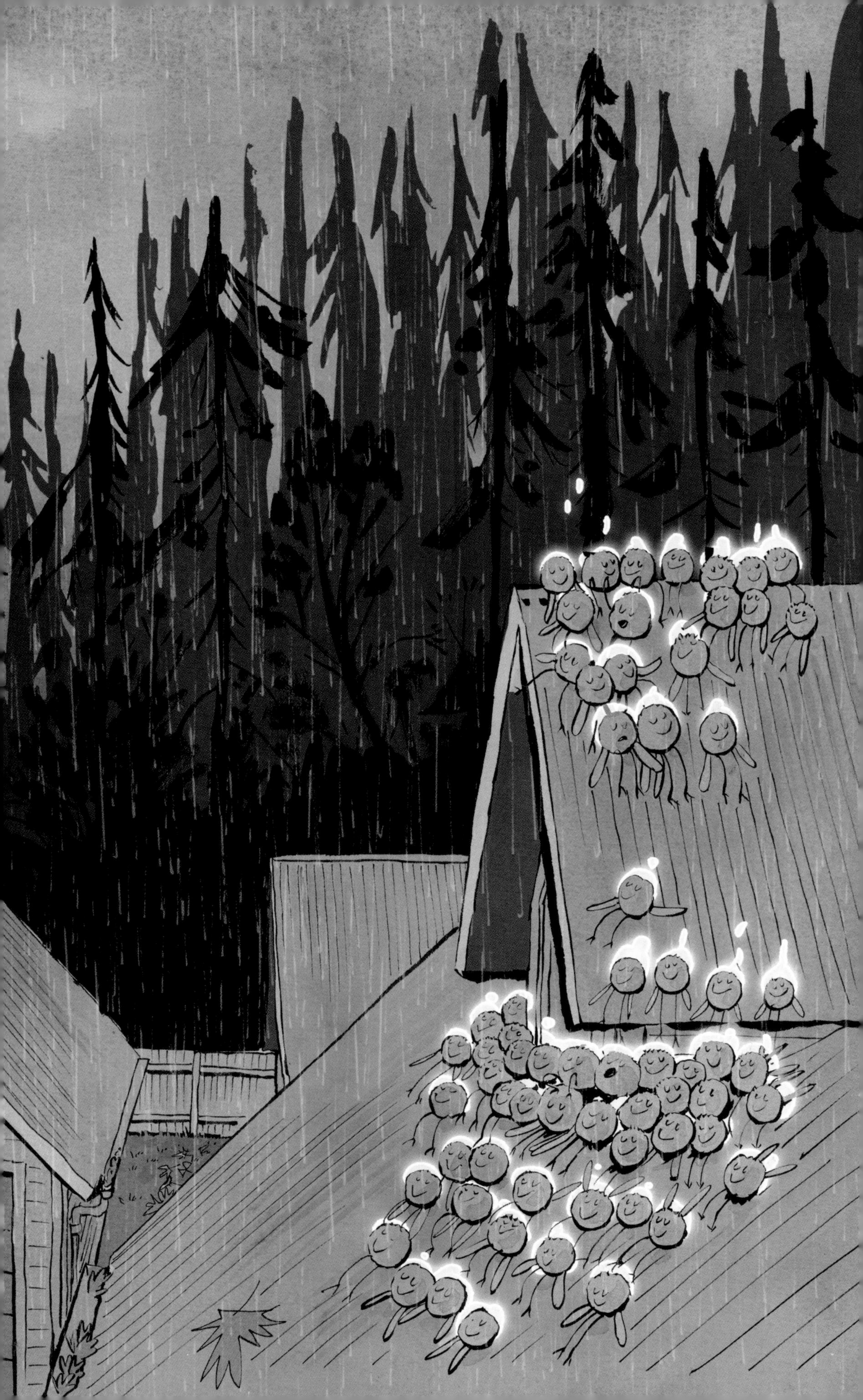

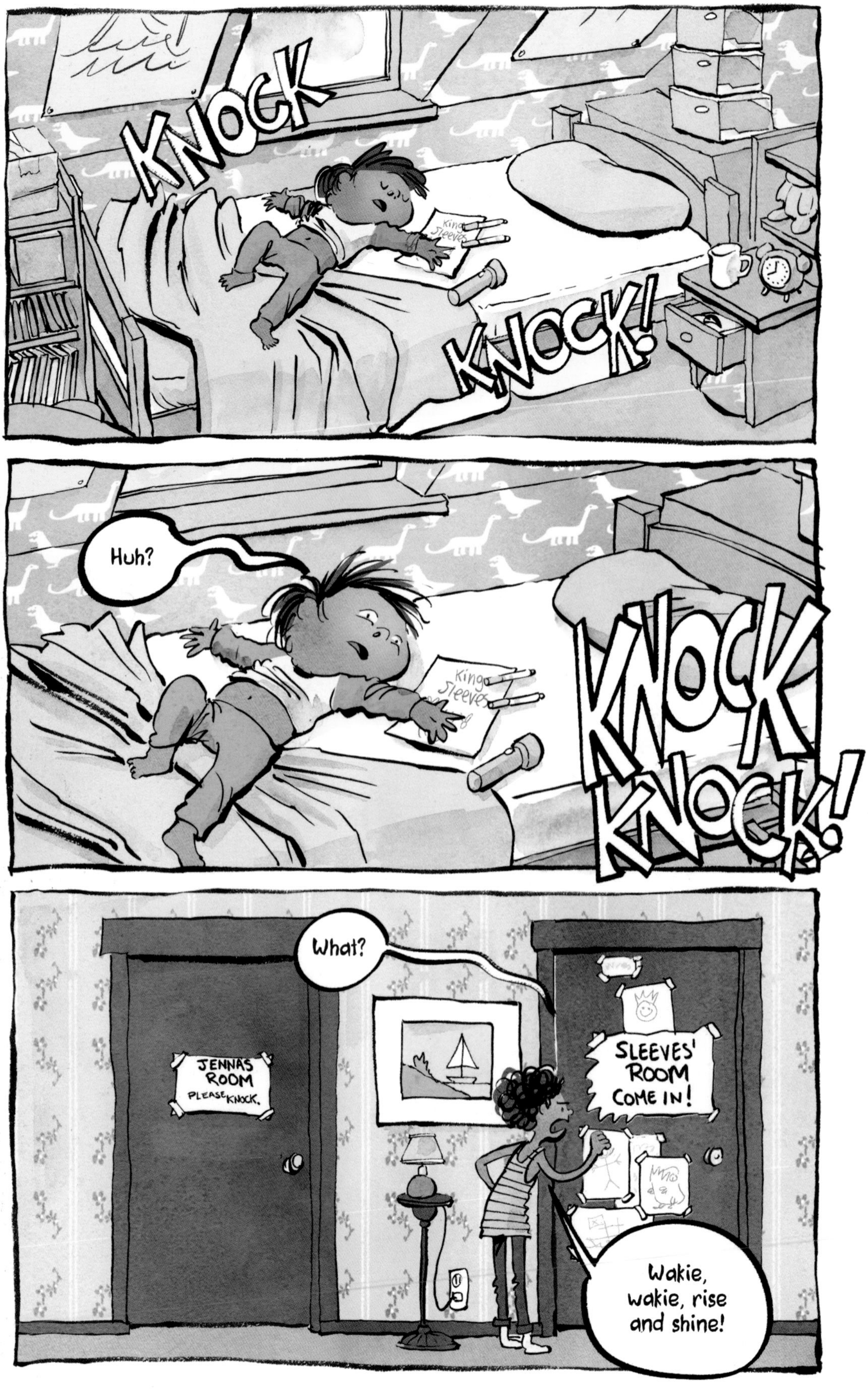
KNOCK
King Sleeves
KNOCK!
Huh?
King Sleeves
KNOCK
KNOCK!
What?
JENNA'S ROOM PLEASE KNOCK.
SLEEVES' ROOM COME IN!
Wakie, wakie, rise and shine!

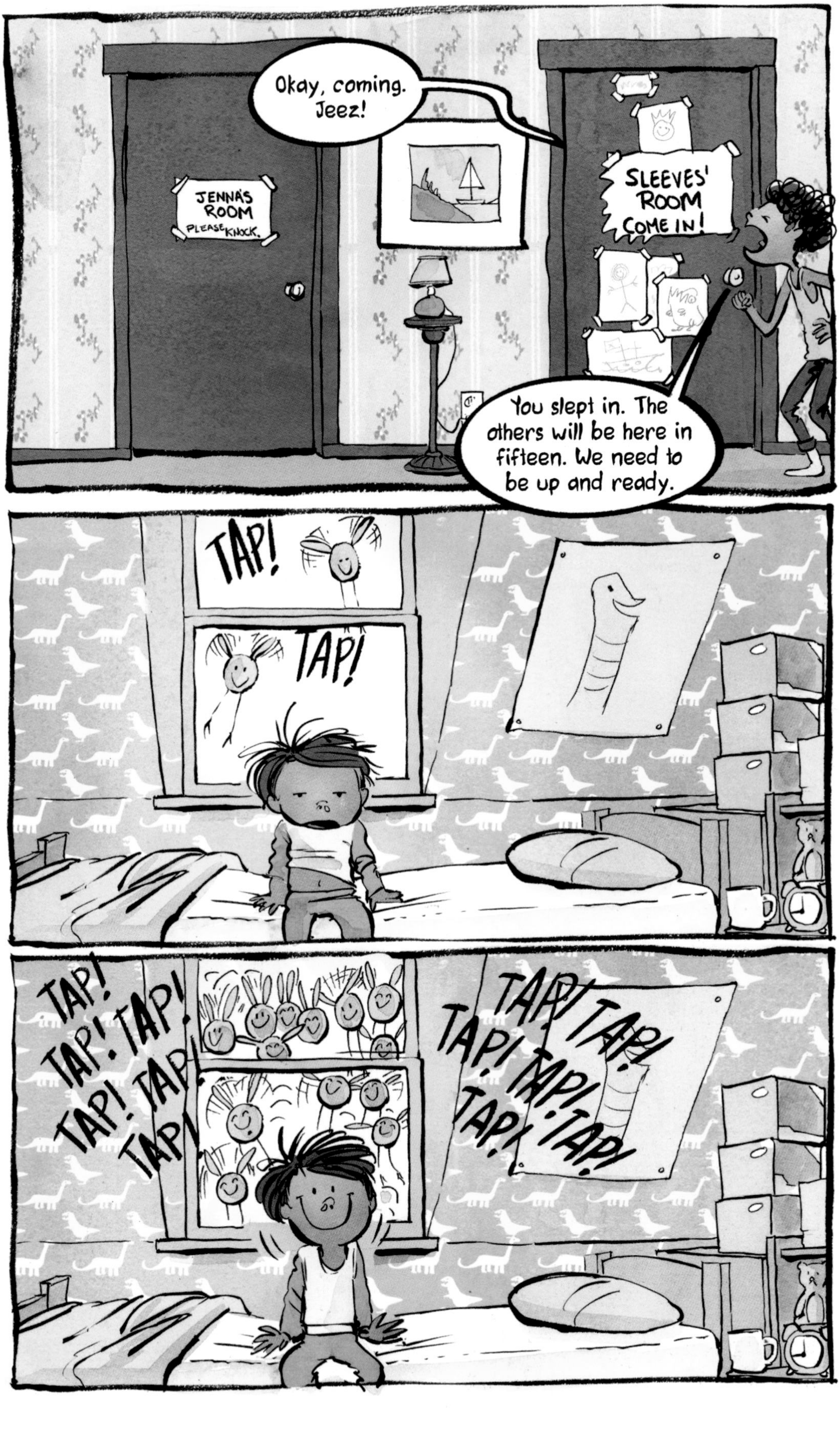
Okay, coming. Jeez!
JENNA'S ROOM PLEASE KNOCK.
SLEEVES' ROOM COME IN!
You slept in. The others will be here in fifteen. We need to be up and ready.
TAP!
TAP!
TAP! TAP! TAP! TAP! TAP! TAP!
TAP! TAP! TAP! TAP! TAP! TAP! TAP!

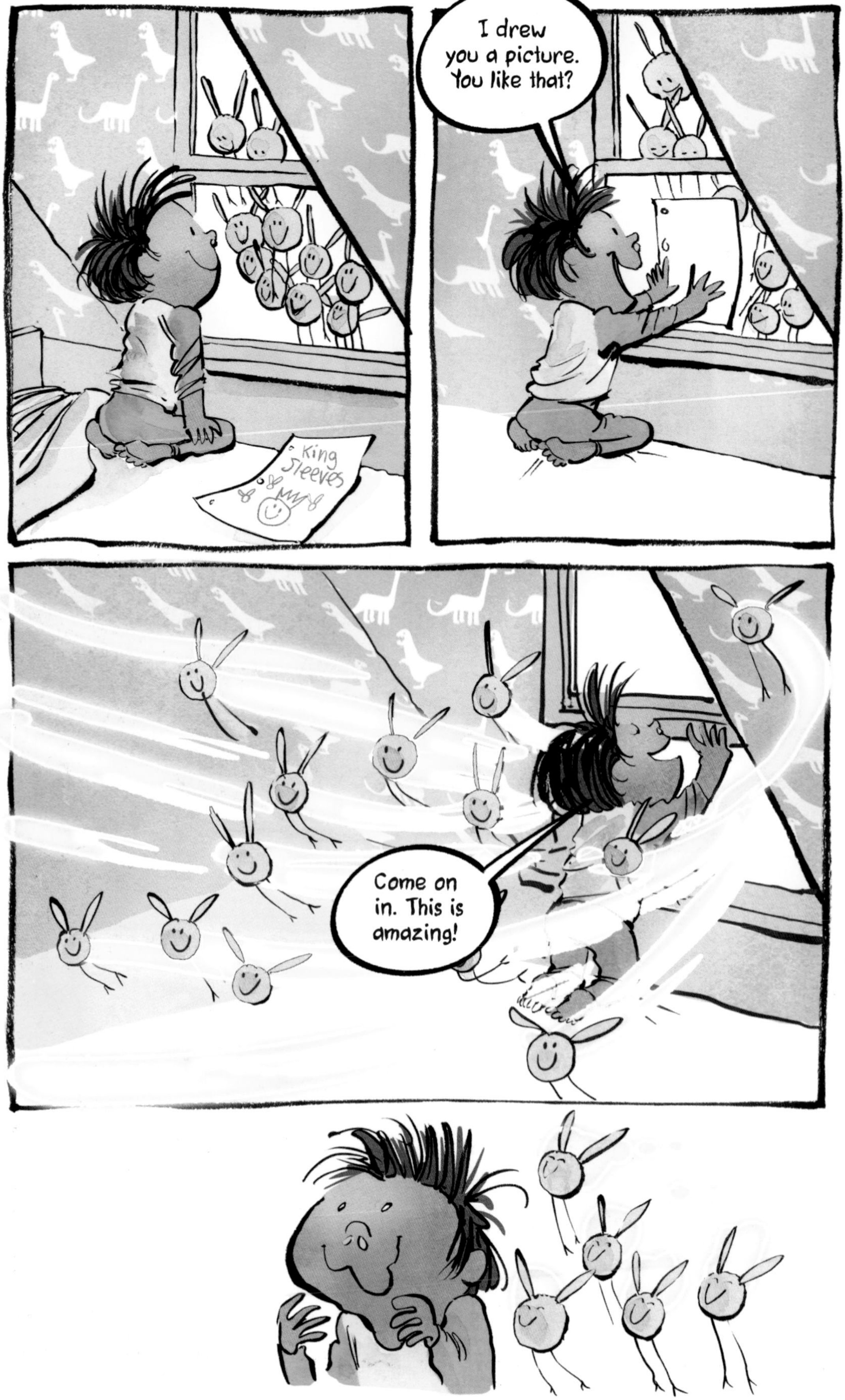
King Sleeves
I drew you a picture. You like that?
Come on in. This is amazing!

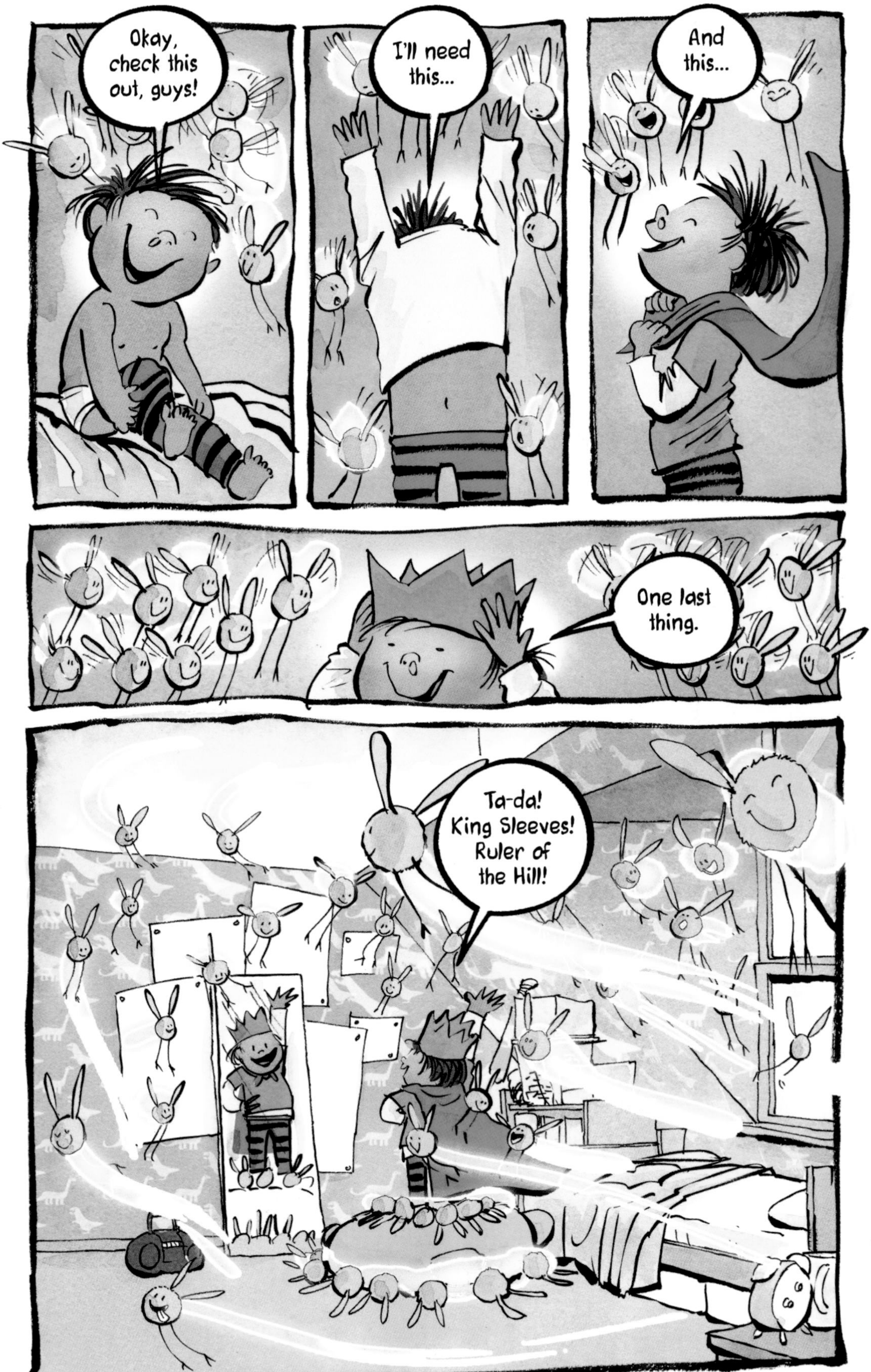
Okay, check this out, guys!
I'll need this...
And this...
One last thing.
Ta-da! King Sleeves! Ruler of the Hill!

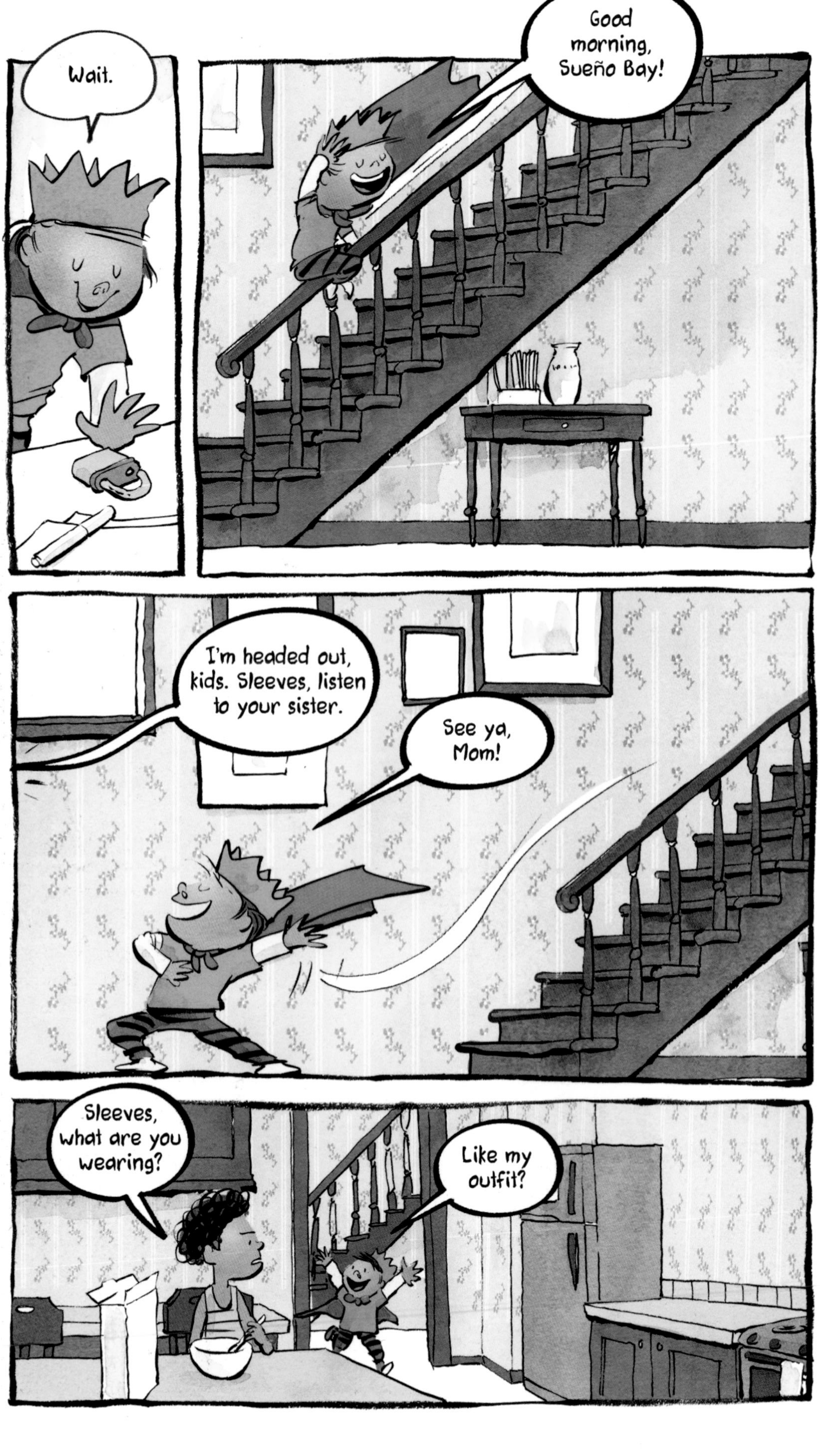
Wait.
Good morning, Sueño Bay!
I'm headed out, kids. Sleeves, listen to your sister.
See ya, Mom!
Sleeves, what are you wearing?
Like my outfit?

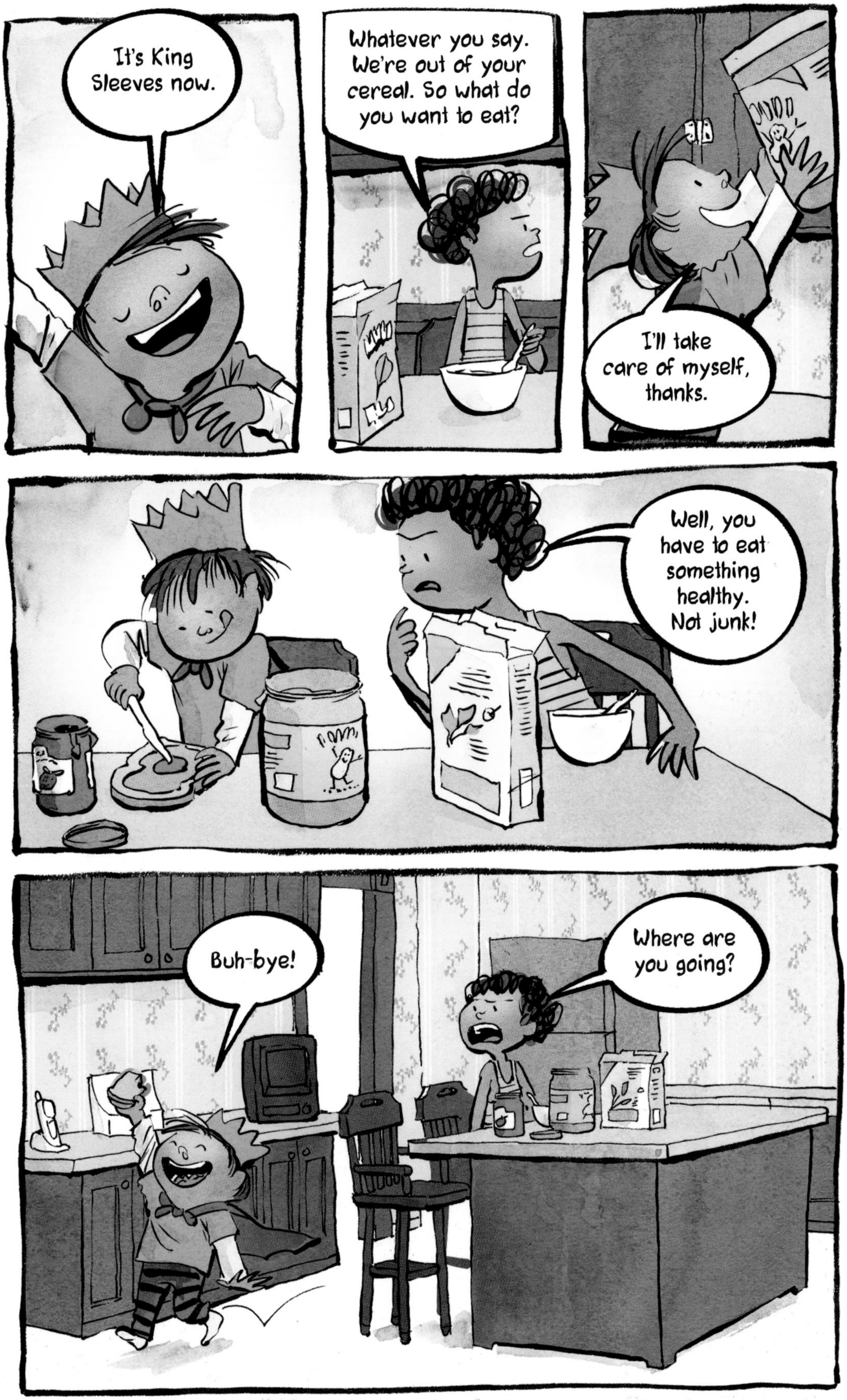
It's King Sleeves now.
Whatever you say. We're out of your cereal. So what do you want to eat?
I'll take care of myself, thanks.
Well, you have to eat something healthy. Not junk!
Buh-bye!
Where are you going?

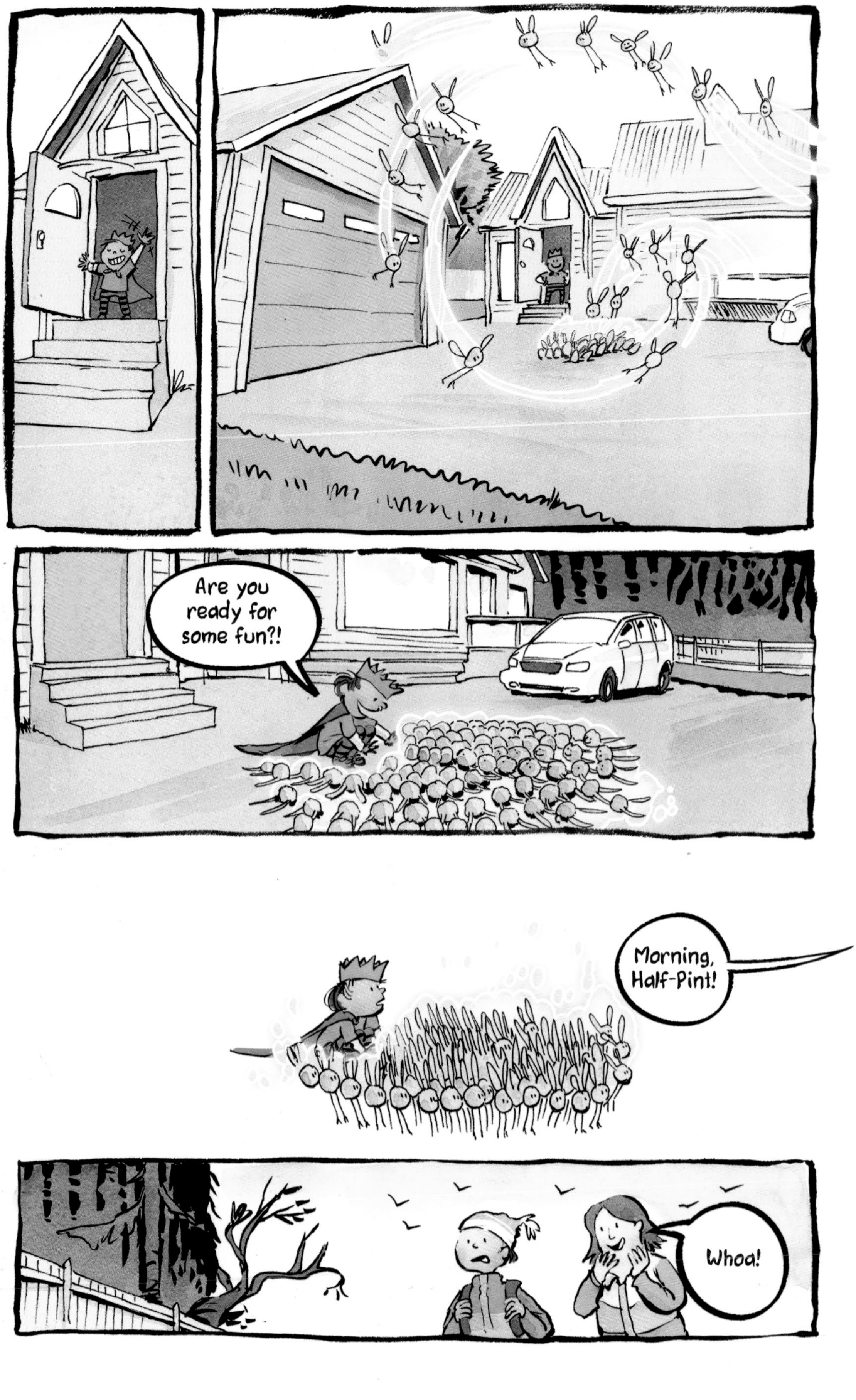
Are you ready for some fun?!
Morning, Half-Pint!
Whoa!

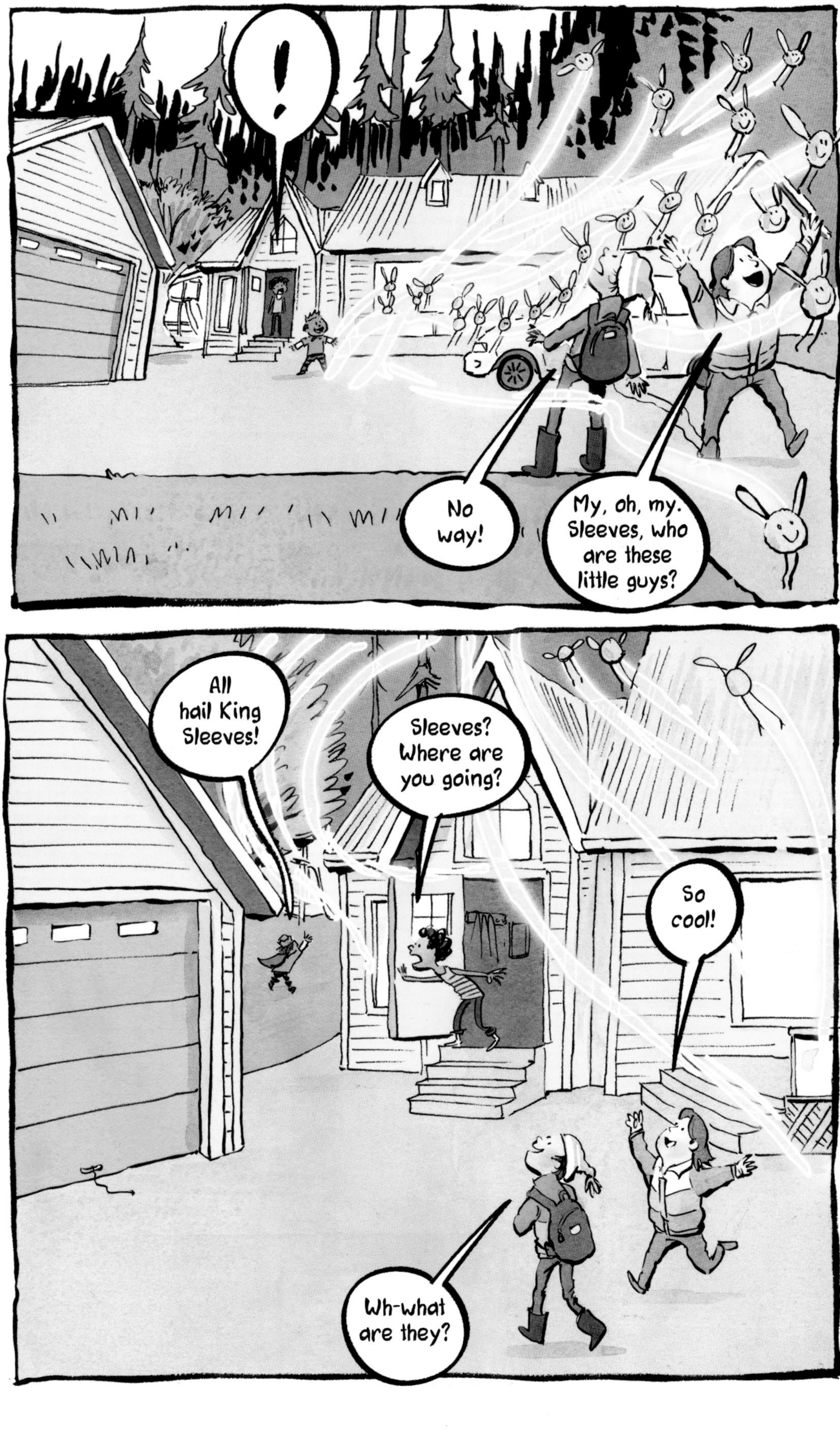
!
No way!
My, oh, my. Sleeves, who are these little guys?
All hail King Sleeves!
Sleeves? Where are you going?
So cool!
Wh-what are they?

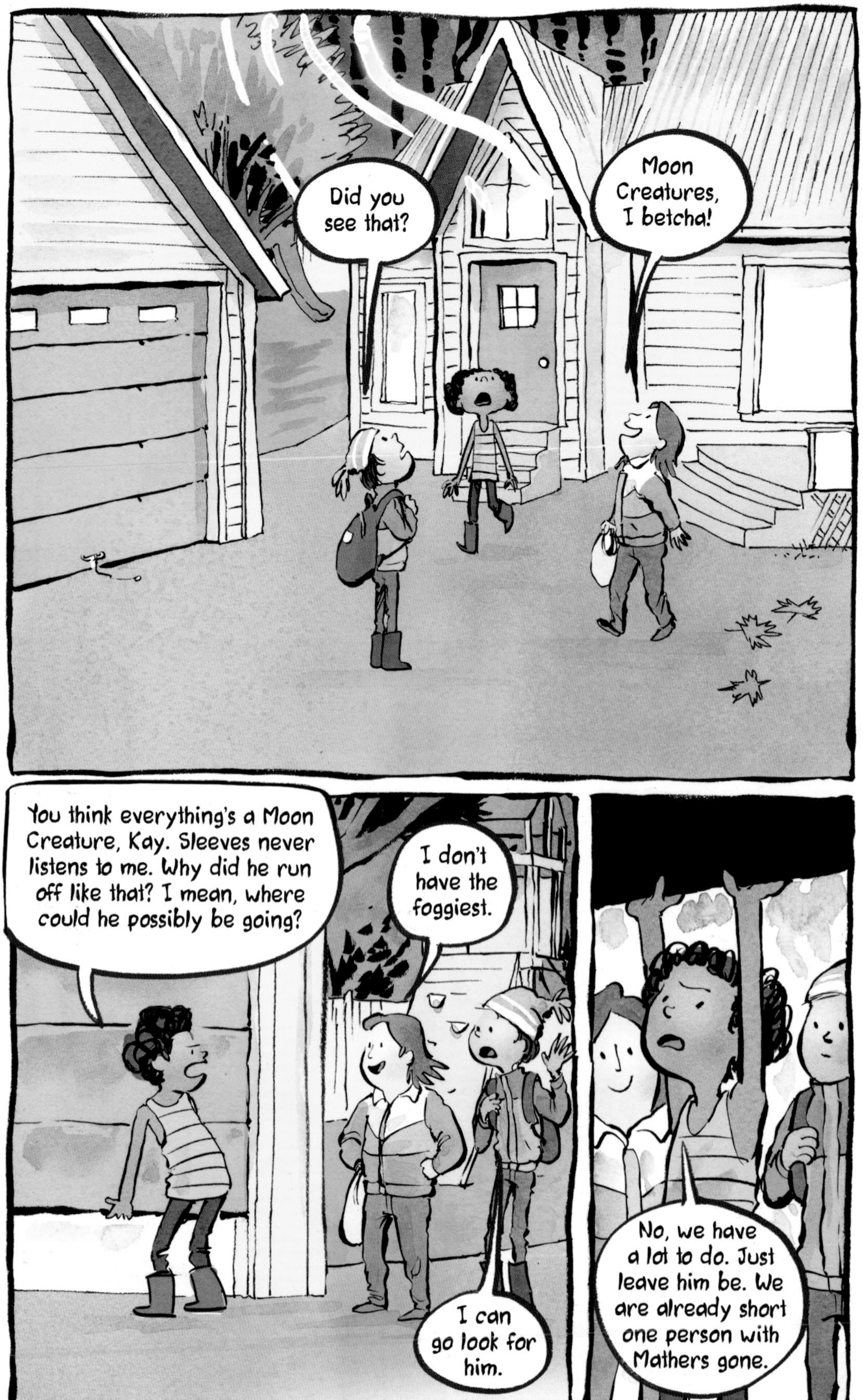
Did you see that?
Moon Creatures, I betcha!
You think everything's a Moon Creature, Kay. Sleeves never listens to me. Why did he run off like that? I mean, where could he possibly be going?
I don't have the foggiest.
I can go look for him.
No, we have a lot to do. Just leave him be. We are already short one person with Mathers gone.

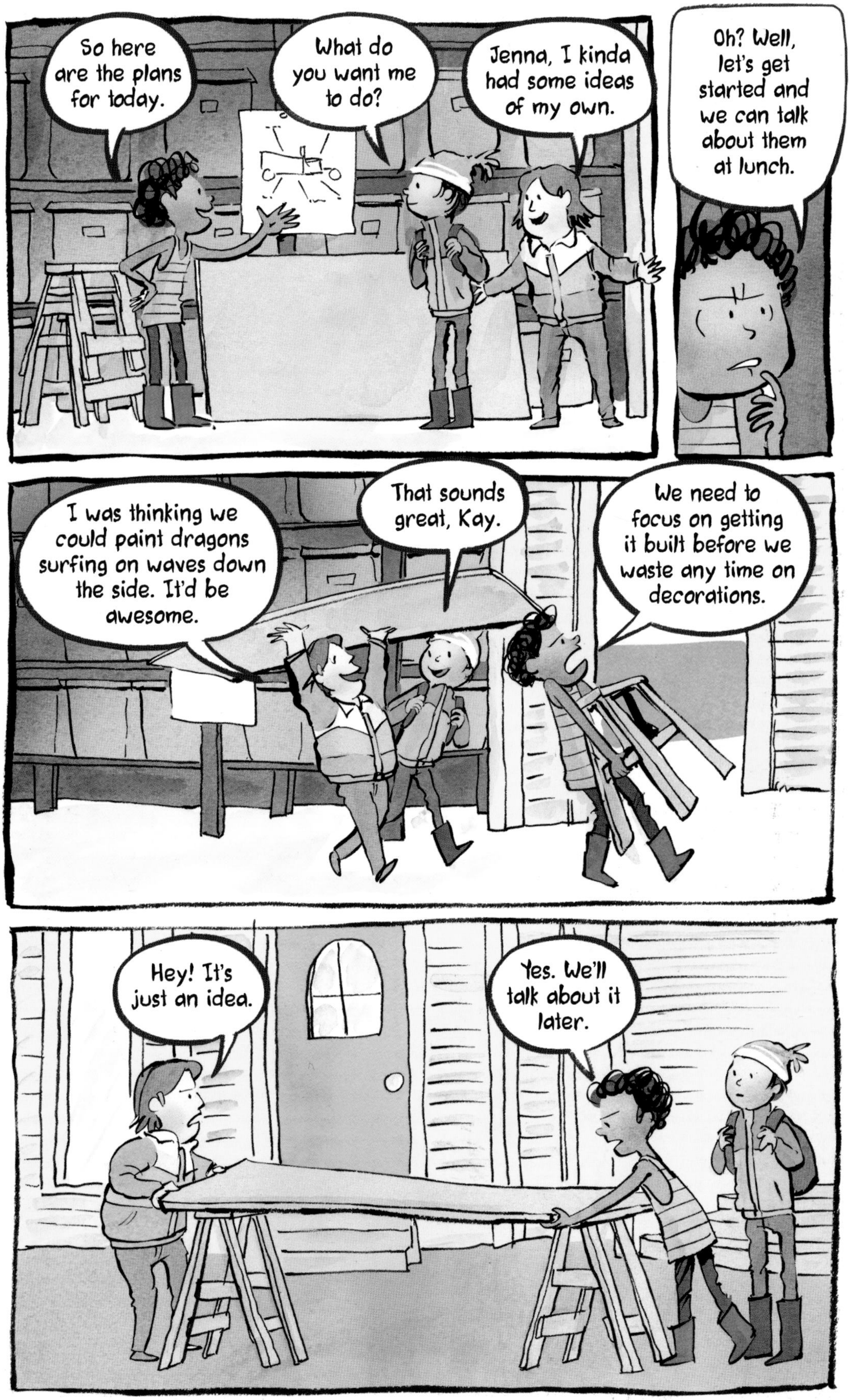
So here are the plans for today.
What do you want me to do?
Jenna, I kinda had some ideas of my own.
Oh? Well, let's get started and we can talk about them at lunch.
I was thinking we could paint dragons surfing on waves down the side. It'd be awesome.
That sounds great, Kay.
We need to focus on getting it built before we waste any time on decorations.
Hey! It's just an idea.
Yes. We'll talk about it later.

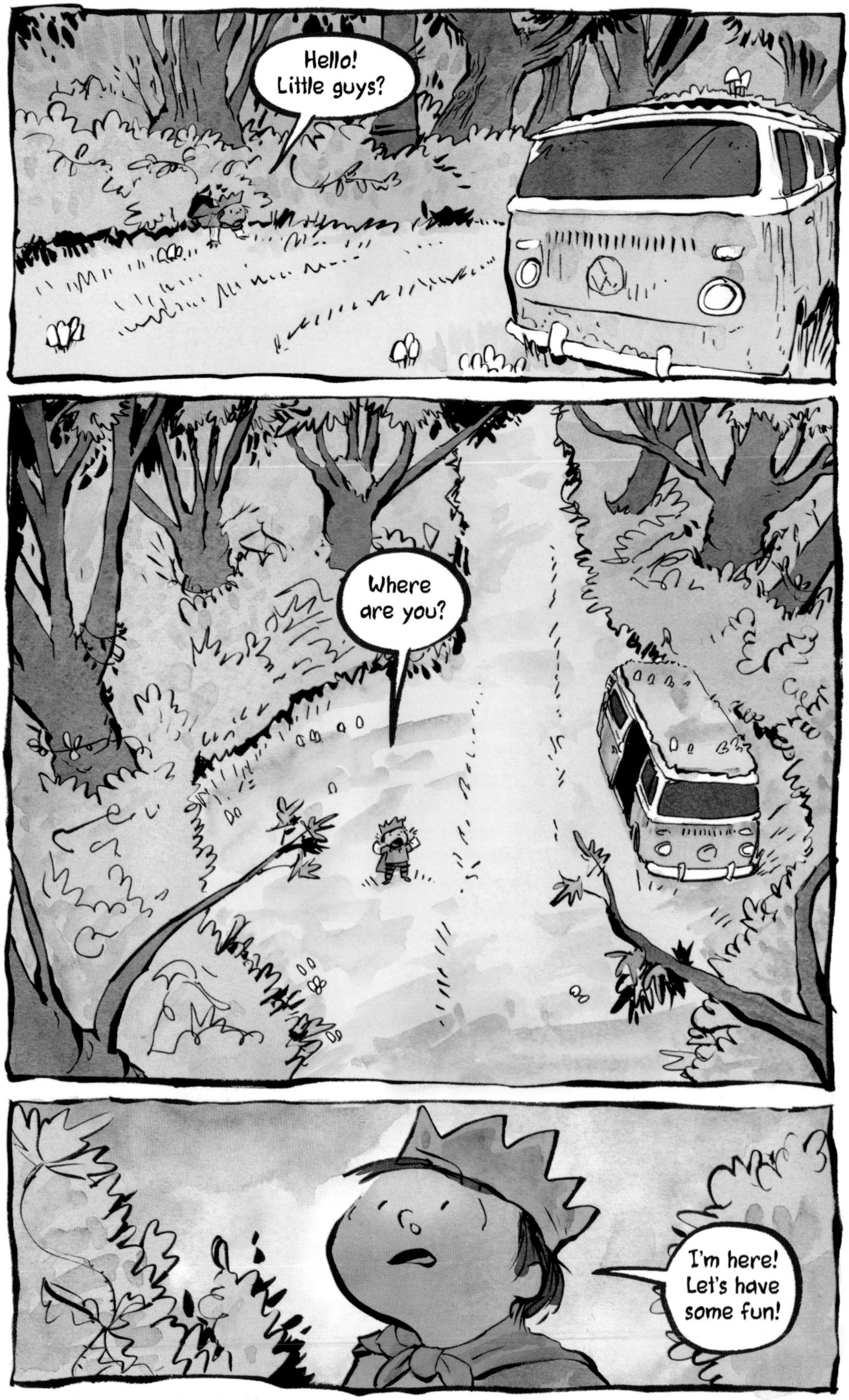
Hello! Little guys?
Where are you?
I'm here! Let's have some fun!

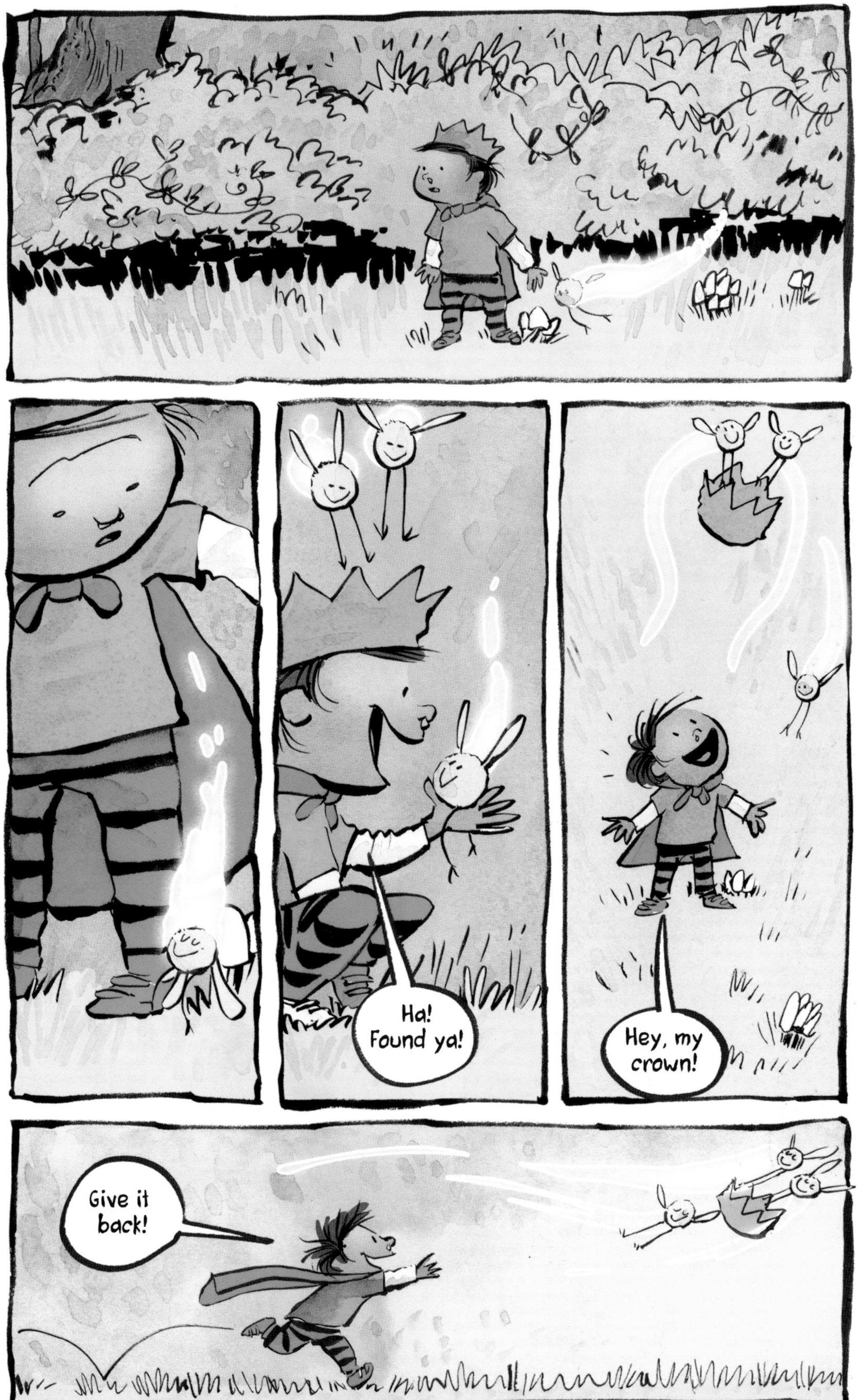
Ha! Found ya!
Hey, my crown!
Give it back!

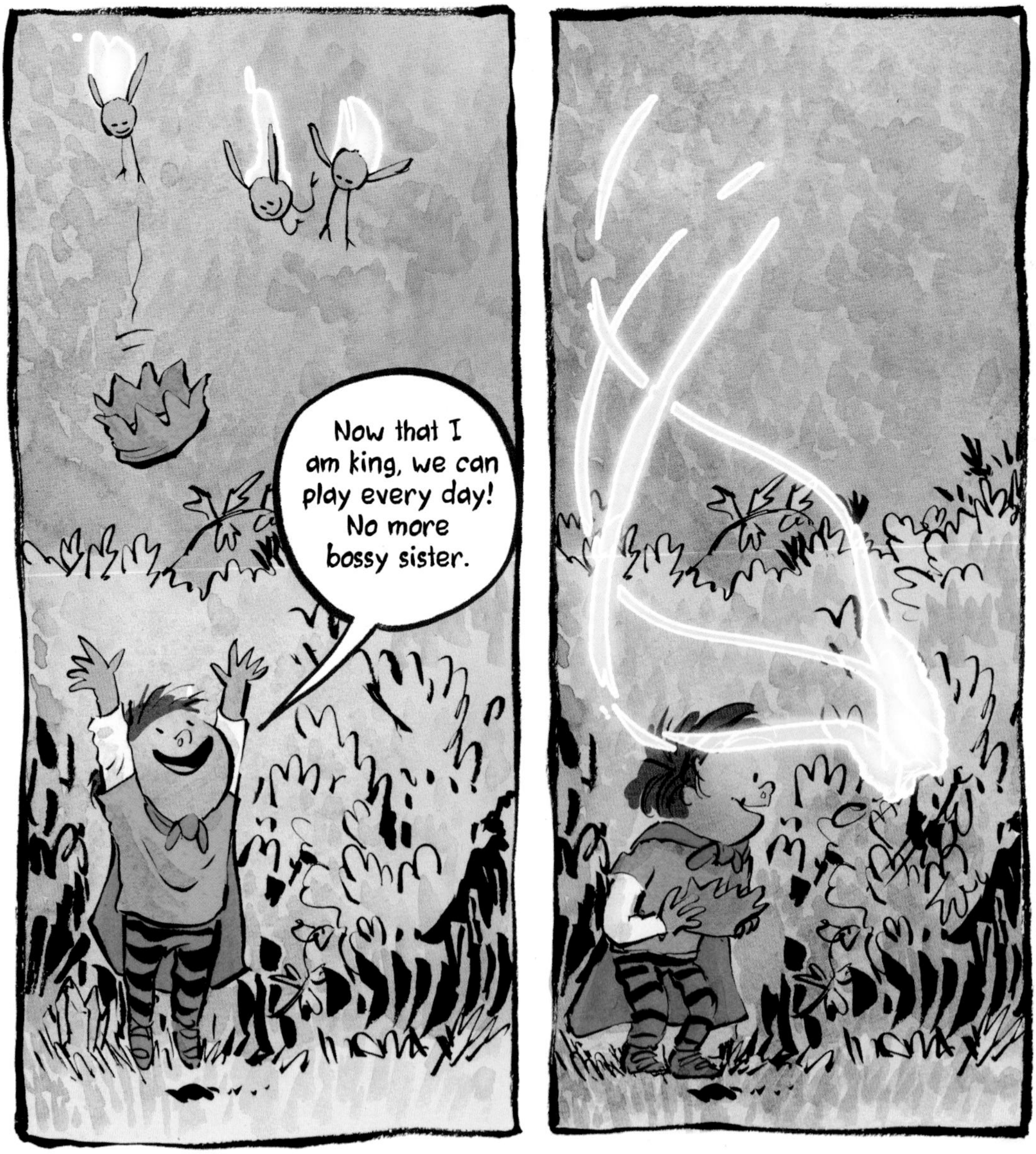
Now that I am king, we can play every day! No more bossy sister.

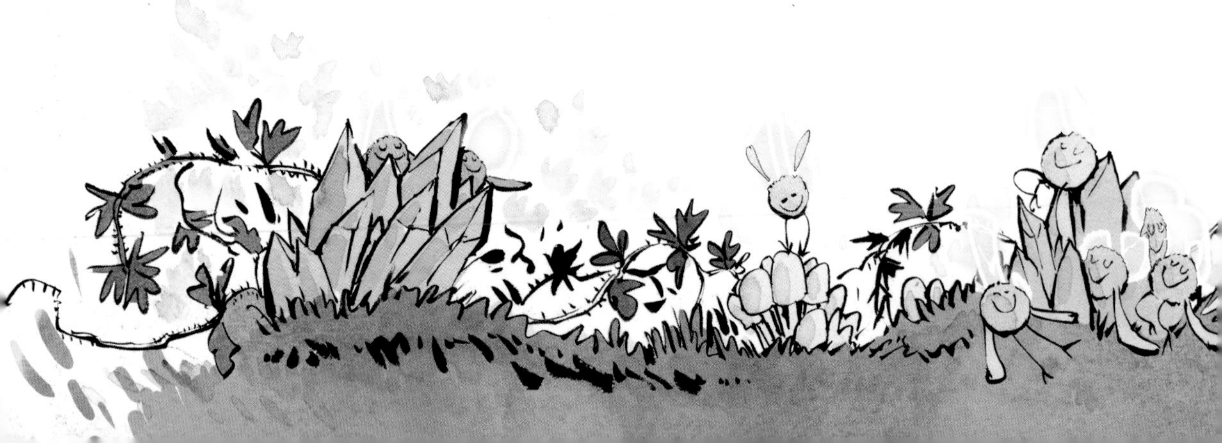

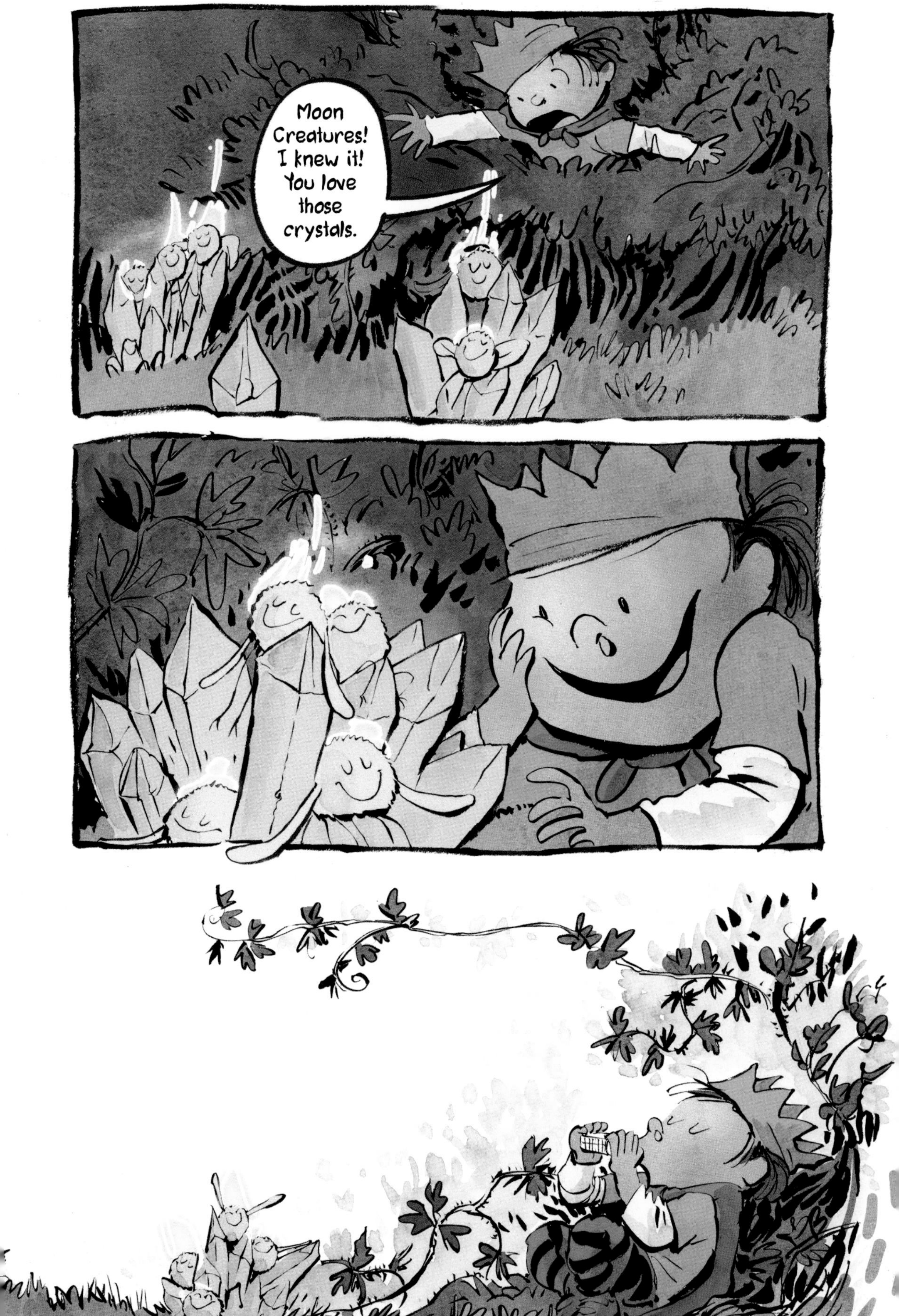
Moon Creatures! I knew it! You love those crystals.

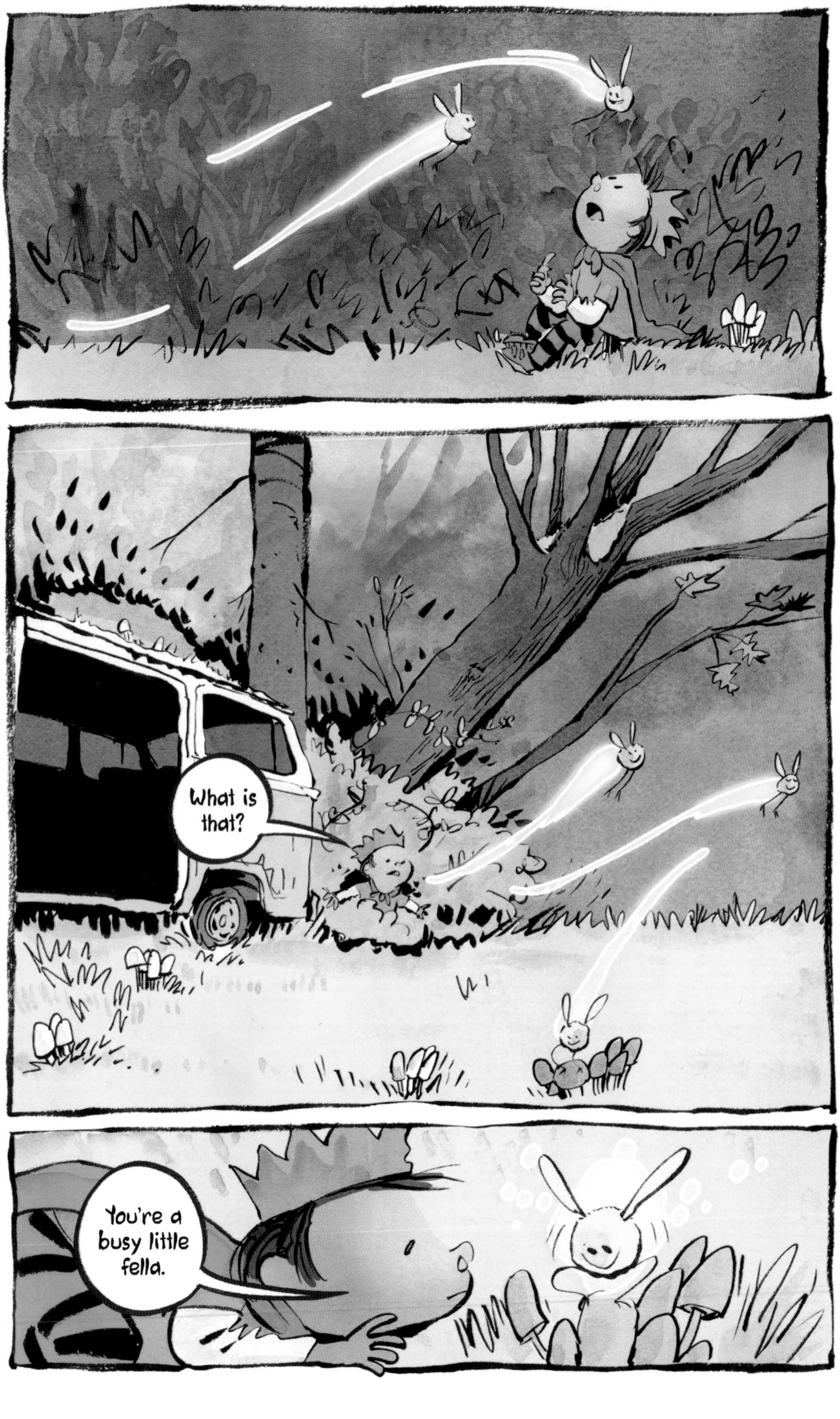
What is that?
You're a busy little fella.

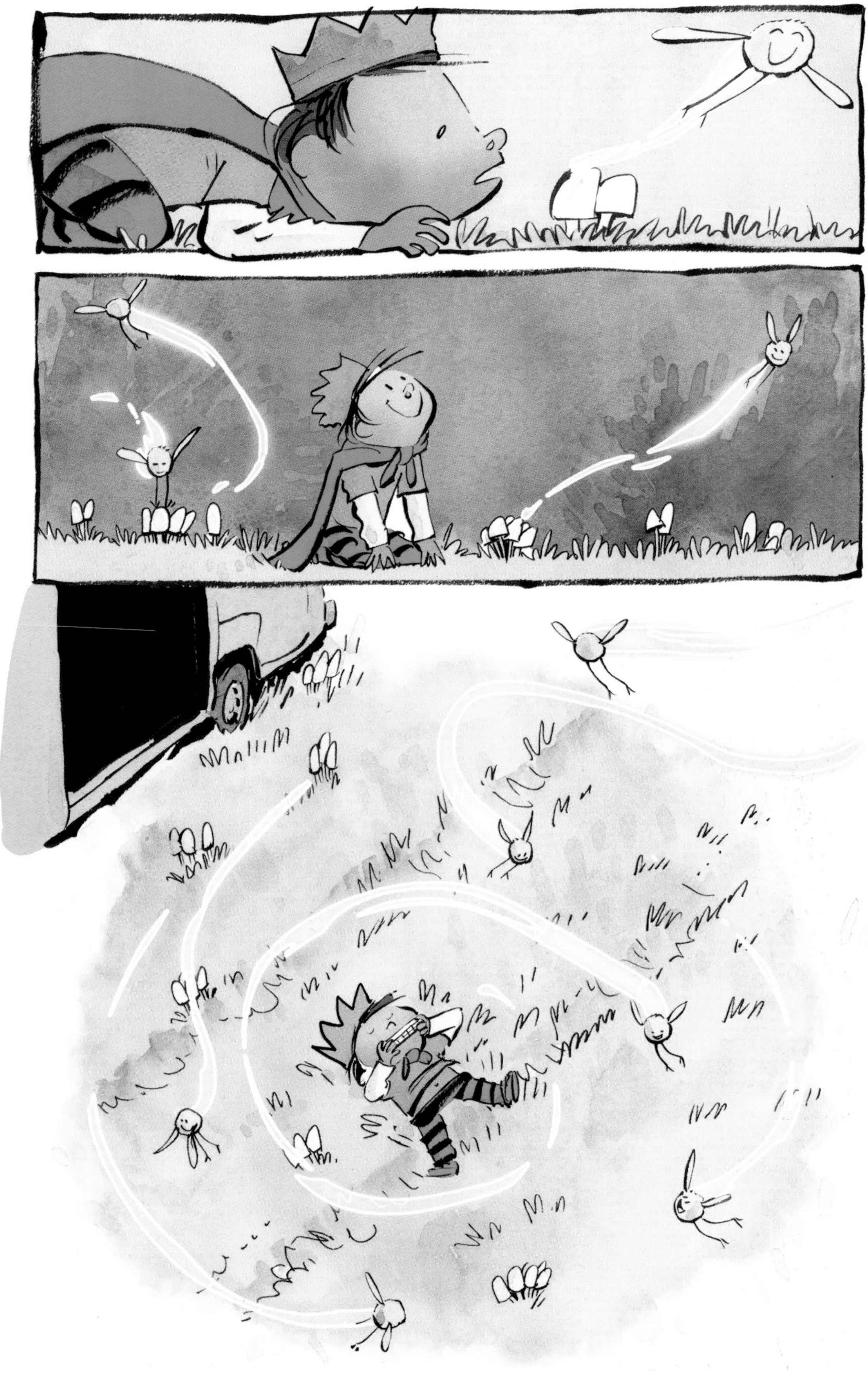

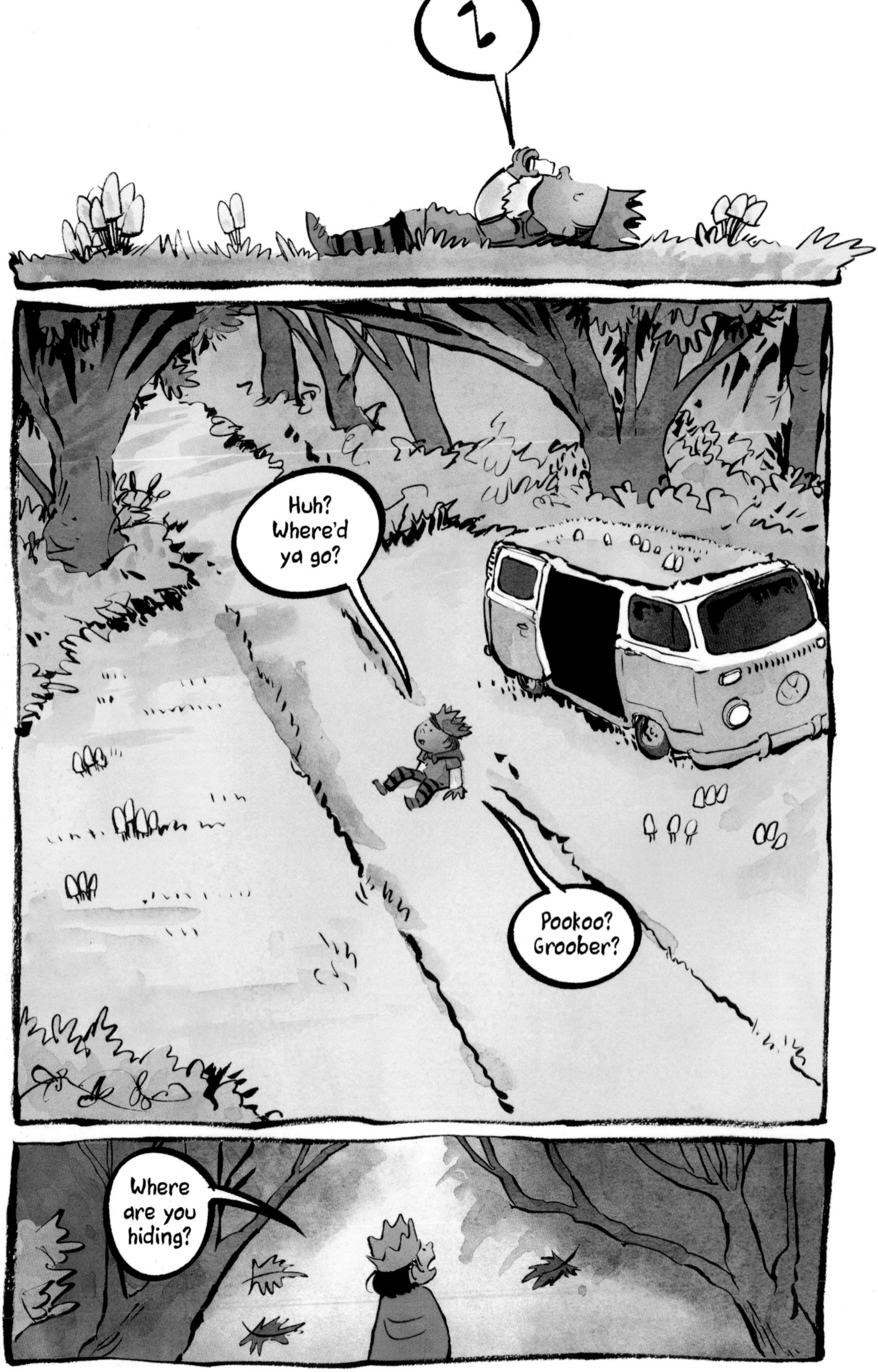
Z
Huh? Where'd ya go?
Pookoo? Groober?
Where are you hiding?

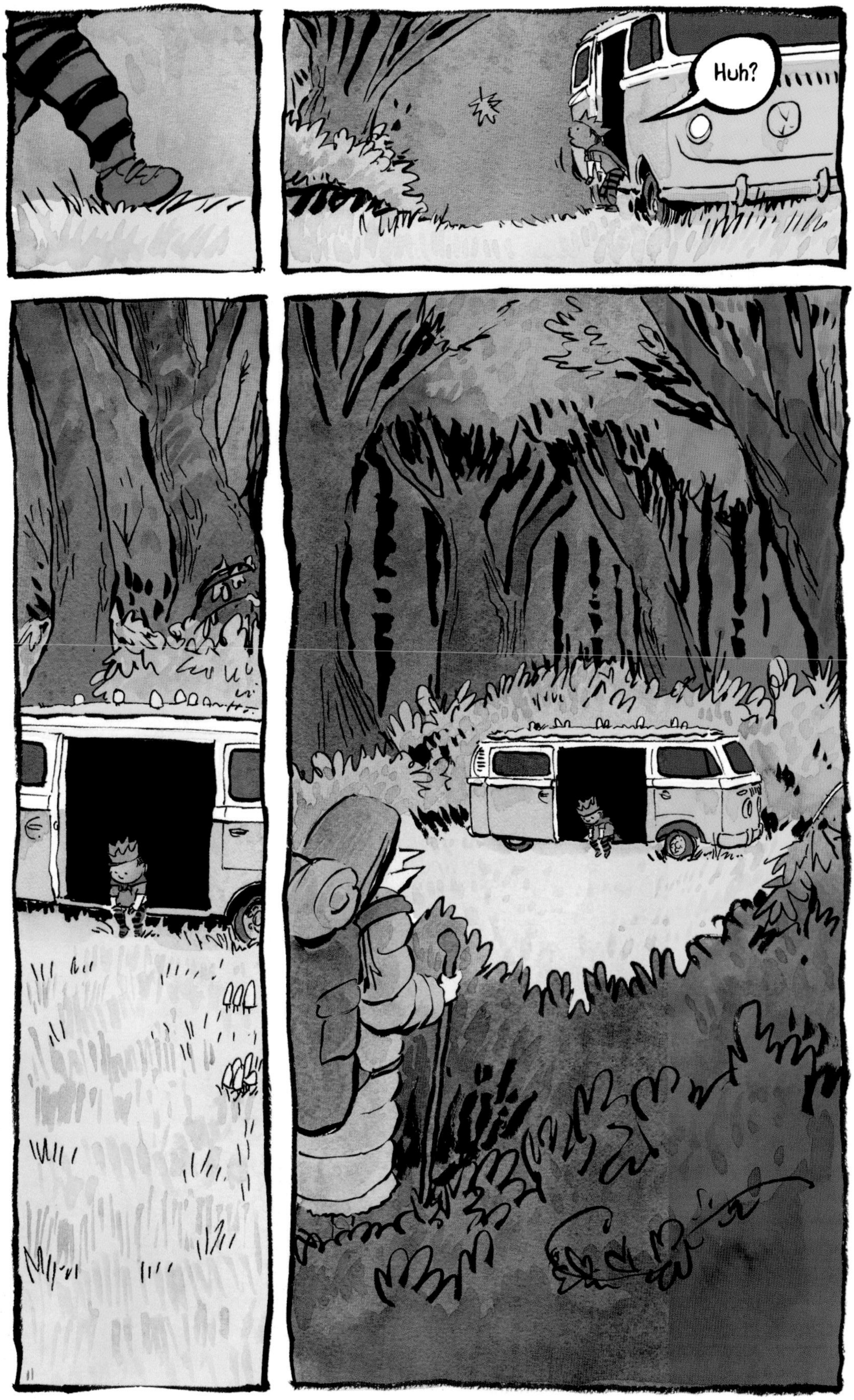
Huh?

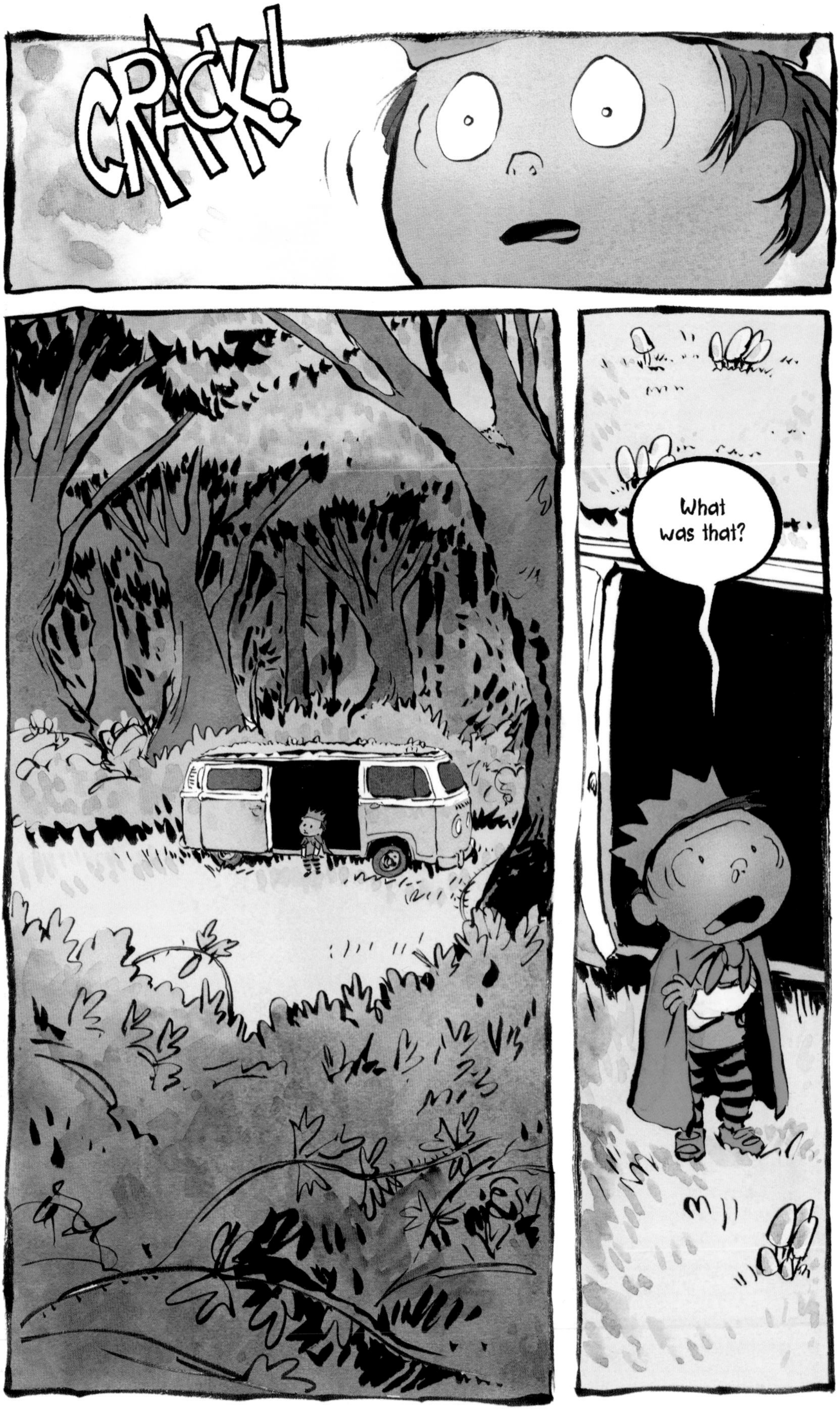
CRACK!
What was that?

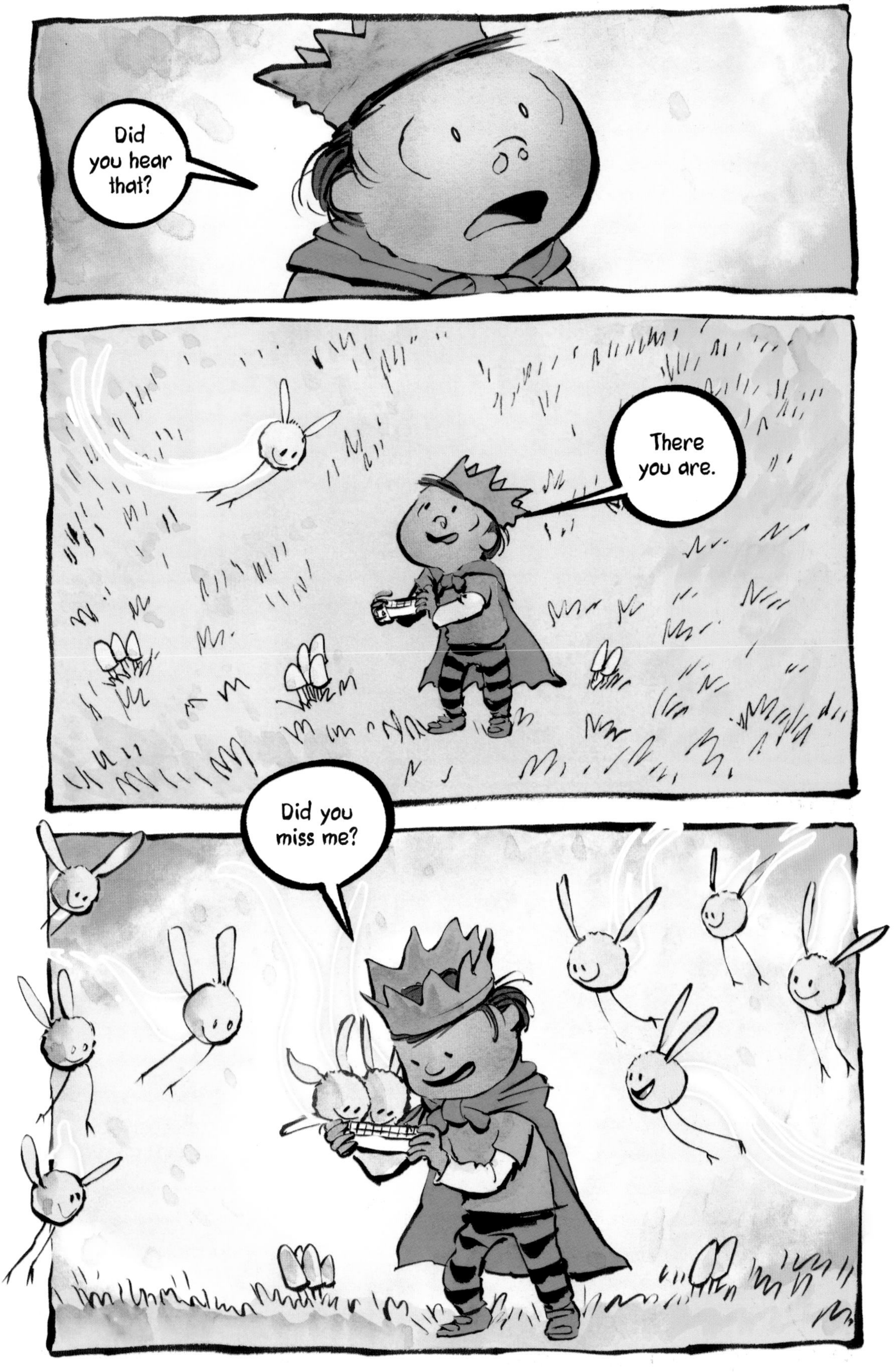
Did you hear that?
There you are.
Did you miss me?

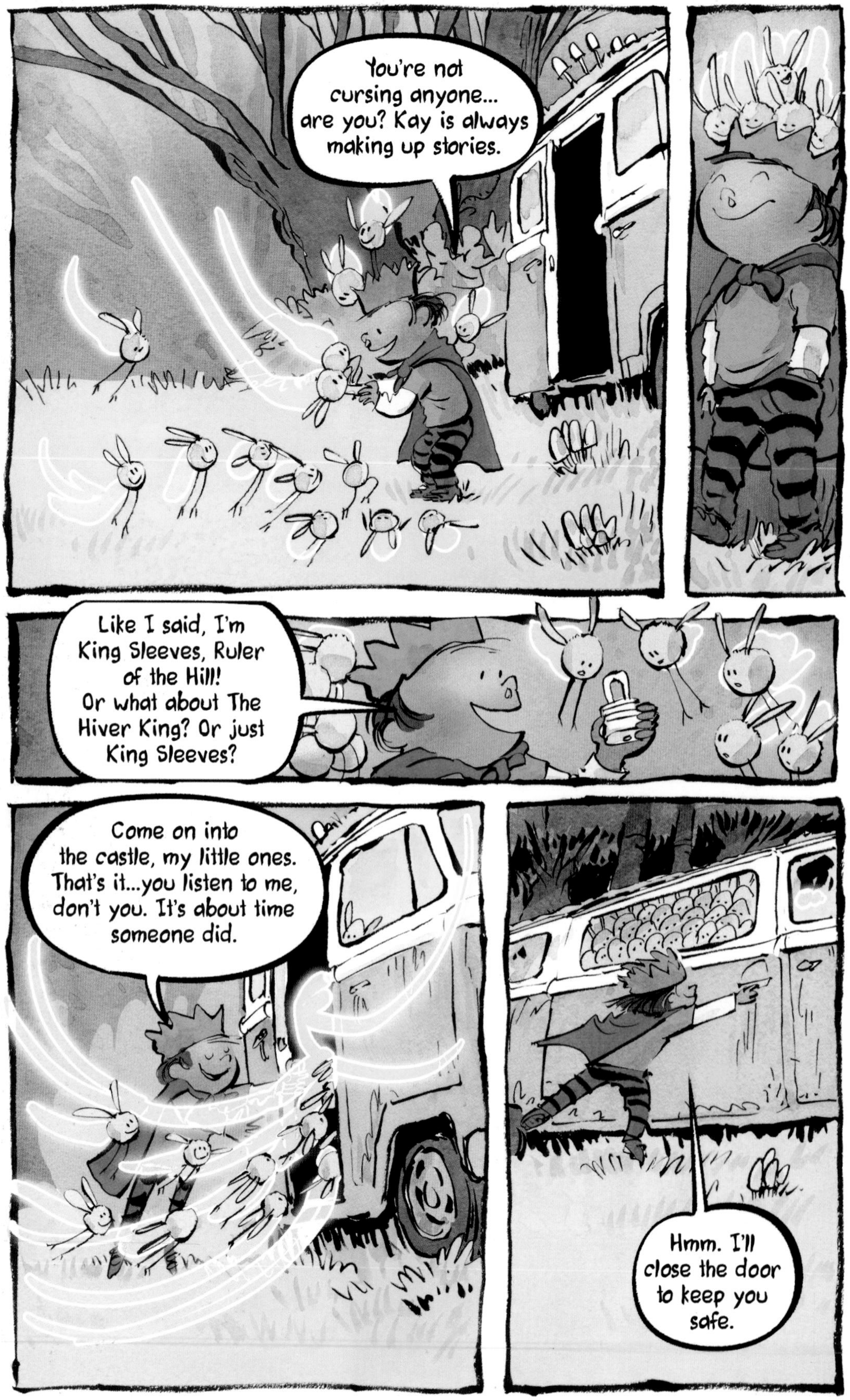
You're not cursing anyone... are you? Kay is always making up stories.
Like I said, I'm King Sleeves, Ruler of the Hill! Or what about The Hiver King? Or just King Sleeves?
Come on into the castle, my little ones. That's it...you listen to me, don't you. It's about time someone did.
Hmm. I'll close the door to keep you safe.

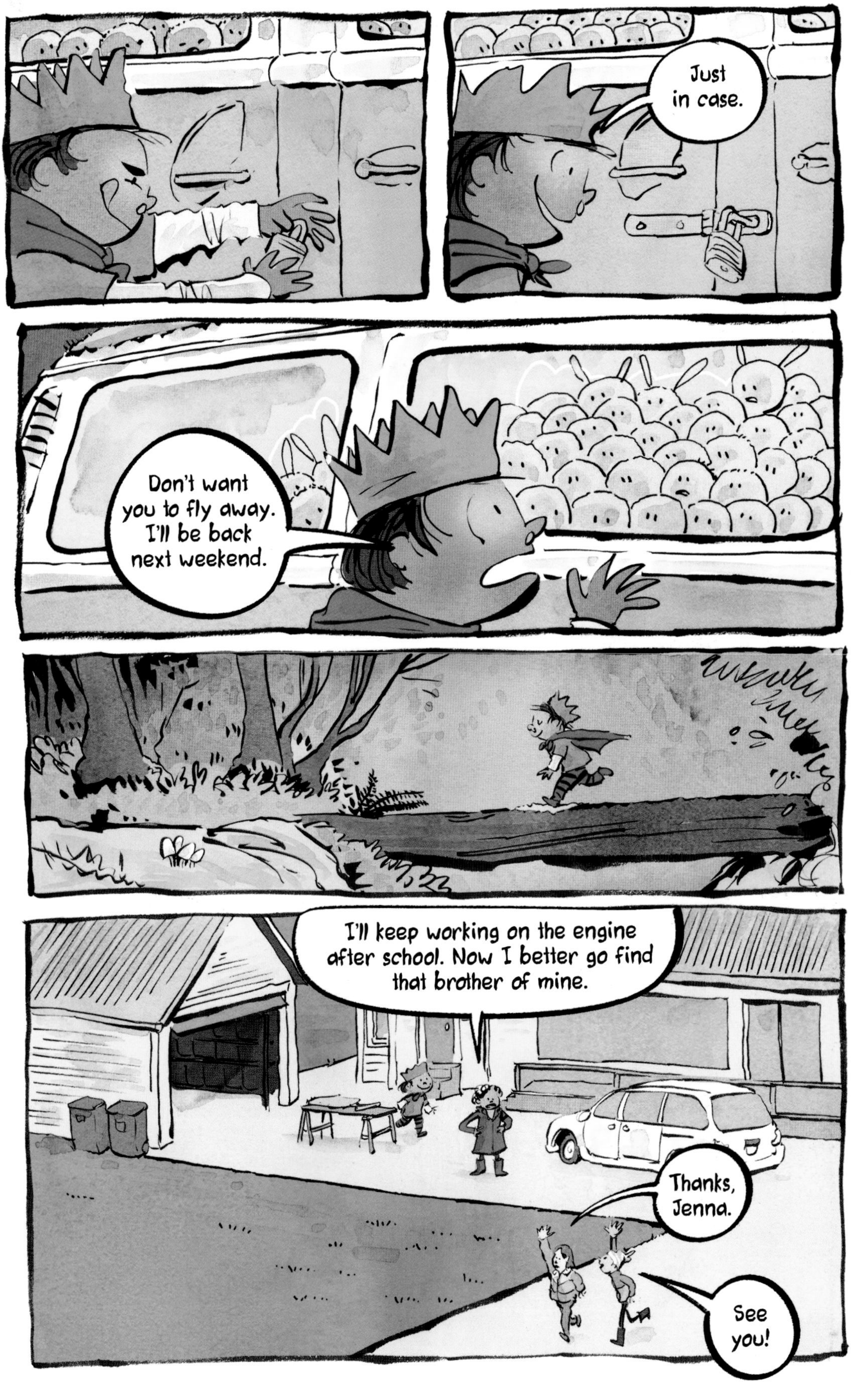
Just in case.
Don't want you to fly away. I'll be back next weekend.
I'll keep working on the engine after school. Now I better go find that brother of mine.
Thanks, Jenna.
See you!

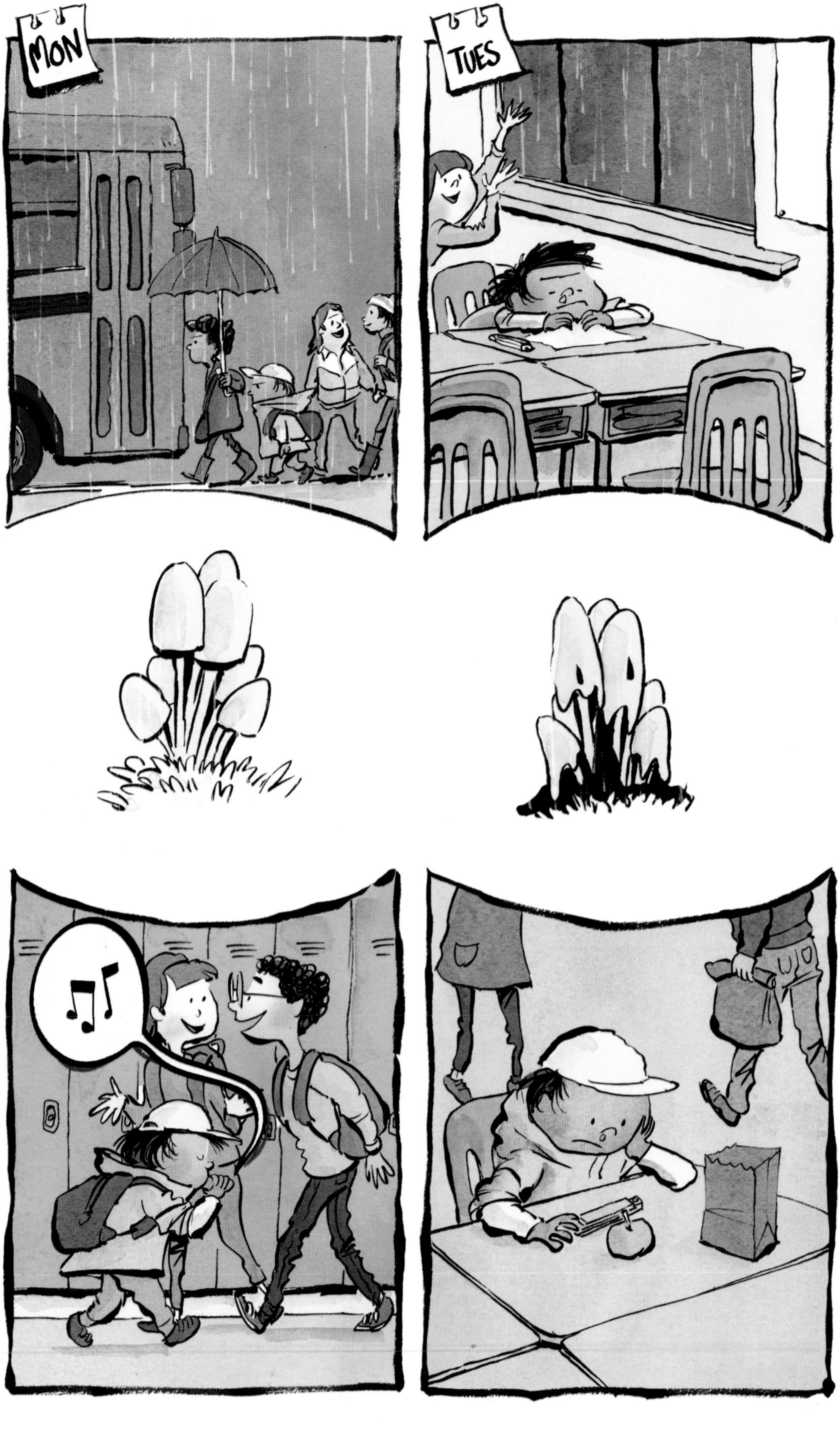
MON
TUES

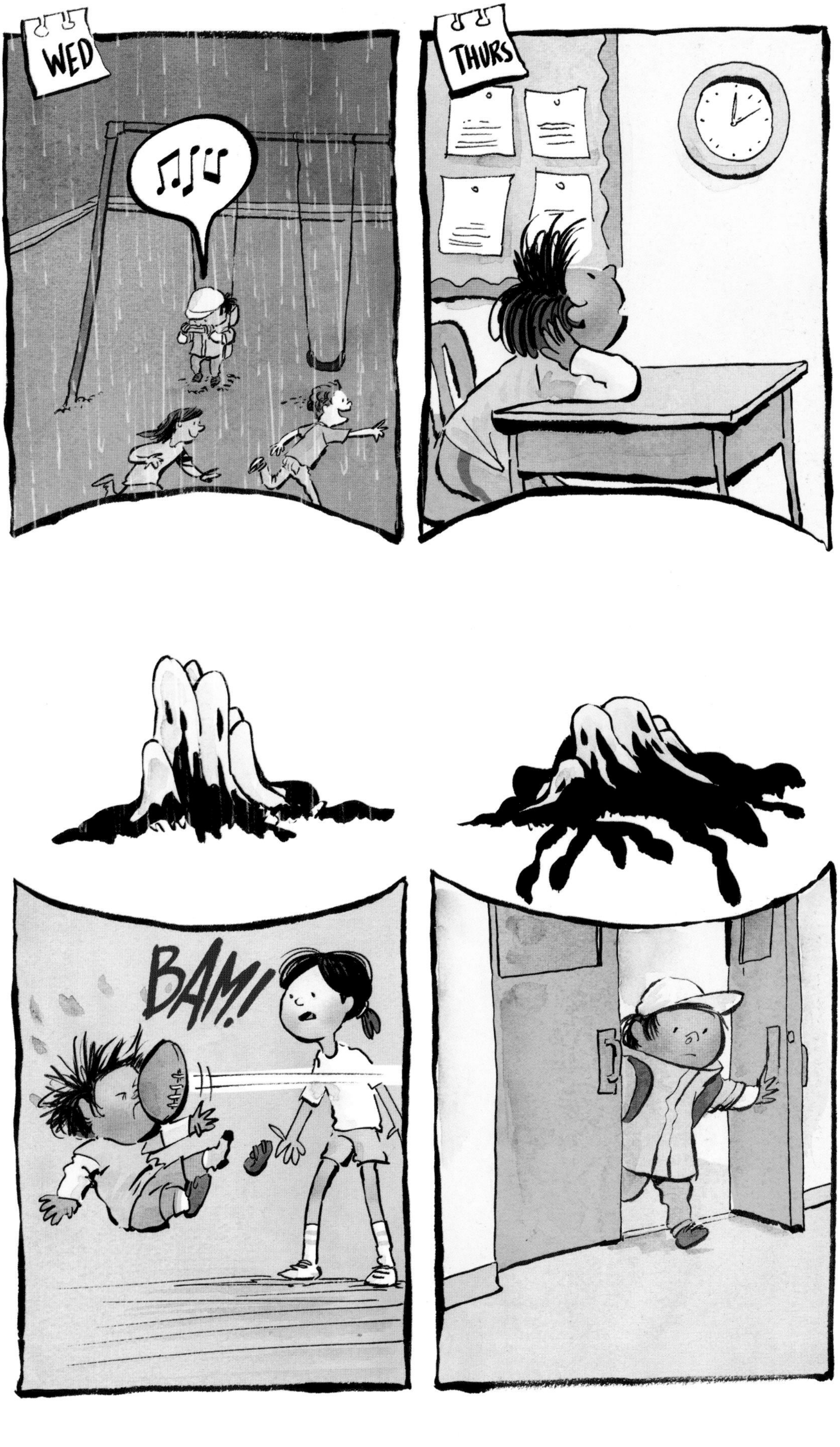
WED
THURS
BAM!

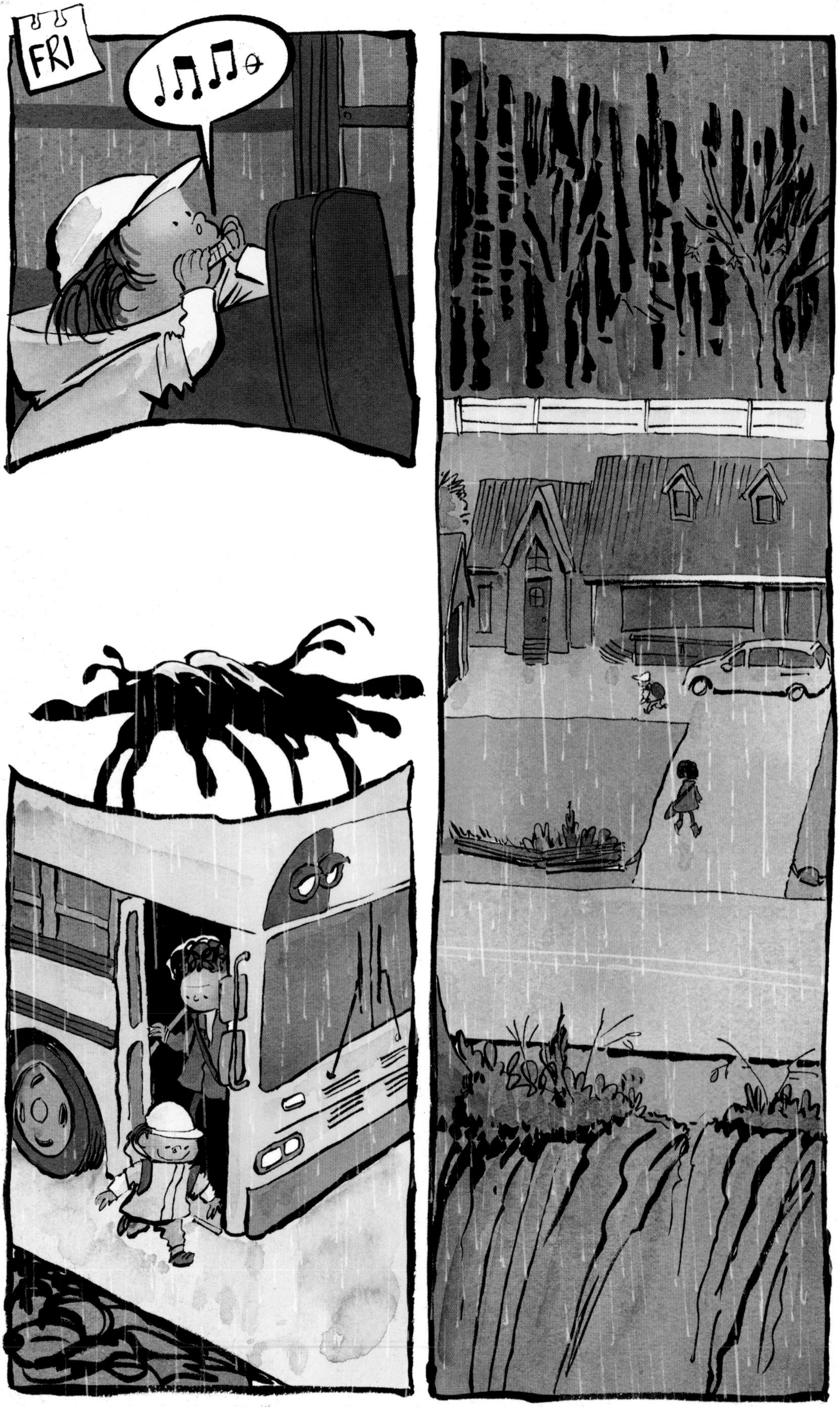
FRI

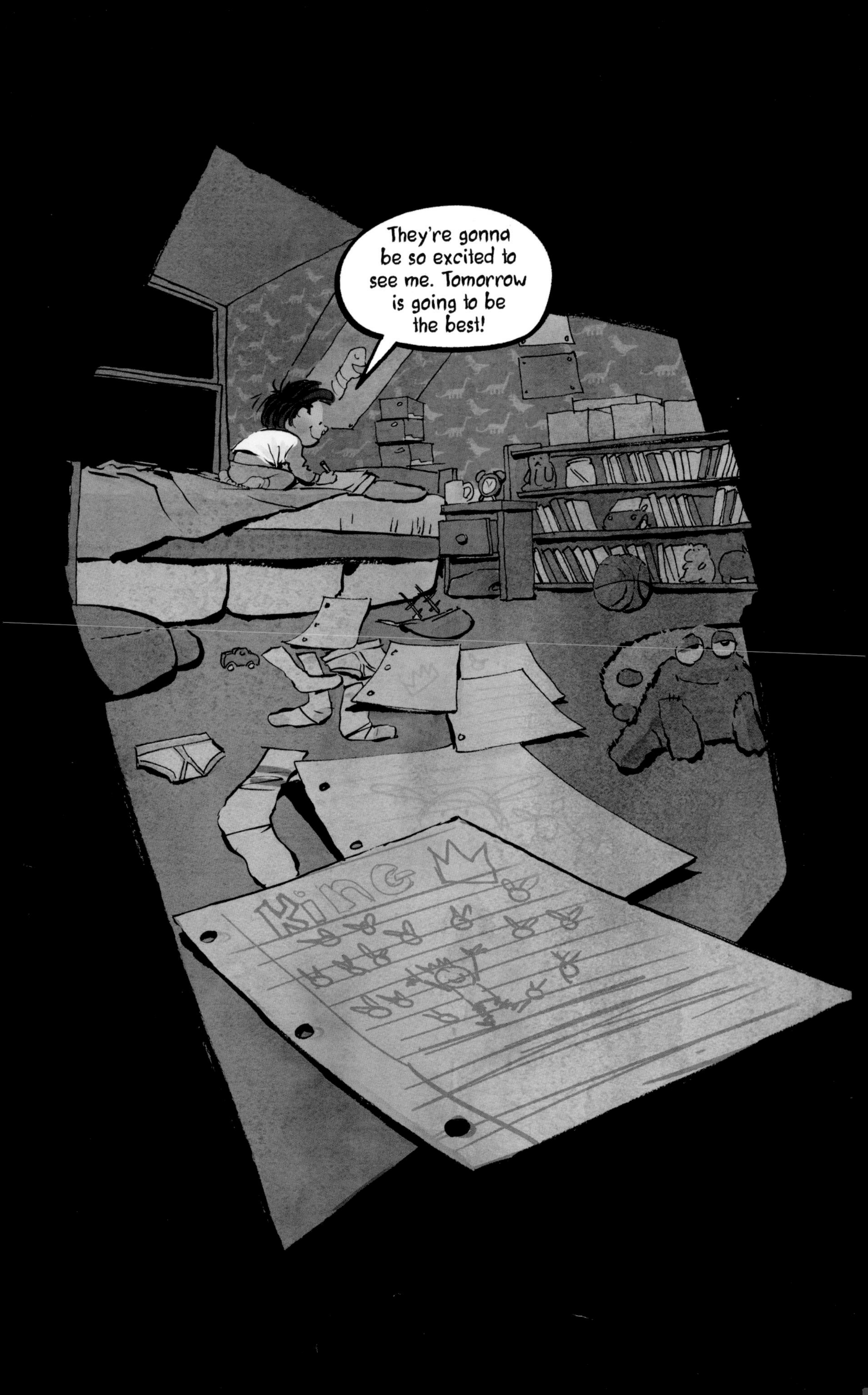
They're gonna be so excited to see me. Tomorrow is going to be the best!
King

CHAPTER FOUR

I Wouldn't Do That If I Were You

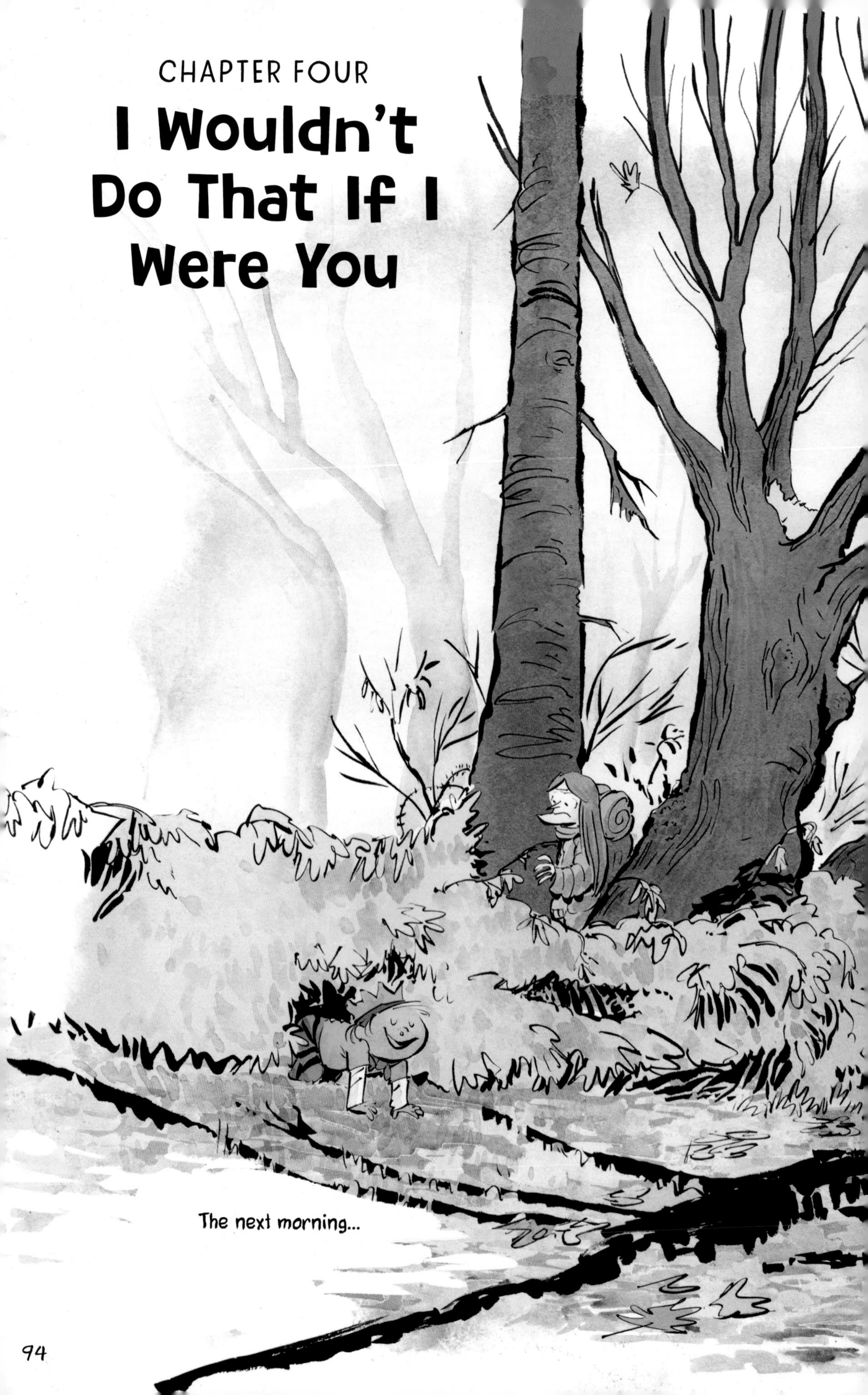
The next morning...

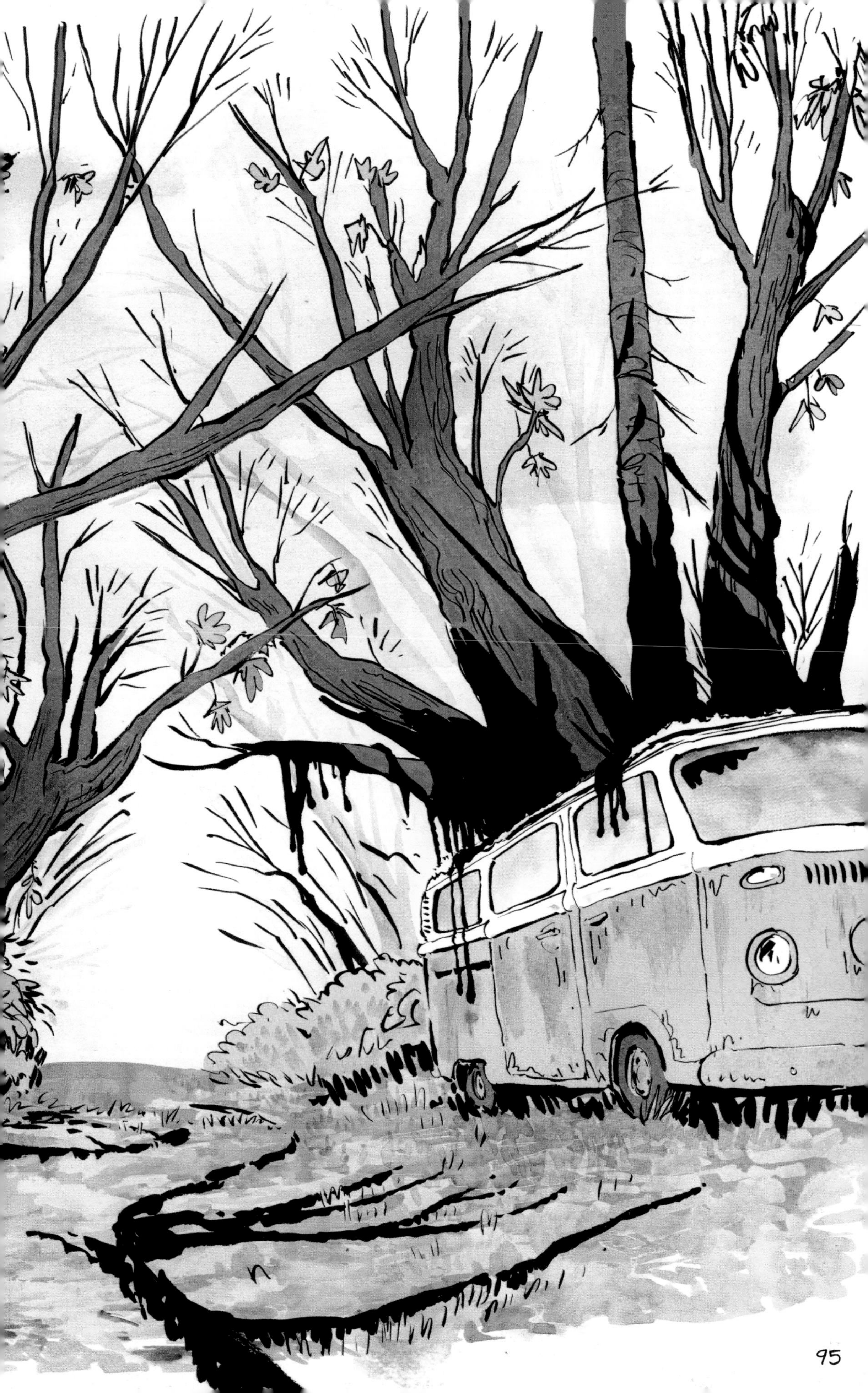

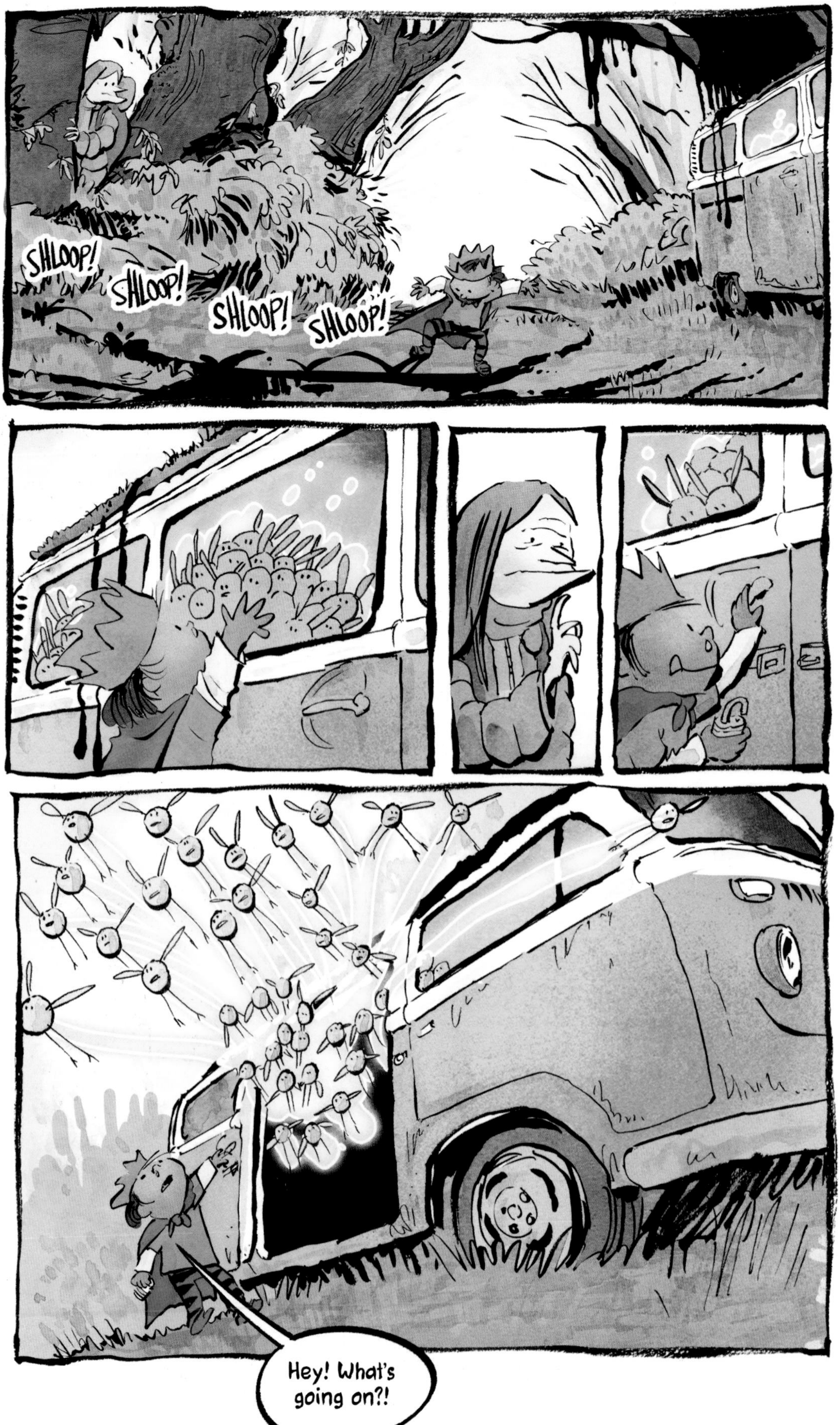
SHLOOP!
SHLOOP!
SHLOOP!
SHLOOP!
Hey! What's going on?!

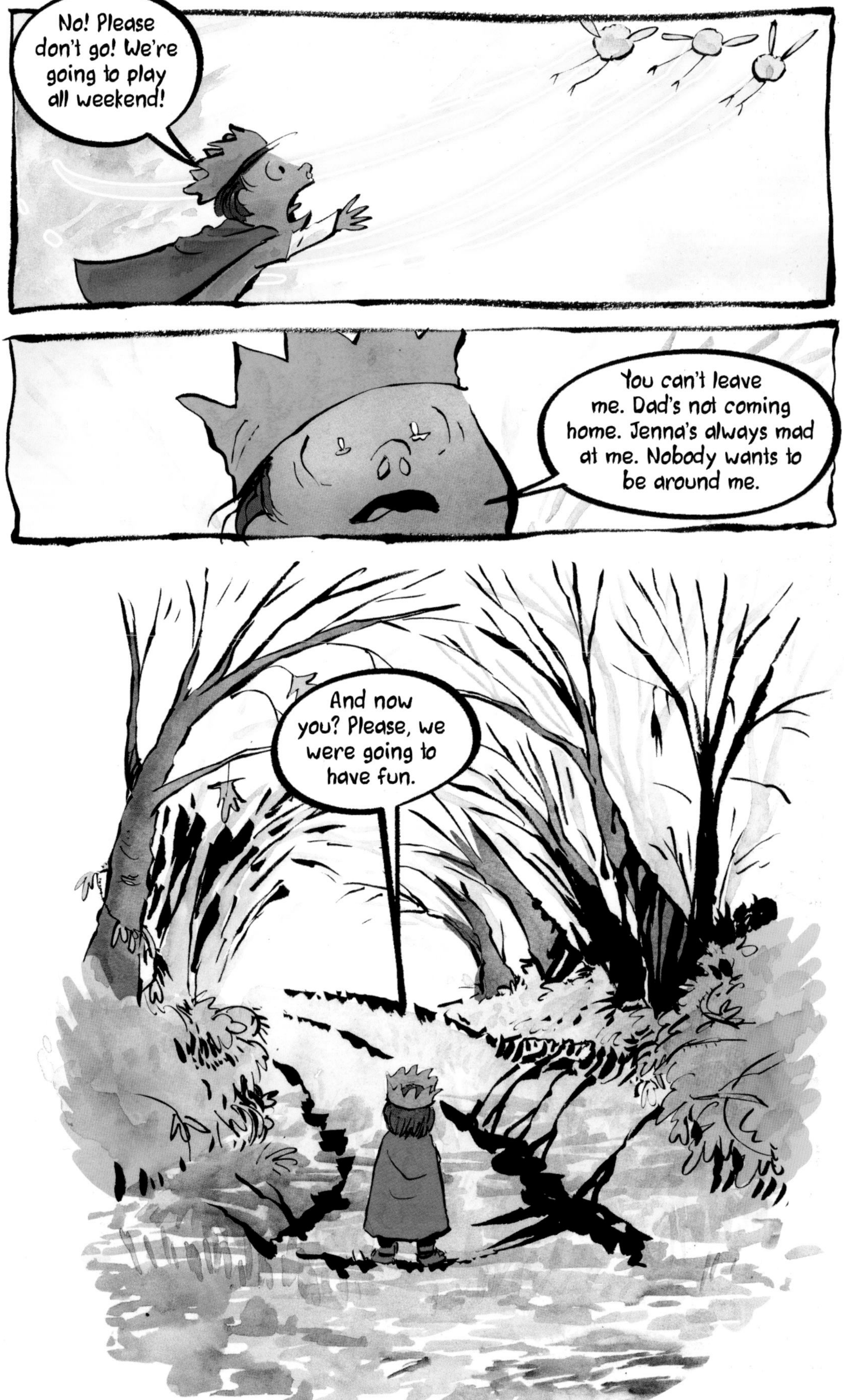
No! Please don't go! We're going to play all weekend!
You can't leave me. Dad's not coming home. Jenna's always mad at me. Nobody wants to be around me.
And now you? Please, we were going to have fun.

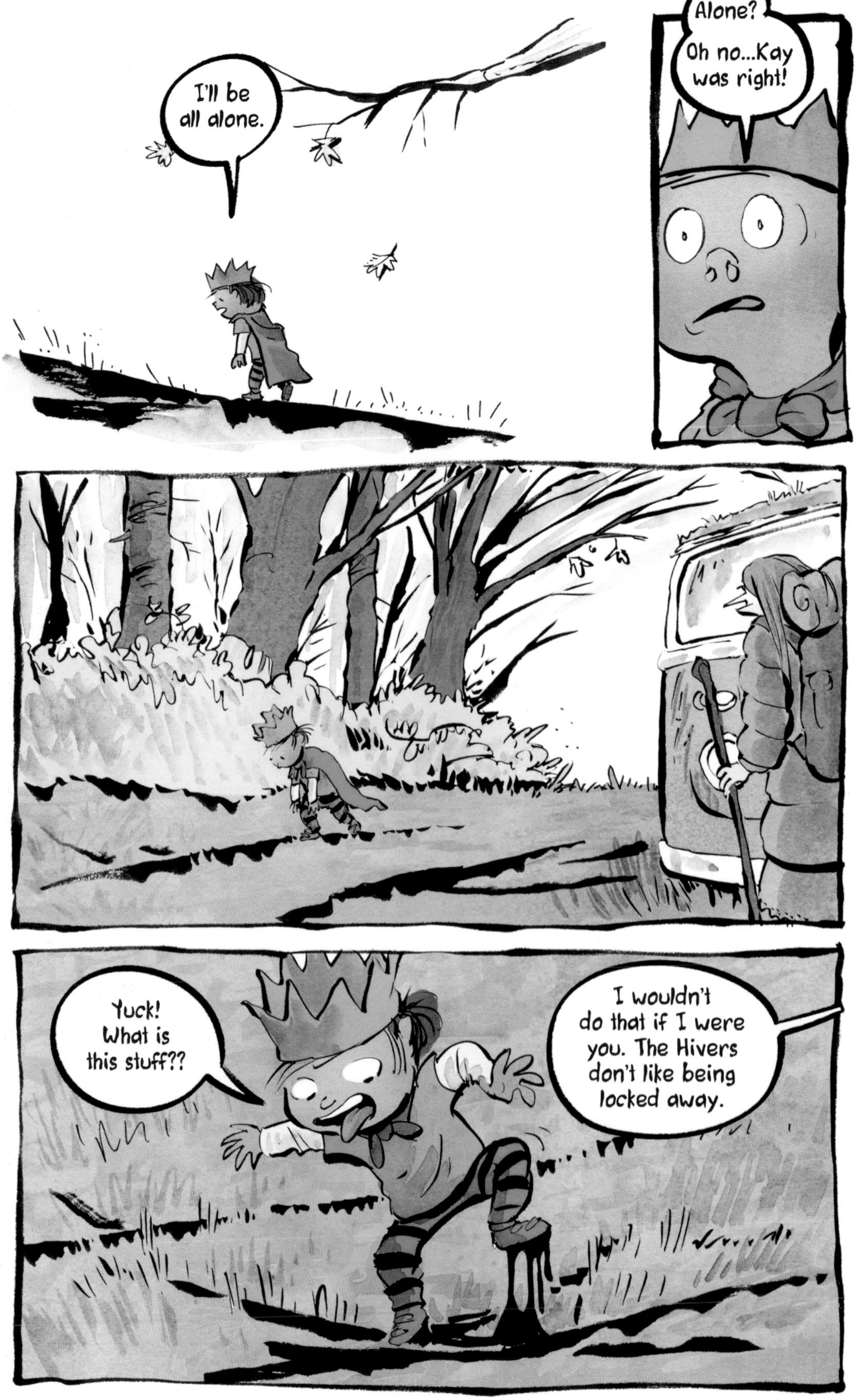

I'll be all alone.
Alone?
Oh no...Kay was right!
Yuck! What is this stuff??
I wouldn't do that if I were you. The Hivers don't like being locked away.

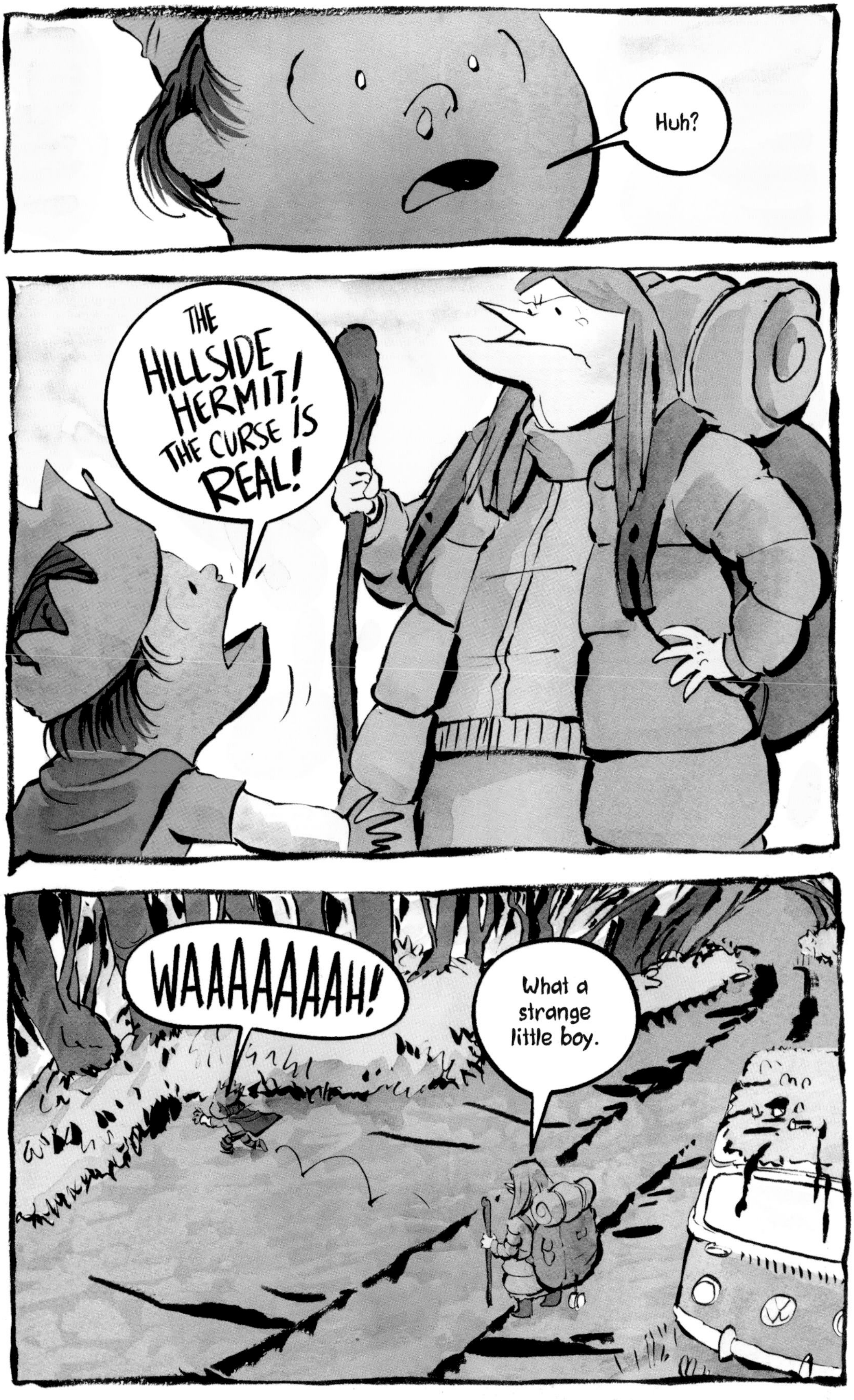
Huh?
THE HILLSIDE HERMIT! THE CURSE IS REAL!
WAAAAAAAH!
What a strange little boy.

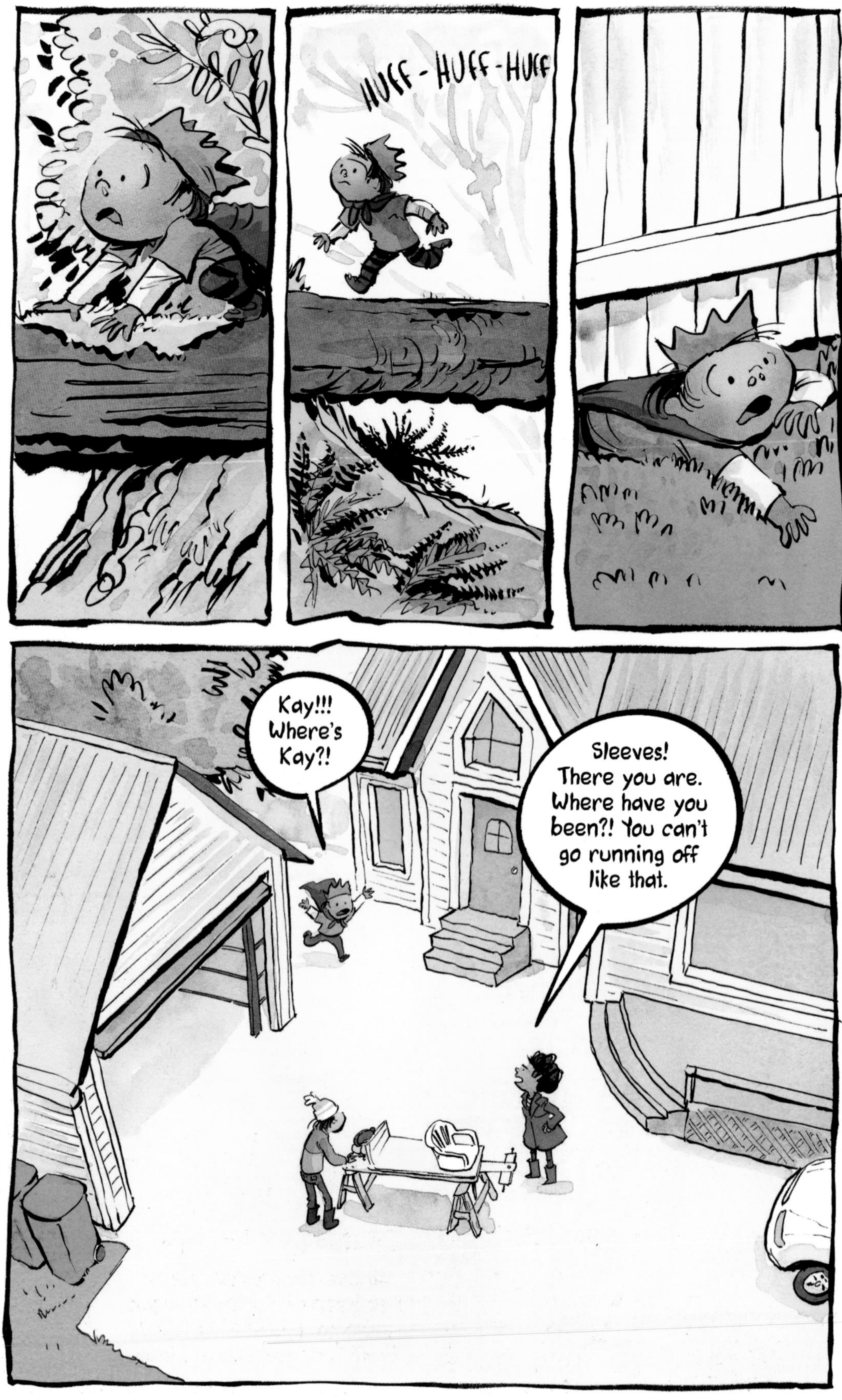
HUFF - HUFF - HUFF
Kay!!! Where's Kay?!
Sleeves! There you are. Where have you been?! You can't go running off like that.

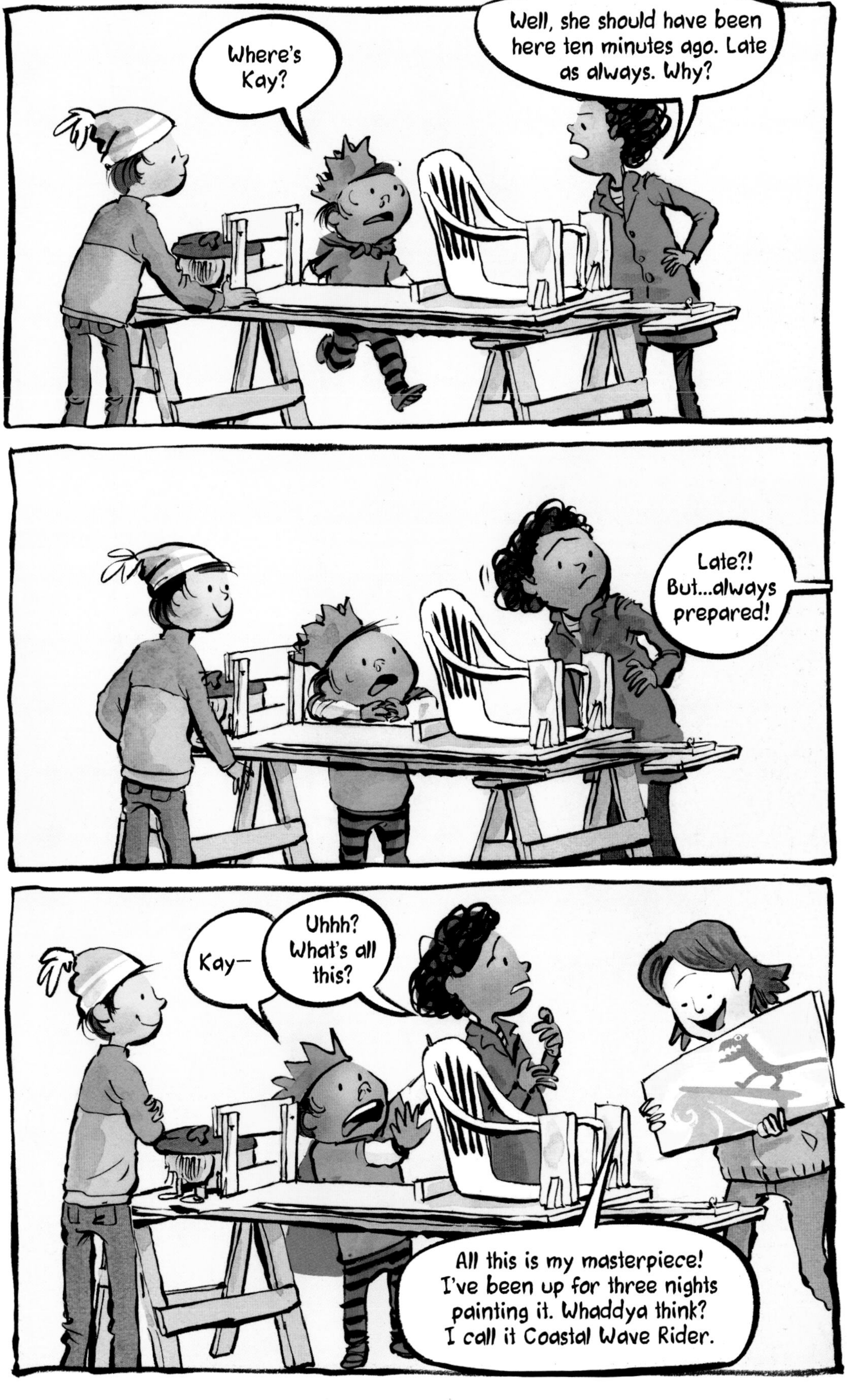
Where's Kay?
Well, she should have been here ten minutes ago. Late as always. Why?
Late?! But...always prepared!
Kay—
Uhhh? What's all this?
All this is my masterpiece! I've been up for three nights painting it. Whaddya think? I call it Coastal Wave Rider.

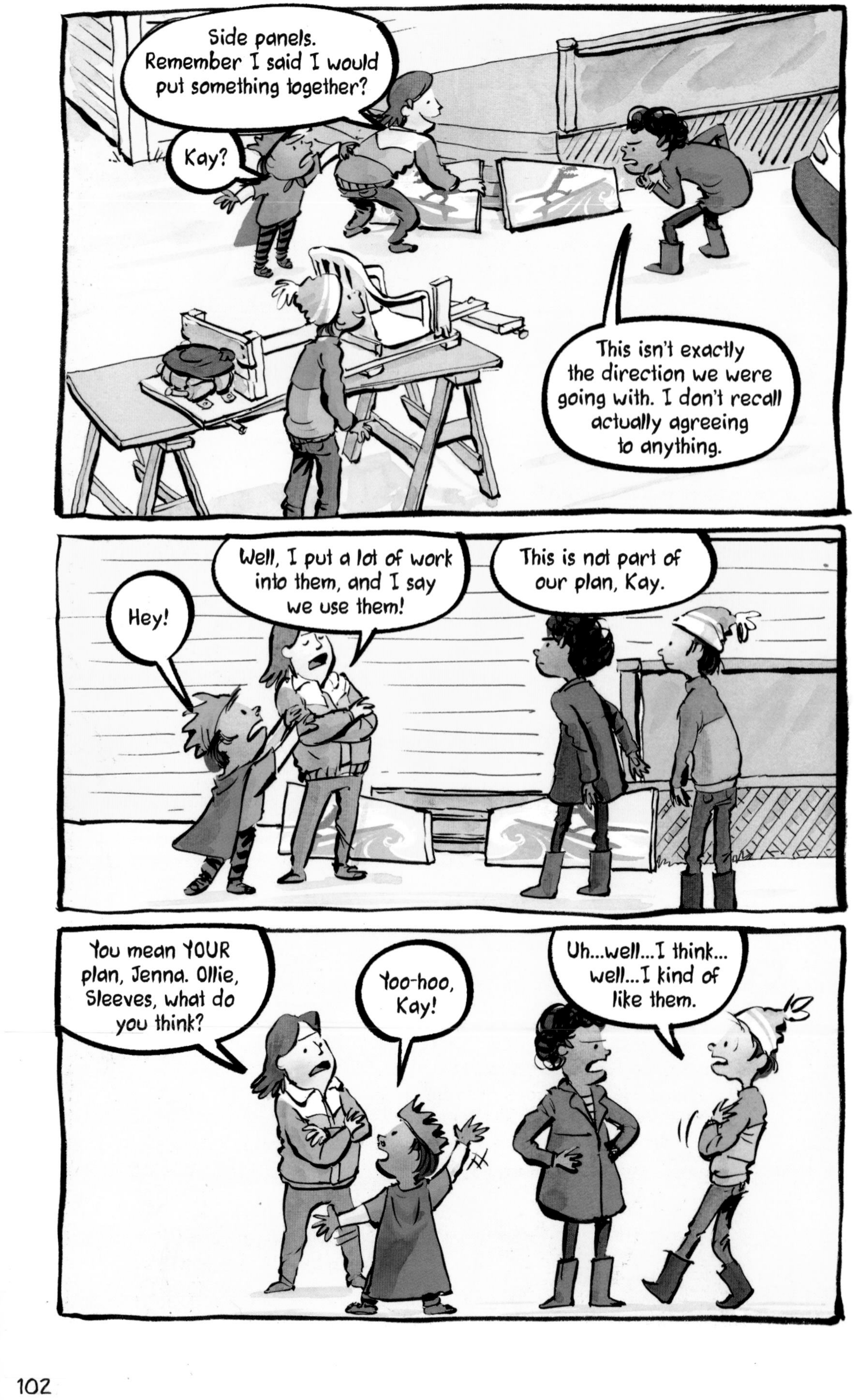
Side panels. Remember I said I would put something together?
Kay?
This isn't exactly the direction we were going with. I don't recall actually agreeing to anything.
Hey!
Well, I put a lot of work into them, and I say we use them!
This is not part of our plan, Kay.
You mean YOUR plan, Jenna. Ollie, Sleeves, what do you think?
Yoo-hoo, Kay!
Uh...well...I think... well...I kind of like them.

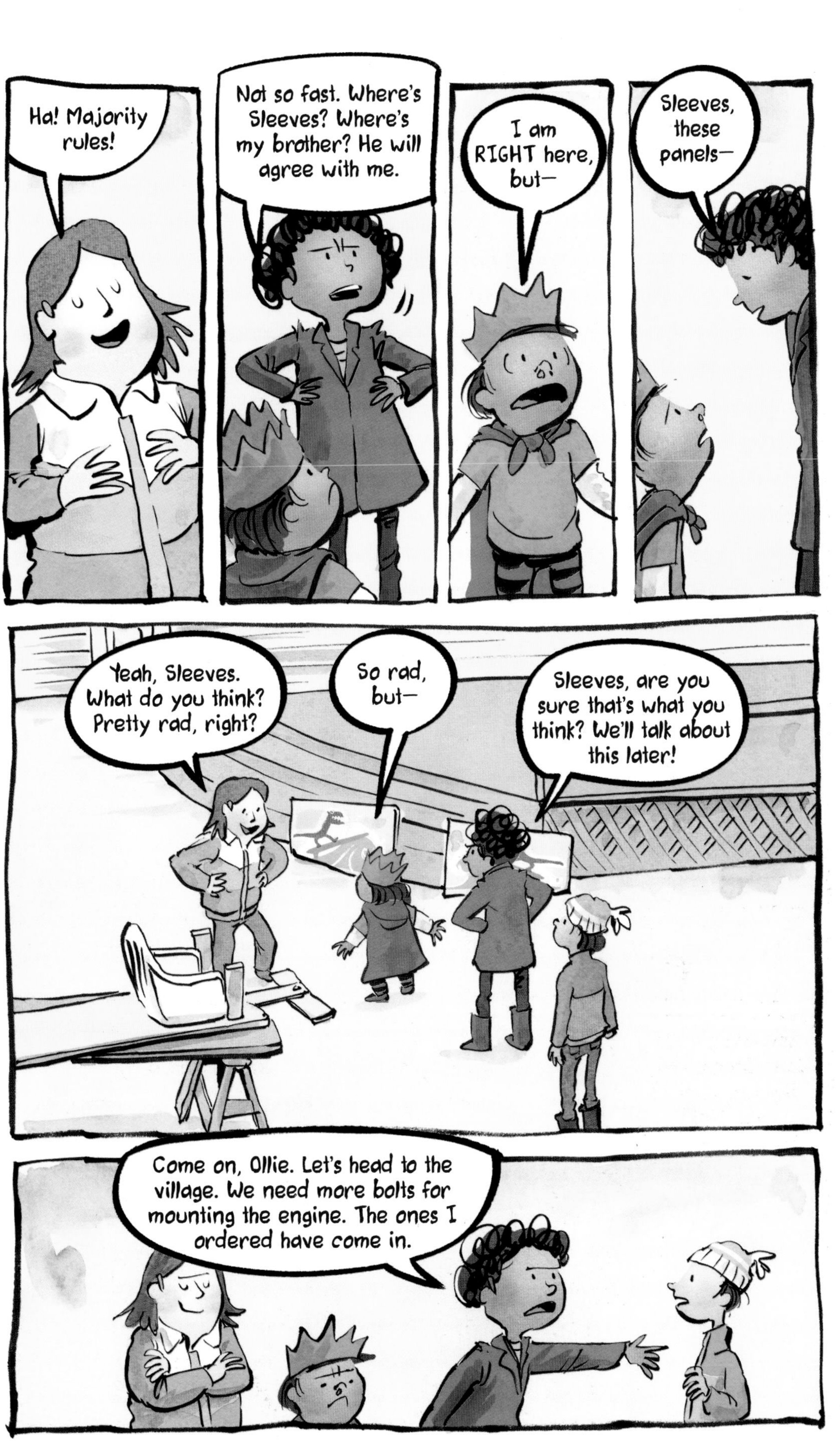
Ha! Majority rules!
Not so fast. Where's Sleeves? Where's my brother? He will agree with me.
I am RIGHT here, but—
Sleeves, these panels—
Yeah, Sleeves. What do you think? Pretty rad, right?
So rad, but—
Sleeves, are you sure that's what you think? We'll talk about this later!
Come on, Ollie. Let's head to the village. We need more bolts for mounting the engine. The ones I ordered have come in.

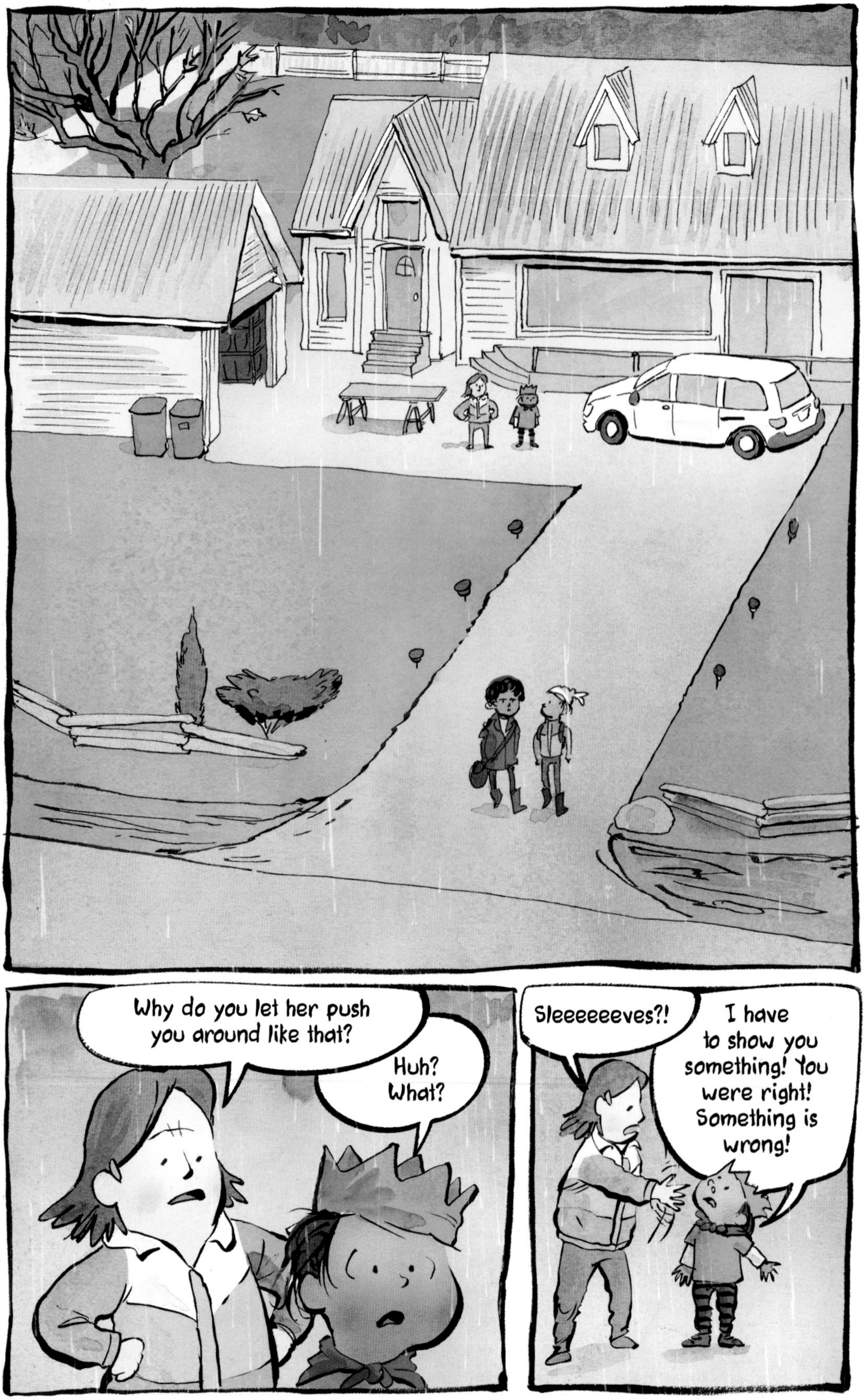
Why do you let her push you around like that?
Huh? What?
Sleeeeeeves?!
I have to show you something! You were right! Something is wrong!

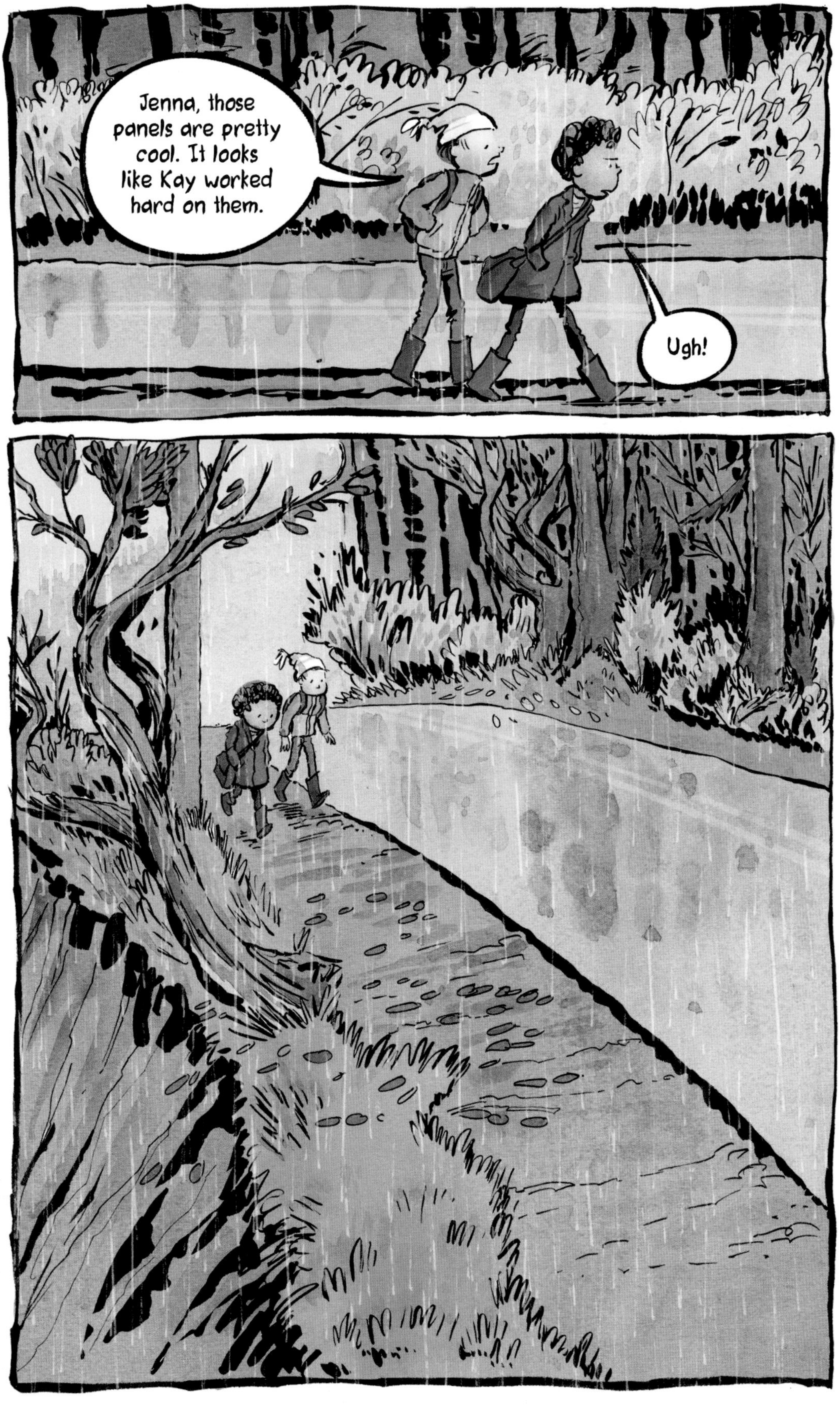
Jenna, those panels are pretty cool. It looks like Kay worked hard on them.
Ugh!

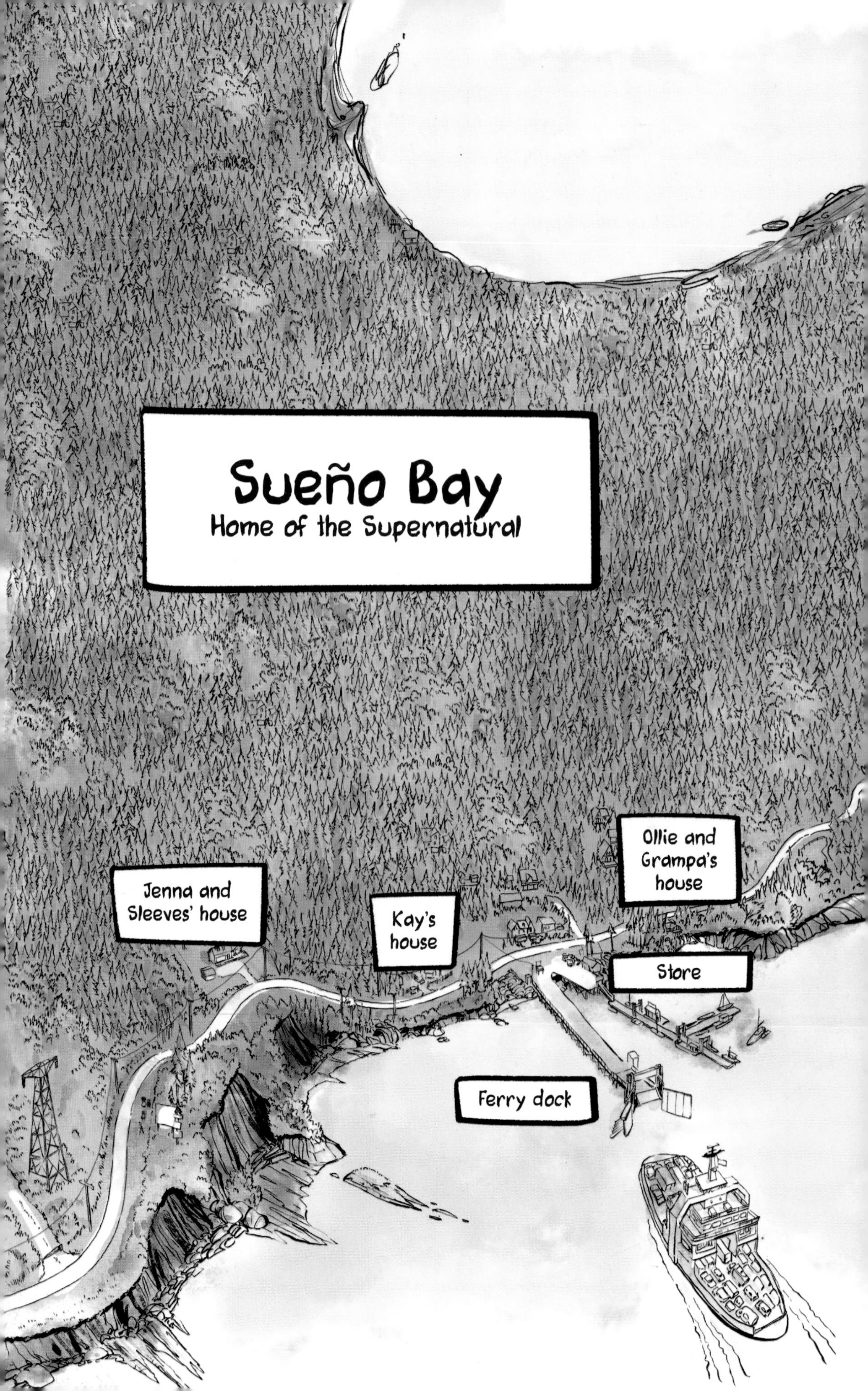
Sueño Bay
Home of the Supernatural
Ollie and Grampa's house
Jenna and Sleeves' house
Kay's house
Store
Ferry dock

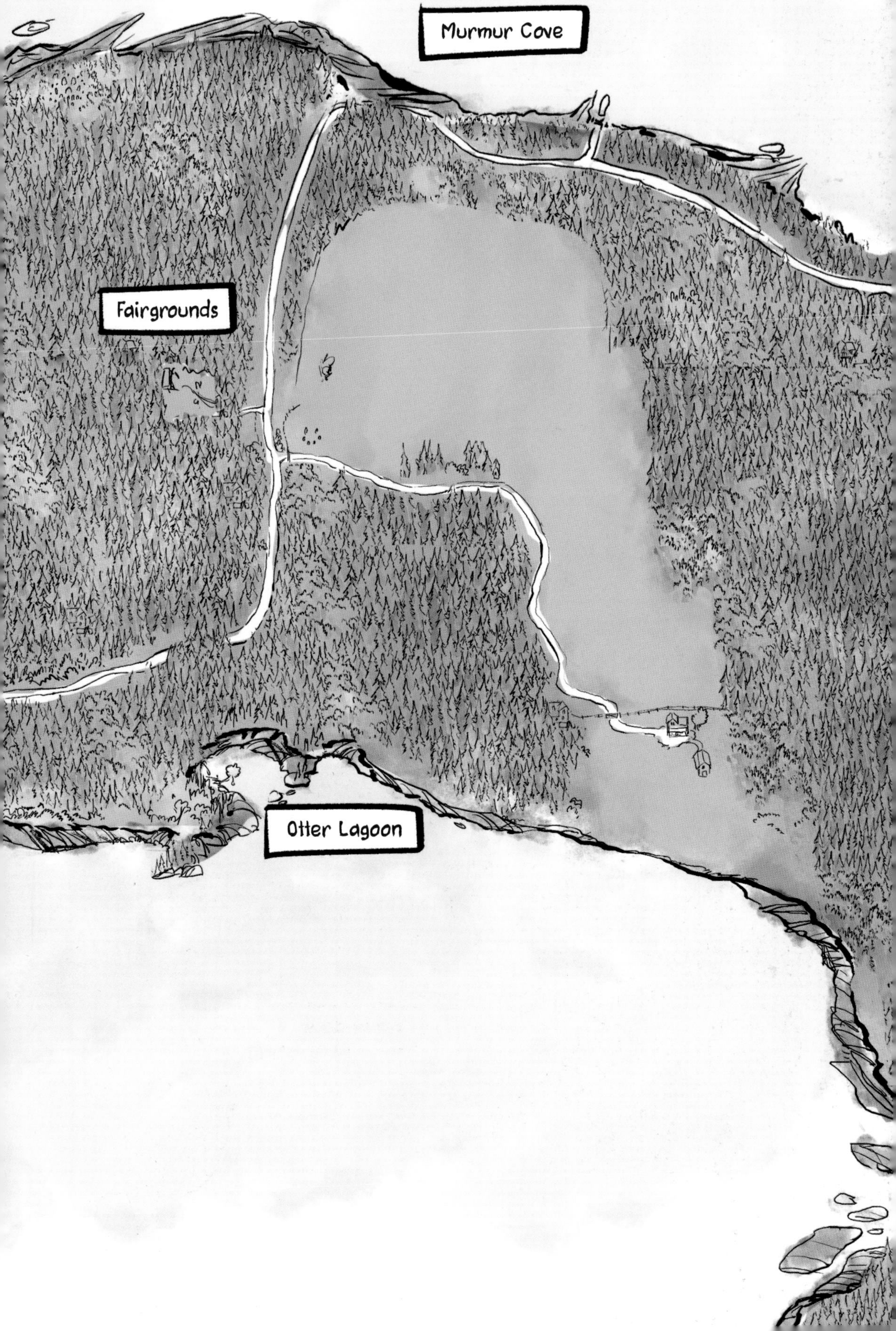
Murmur Cove
Fairgrounds
Otter Lagoon

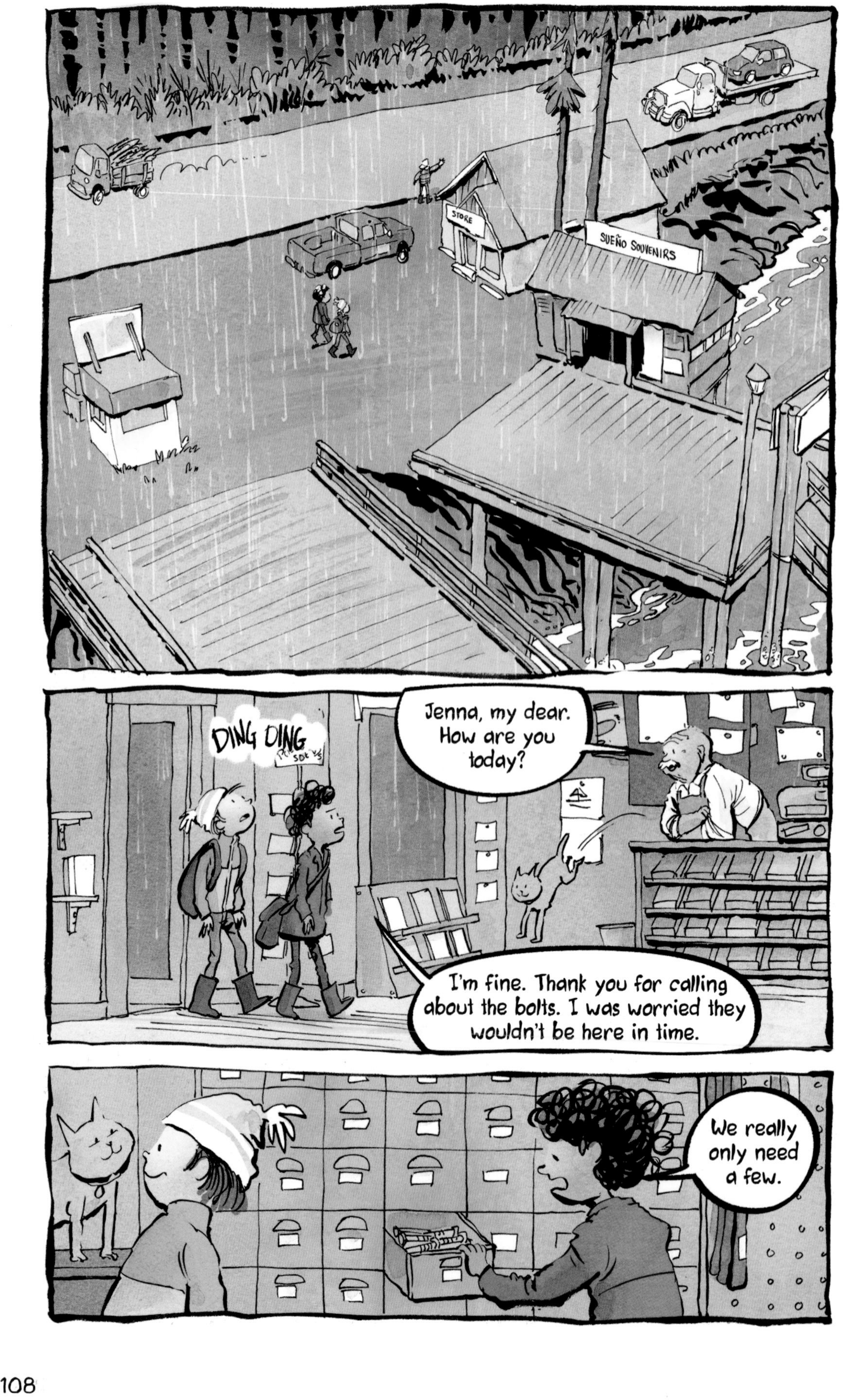
STORE
SUEÑO SOUVENIRS
DING DING
Jenna, my dear. How are you today?
I'm fine. Thank you for calling about the bolts. I was worried they wouldn't be here in time.
We really only need a few.

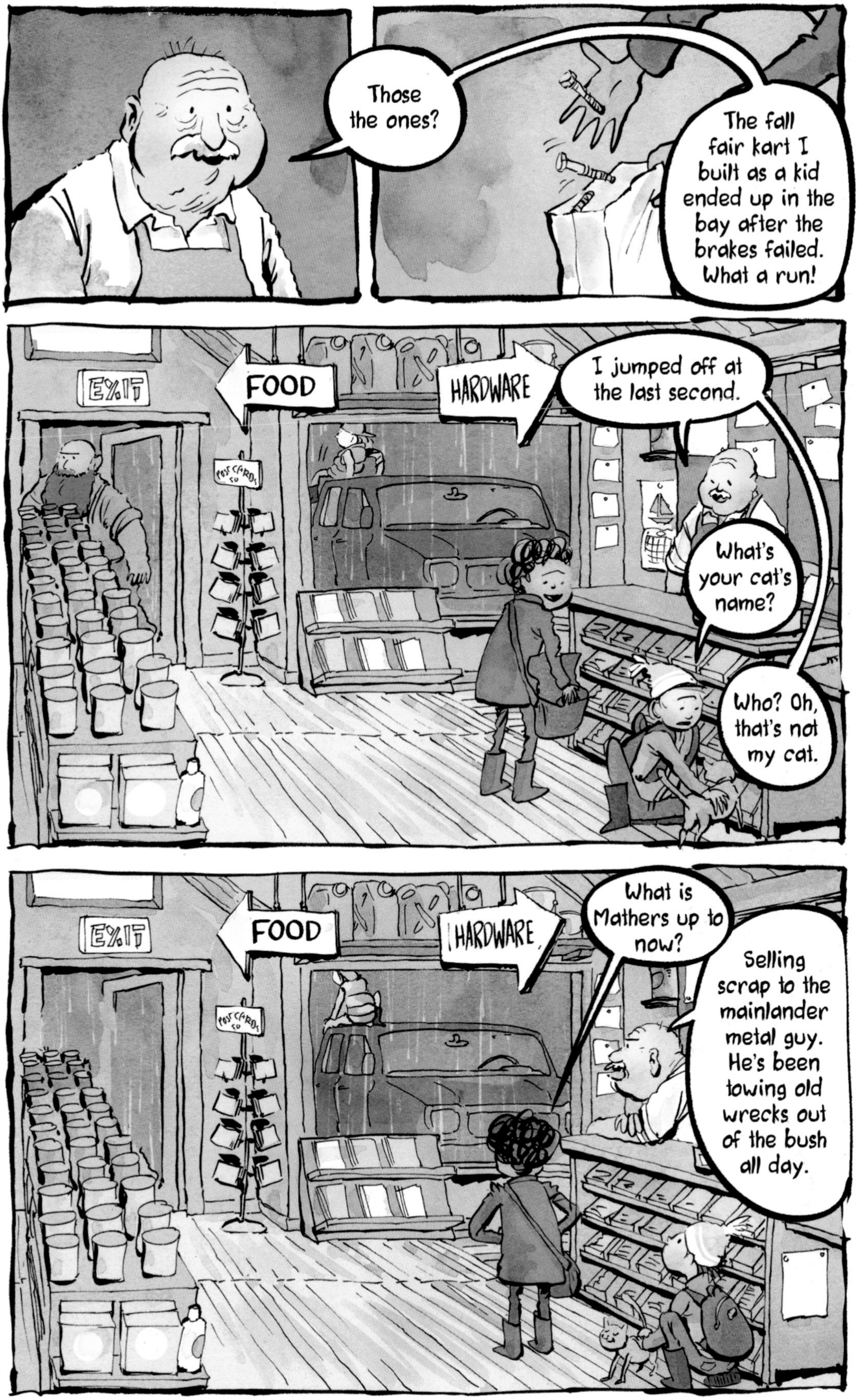
Those the ones?
The fall fair kart I built as a kid ended up in the bay after the brakes failed. What a run!
EXIT
FOOD
HARDWARE
I jumped off at the last second.
What's your cat's name?
Who? Oh, that's not my cat.
EXIT
FOOD
HARDWARE
What is Mathers up to now?
Selling scrap to the mainlander metal guy. He's been towing old wrecks out of the bush all day.

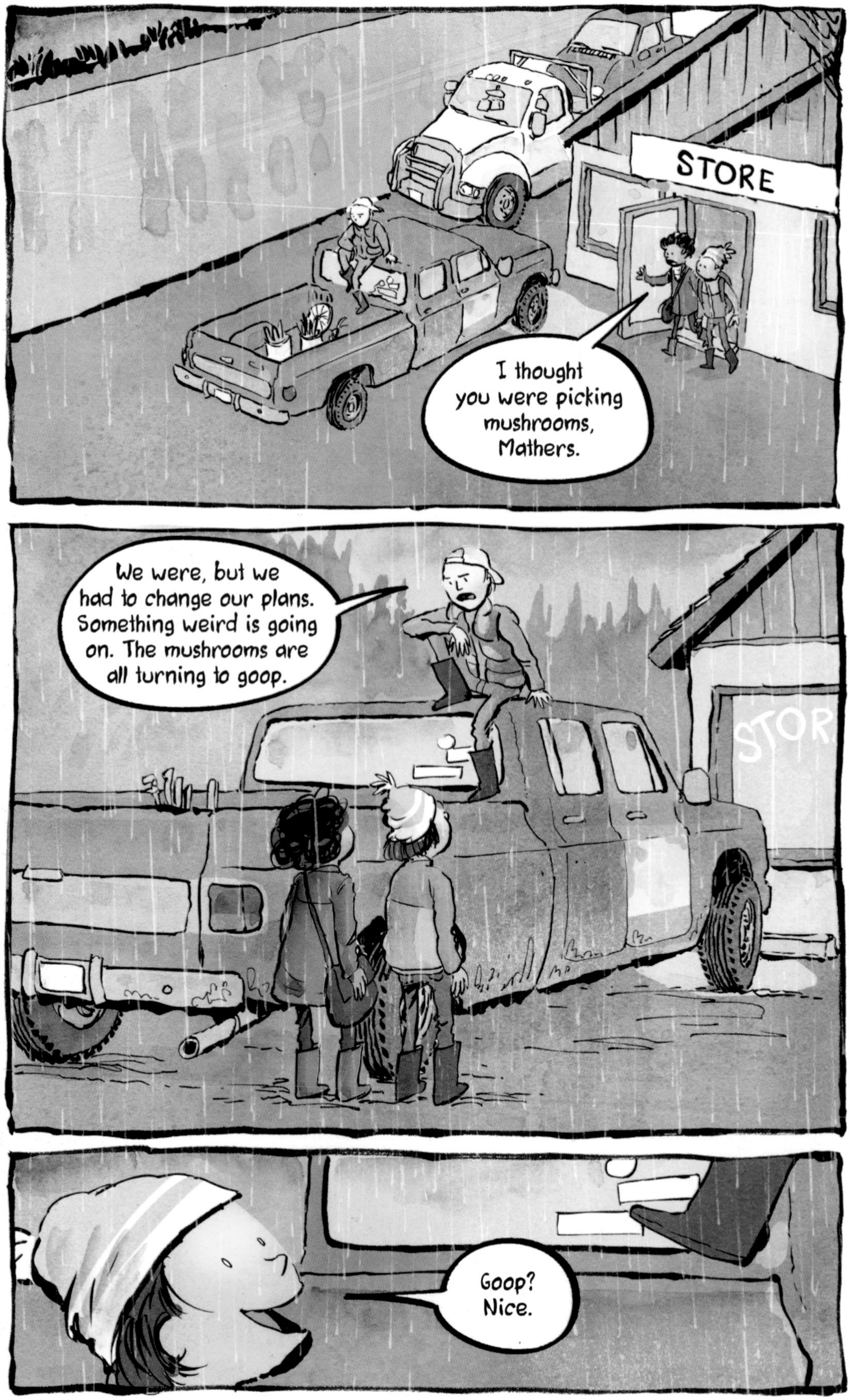
STORE
I thought you were picking mushrooms, Mathers.
We were, but we had to change our plans. Something weird is going on. The mushrooms are all turning to goop.
STORE
Goop? Nice.

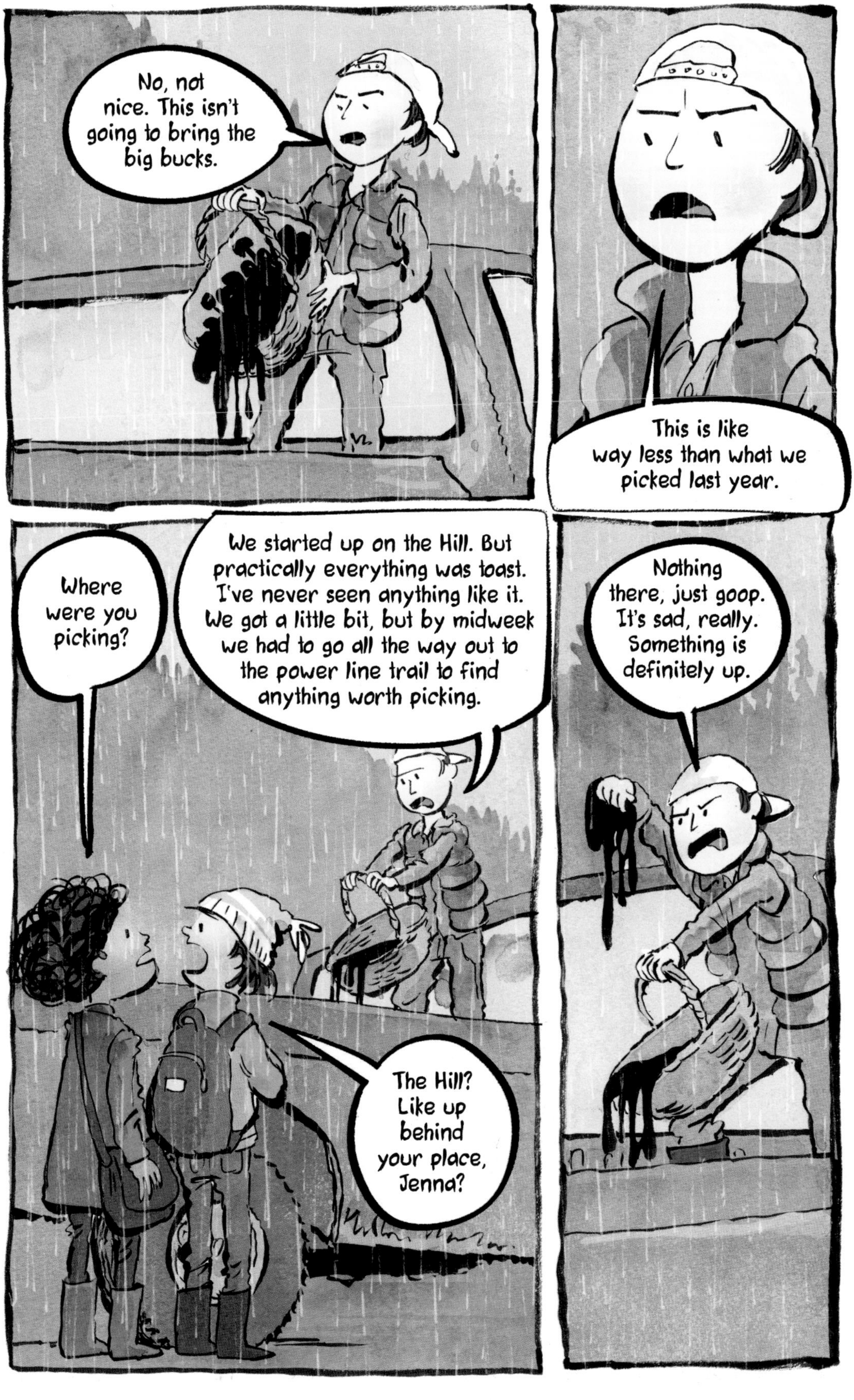
No, not nice. This isn't going to bring the big bucks.
This is like way less than what we picked last year.
Where were you picking?
We started up on the Hill. But practically everything was toast. I've never seen anything like it. We got a little bit, but by midweek we had to go all the way out to the power line trail to find anything worth picking.
The Hill? Like up behind your place, Jenna?
Nothing there, just goop. It's sad, really. Something is definitely up.

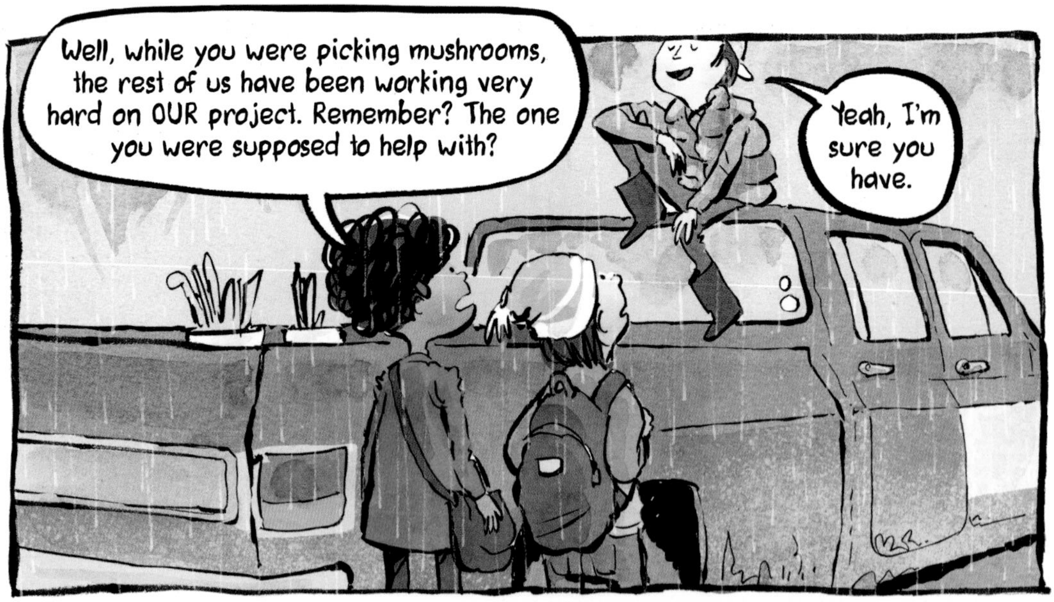
Well, while you were picking mushrooms, the rest of us have been working very hard on OUR project. Remember? The one you were supposed to help with?
Yeah, I'm sure you have.

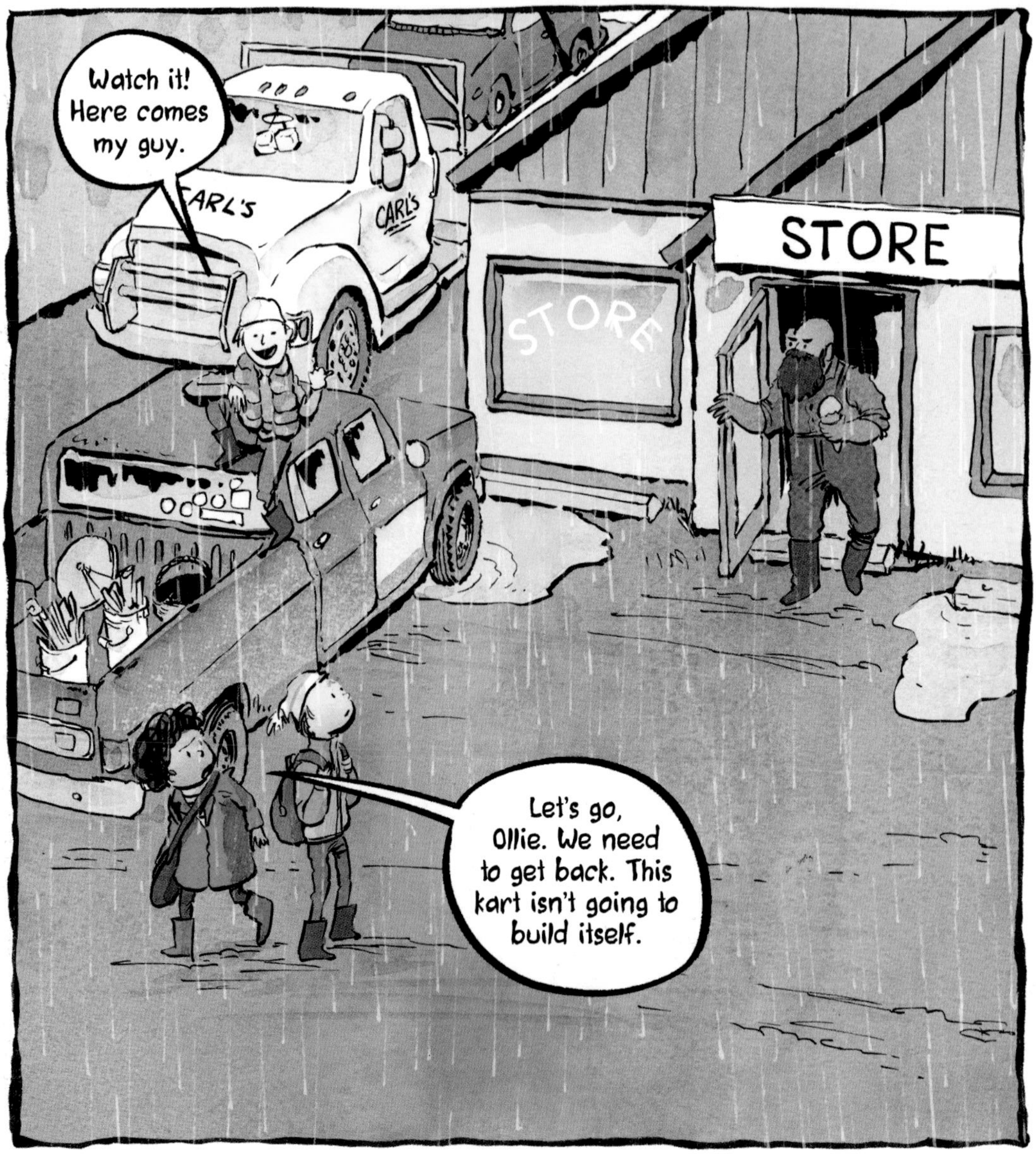
Watch it! Here comes my guy.
CARL'S
CARL'S
STORE
STORE
Let's go, Ollie. We need to get back. This kart isn't going to build itself.

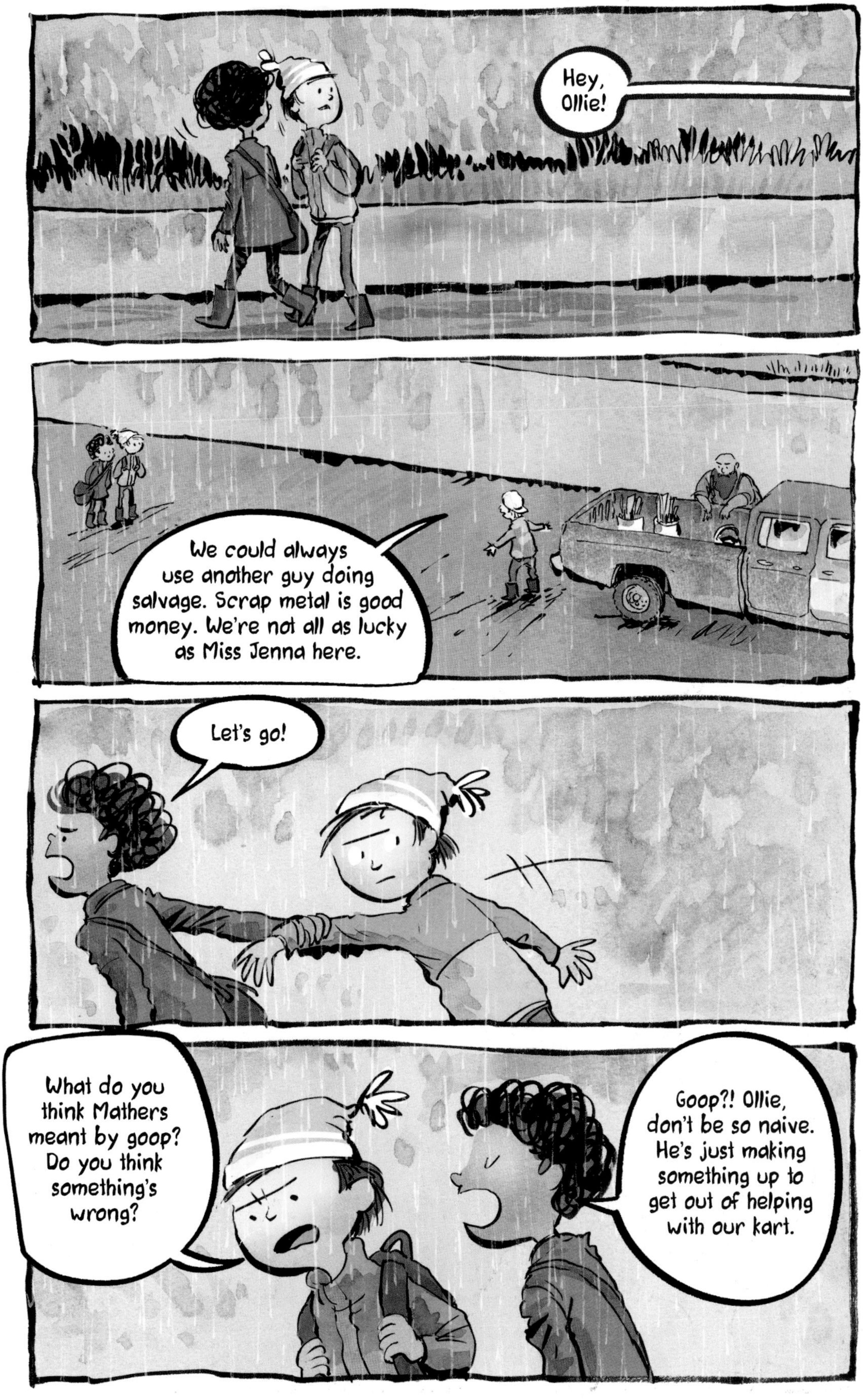
Hey, Ollie!
We could always use another guy doing salvage. Scrap metal is good money. We're not all as lucky as Miss Jenna here.
Let's go!
What do you think Mathers meant by goop? Do you think something's wrong?
Goop?! Ollie, don't be so naive. He's just making something up to get out of helping with our kart.

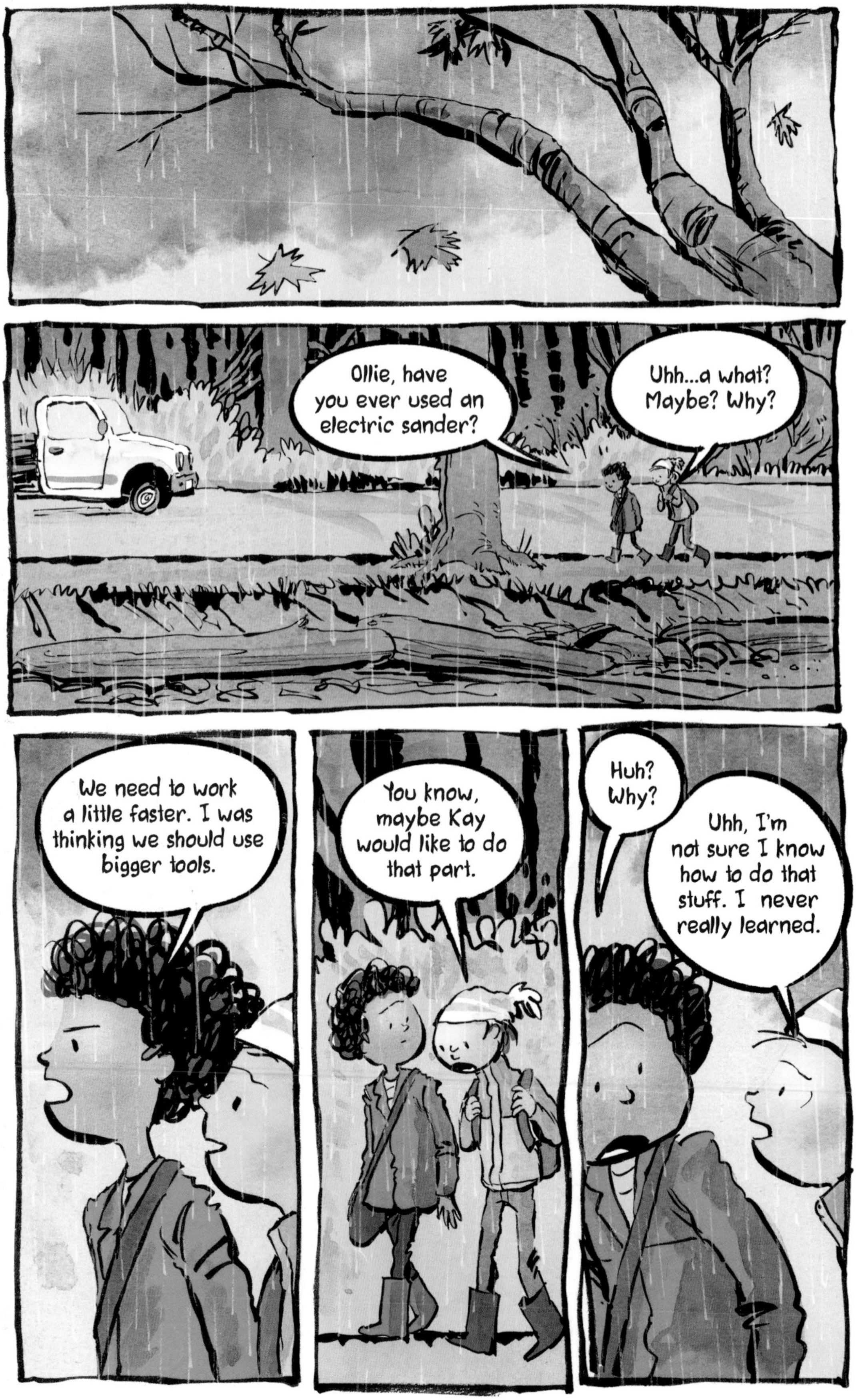
Ollie, have you ever used an electric sander?
Uhh...a what? Maybe? Why?
We need to work a little faster. I was thinking we should use bigger tools.
You know, maybe Kay would like to do that part.
Huh? Why?
Uhh, I'm not sure I know how to do that stuff. I never really learned.

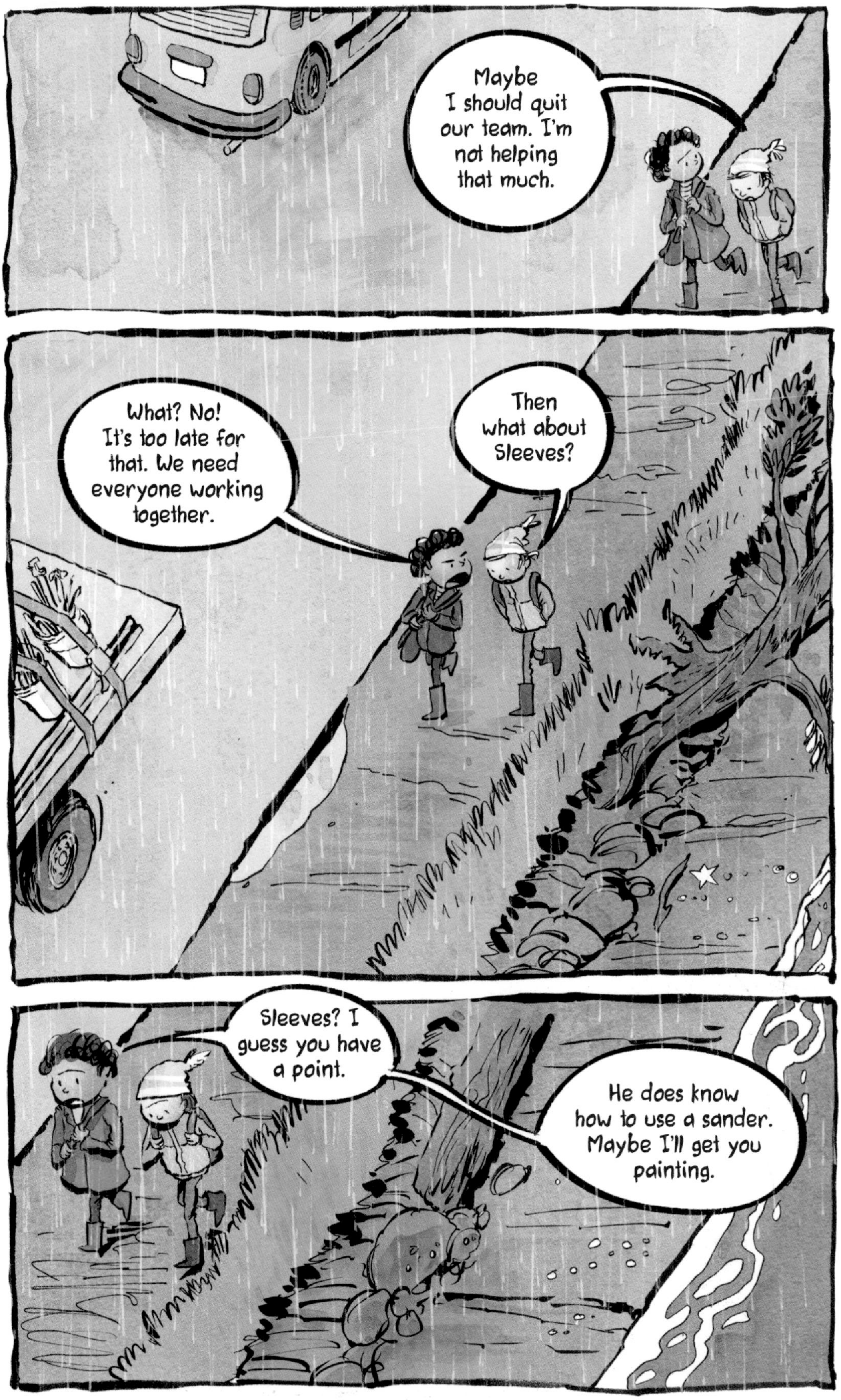
Maybe I should quit our team. I'm not helping that much.
What? No! It's too late for that. We need everyone working together.
Then what about Sleeves?
Sleeves? I guess you have a point.
He does know how to use a sander. Maybe I'll get you painting.

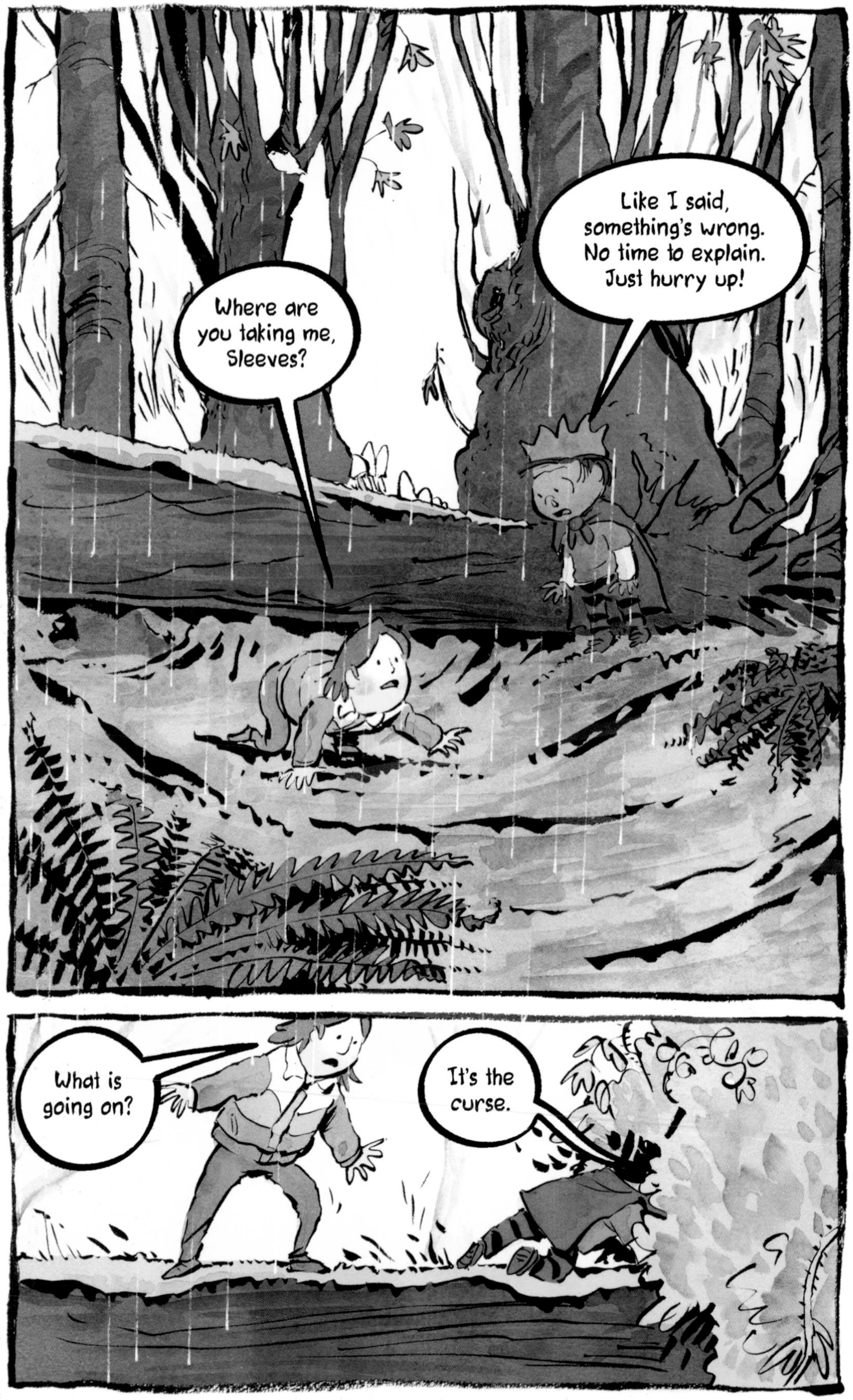
Where are you taking me, Sleeves?
Like I said, something's wrong. No time to explain. Just hurry up!
What is going on?
It's the curse.

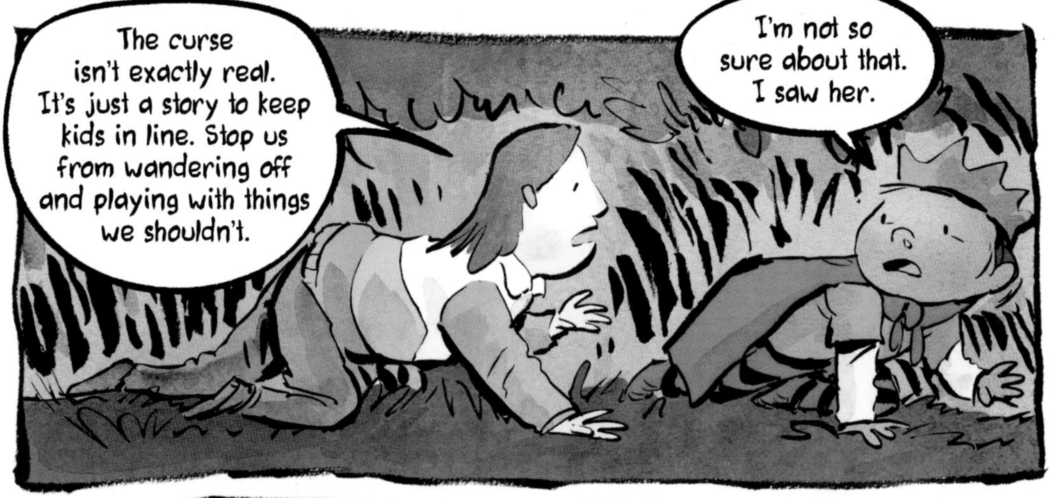
The curse isn't exactly real. It's just a story to keep kids in line. Stop us from wandering off and playing with things we shouldn't.
I'm not so sure about that. I saw her.

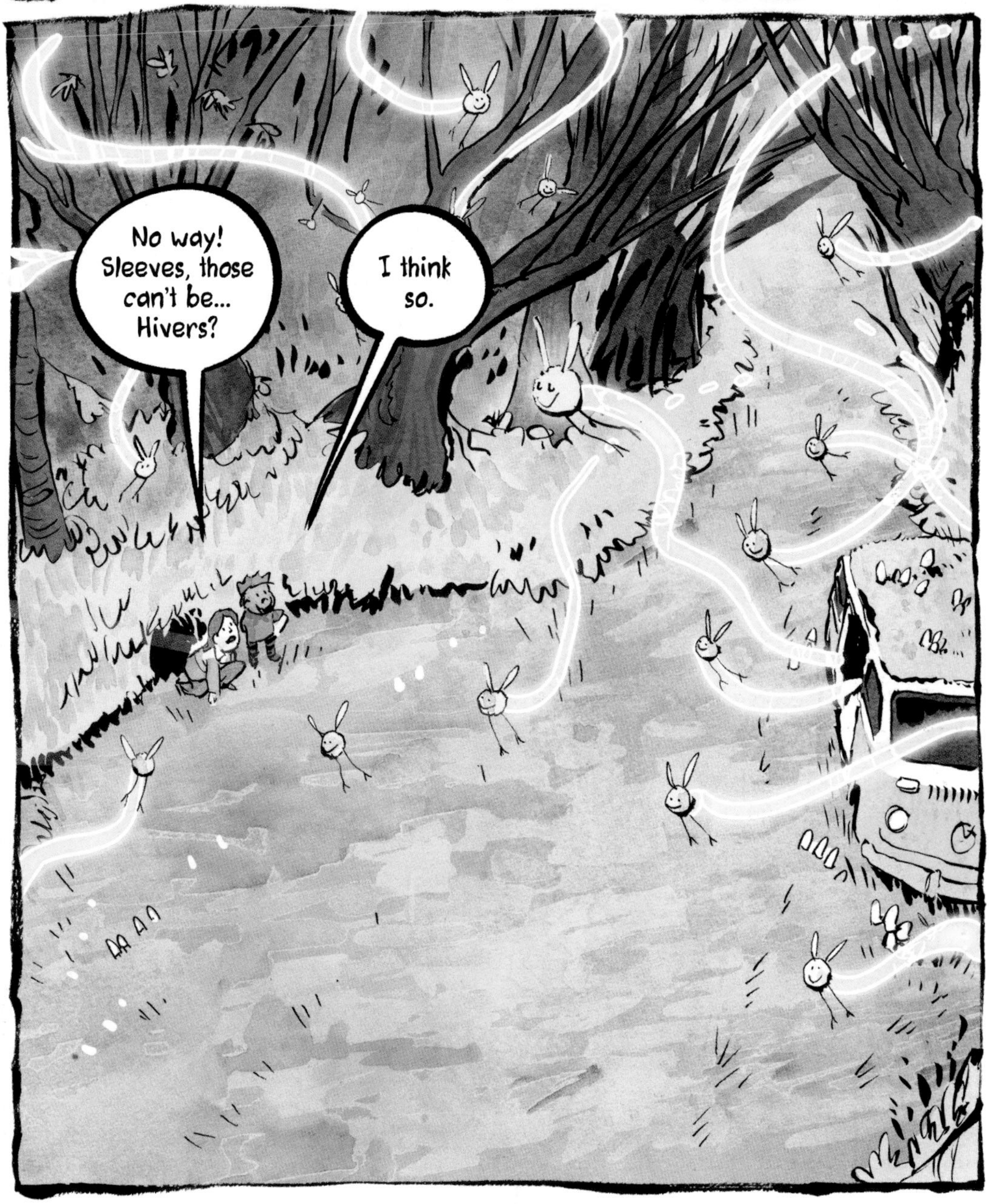
No way! Sleeves, those can't be... Hivers?
I think so.

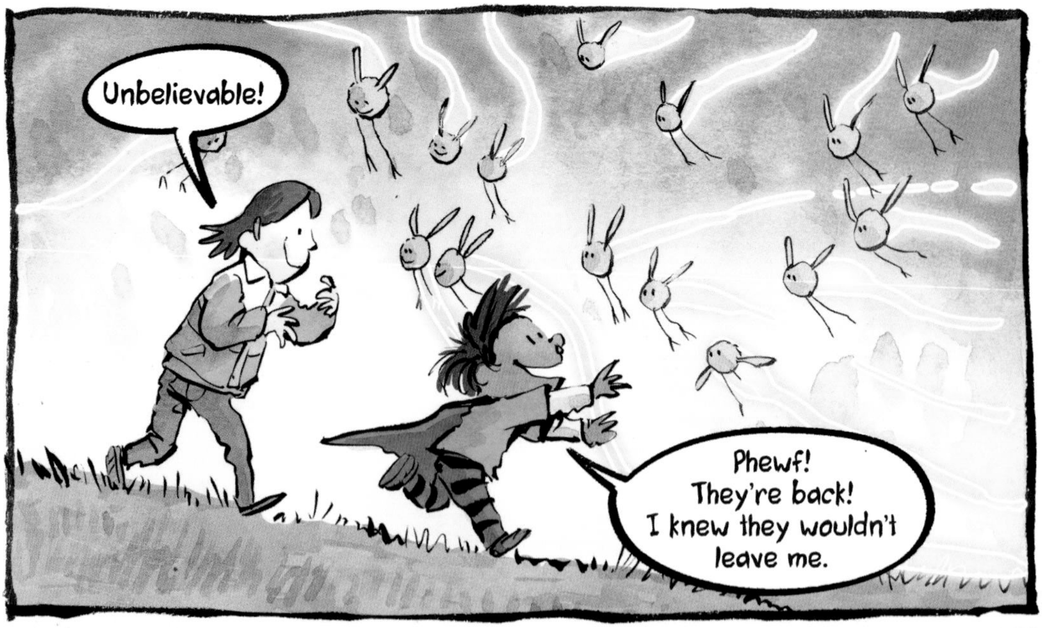
Unbelievable!
Phewf! They're back! I knew they wouldn't leave me.

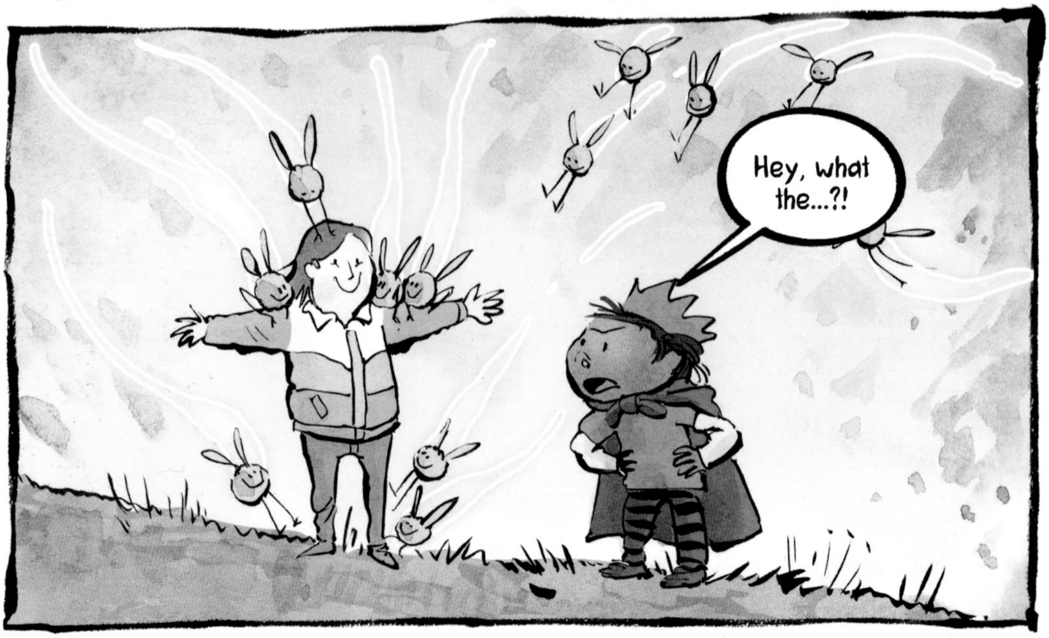
Hey, what the...?!

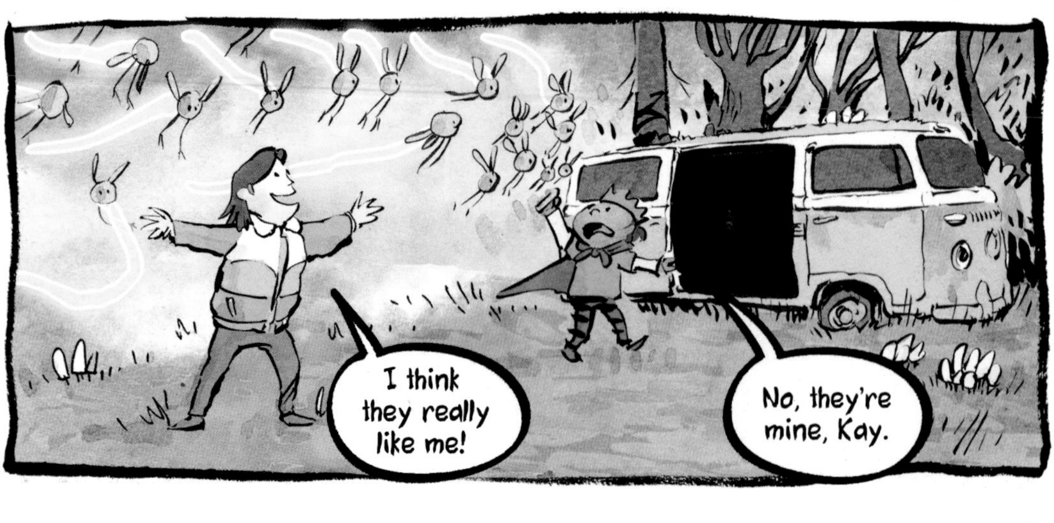
I think they really like me!
No, they're mine, Kay.

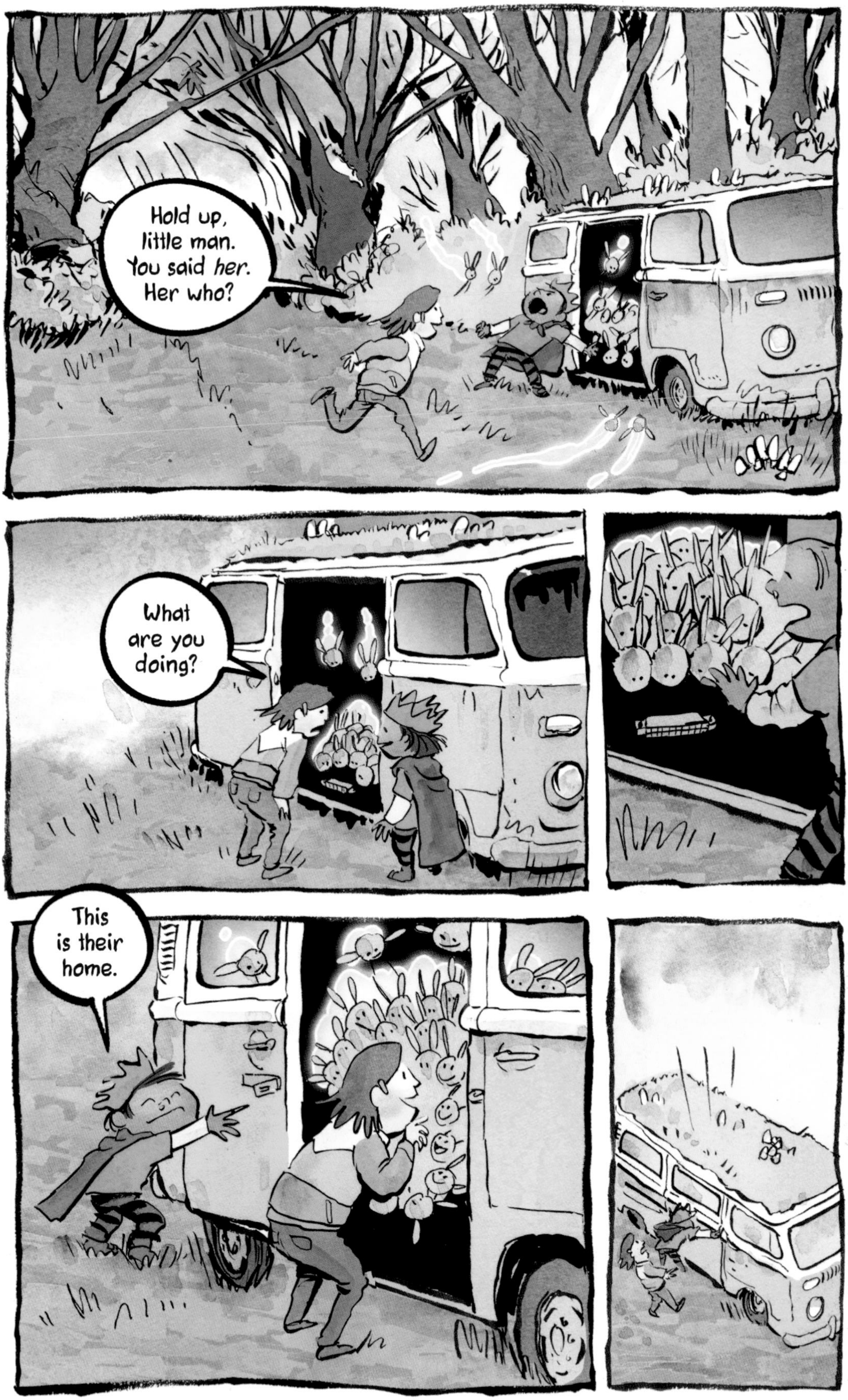

Hold up, little man. You said *her*. Her who?
What are you doing?
This is their home.

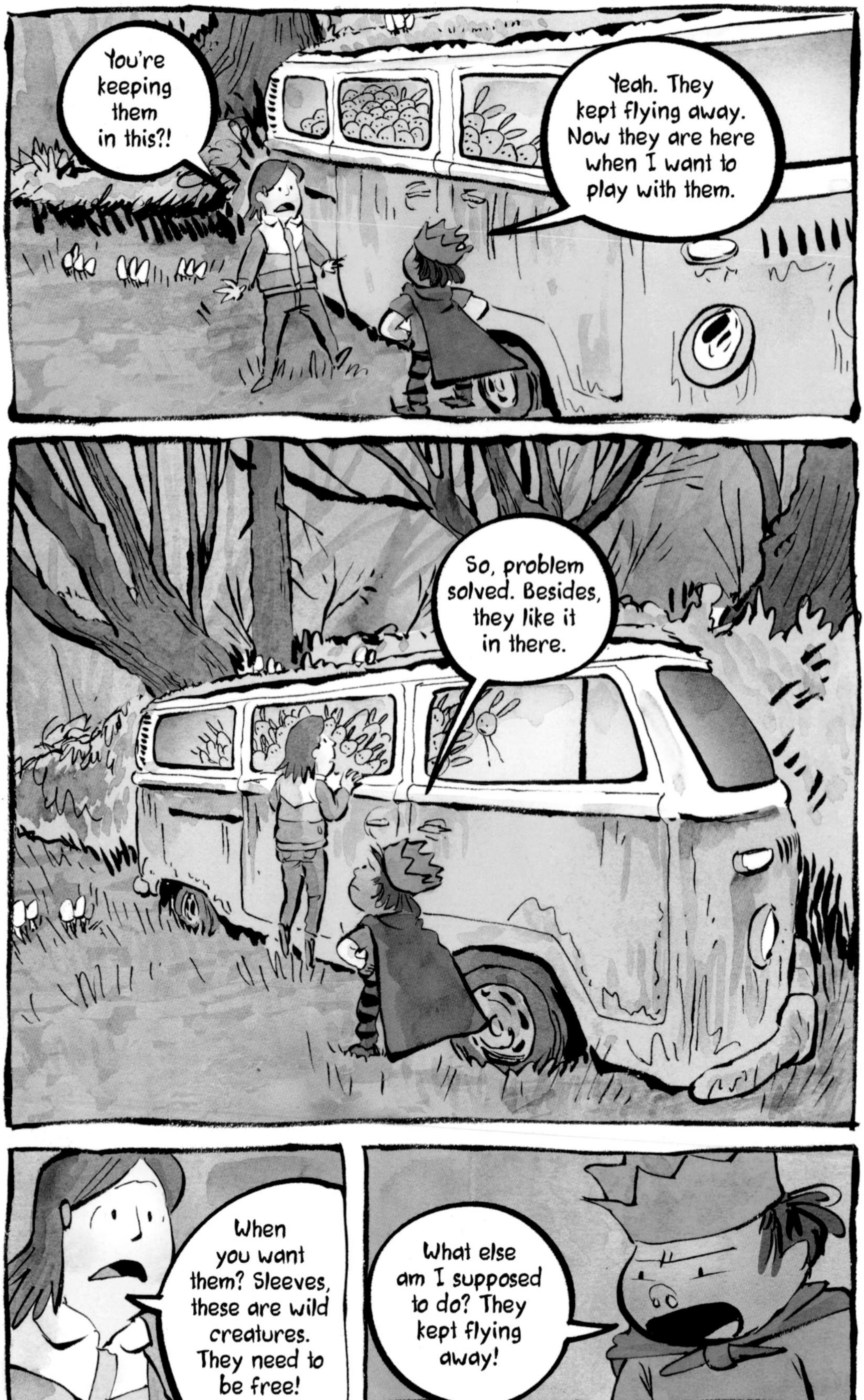
You're keeping them in this?!
Yeah. They kept flying away. Now they are here when I want to play with them.
So, problem solved. Besides, they like it in there.
When you want them? Sleeves, these are wild creatures. They need to be free!
What else am I supposed to do? They kept flying away!

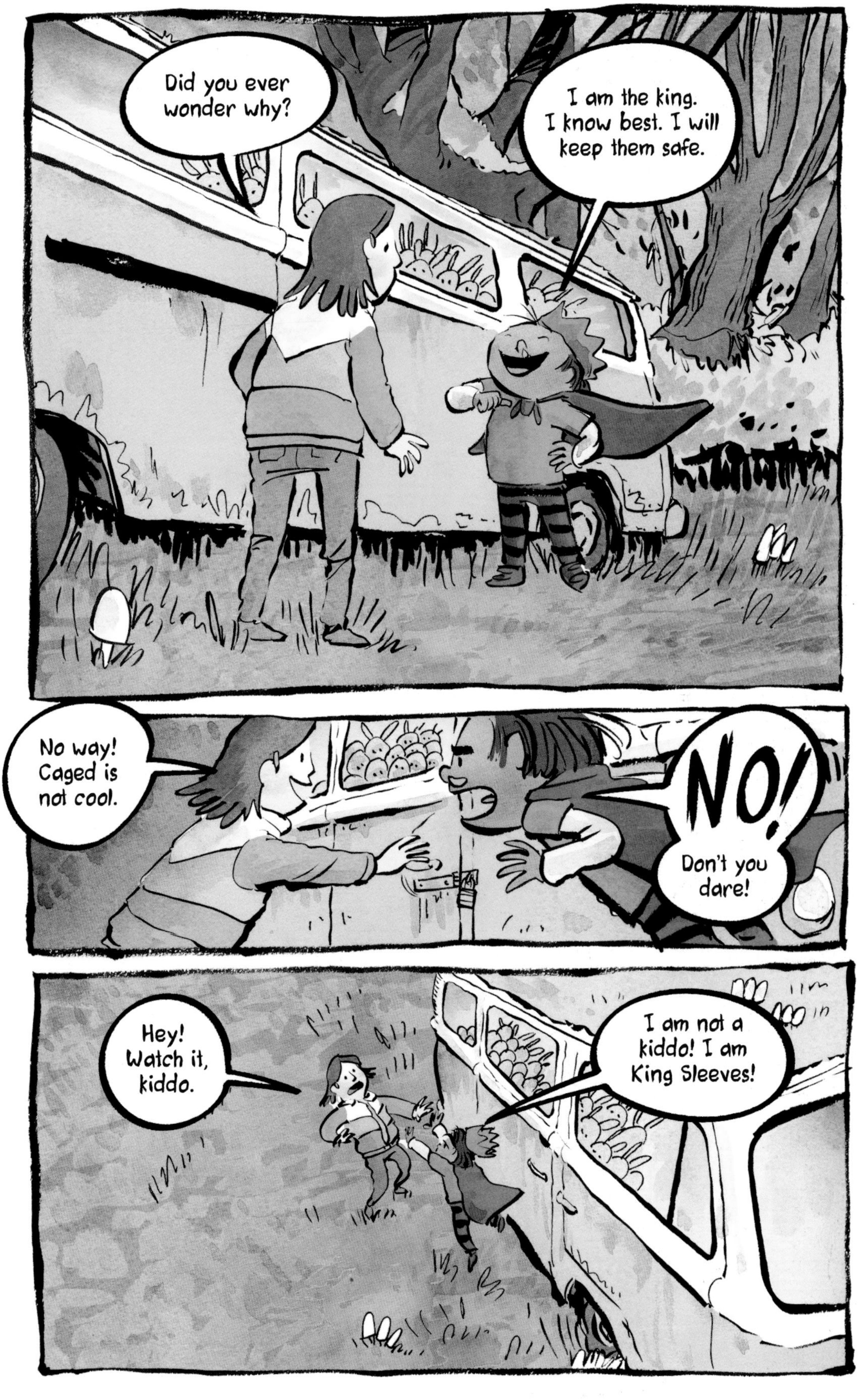
Did you ever wonder why?
I am the king. I know best. I will keep them safe.
No way! Caged is not cool.
NO!
Don't you dare!
Hey! Watch it, kiddo.
I am not a kiddo! I am King Sleeves!

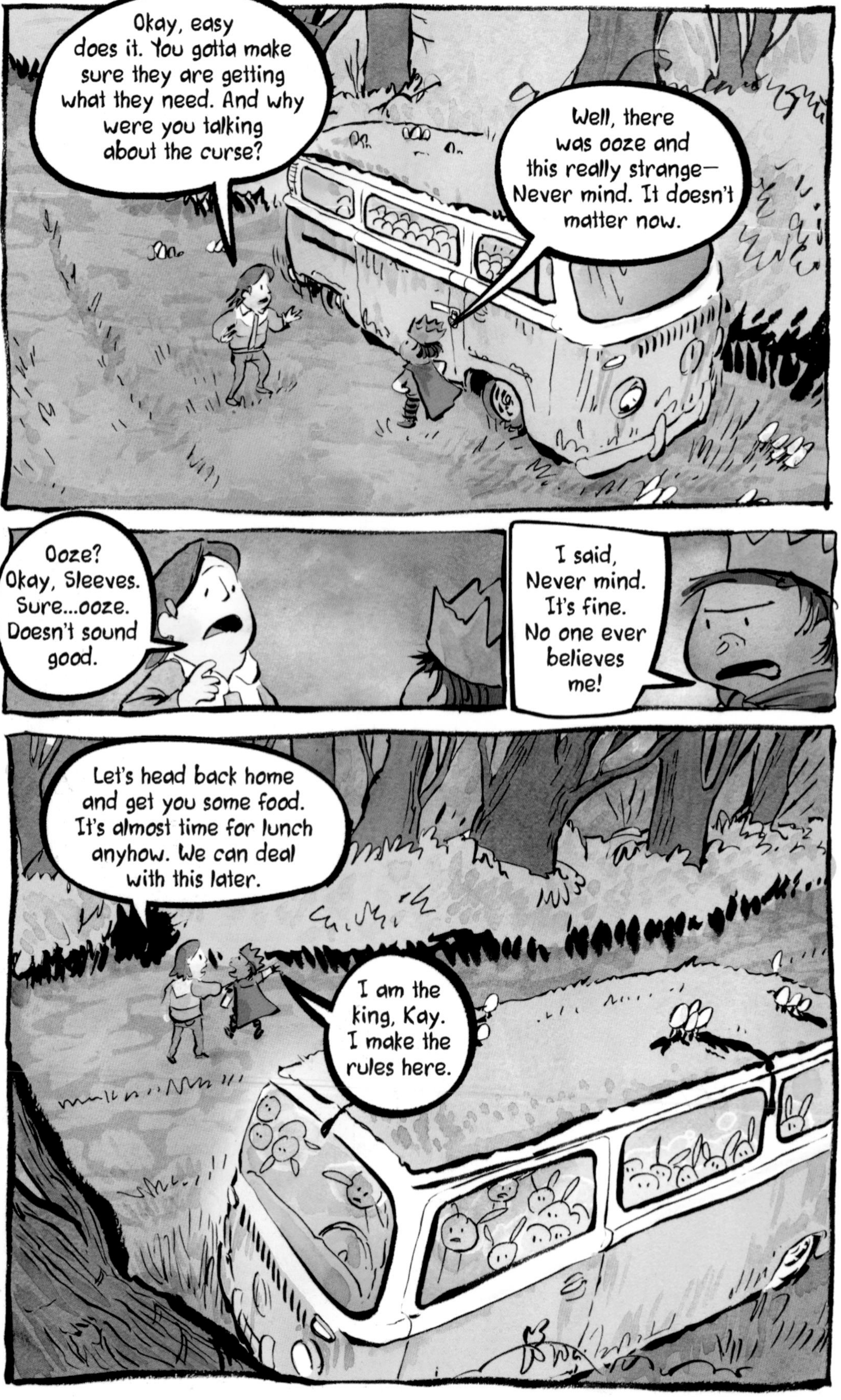
Okay, easy does it. You gotta make sure they are getting what they need. And why were you talking about the curse?
Well, there was ooze and this really strange— Never mind. It doesn't matter now.
Ooze? Okay, Sleeves. Sure...ooze. Doesn't sound good.
I said, Never mind. It's fine. No one ever believes me!
Let's head back home and get you some food. It's almost time for lunch anyhow. We can deal with this later.
I am the king, Kay. I make the rules here.

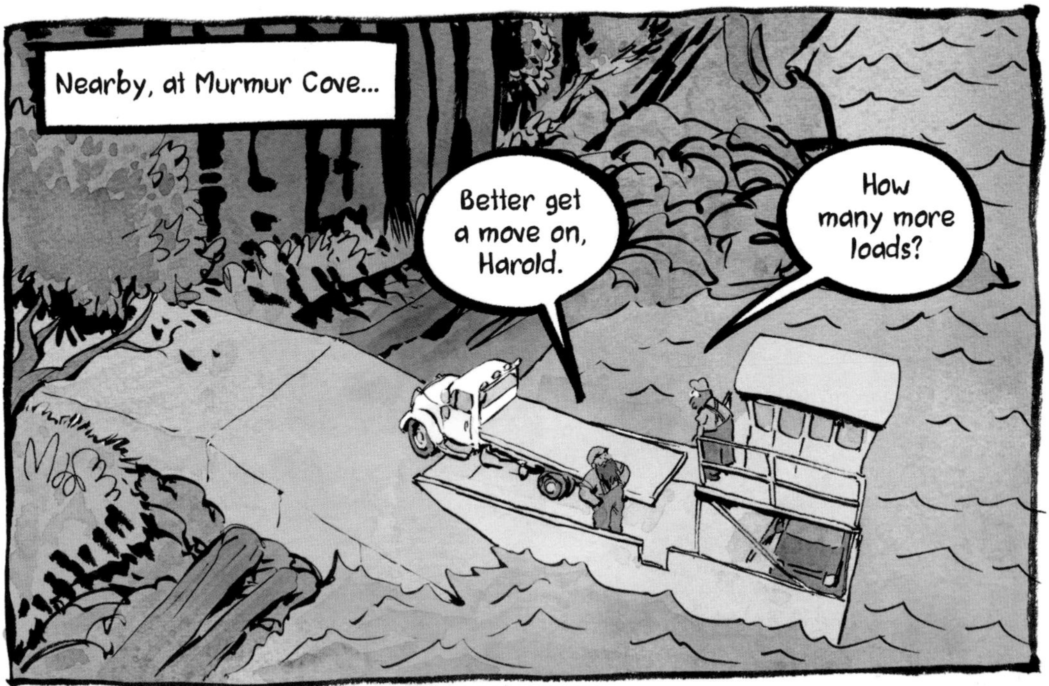

Nearby, at Murmur Cove...
Better get a move on, Harold.
How many more loads?

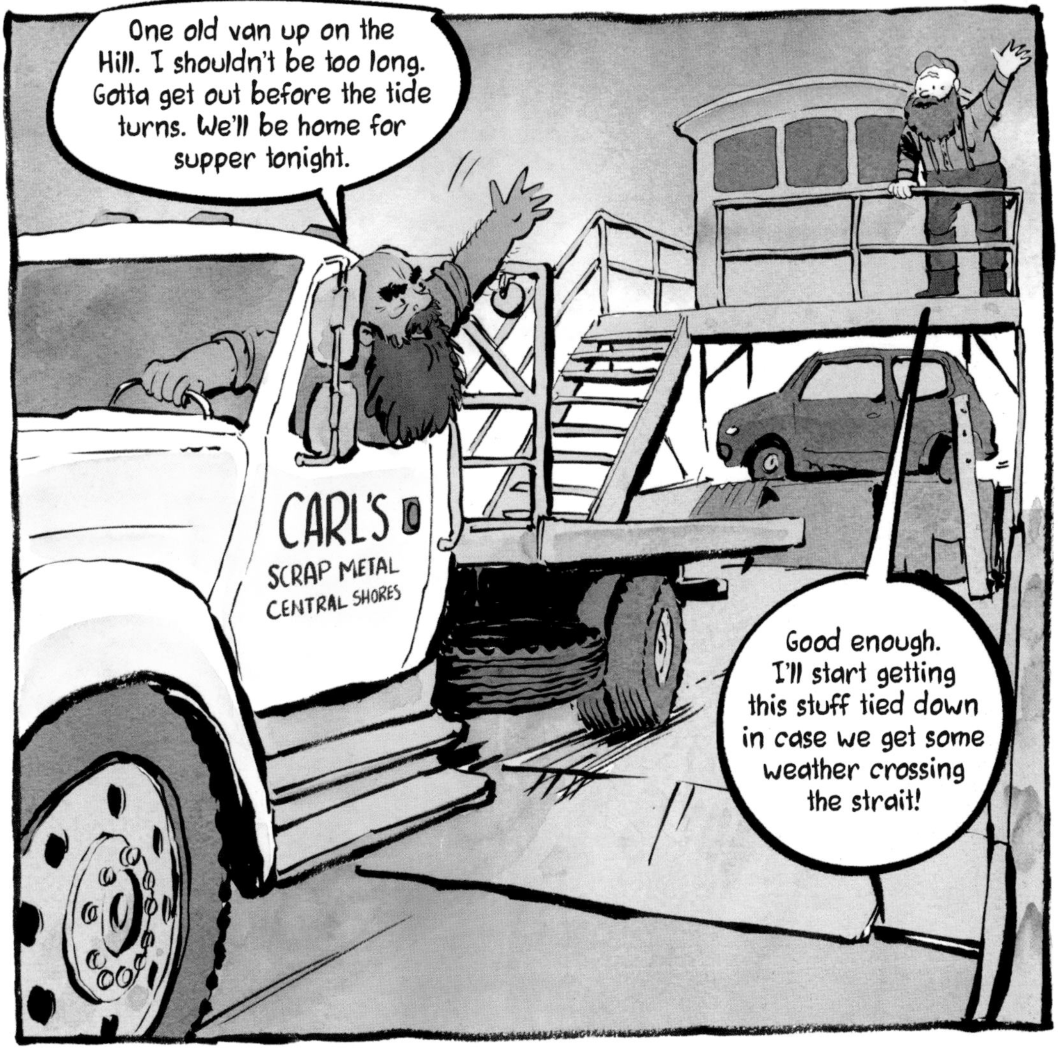

One old van up on the Hill. I shouldn't be too long. Gotta get out before the tide turns. We'll be home for supper tonight.
CARL'S
SCRAP METAL
CENTRAL SHORES
Good enough. I'll start getting this stuff tied down in case we get some weather crossing the strait!

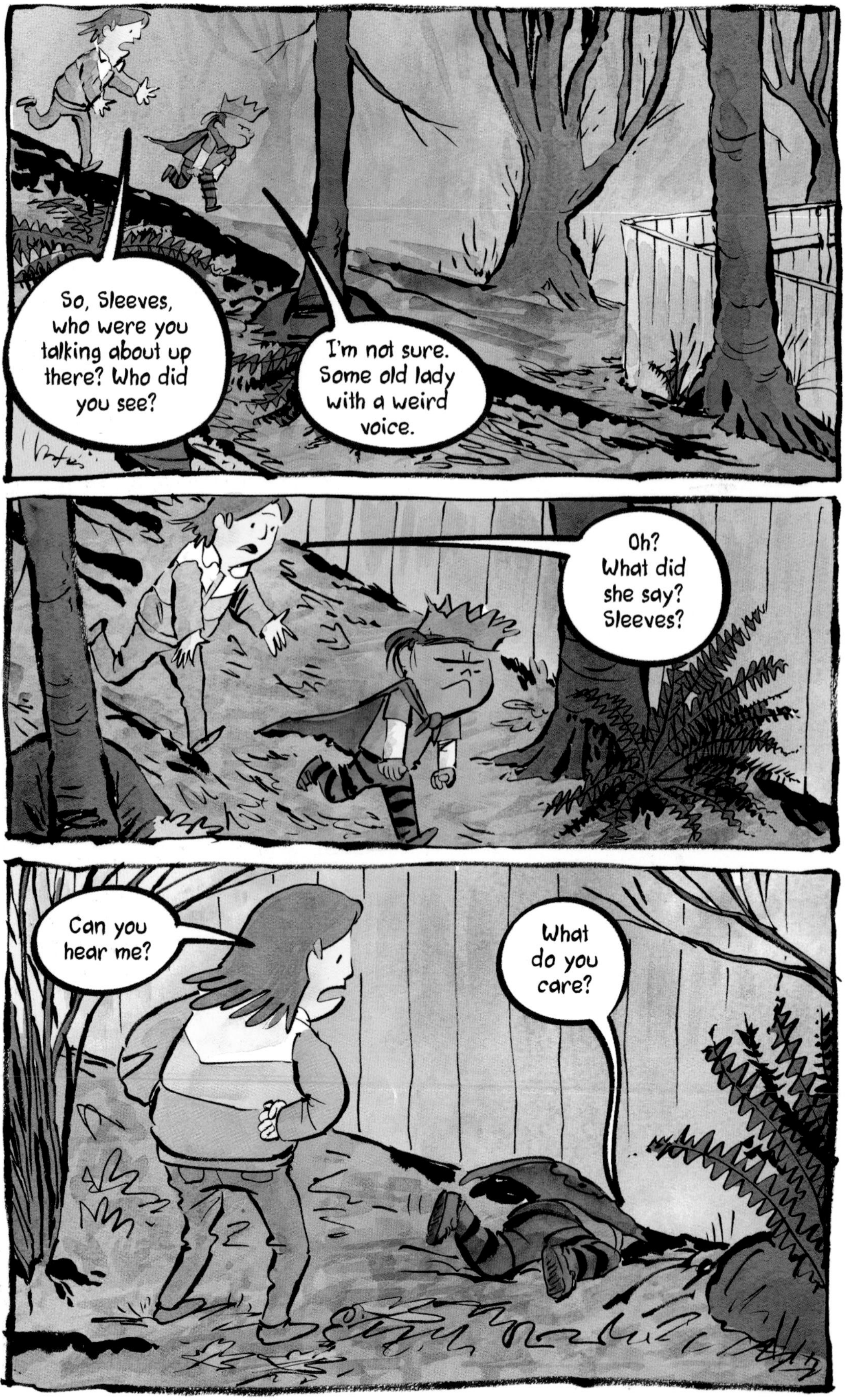
So, Sleeves, who were you talking about up there? Who did you see?
I'm not sure. Some old lady with a weird voice.
Oh? What did she say? Sleeves?
Can you hear me?
What do you care?

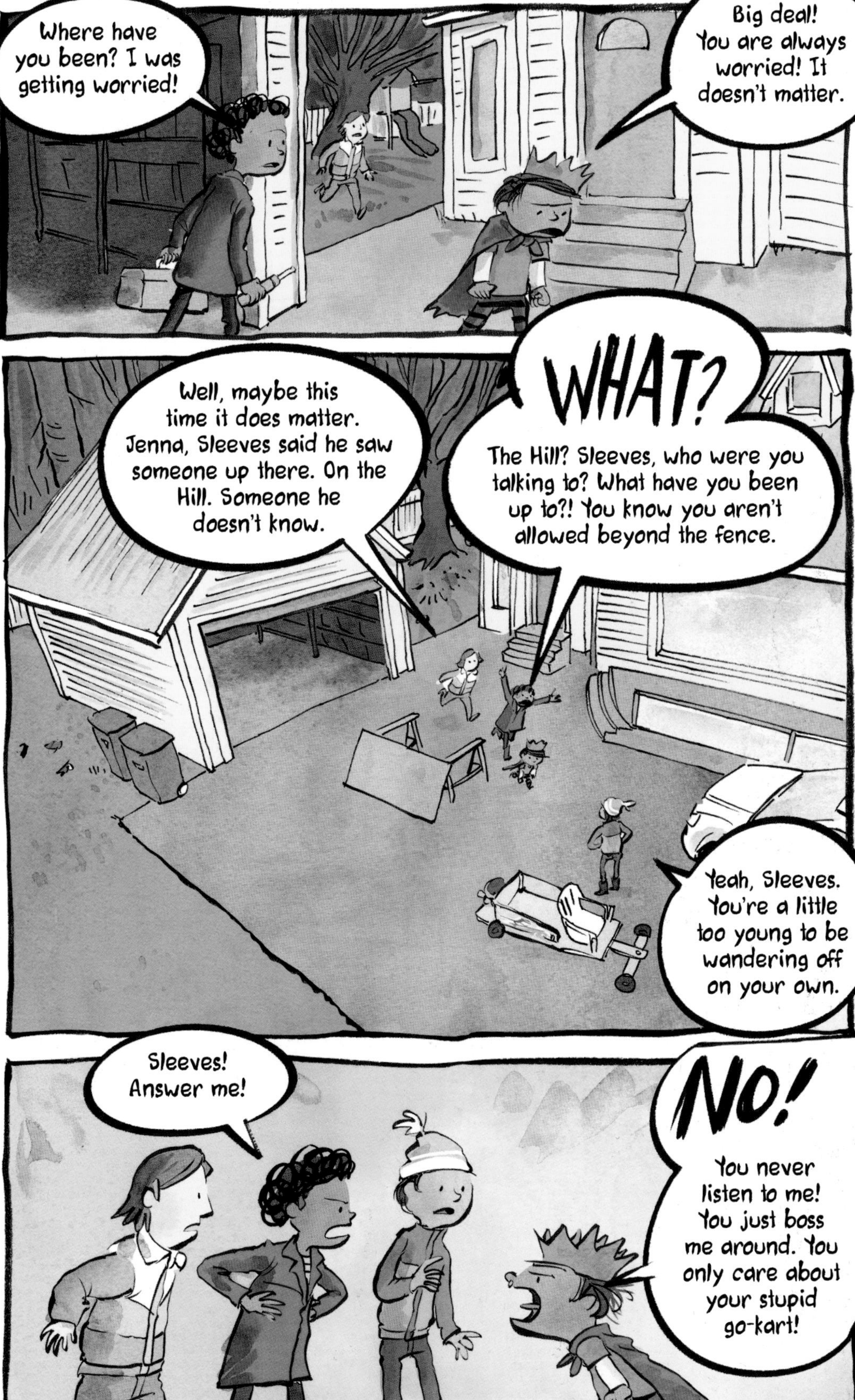
Where have you been? I was getting worried!
Big deal! You are always worried! It doesn't matter.
Well, maybe this time it does matter. Jenna, Sleeves said he saw someone up there. On the Hill. Someone he doesn't know.
WHAT?
The Hill? Sleeves, who were you talking to? What have you been up to?! You know you aren't allowed beyond the fence.
Yeah, Sleeves. You're a little too young to be wandering off on your own.
Sleeves! Answer me!
NO!
You never listen to me! You just boss me around. You only care about your stupid go-kart!

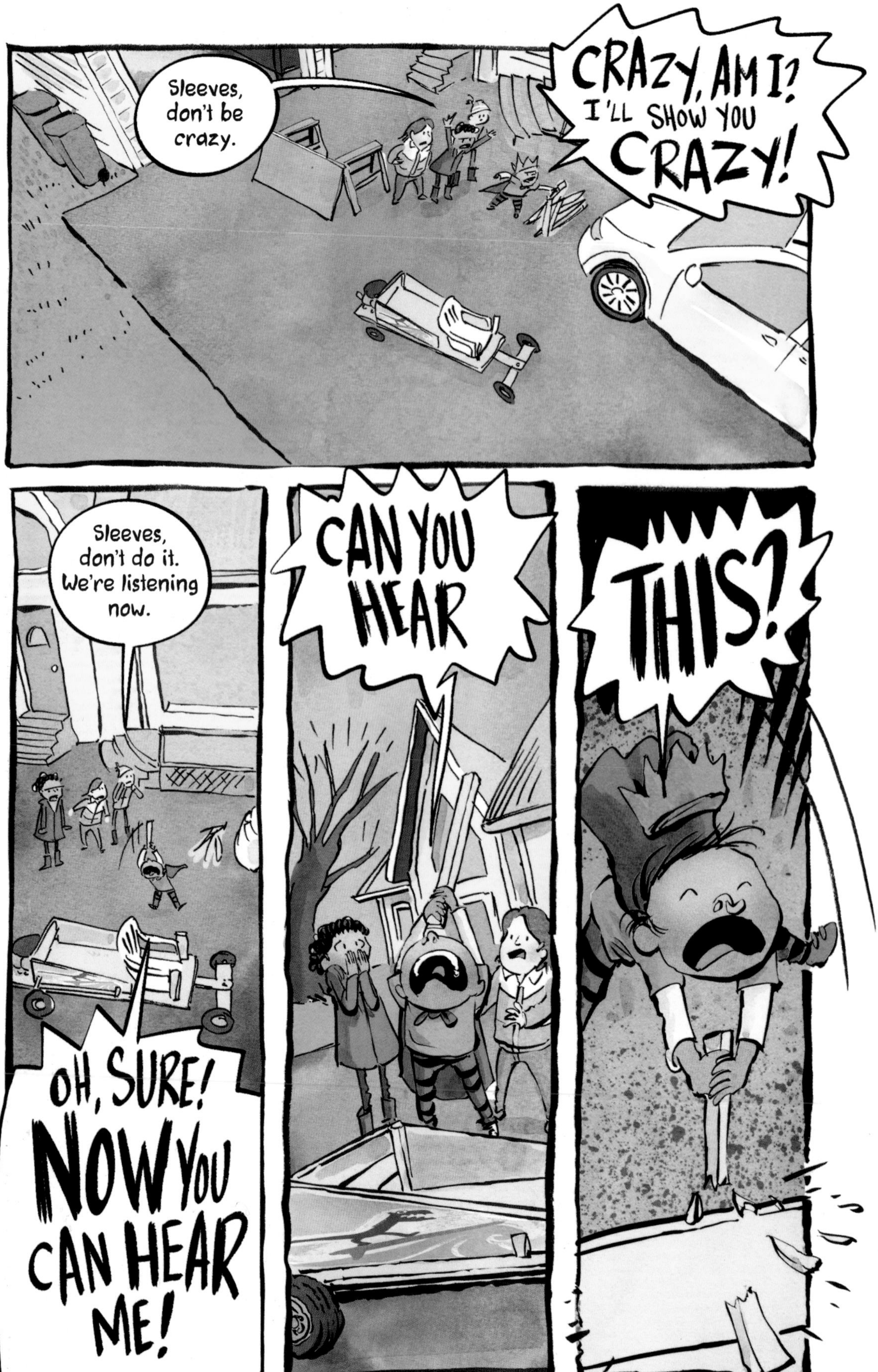
Sleeves, don't be crazy.
CRAZY, AM I? I'LL SHOW YOU CRAZY!
Sleeves, don't do it. We're listening now.
OH, SURE! NOW YOU CAN HEAR ME!
CAN YOU HEAR
THIS?!

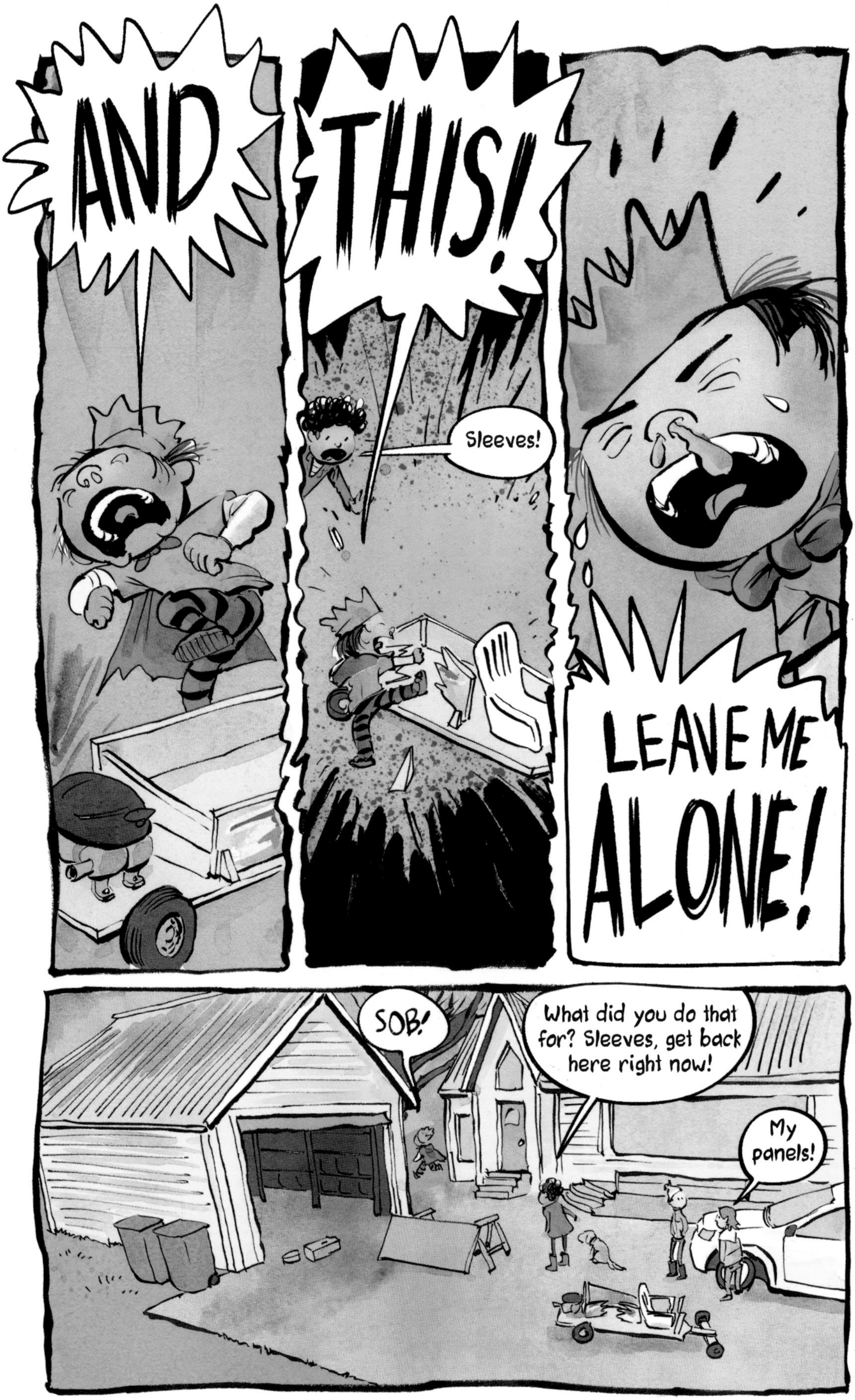
AND
THIS!
Sleeves!
LEAVE ME ALONE!
SOB!
What did you do that for? Sleeves, get back here right now!
My panels!

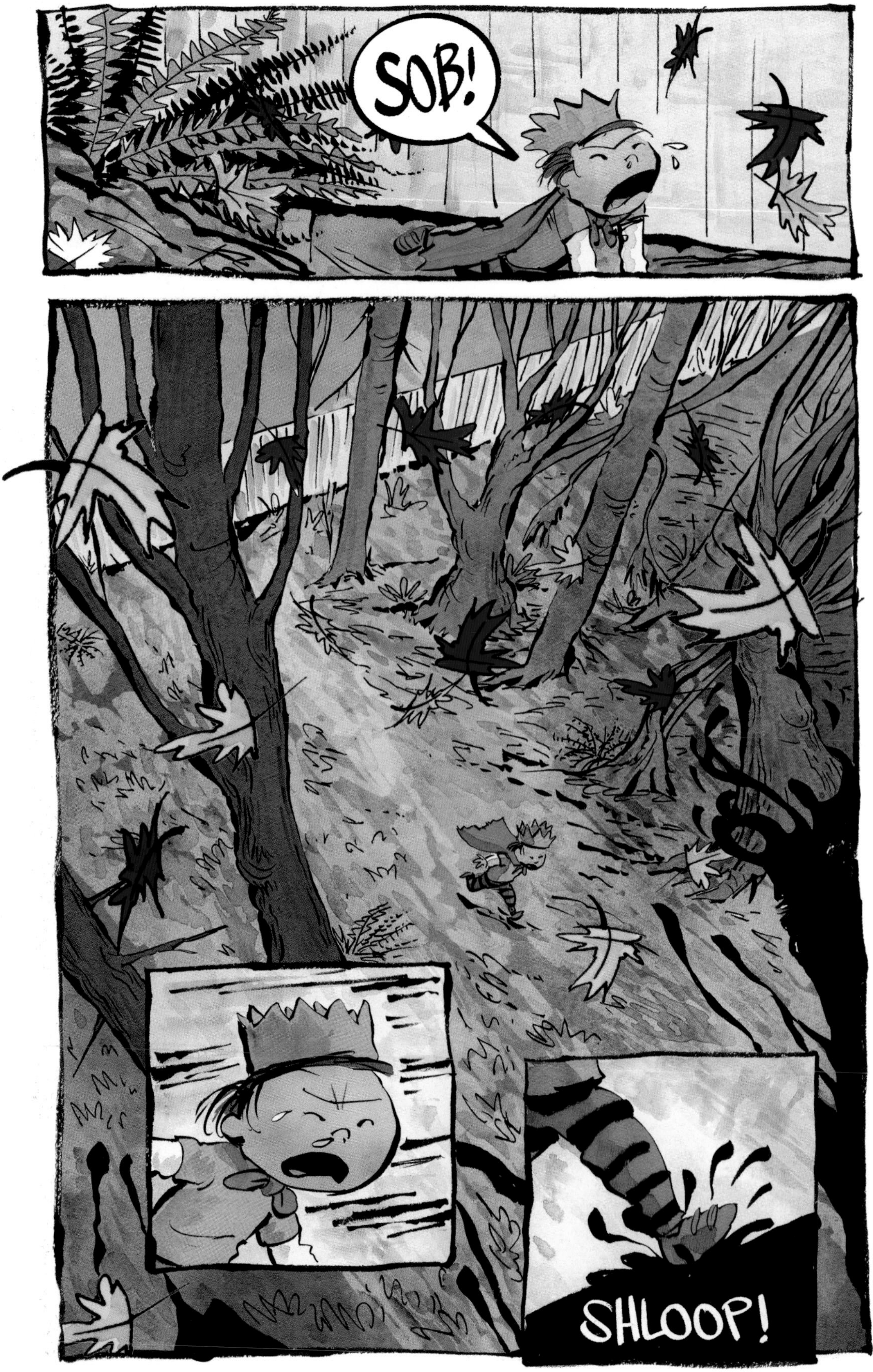
SOB!
SHLOOP!

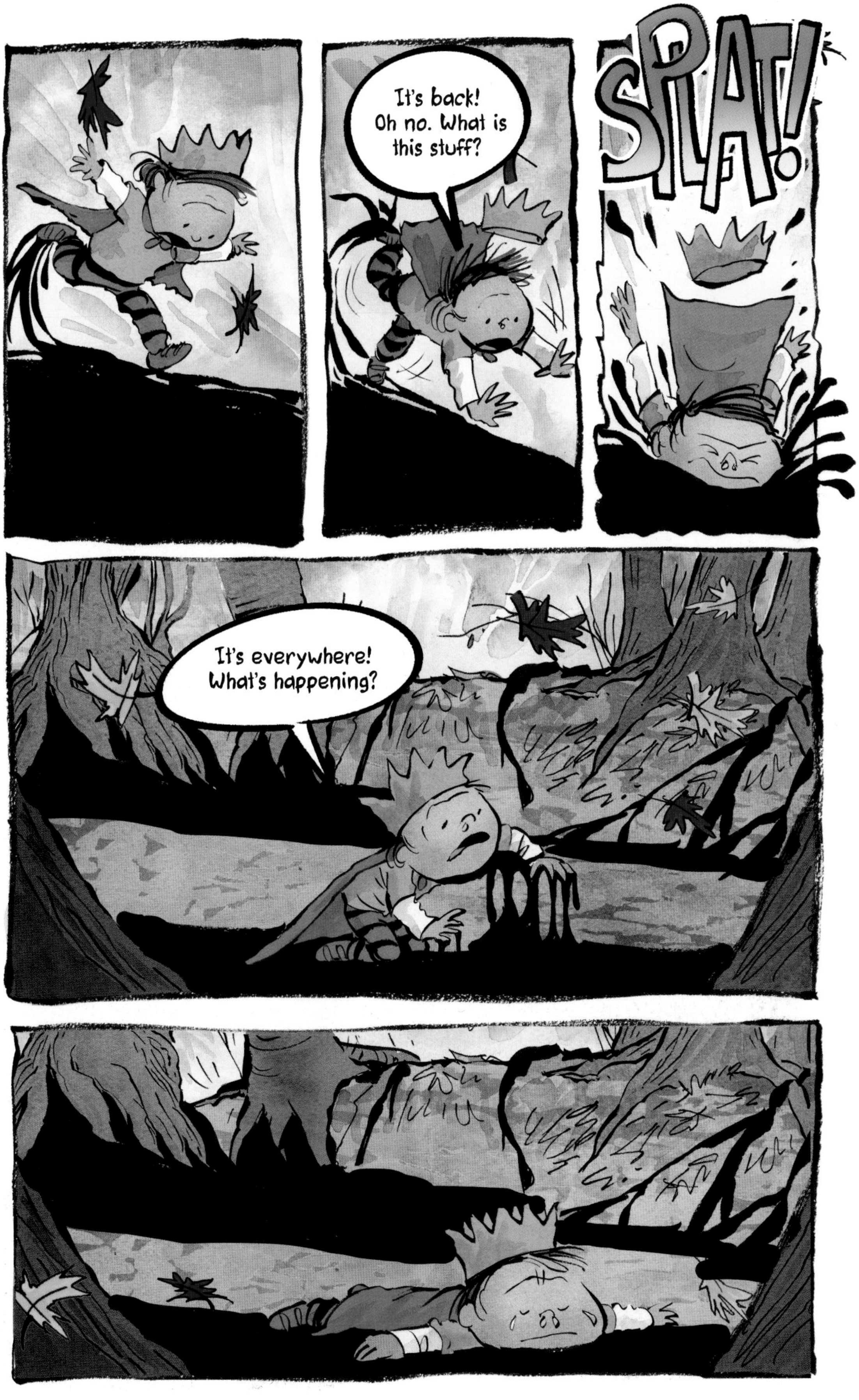
It's back! Oh no. What is this stuff?
SPLAT!
It's everywhere! What's happening?

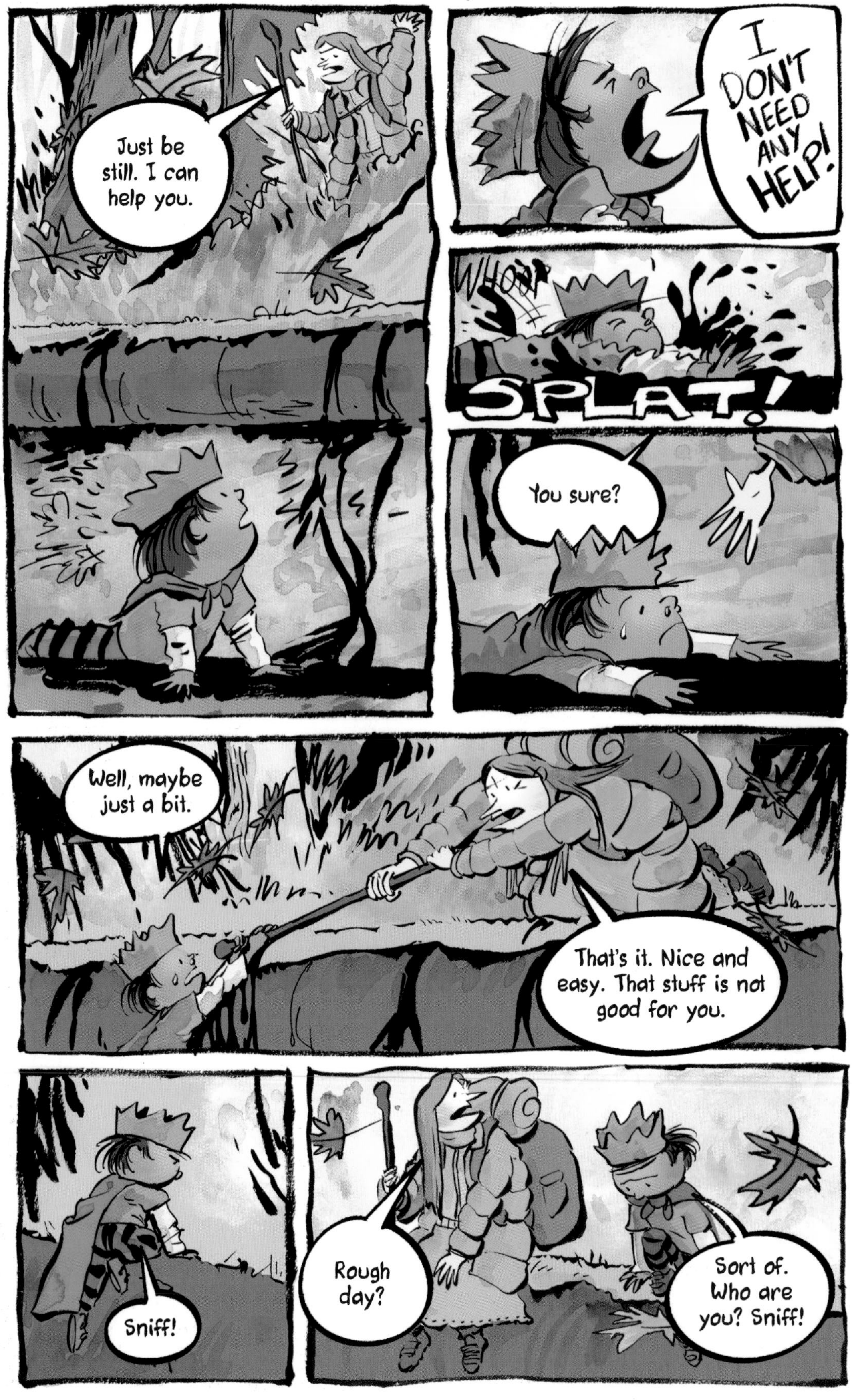
Just be still. I can help you.
I DON'T NEED ANY HELP!
SPLAT!
You sure?
Well, maybe just a bit.
That's it. Nice and easy. That stuff is not good for you.
Sniff!
Rough day?
Sort of. Who are you? Sniff!

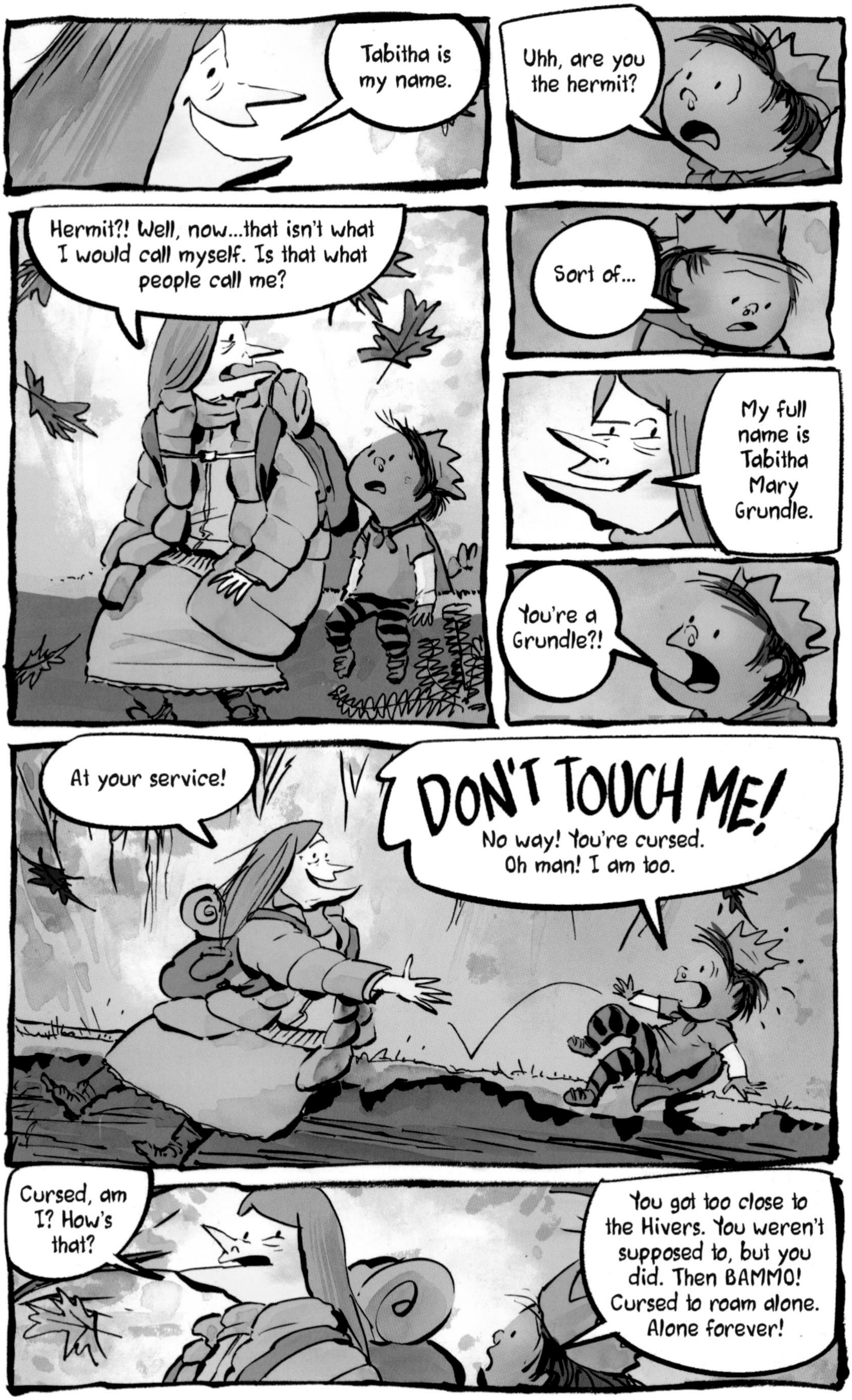
Tabitha is my name.
Uhh, are you the hermit?
Hermit?! Well, now...that isn't what I would call myself. Is that what people call me?
Sort of...
My full name is Tabitha Mary Grundle.
You're a Grundle?!
At your service!
DON'T TOUCH ME!
No way! You're cursed. Oh man! I am too.
Cursed, am I? How's that?
You got too close to the Hivers. You weren't supposed to, but you did. Then BAMMO! Cursed to roam alone. Alone forever!

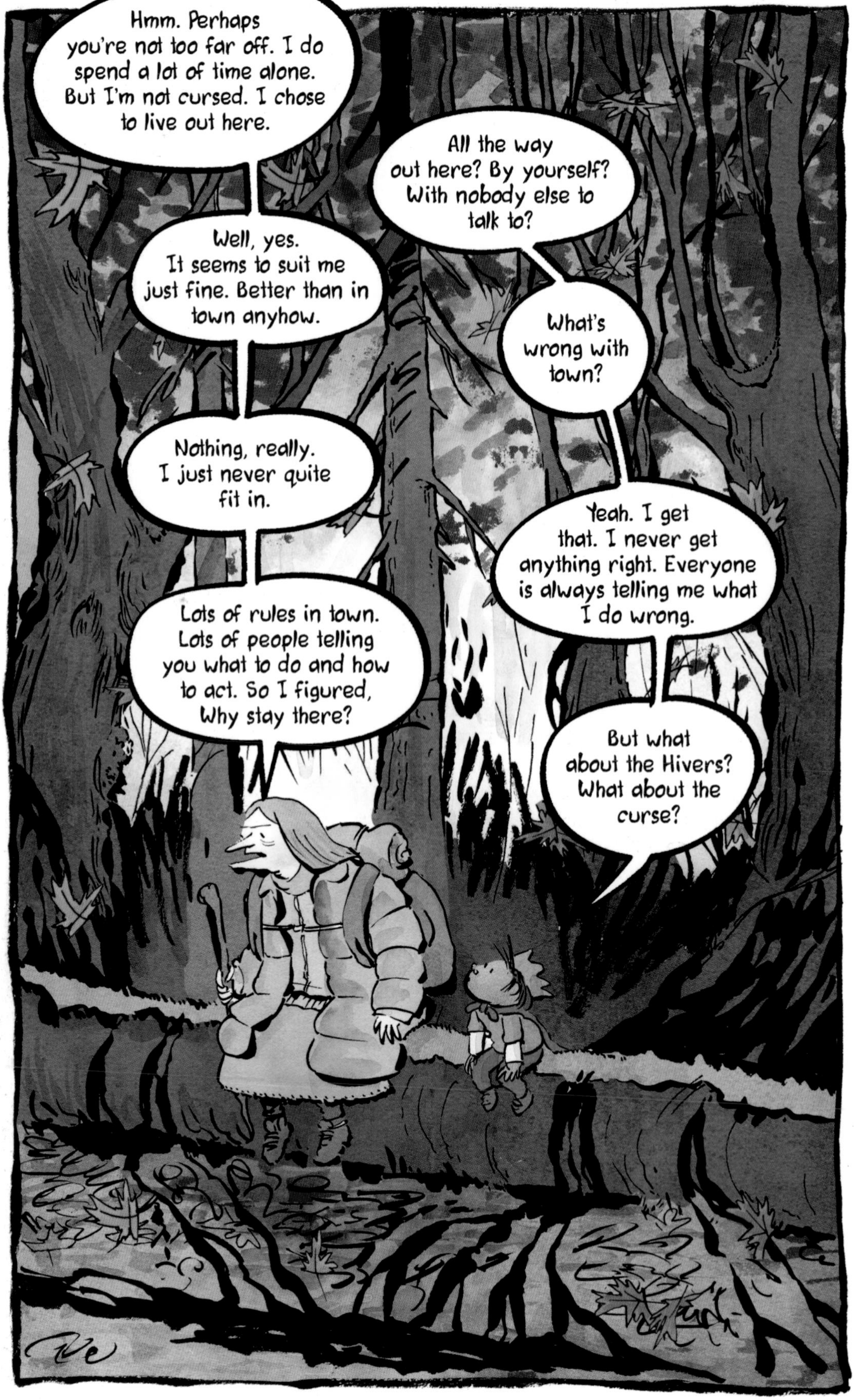
Hmm. Perhaps you're not too far off. I do spend a lot of time alone. But I'm not cursed. I chose to live out here.
All the way out here? By yourself? With nobody else to talk to?
Well, yes. It seems to suit me just fine. Better than in town anyhow.
What's wrong with town?
Nothing, really. I just never quite fit in.
Yeah. I get that. I never get anything right. Everyone is always telling me what I do wrong.
Lots of rules in town. Lots of people telling you what to do and how to act. So I figured, Why stay there?
But what about the Hivers? What about the curse?

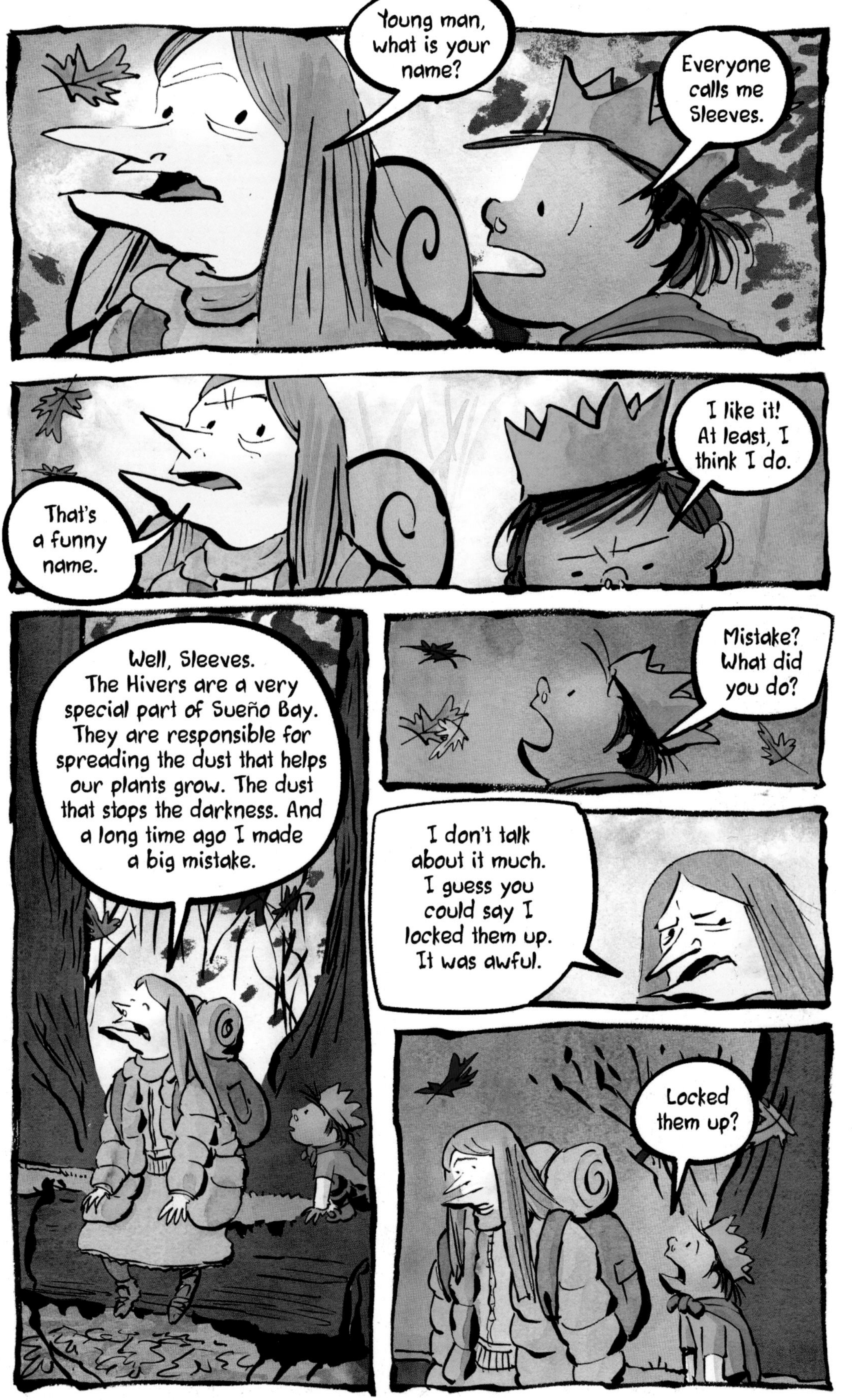
Young man, what is your name?
Everyone calls me Sleeves.
That's a funny name.
I like it! At least, I think I do.
Well, Sleeves. The Hivers are a very special part of Sueño Bay. They are responsible for spreading the dust that helps our plants grow. The dust that stops the darkness. And a long time ago I made a big mistake.
Mistake? What did you do?
I don't talk about it much. I guess you could say I locked them up. It was awful.
Locked them up?

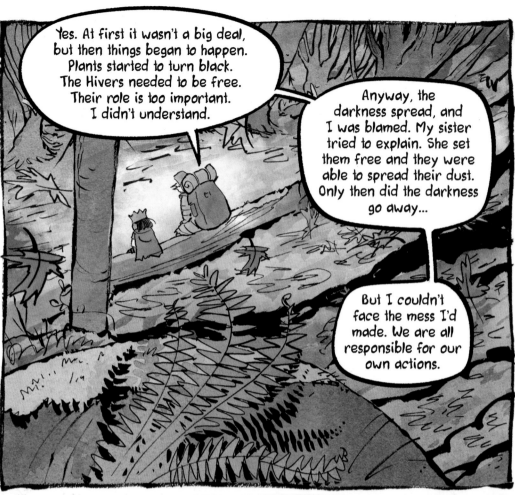

Yes. At first it wasn't a big deal, but then things began to happen. Plants started to turn black. The Hivers needed to be free. Their role is too important. I didn't understand.

Anyway, the darkness spread, and I was blamed. My sister tried to explain. She set them free and they were able to spread their dust. Only then did the darkness go away...

But I couldn't face the mess I'd made. We are all responsible for our own actions.

What about your sister? Where is she?

Kate? My twin sister? I don't know. I haven't spoken to her in nearly thirty years.

Thirty years?! I bet she misses you. I know I'd miss my sister. You should find her.

It has been a long time, but I'm not sure about any of that. Anyway, the other day I ate a bad mushroom. I felt terrible for about three days. I went back to where I had picked it and saw the darkness.

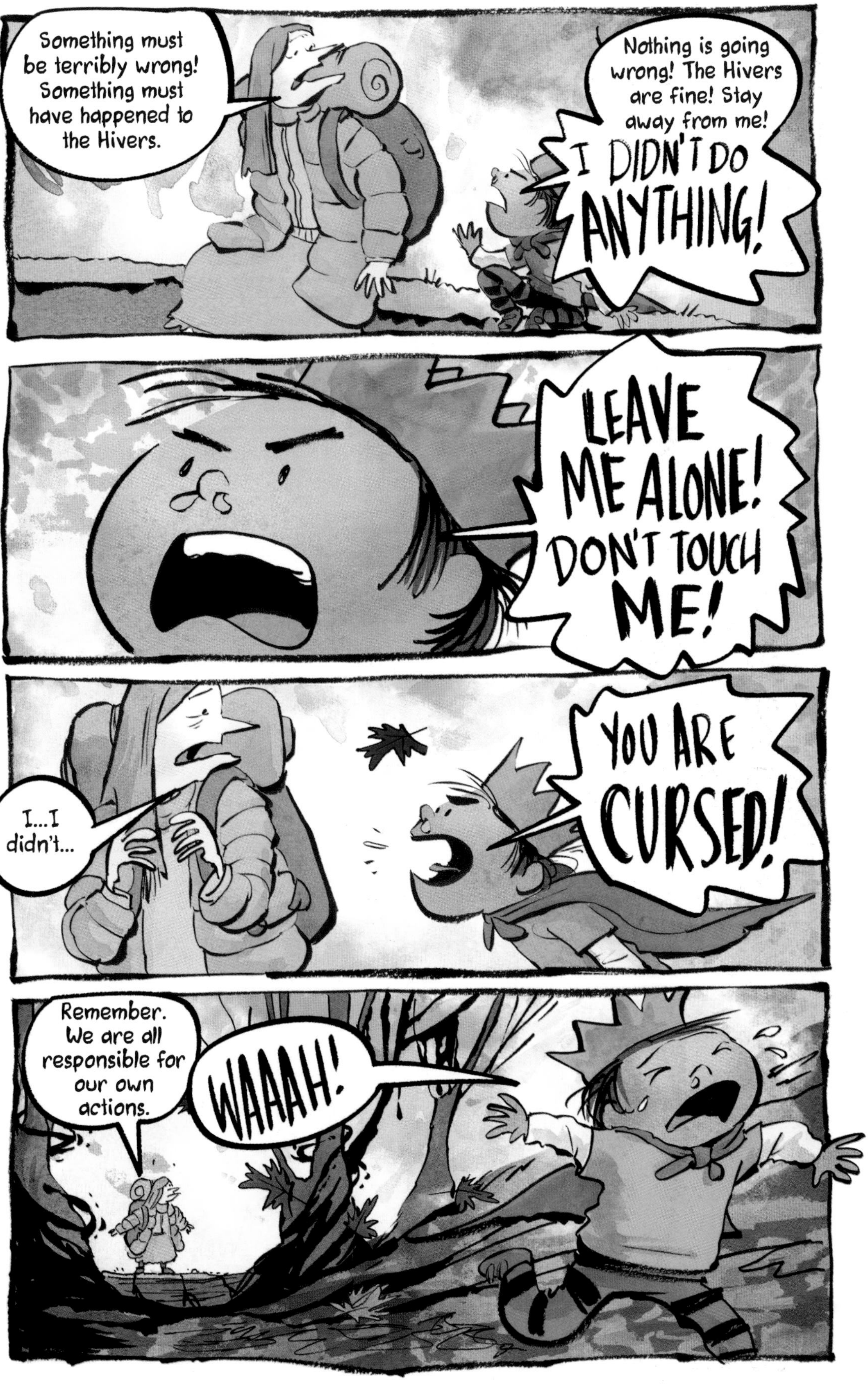
Something must be terribly wrong! Something must have happened to the Hivers.
Nothing is going wrong! The Hivers are fine! Stay away from me!
I DIDN'T DO ANYTHING!
LEAVE ME ALONE! DON'T TOUCH ME!
I...I didn't...
YOU ARE CURSED!
Remember. We are all responsible for our own actions.
WAAAH!

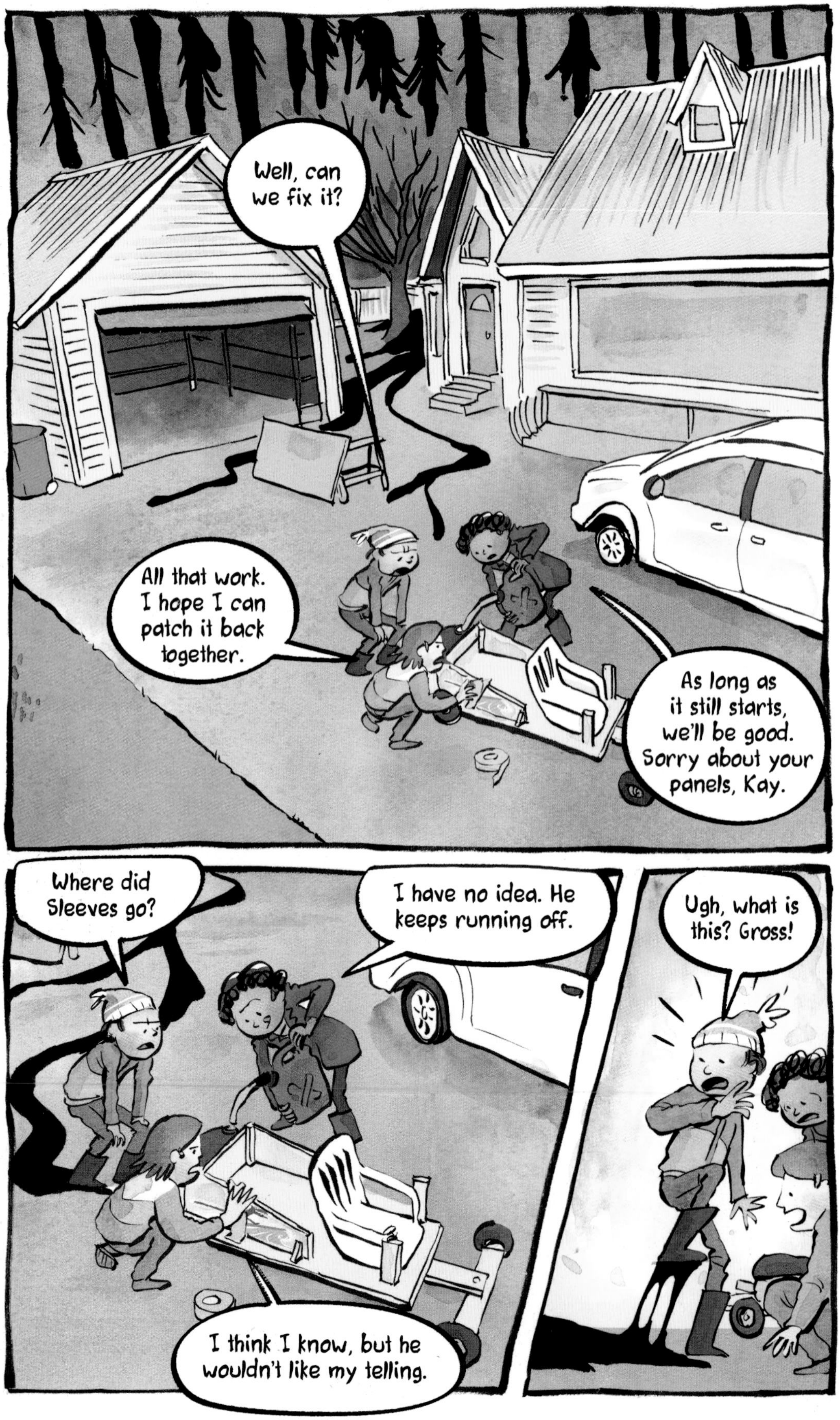
Well, can we fix it?
All that work. I hope I can patch it back together.
As long as it still starts, we'll be good. Sorry about your panels, Kay.
Where did Sleeves go?
I have no idea. He keeps running off.
I think I know, but he wouldn't like my telling.
Ugh, what is this? Gross!

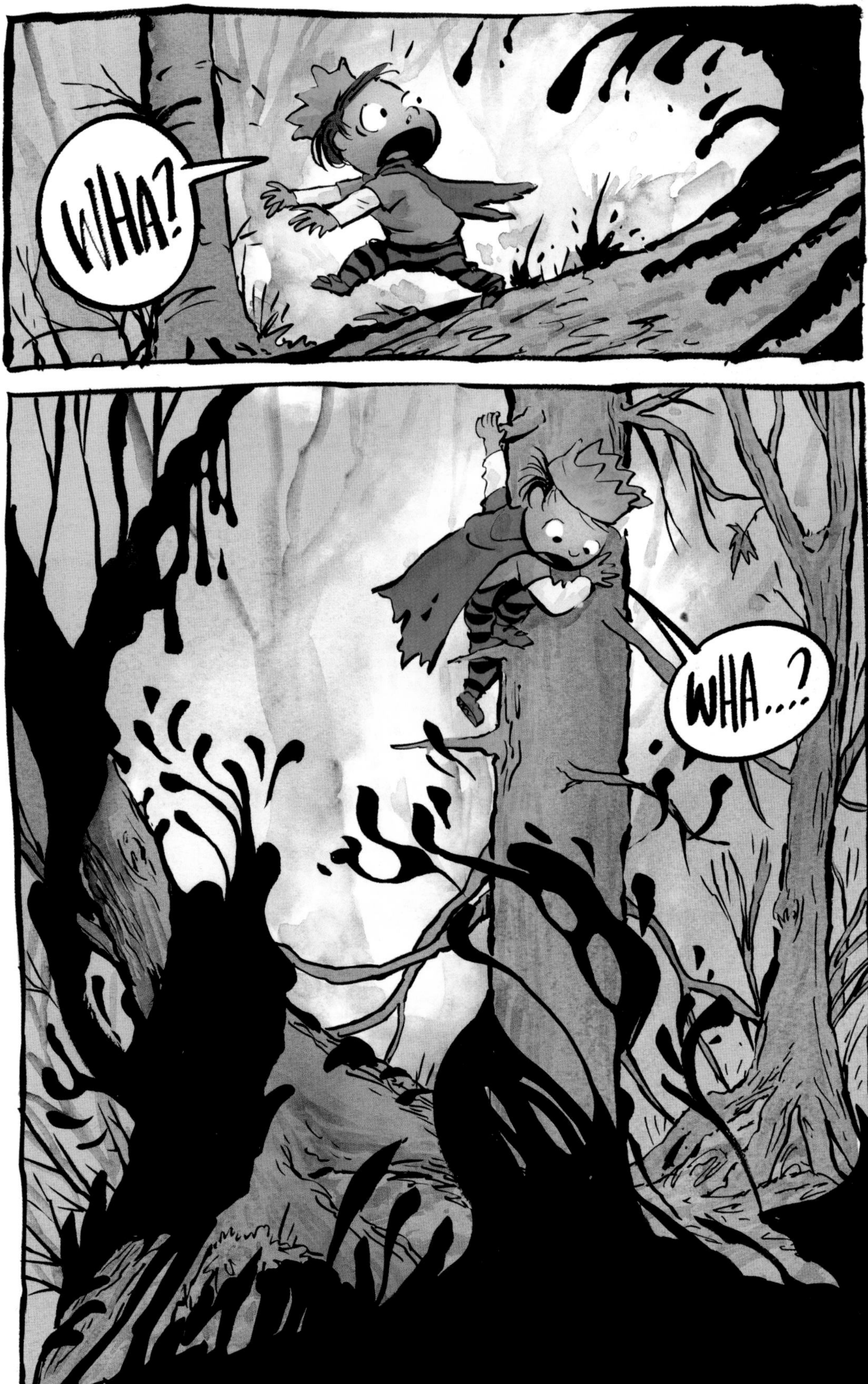
WHA?
WHA...?

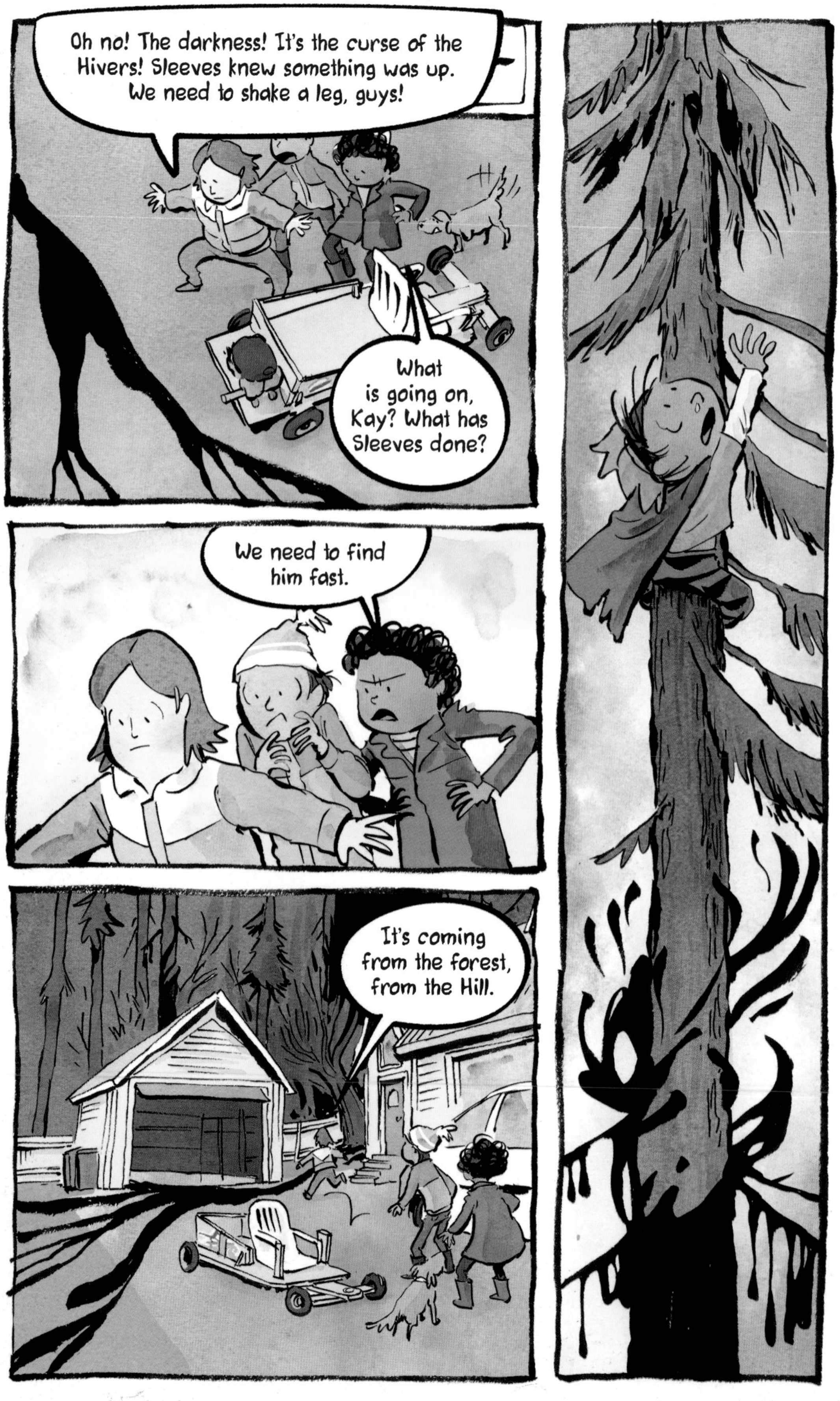
Oh no! The darkness! It's the curse of the Hivers! Sleeves knew something was up. We need to shake a leg, guys!
What is going on, Kay? What has Sleeves done?
We need to find him fast.
It's coming from the forest, from the Hill.

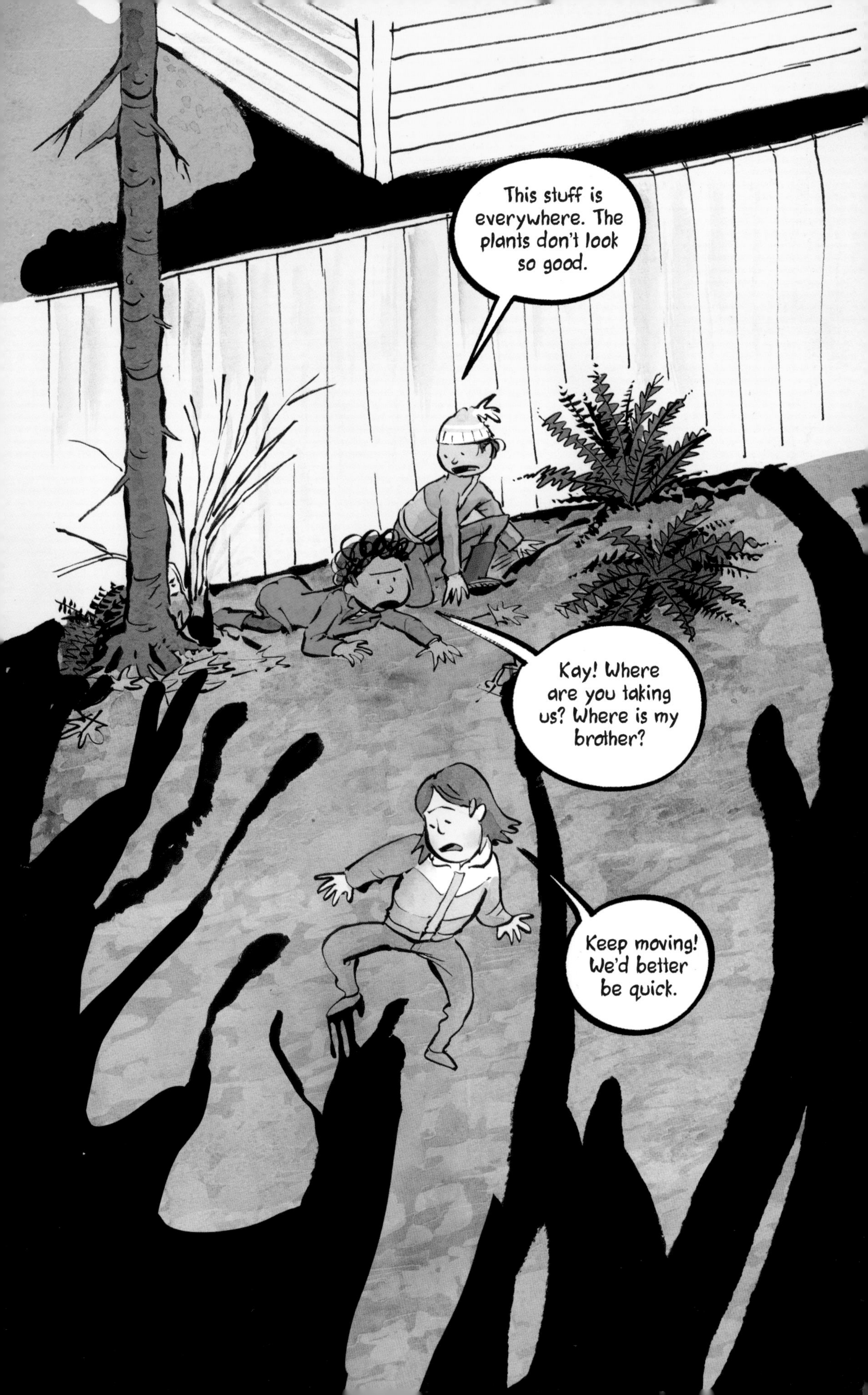
This stuff is everywhere. The plants don't look so good.
Kay! Where are you taking us? Where is my brother?
Keep moving! We'd better be quick.

CHAPTER FIVE

Up a Tree Without a Paddle

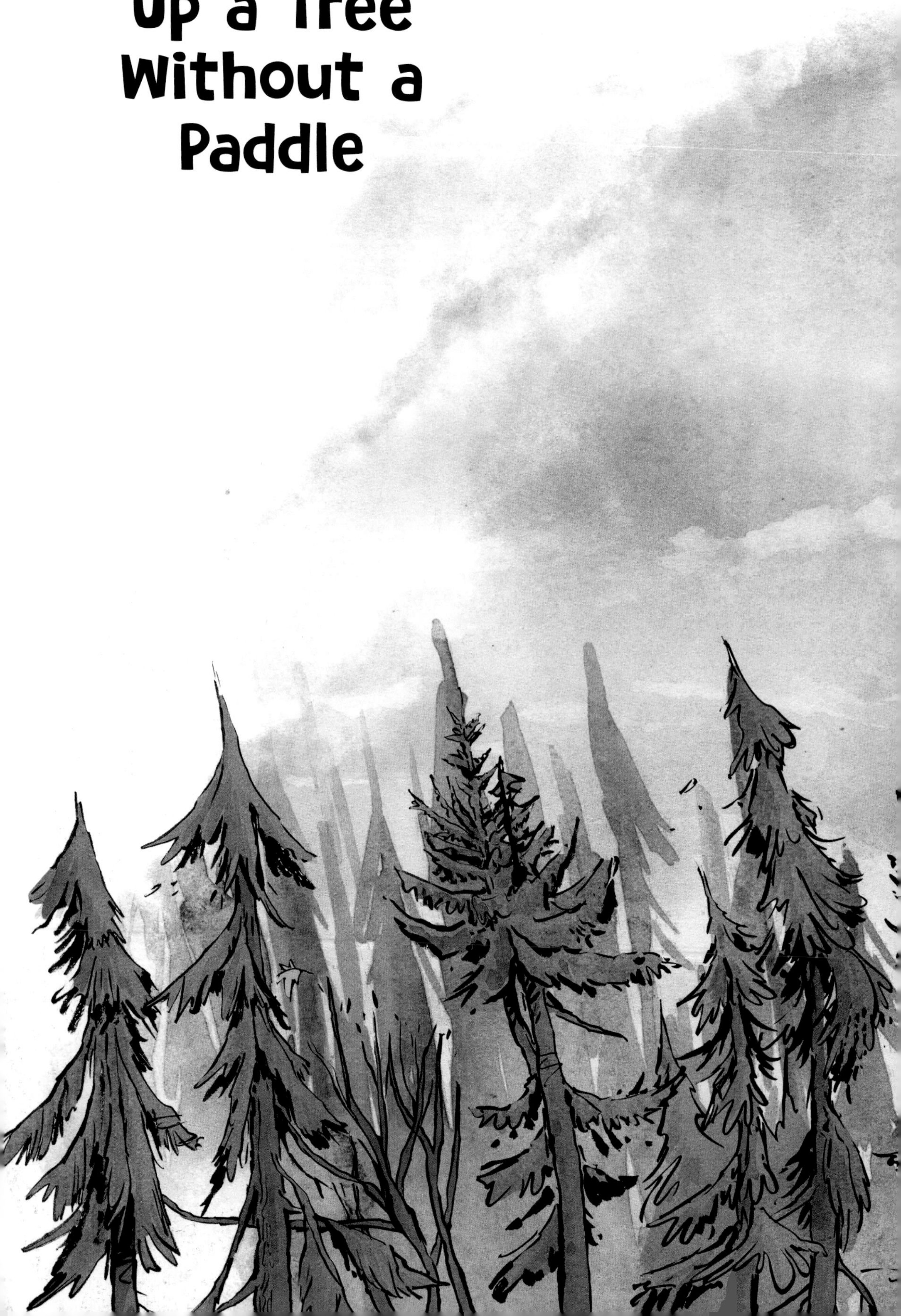

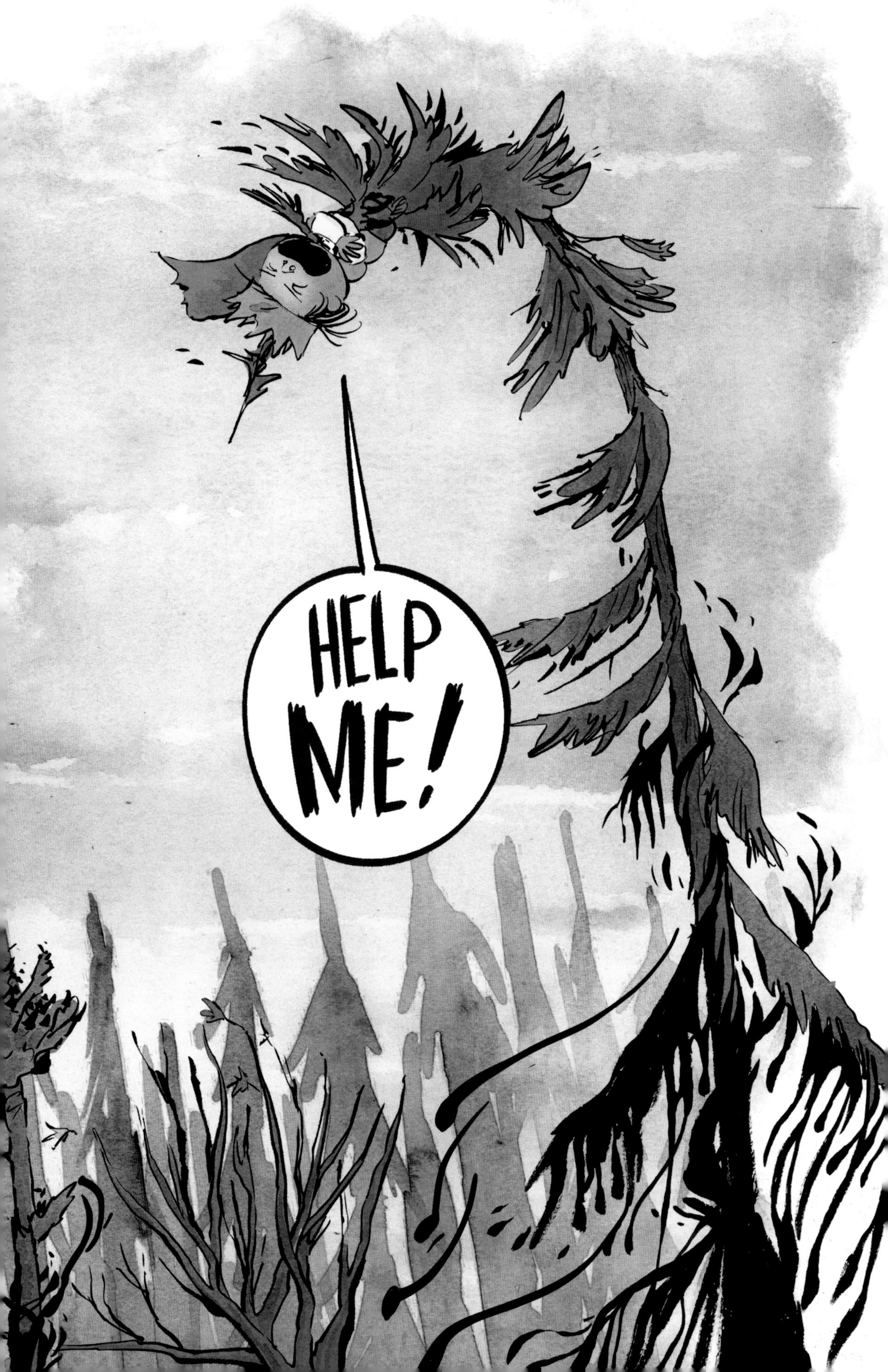
HELP ME!

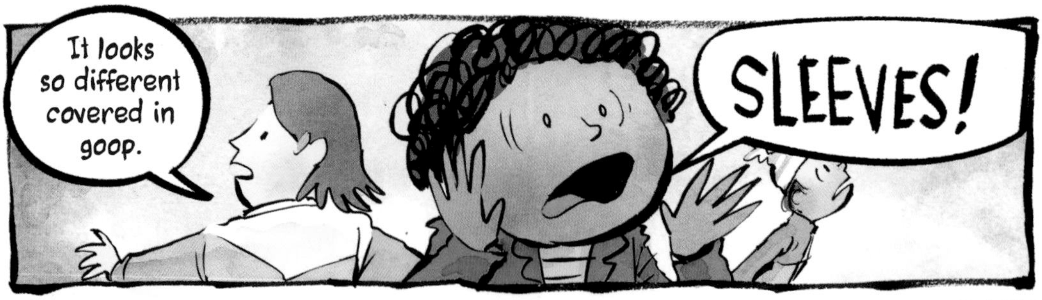
It looks so different covered in goop.
SLEEVES!

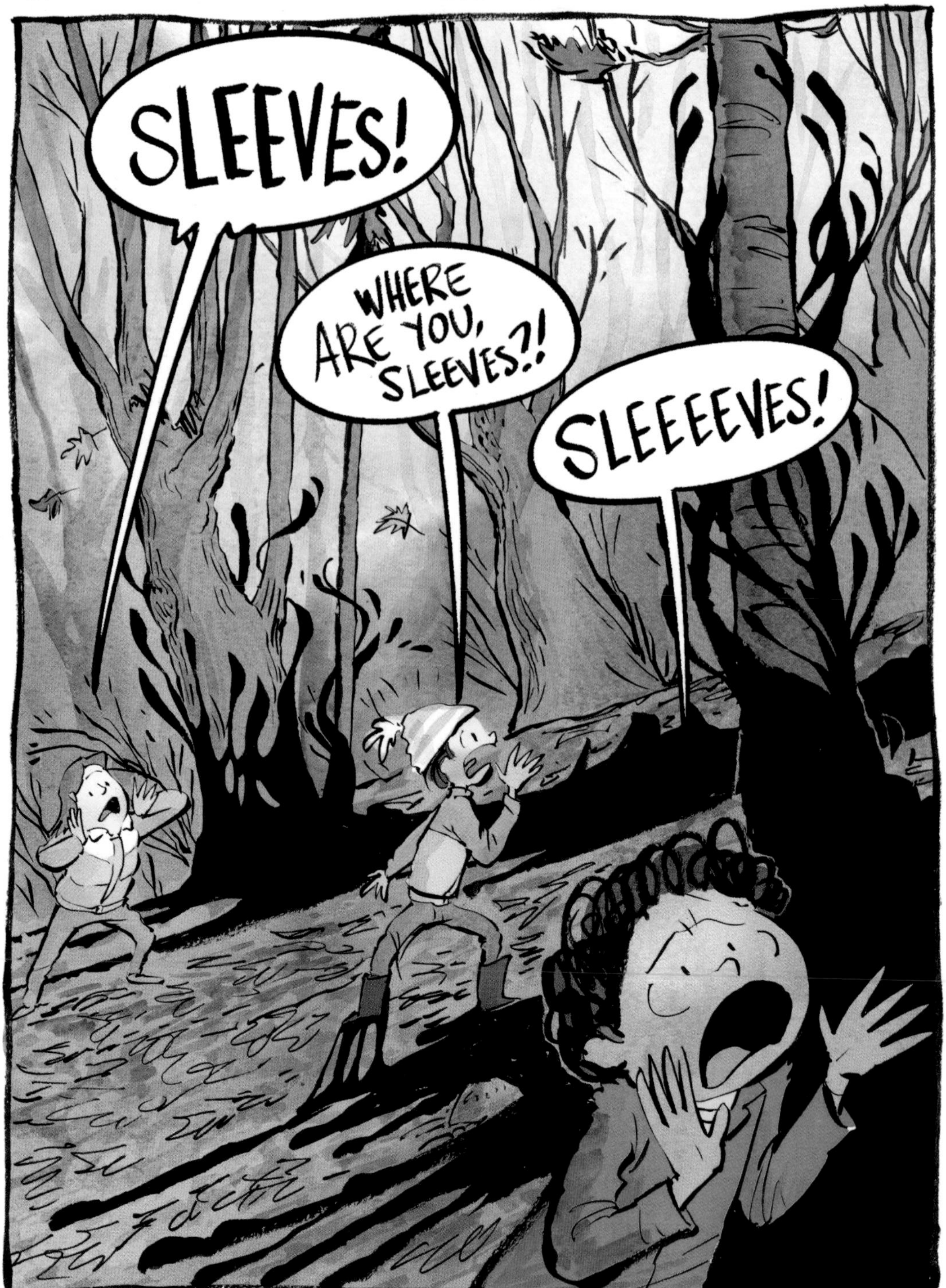
SLEEVES!
WHERE ARE YOU, SLEEVES?!
SLEEEEVES!

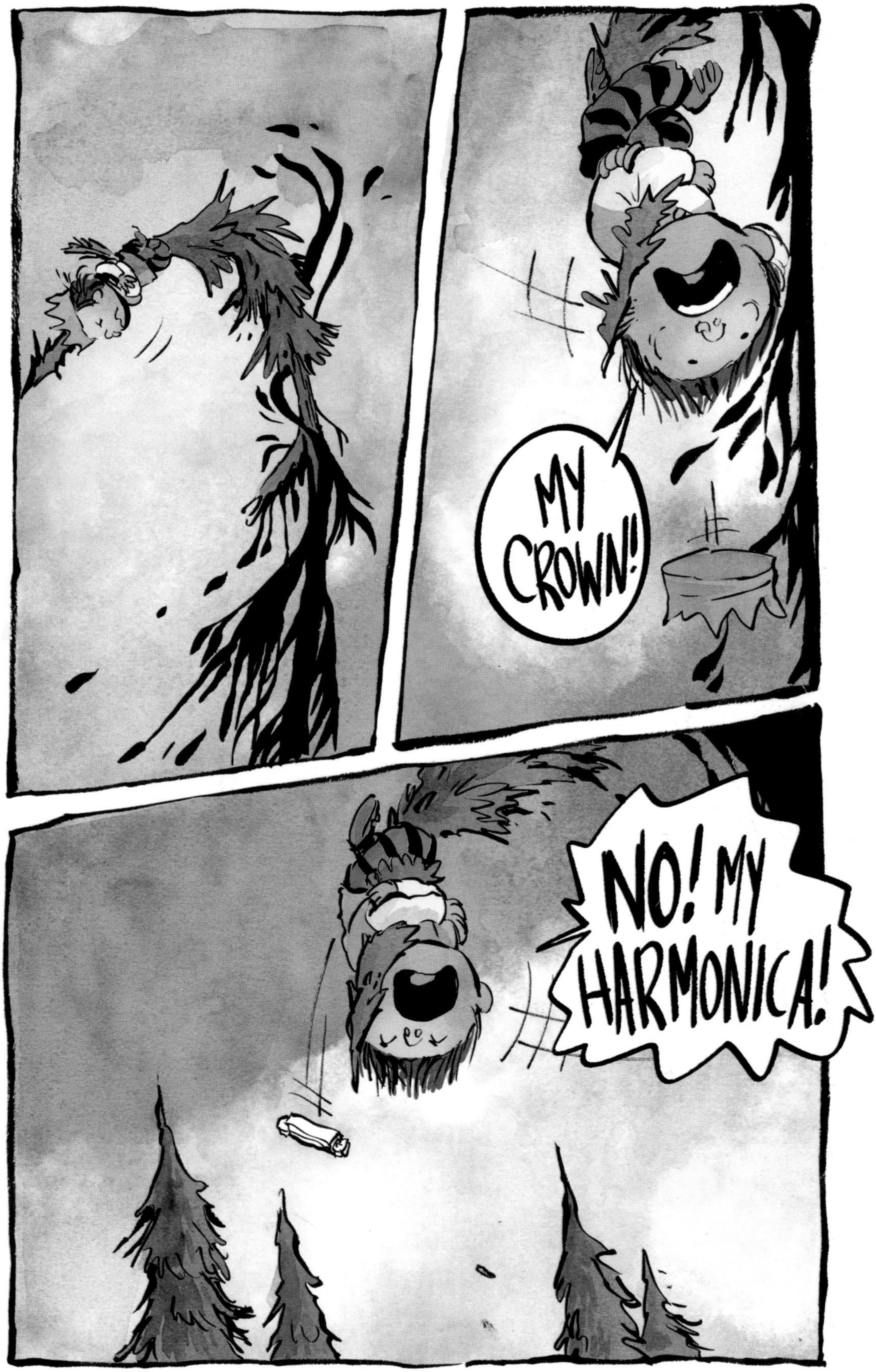
MY CROWN!
NO! MY HARMONICA!

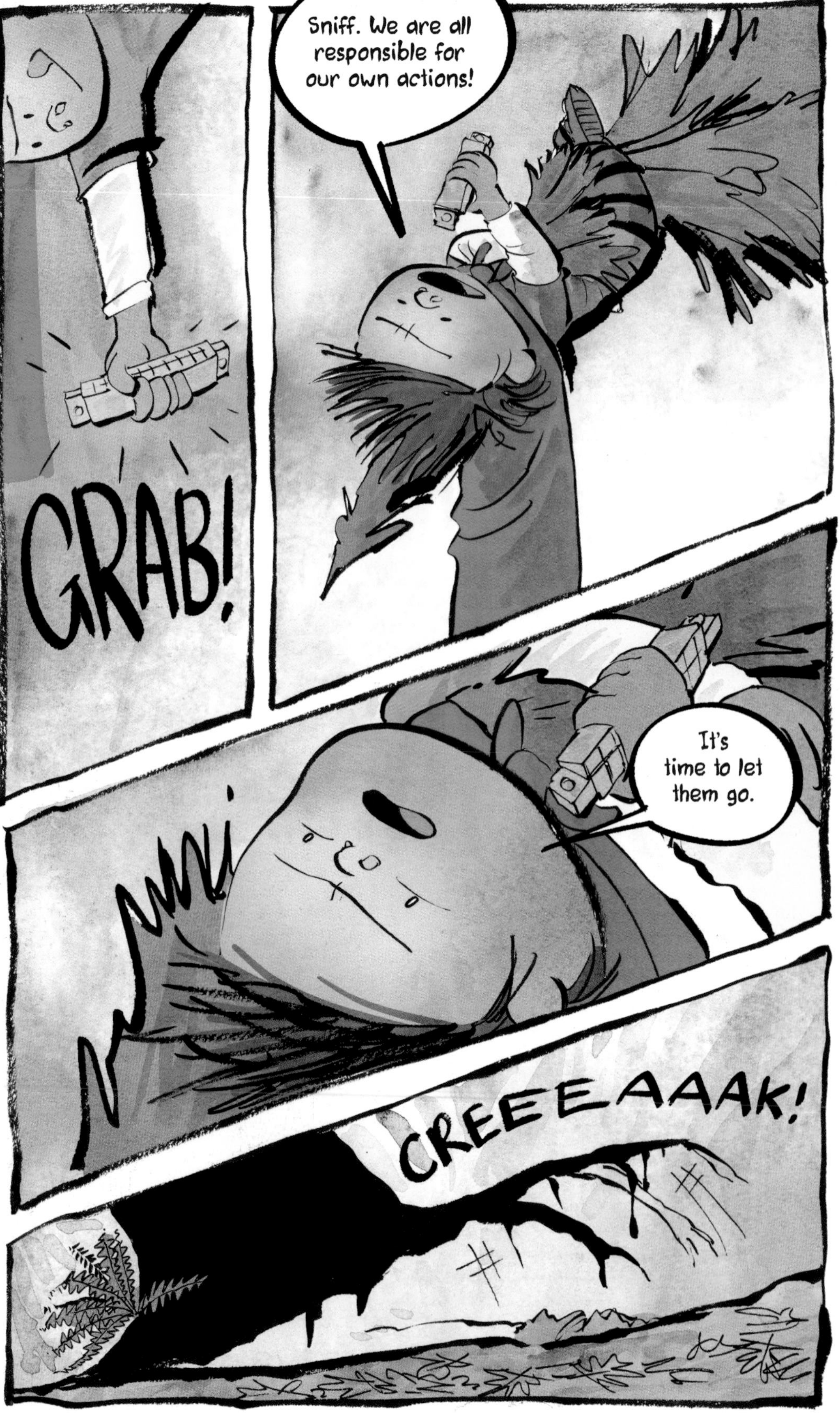
GRAB!
Sniff. We are all responsible for our own actions!
It's time to let them go.
CREEEAAAK!

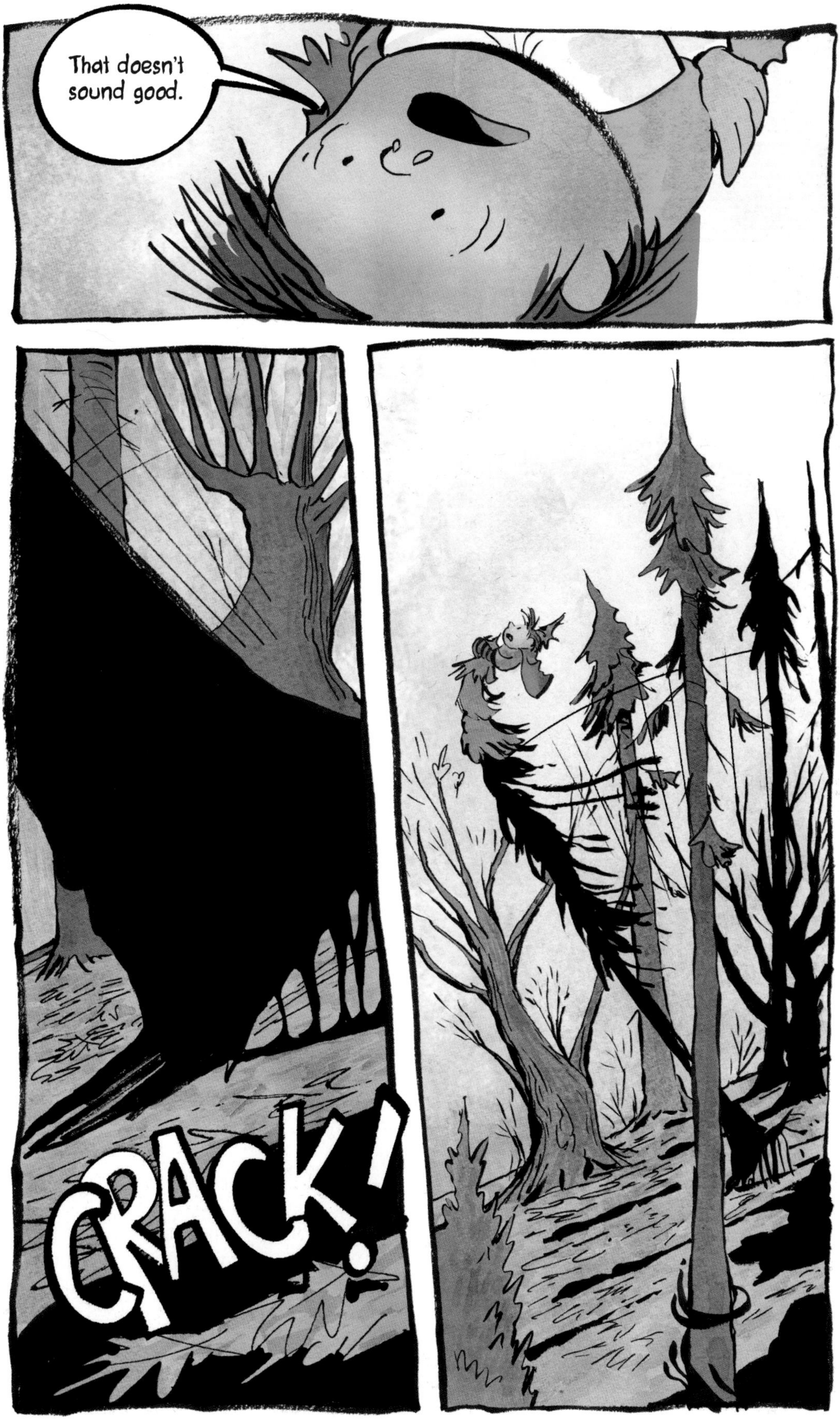
That doesn't sound good.
CRACK!

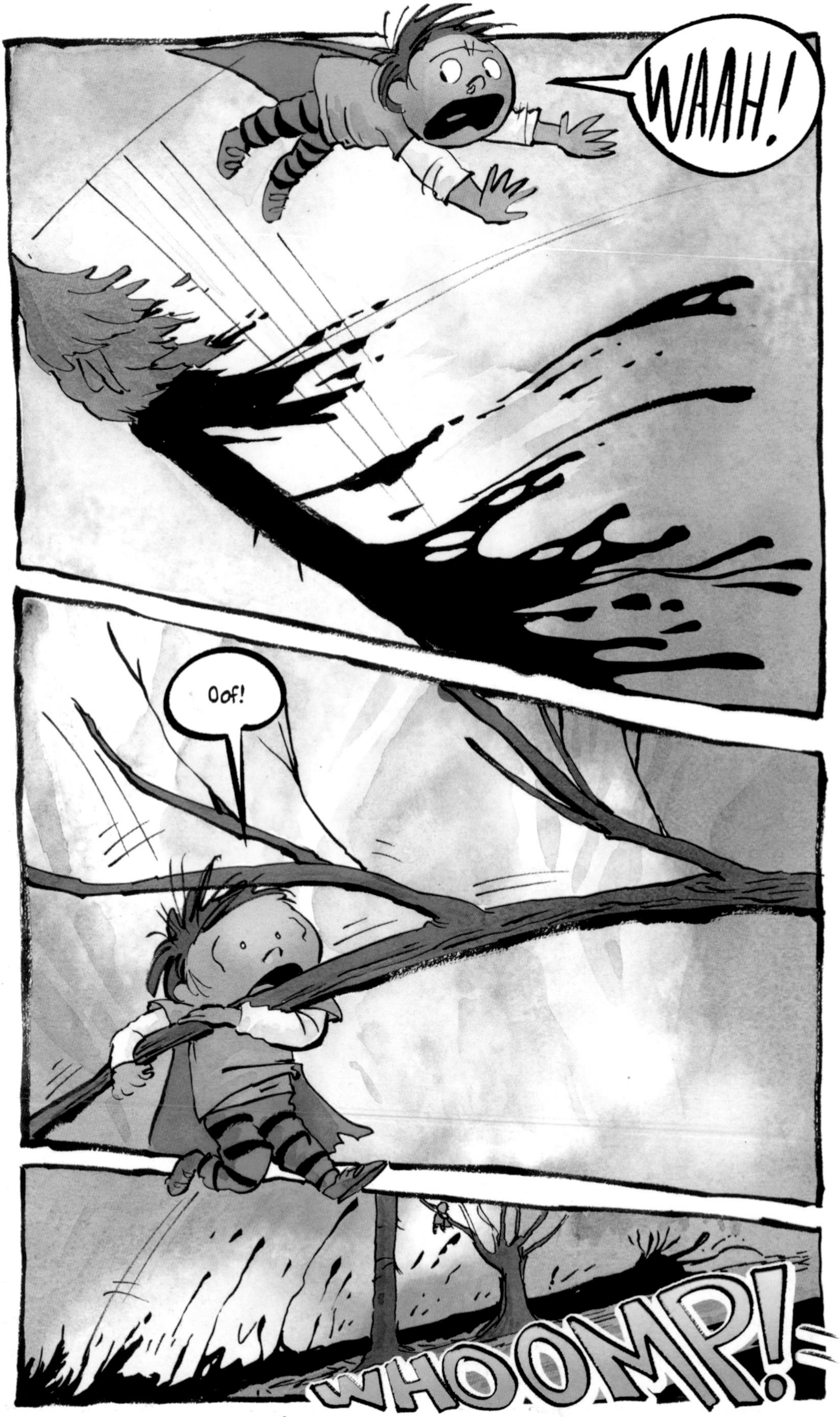
WAAH!
Oof!
WHOOMP!

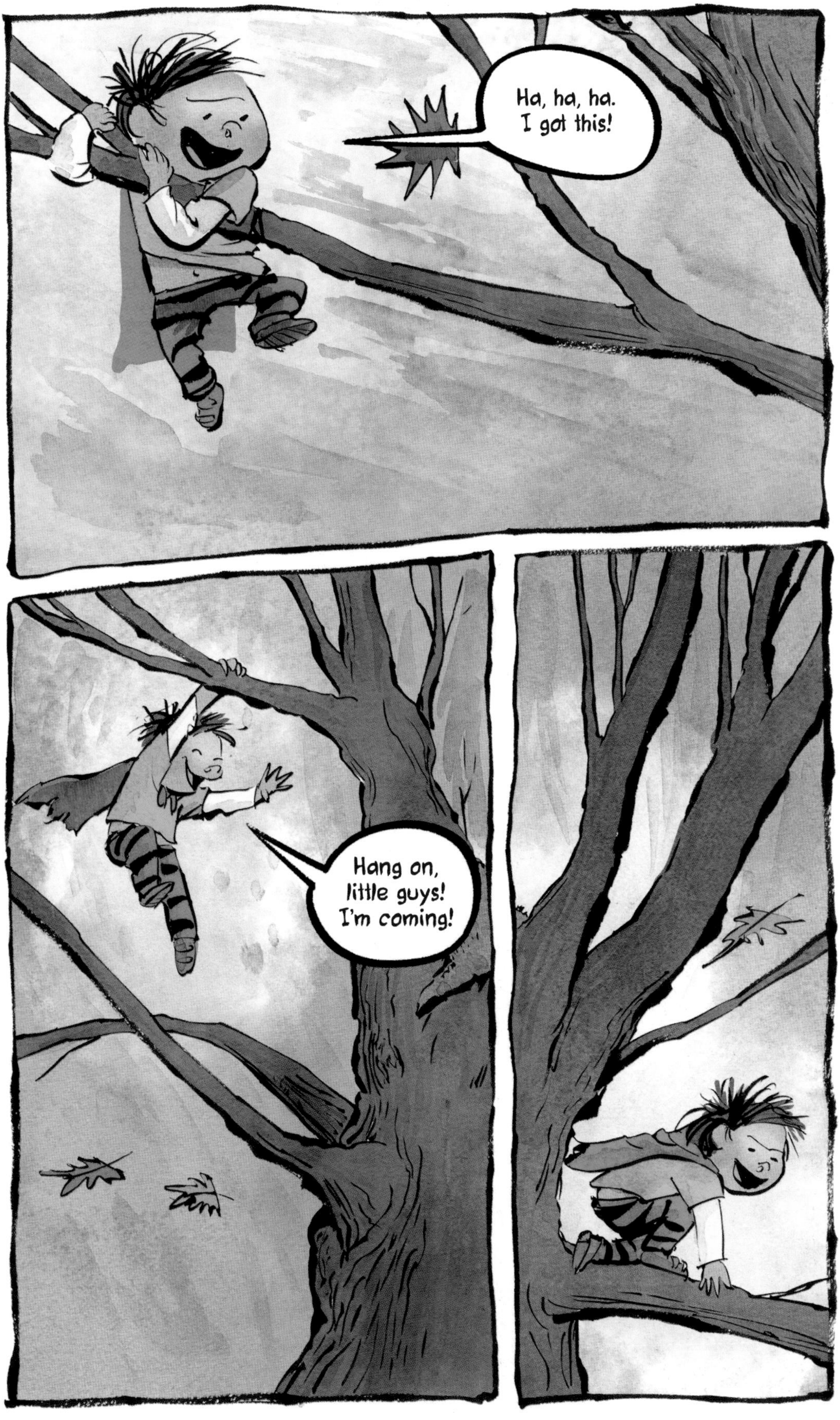
Ha, ha, ha. I got this!
Hang on, little guys! I'm coming!

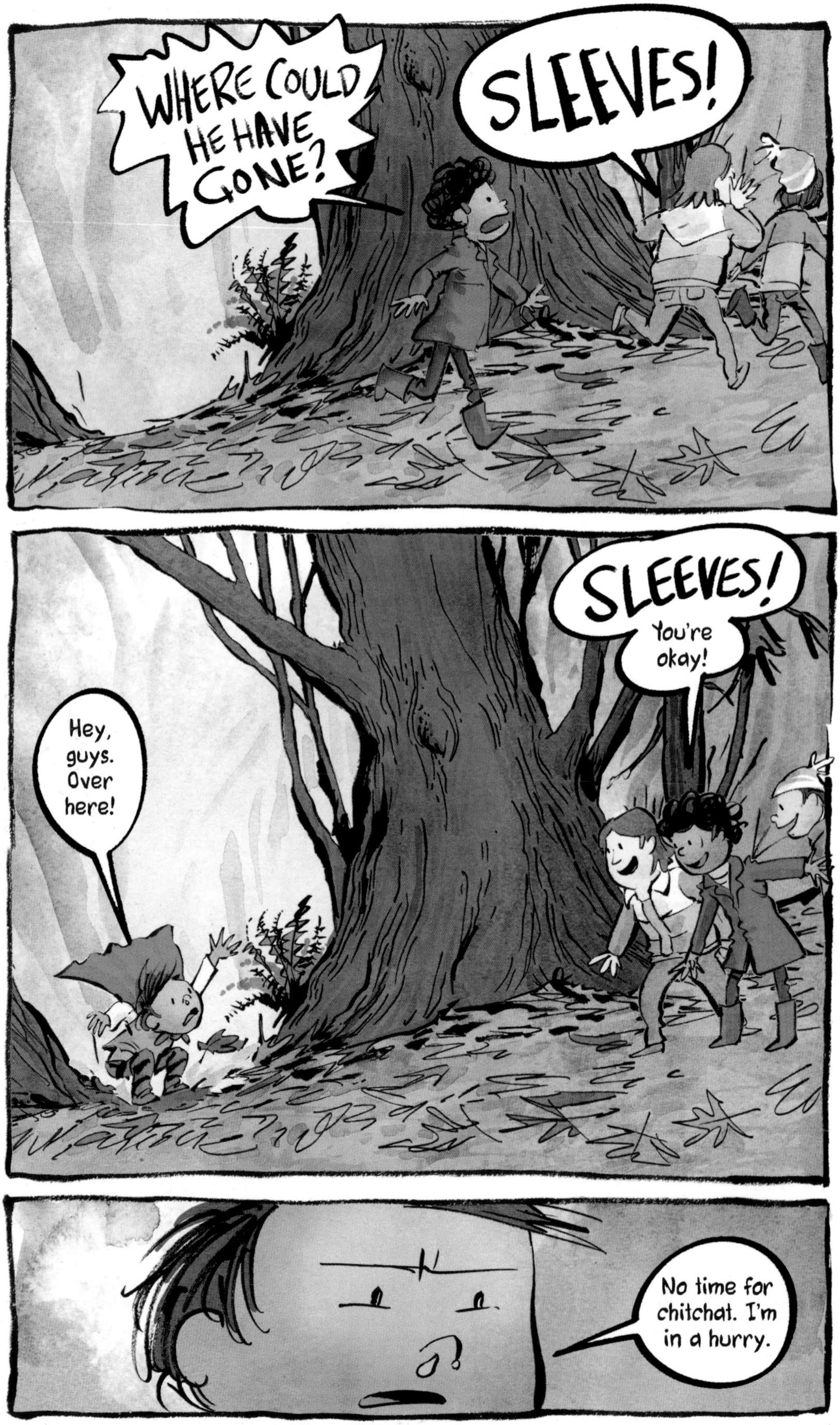
WHERE COULD HE HAVE GONE?
SLEEVES!
SLEEVES! You're okay!
Hey, guys. Over here!
No time for chitchat. I'm in a hurry.

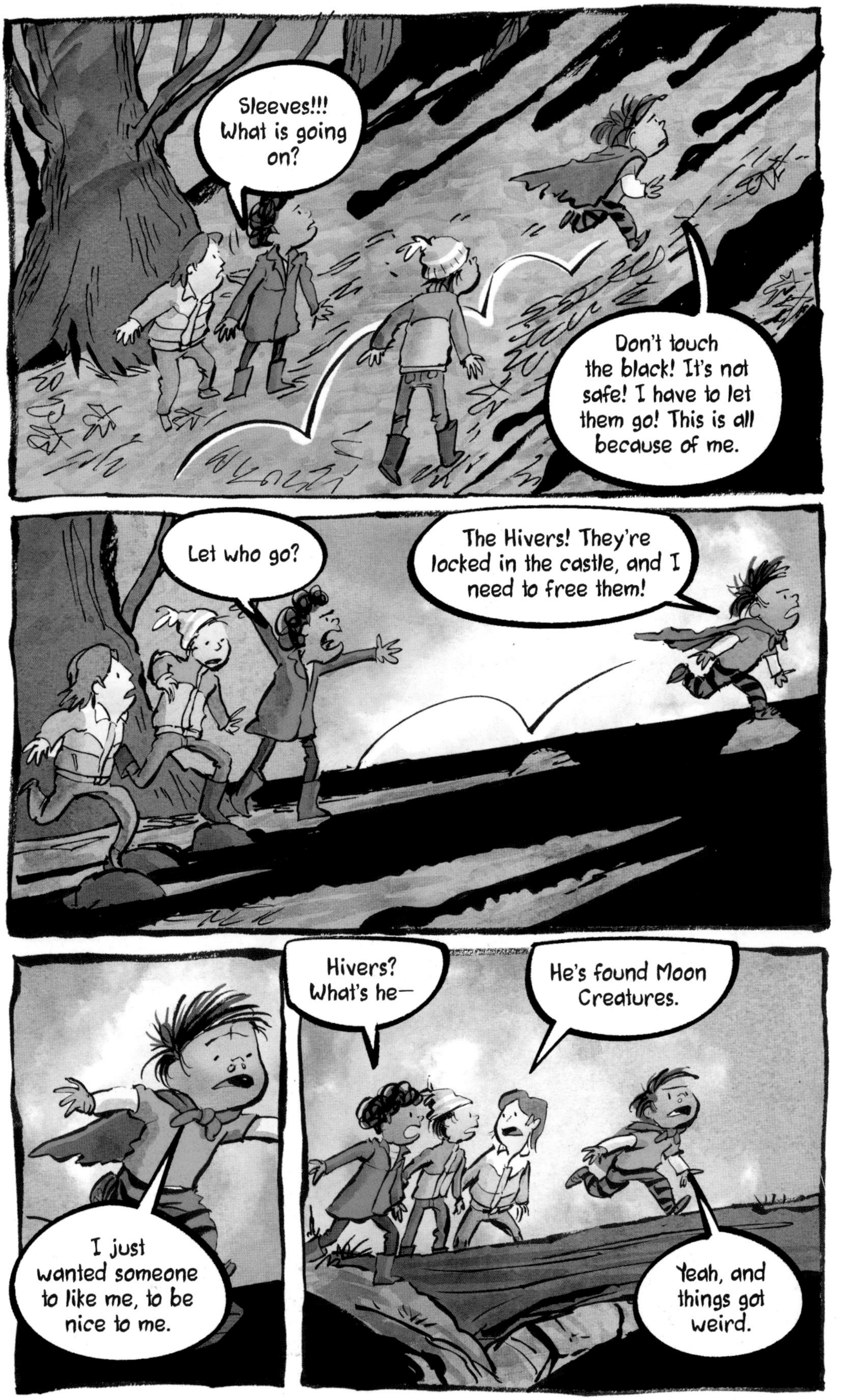
Sleeves!!! What is going on?
Don't touch the black! It's not safe! I have to let them go! This is all because of me.
Let who go?
The Hivers! They're locked in the castle, and I need to free them!
I just wanted someone to like me, to be nice to me.
Hivers? What's he—
He's found Moon Creatures.
Yeah, and things got weird.

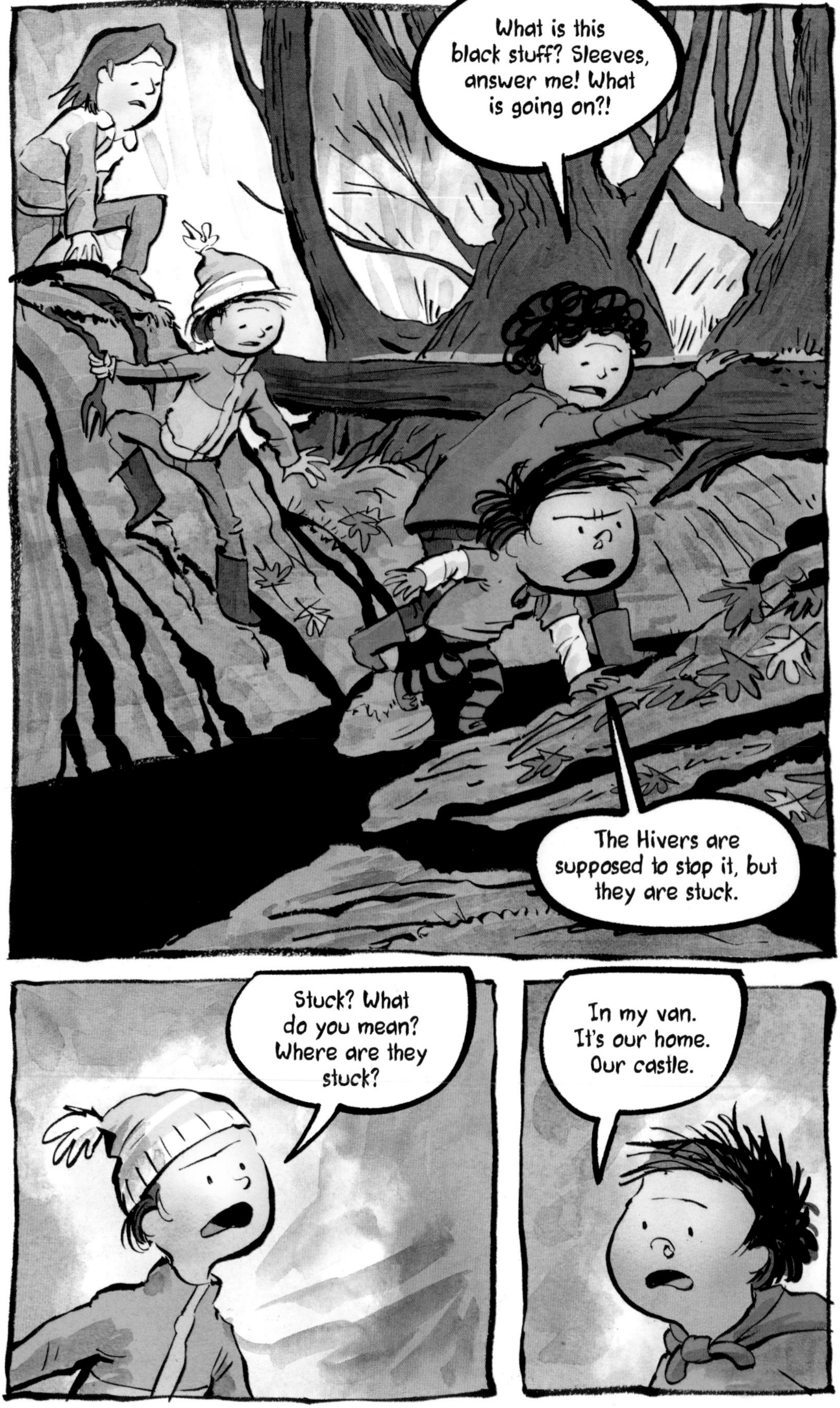
What is this black stuff? Sleeves, answer me! What is going on?!
The Hivers are supposed to stop it, but they are stuck.
Stuck? What do you mean? Where are they stuck?
In my van. It's our home. Our castle.

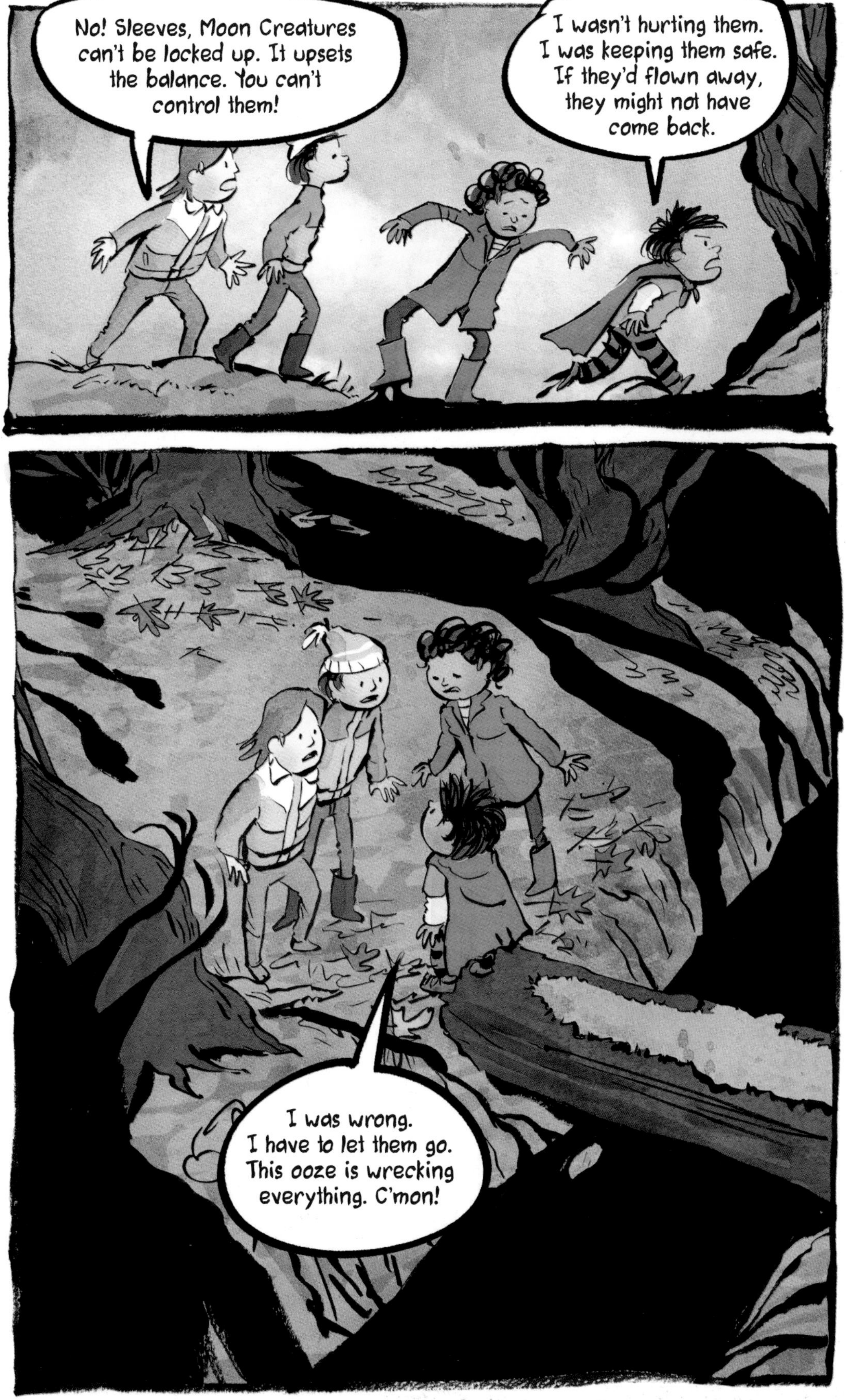
No! Sleeves, Moon Creatures can't be locked up. It upsets the balance. You can't control them!
I wasn't hurting them. I was keeping them safe. If they'd flown away, they might not have come back.
I was wrong. I have to let them go. This ooze is wrecking everything. C'mon!

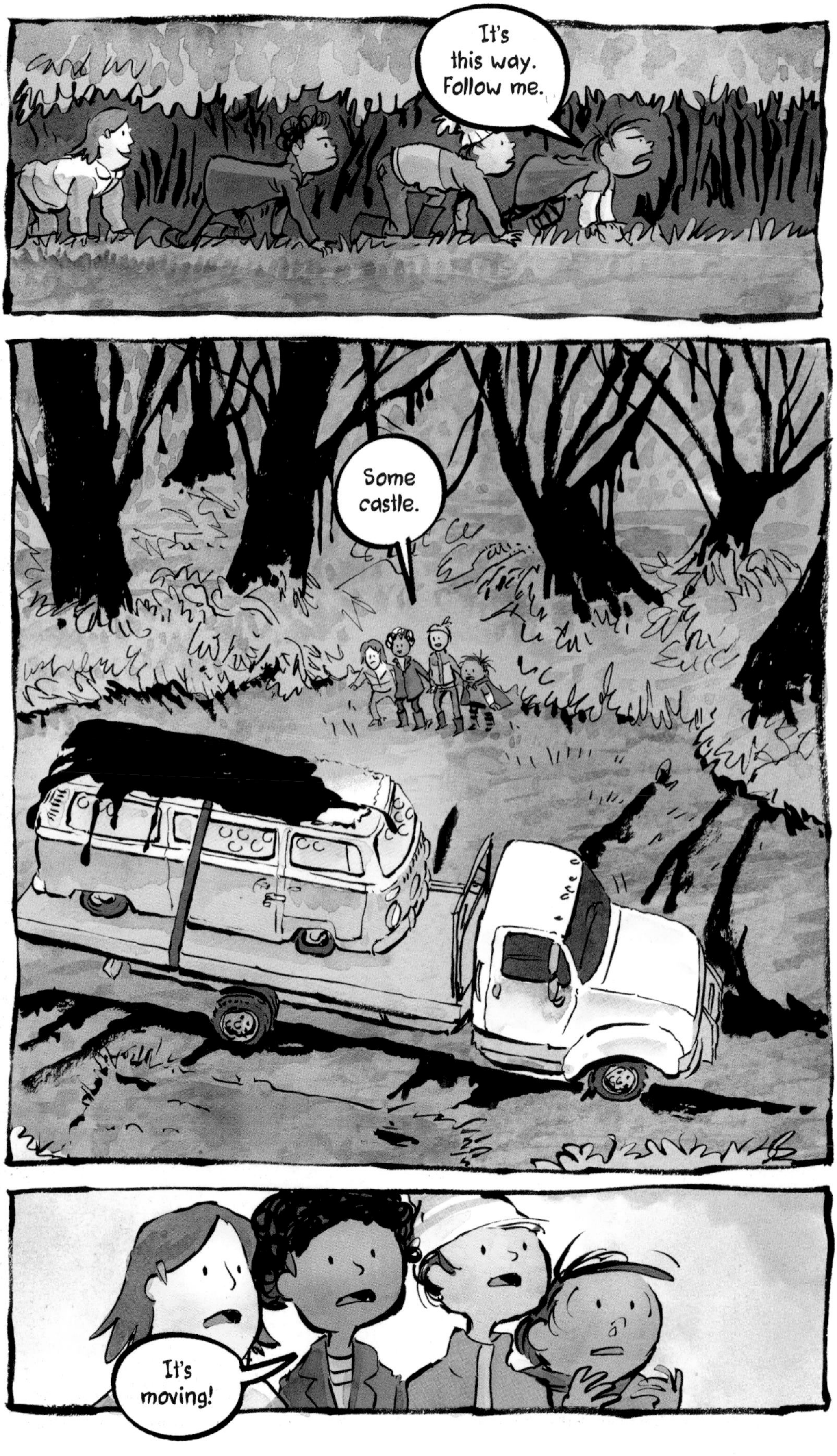
It's this way. Follow me.
Some castle.
It's moving!

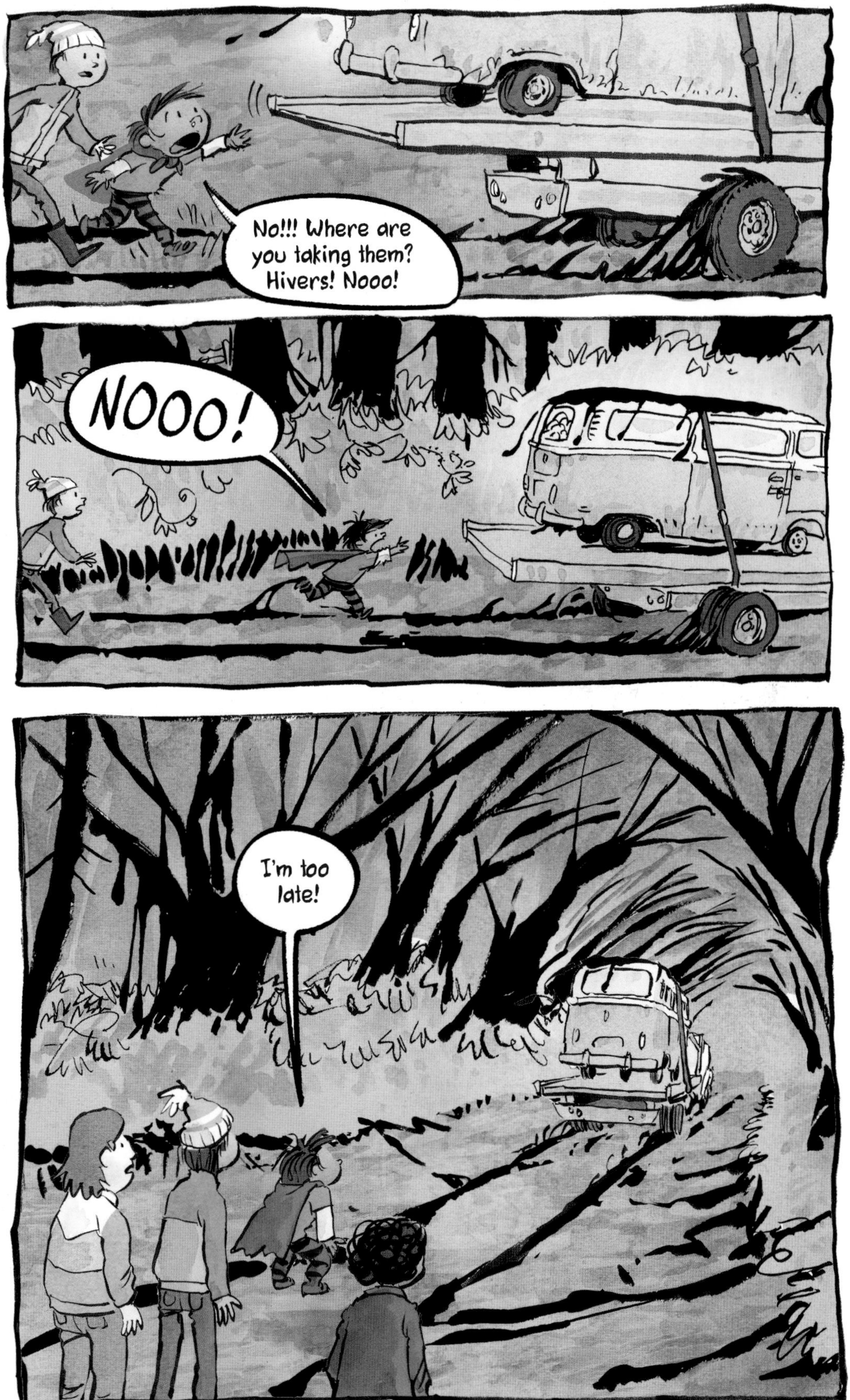
No!!! Where are you taking them? Hivers! Nooo!
NOOO!
I'm too late!

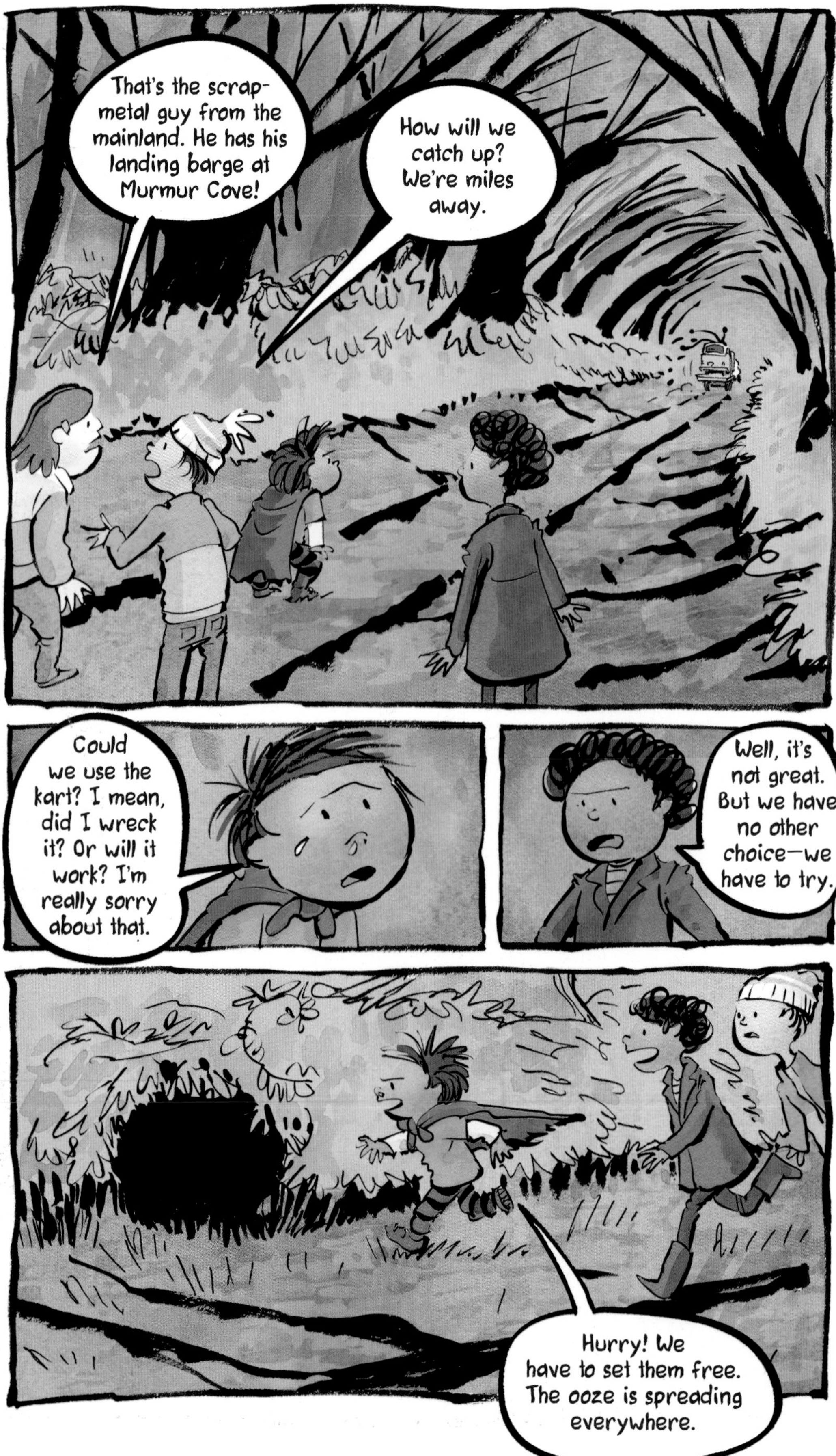
That's the scrap-metal guy from the mainland. He has his landing barge at Murmur Cove!
How will we catch up? We're miles away.
Could we use the kart? I mean, did I wreck it? Or will it work? I'm really sorry about that.
Well, it's not great. But we have no other choice—we have to try.
Hurry! We have to set them free. The ooze is spreading everywhere.

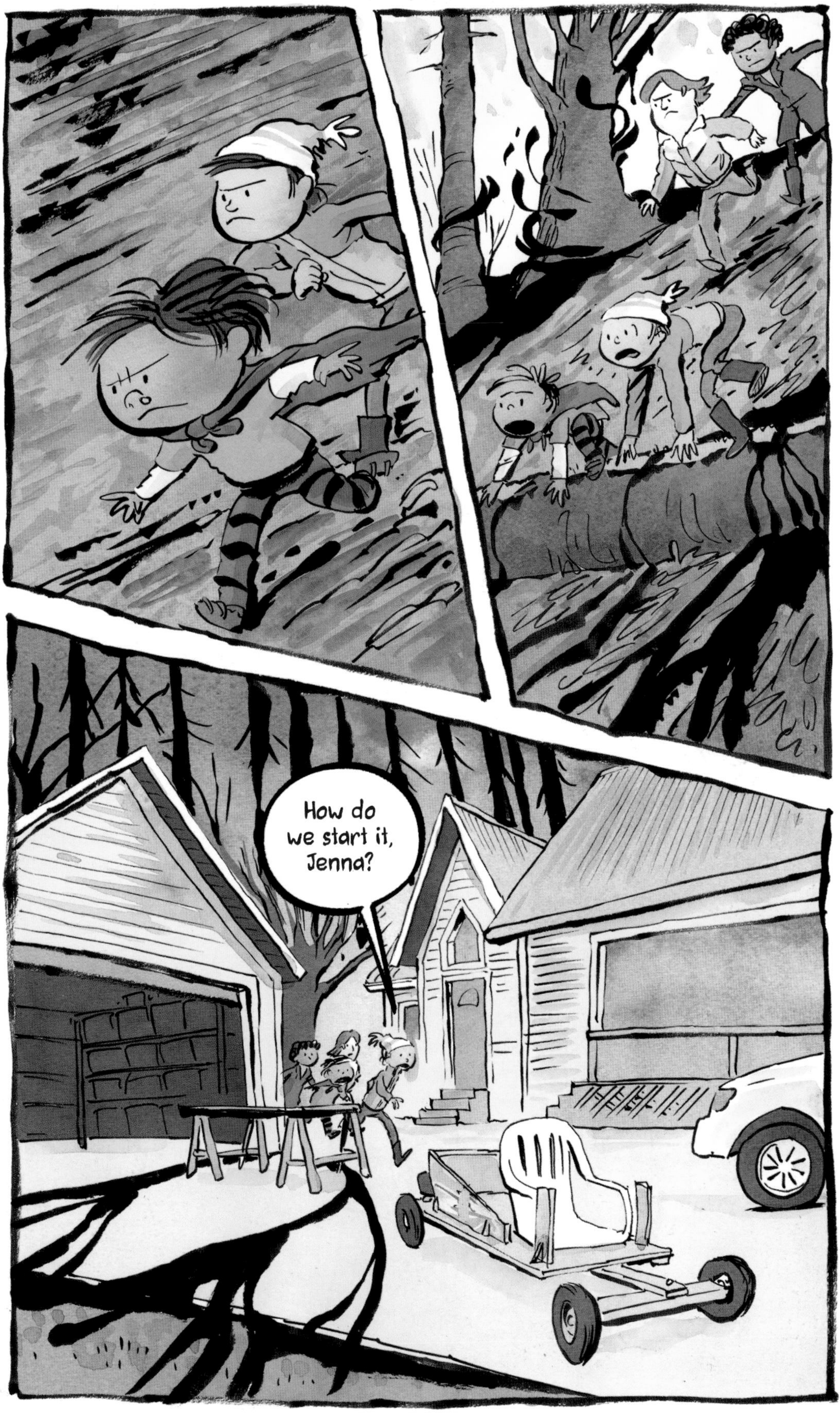
How do we start it, Jenna?

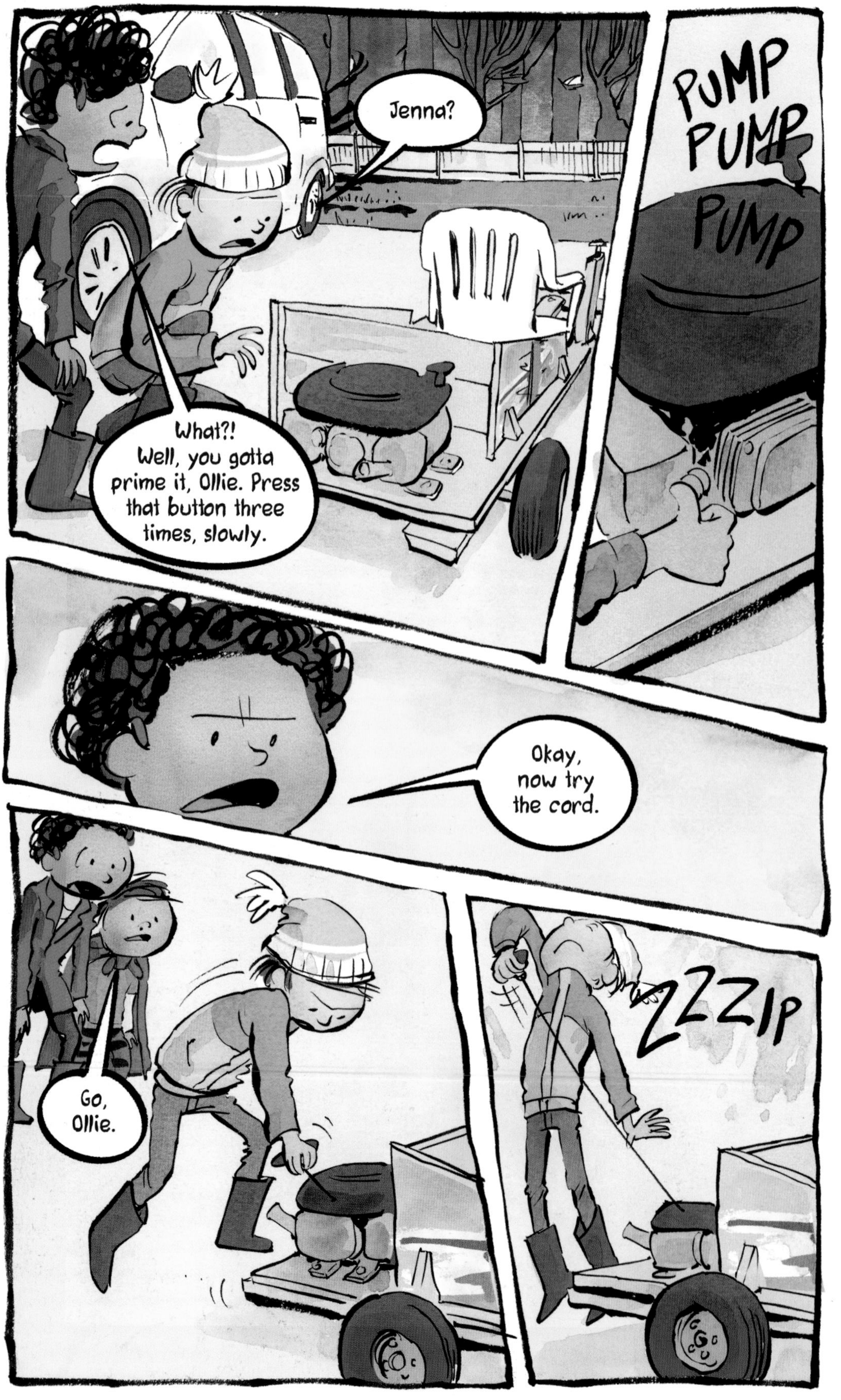
Jenna?
What?! Well, you gotta prime it, Ollie. Press that button three times, slowly.
PUMP PUMP PUMP
Okay, now try the cord.
Go, Ollie.
ZZZIP

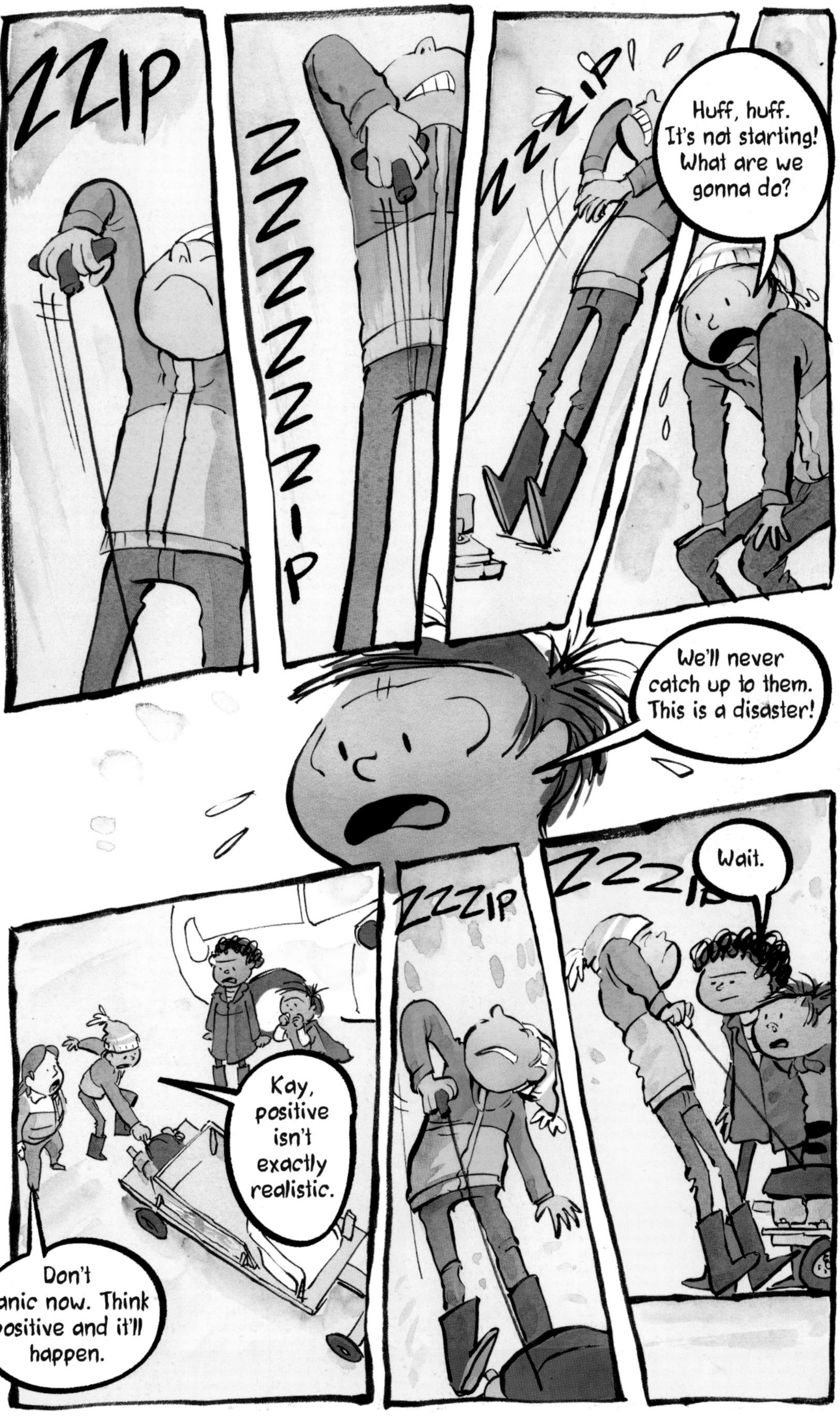
ZZIP
ZZZZZZZZIP
ZZZZIP
Huff, huff. It's not starting! What are we gonna do?
We'll never catch up to them. This is a disaster!
Don't panic now. Think positive and it'll happen.
Kay, positive isn't exactly realistic.
ZZZIP
ZZZZIP
Wait.

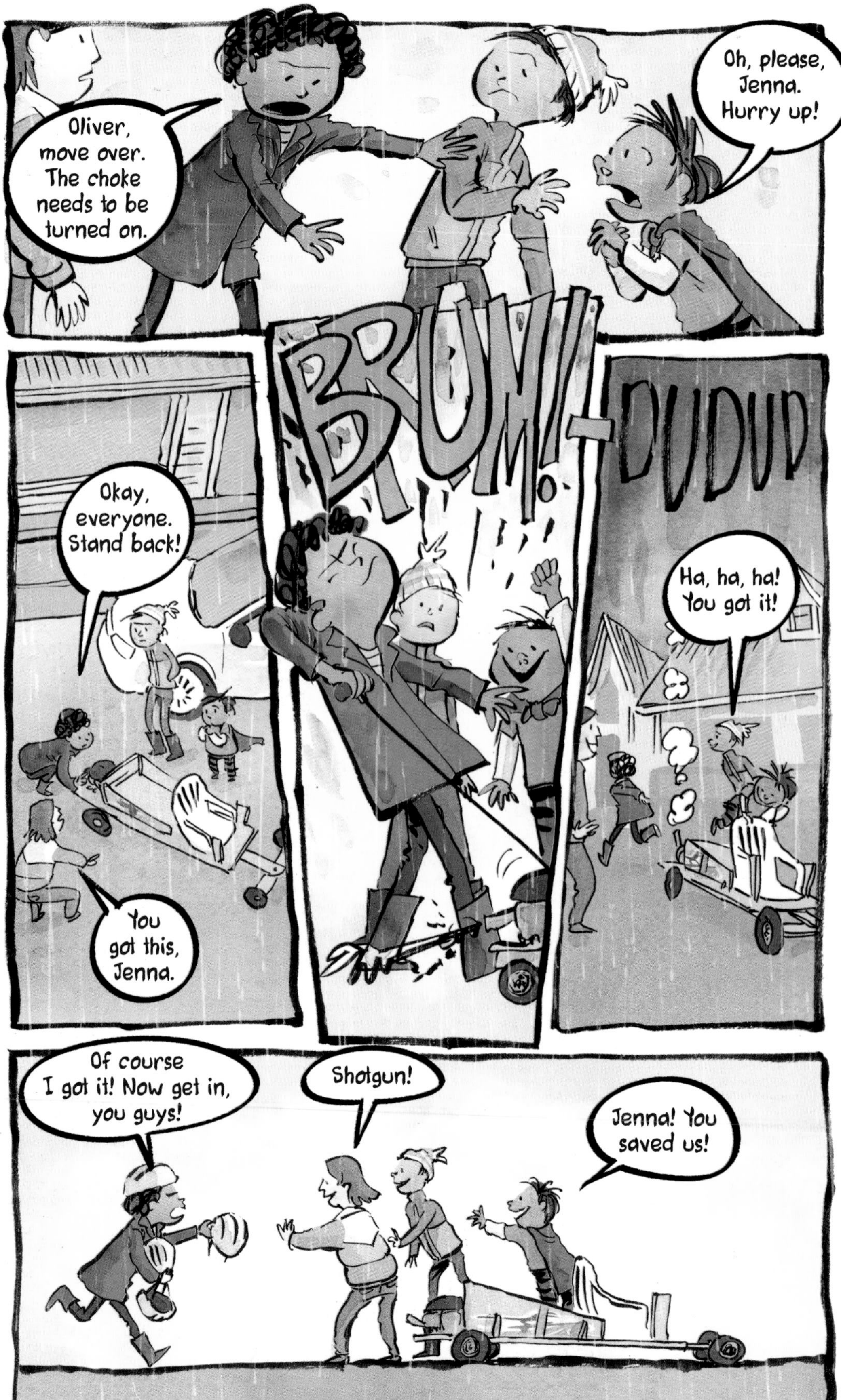
Oliver, move over. The choke needs to be turned on.
Oh, please, Jenna. Hurry up!
Okay, everyone. Stand back!
You got this, Jenna.
BRUM!!-DUDUD
Ha, ha, ha! You got it!
Of course I got it! Now get in, you guys!
Shotgun!
Jenna! You saved us!

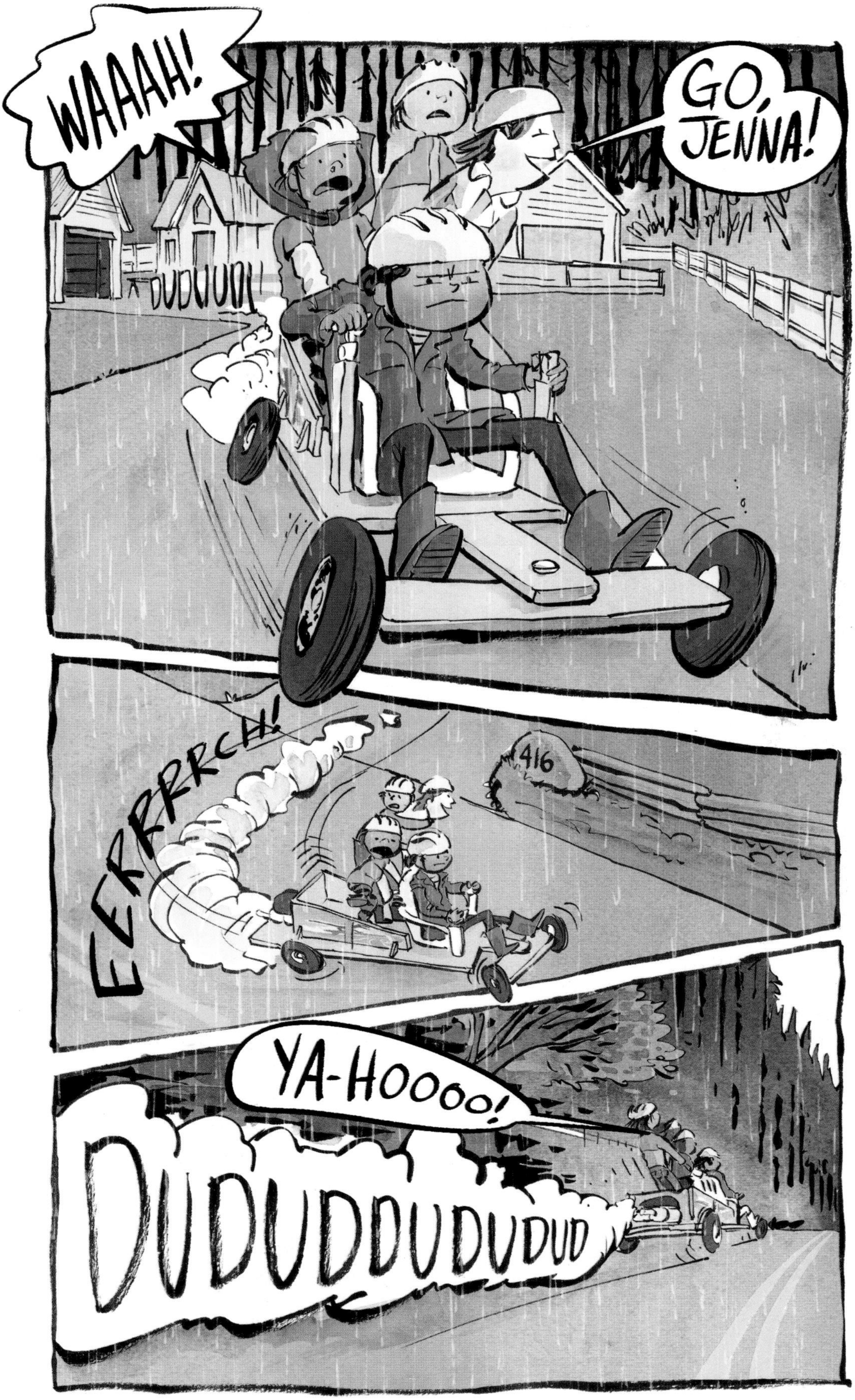
WAAAH!
GO, JENNA!
DUDUUUD
ERRRRCH!
416
YA-HOOOO!
DUDUDDUDUDUD

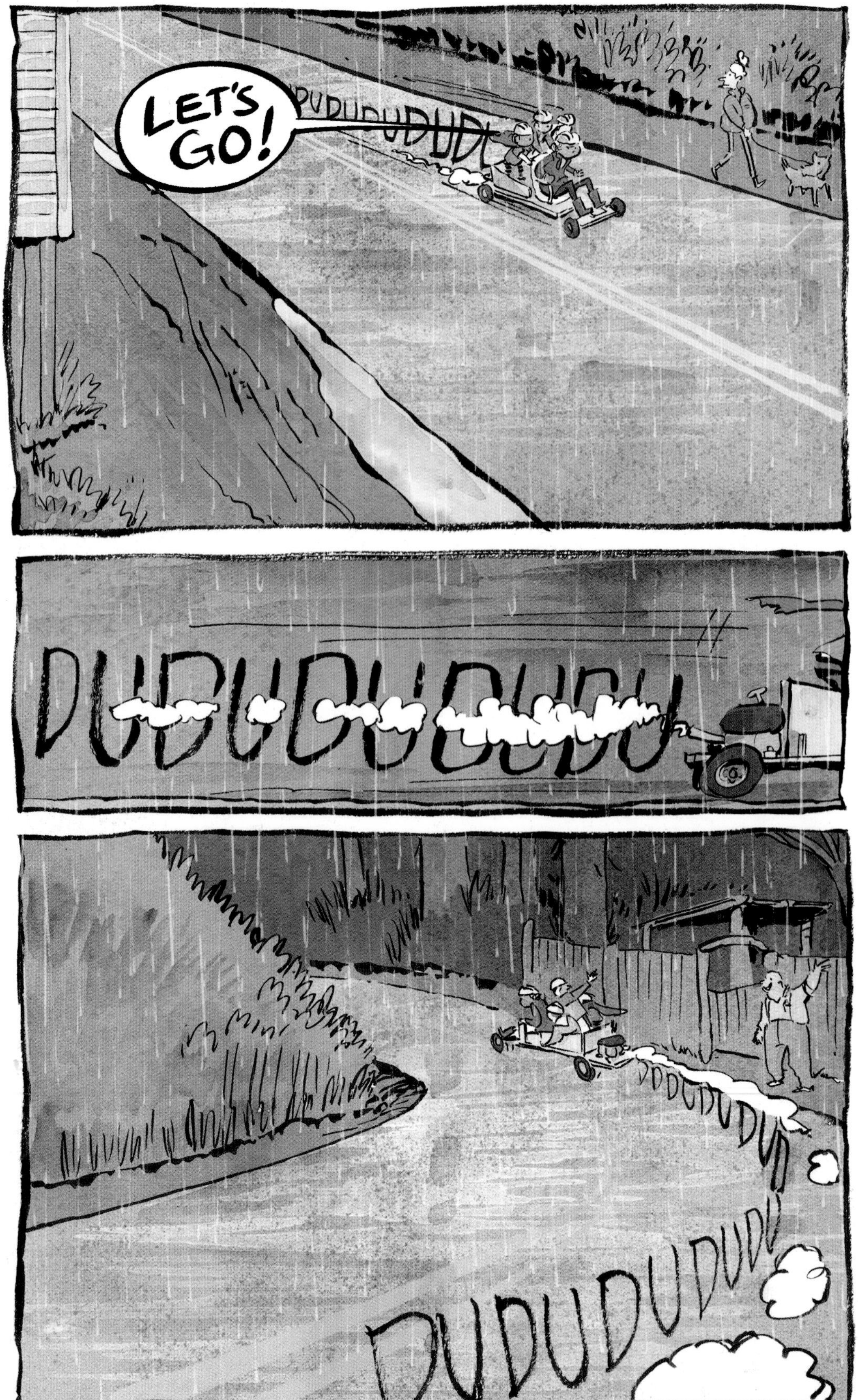
LET'S GO!
DUDUDUDUDUDU
DUDUDUDUDUDU
DUDUDUDUDUDU
DUDUDUDUDU

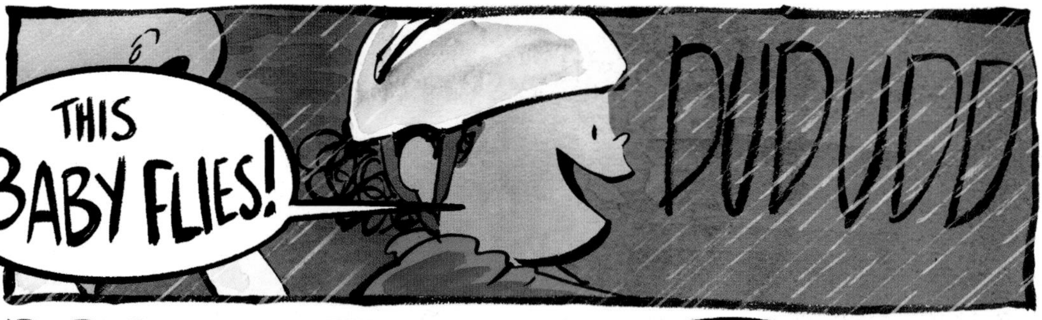
THIS BABY FLIES!
DUDUDD

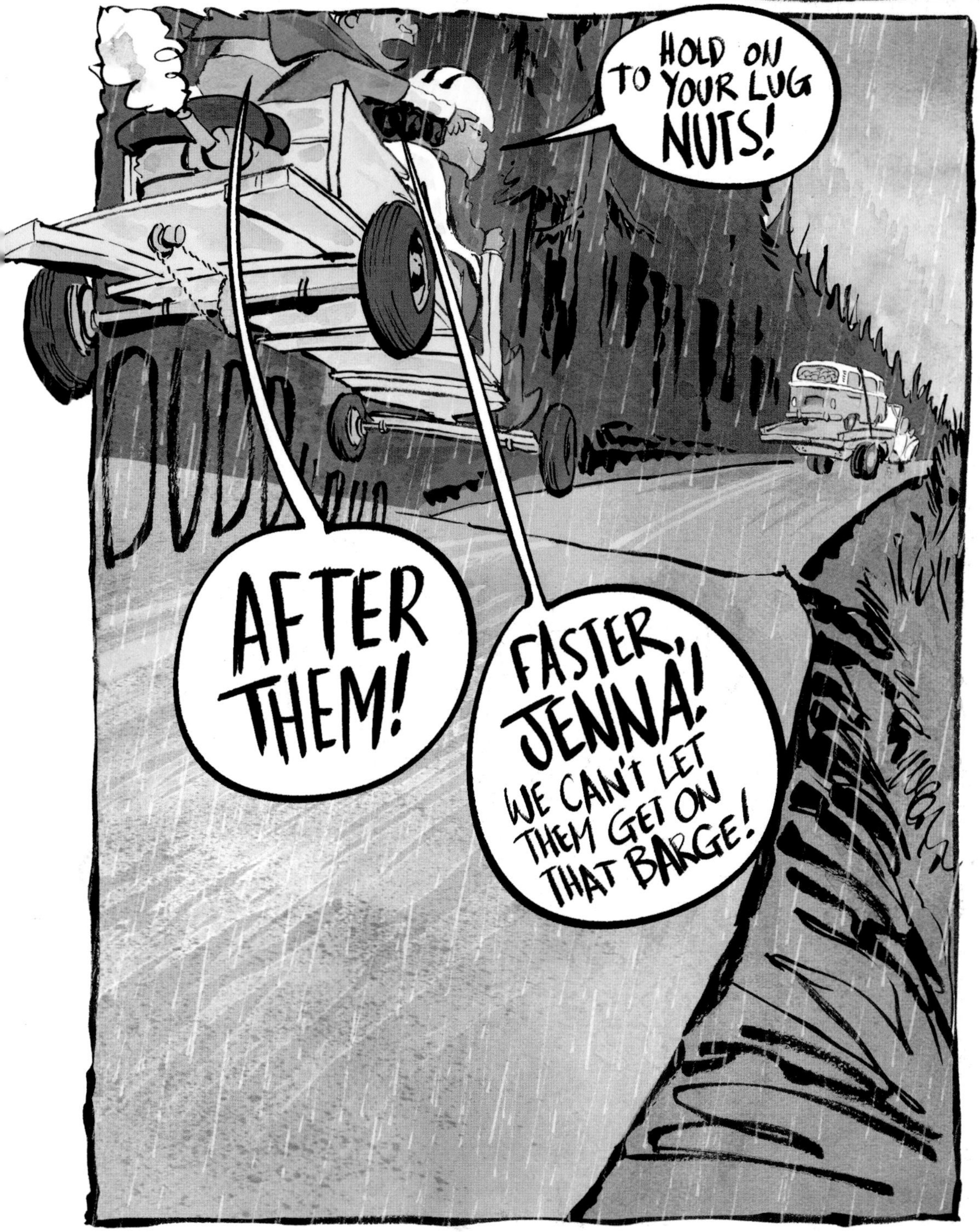
HOLD ON TO YOUR LUG NUTS!
DUDD DUDD DUD
AFTER THEM!
FASTER, JENNA! WE CAN'T LET THEM GET ON THAT BARGE!

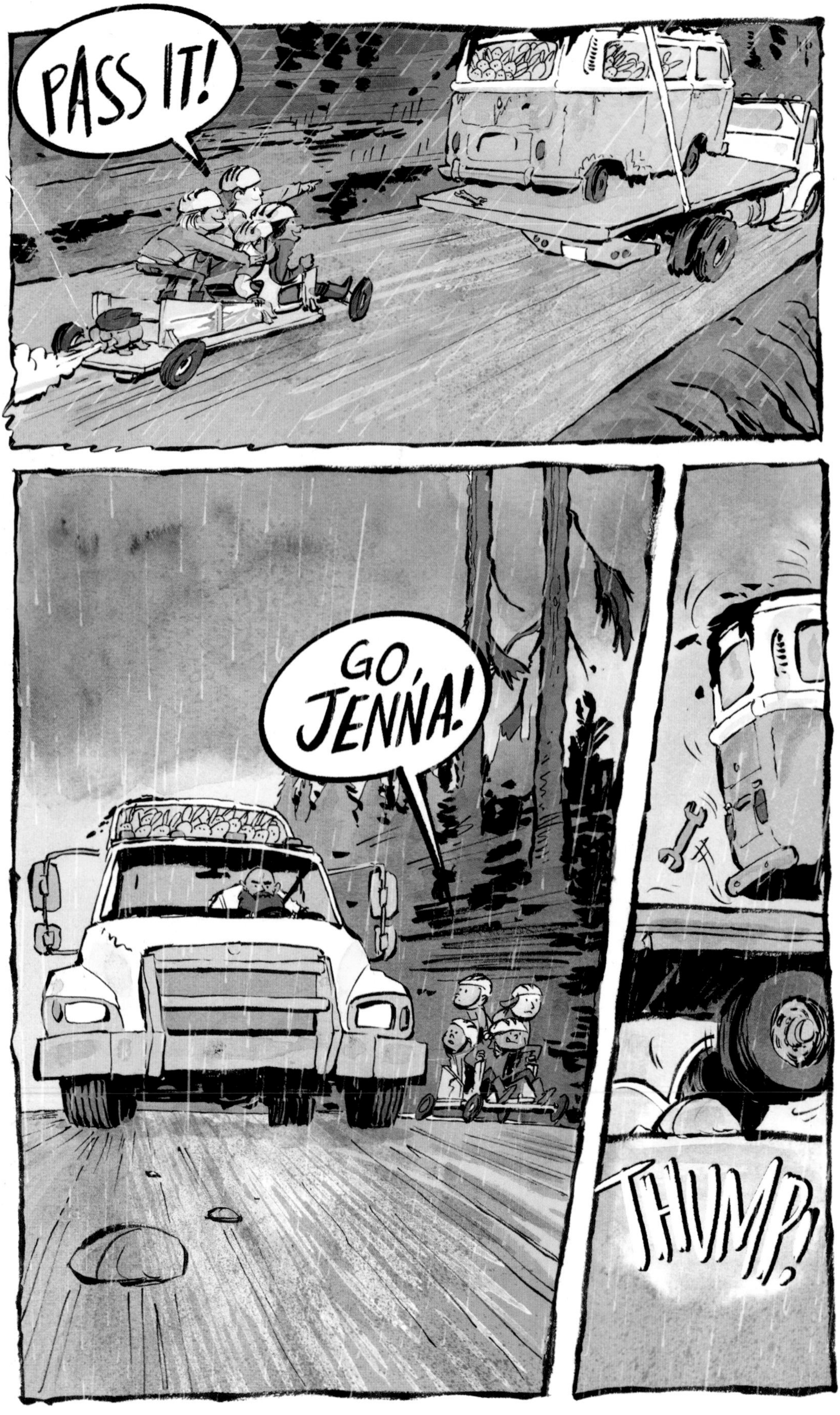
PASS IT!
GO, JENNA!
THUMP!

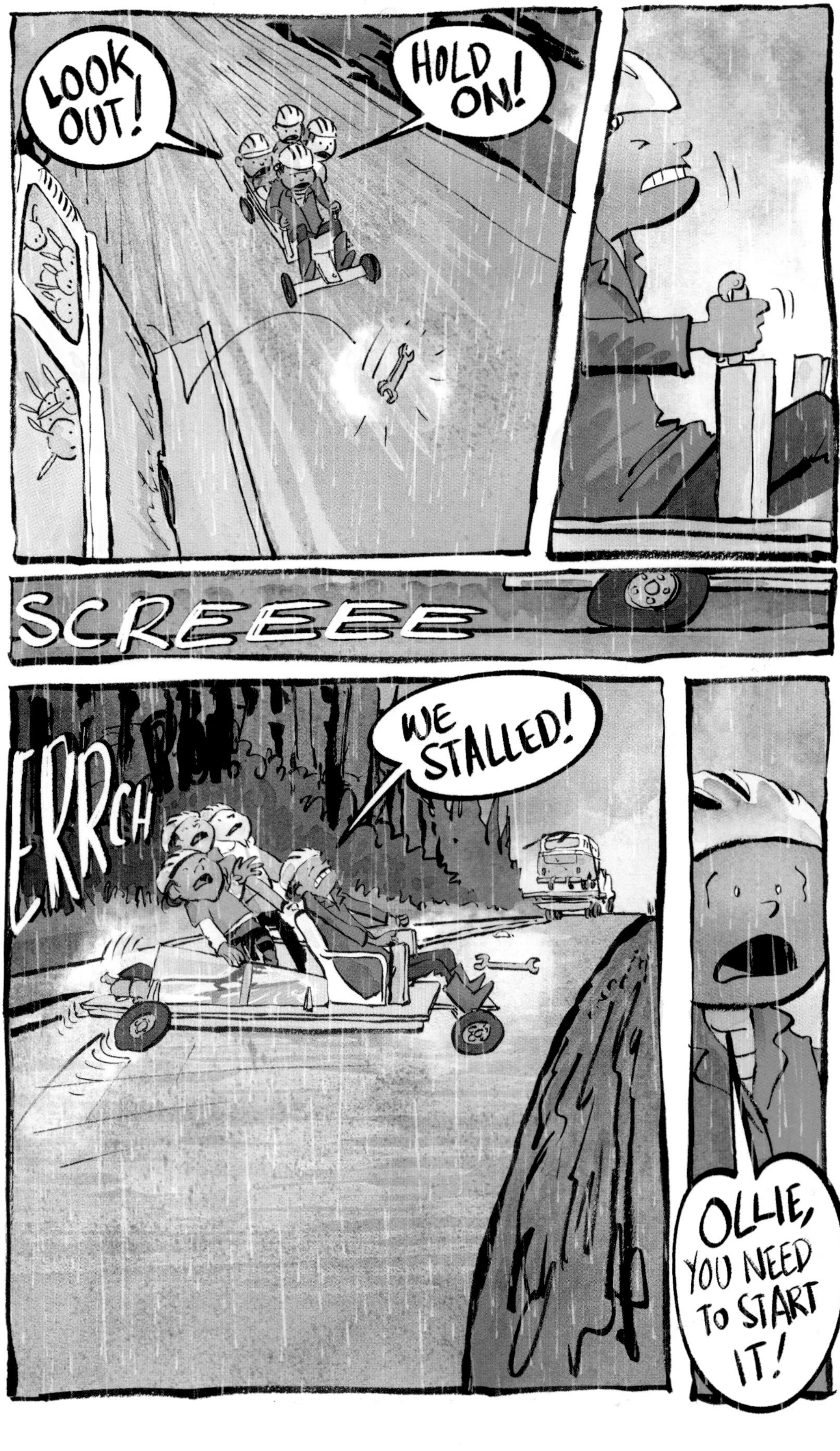
LOOK OUT!
HOLD ON!
SCREEEE
ERRCH
WE STALLED!
OLLIE, YOU NEED TO START IT!

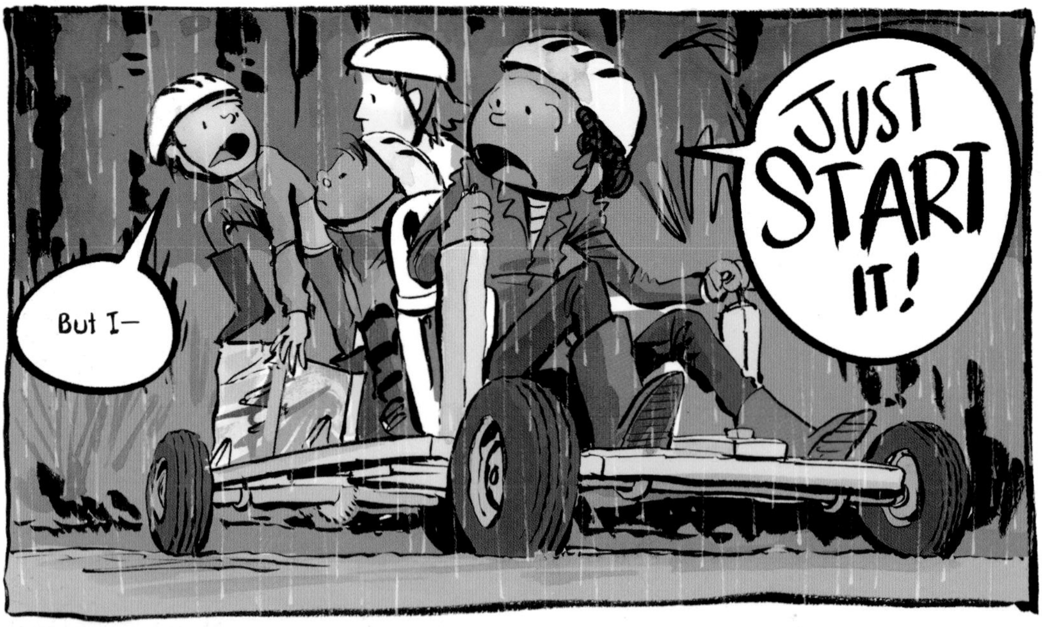
But I—
JUST START IT!

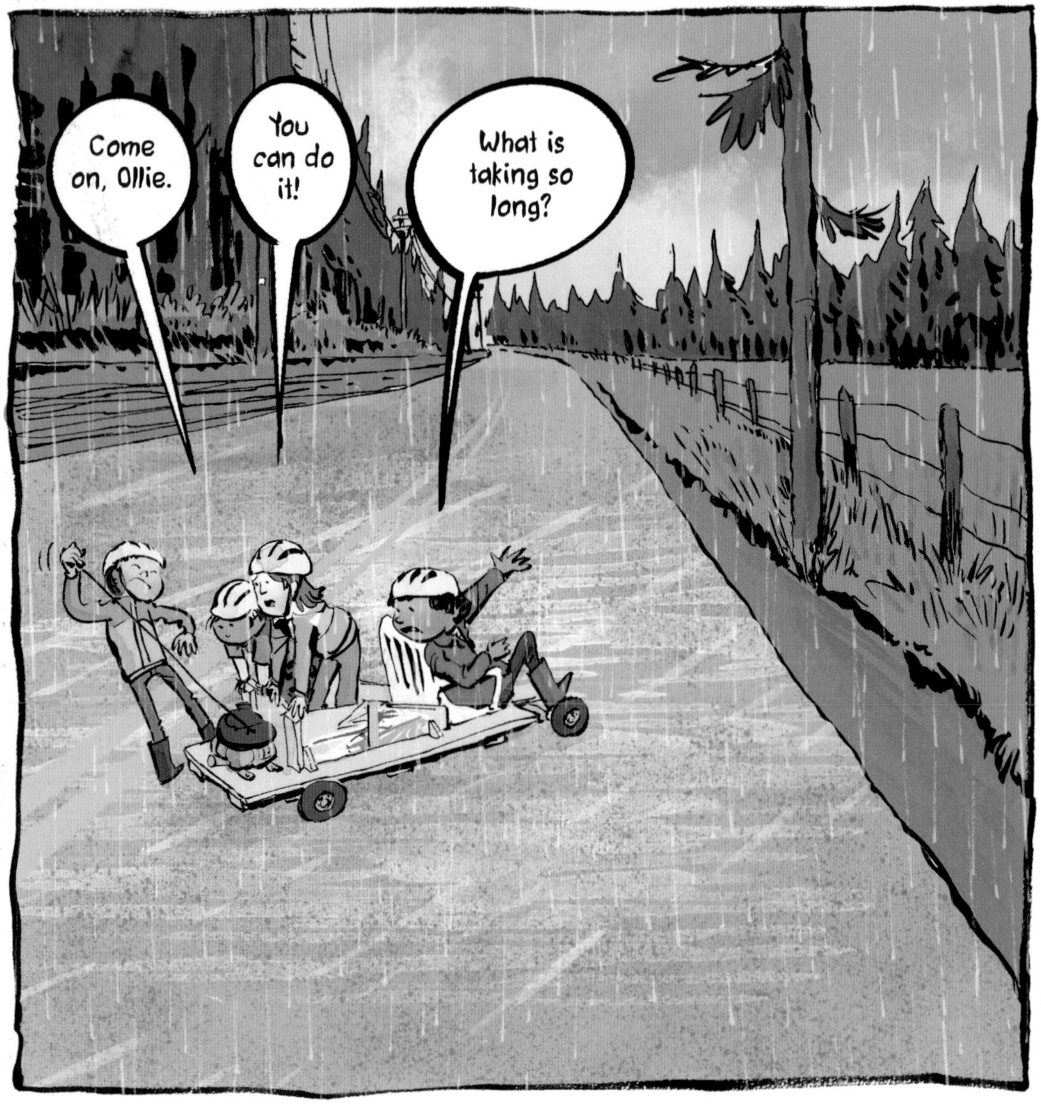
Come on, Ollie.
You can do it!
What is taking so long?

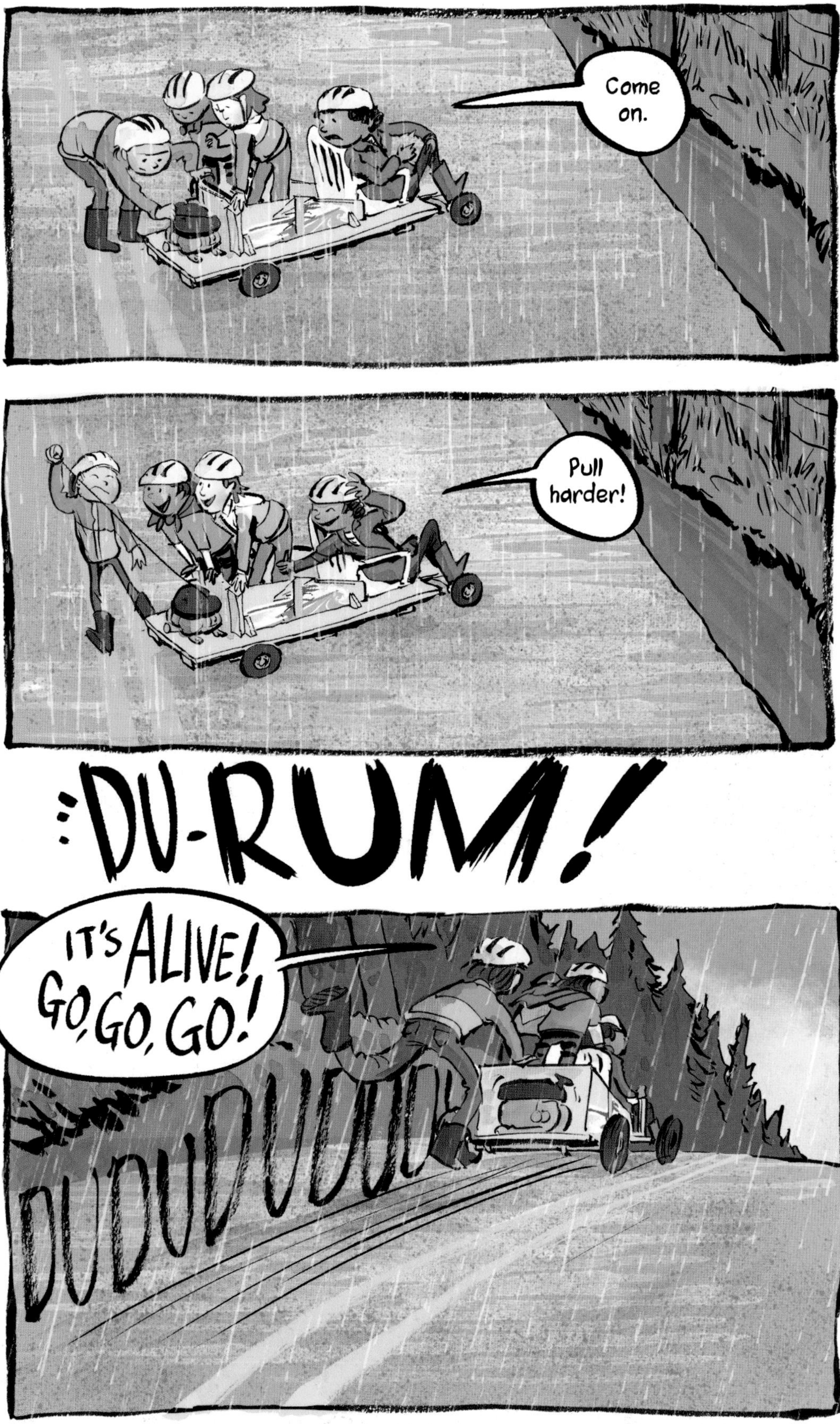
Come on.
Pull harder!
DU-RUM!
IT'S ALIVE! GO, GO, GO!
DUDUDUDUDU

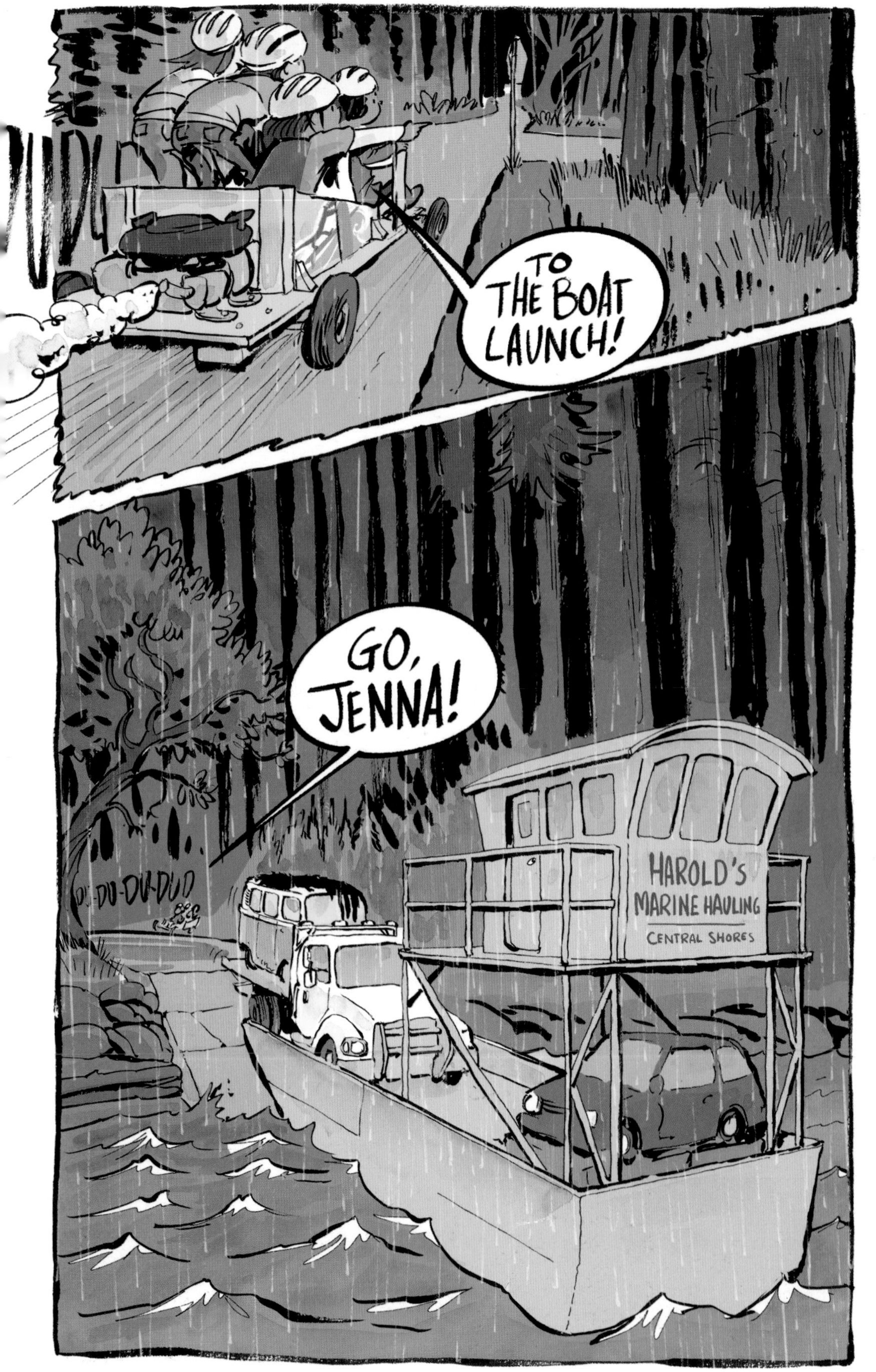
TO THE BOAT LAUNCH!
GO, JENNA!
DU-DU-DU-DUD
HAROLD'S
MARINE HAULING
CENTRAL SHORES

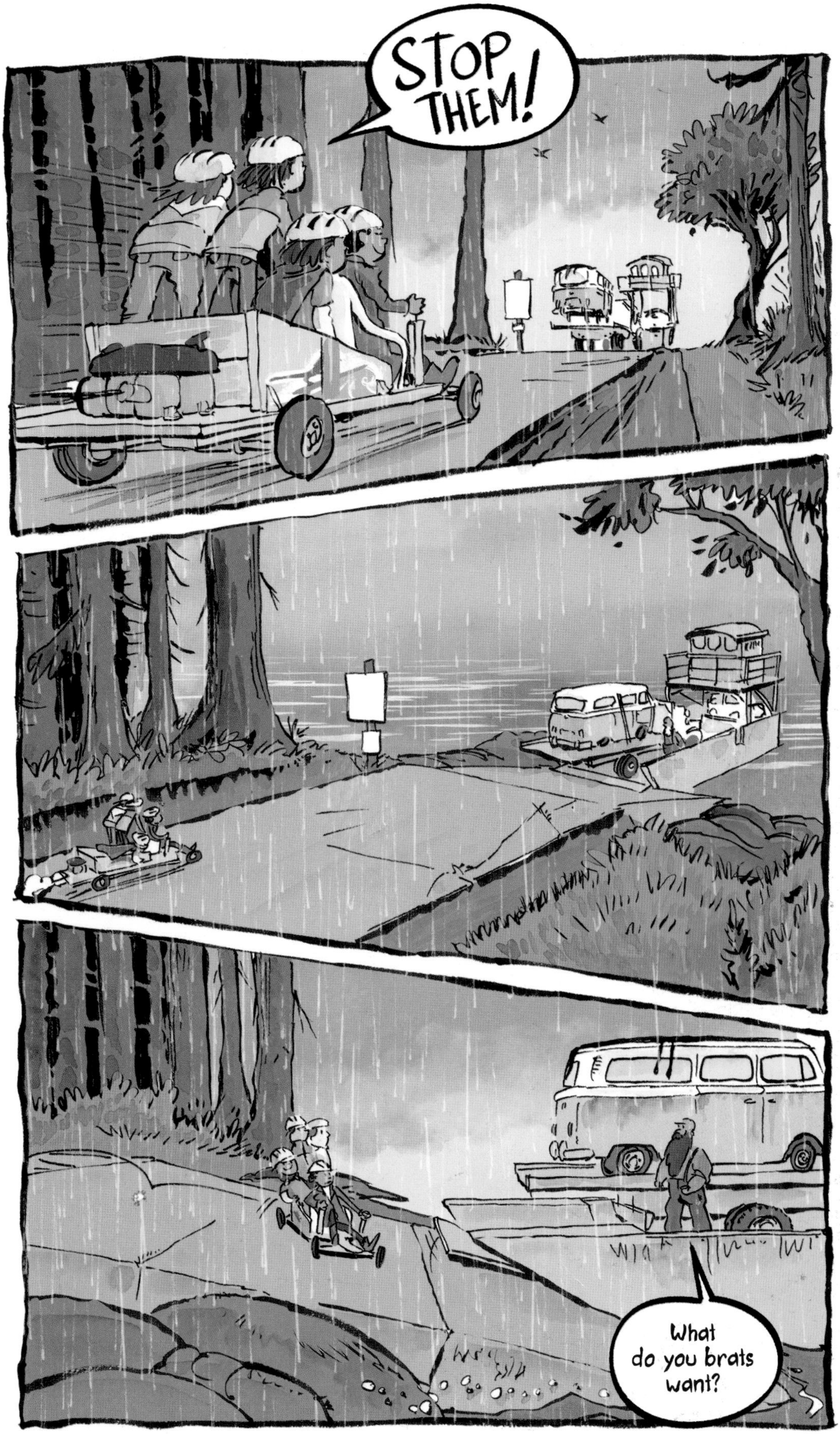
STOP THEM!
What do you brats want?

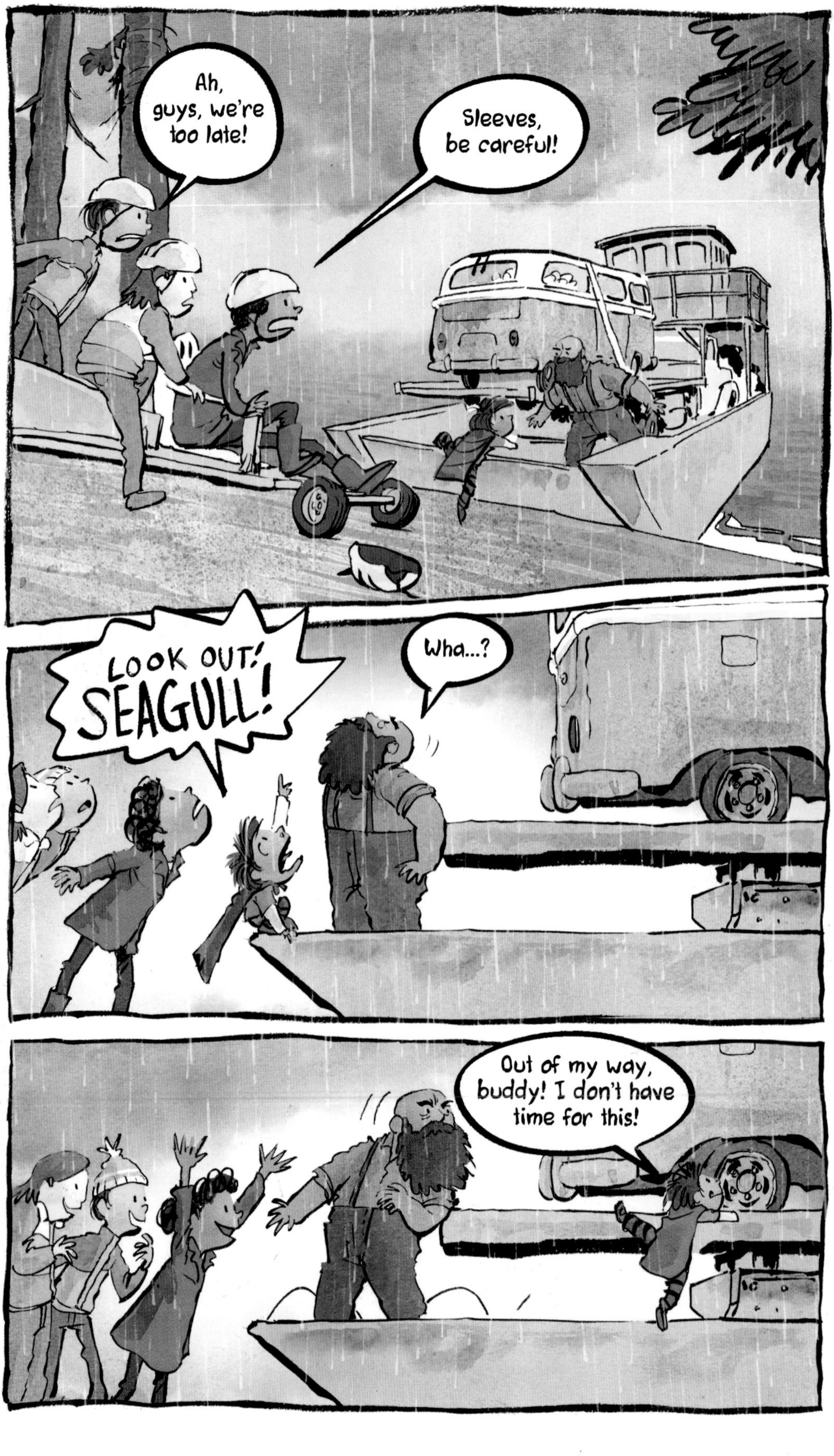
Ah, guys, we're too late!
Sleeves, be careful!
LOOK OUT! SEAGULL!
Wha...?
Out of my way, buddy! I don't have time for this!

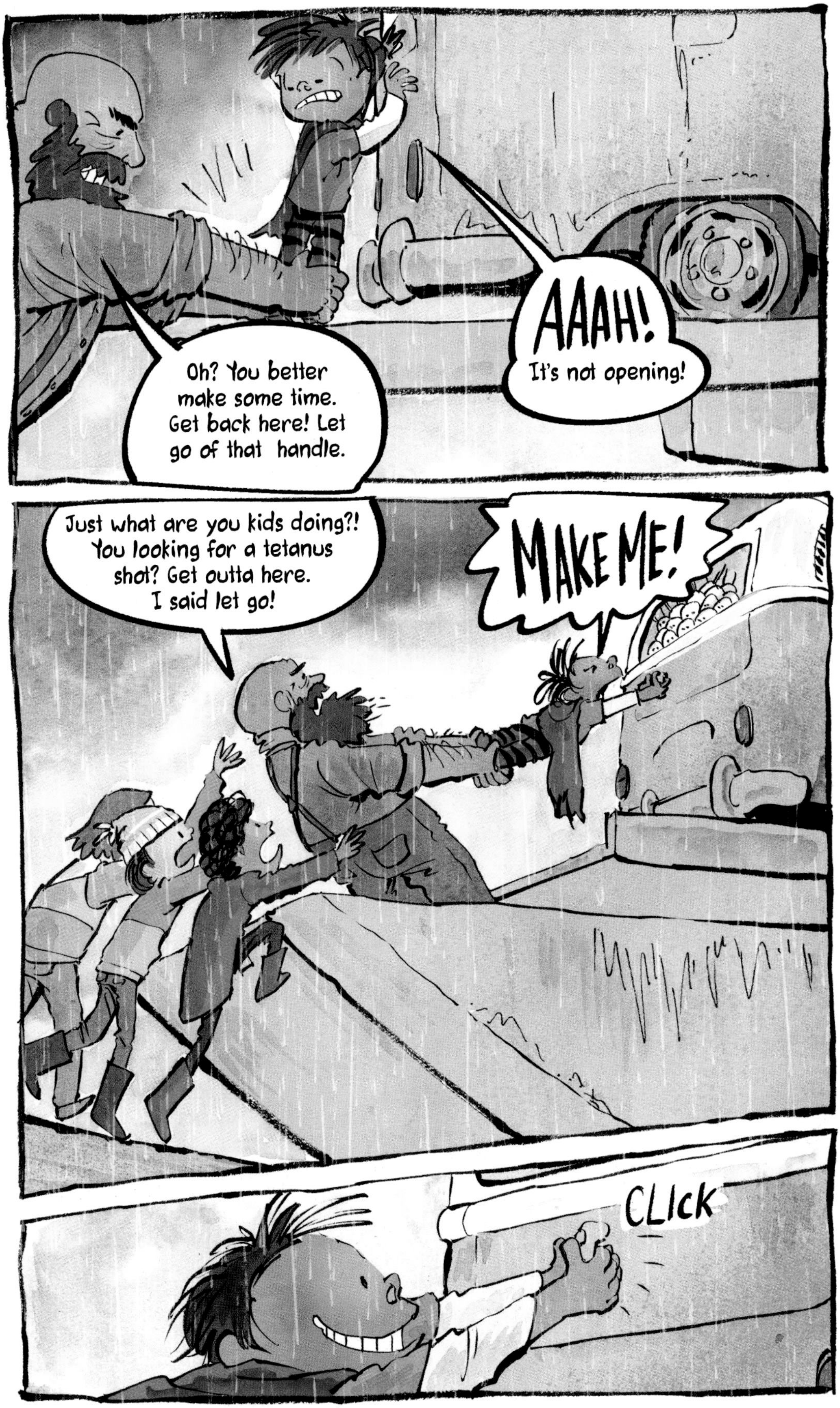

Oh? You better make some time. Get back here! Let go of that handle.
AAAH! It's not opening!
Just what are you kids doing?! You looking for a tetanus shot? Get outta here. I said let go!
MAKE ME!
CLICK

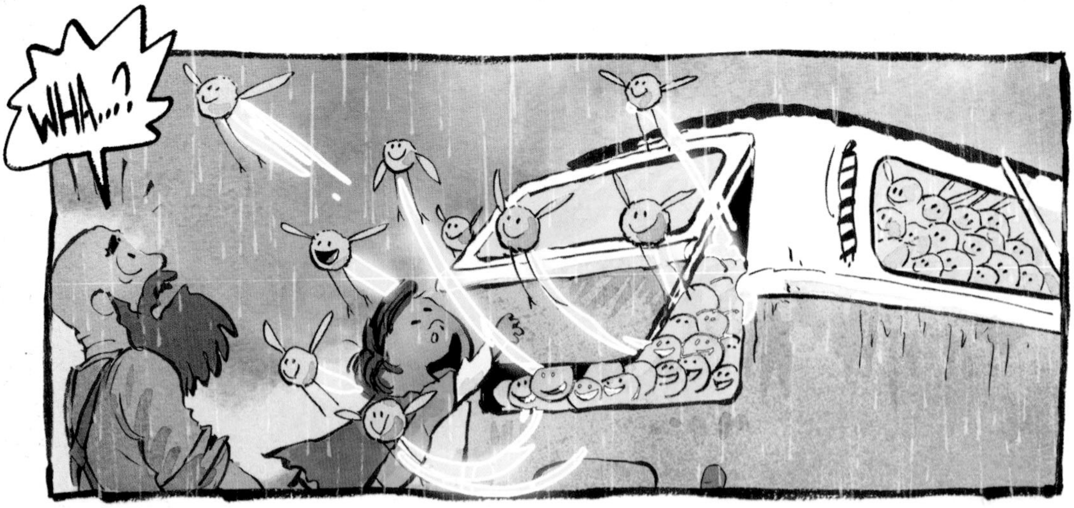
WHA...?

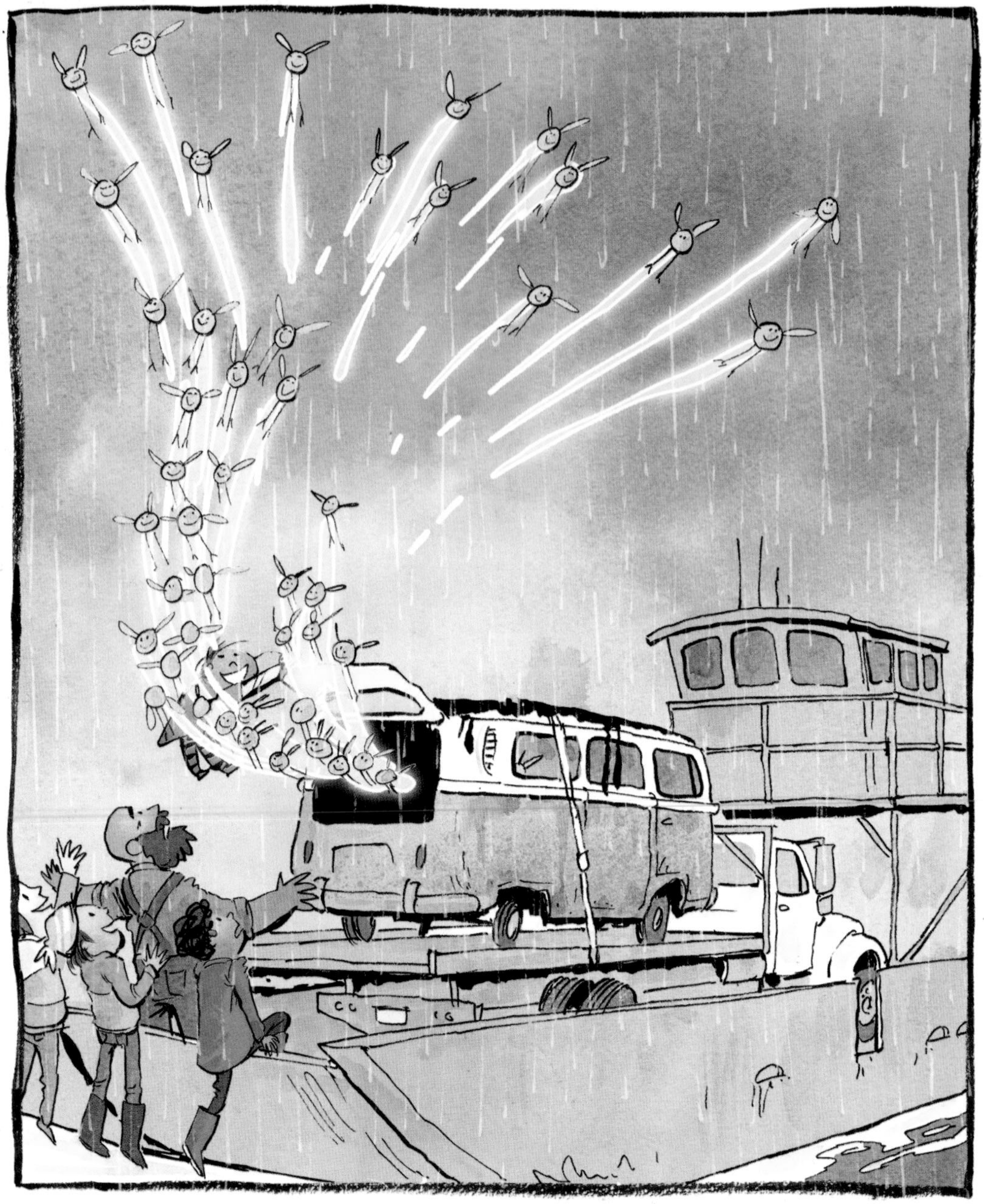

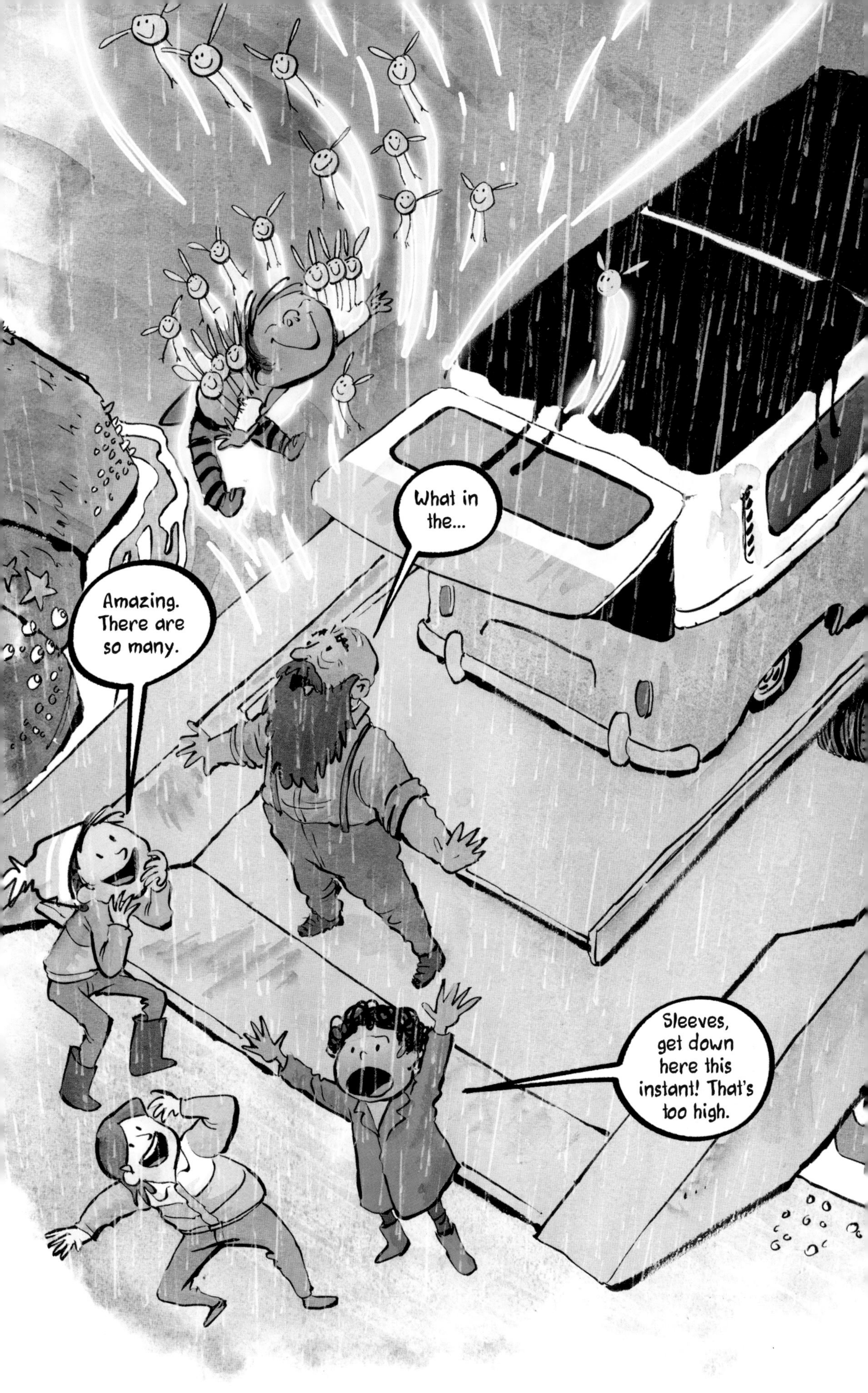
What in the...
Amazing. There are so many.
Sleeves, get down here this instant! That's too high.

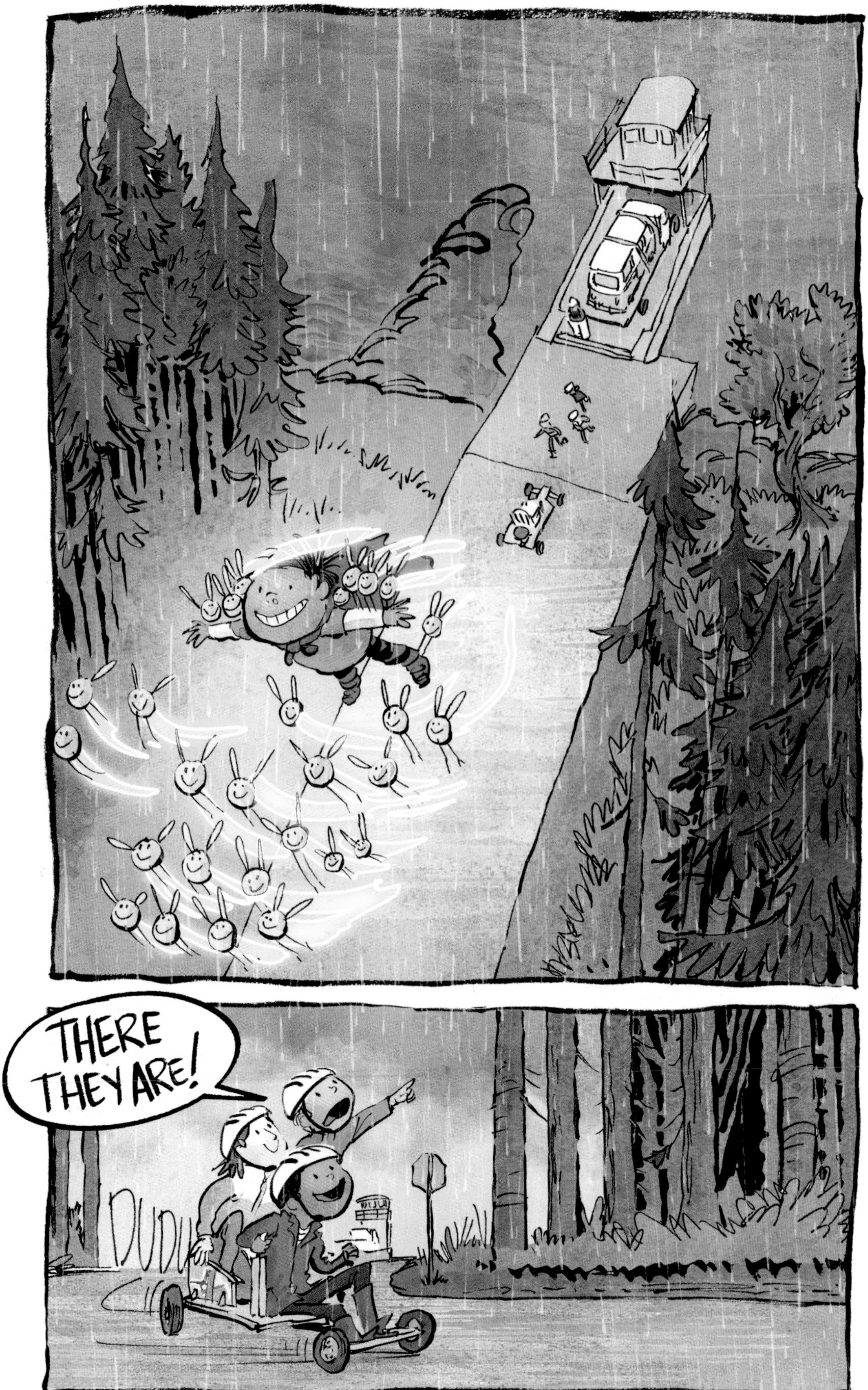
THERE THEY ARE!
DUDU

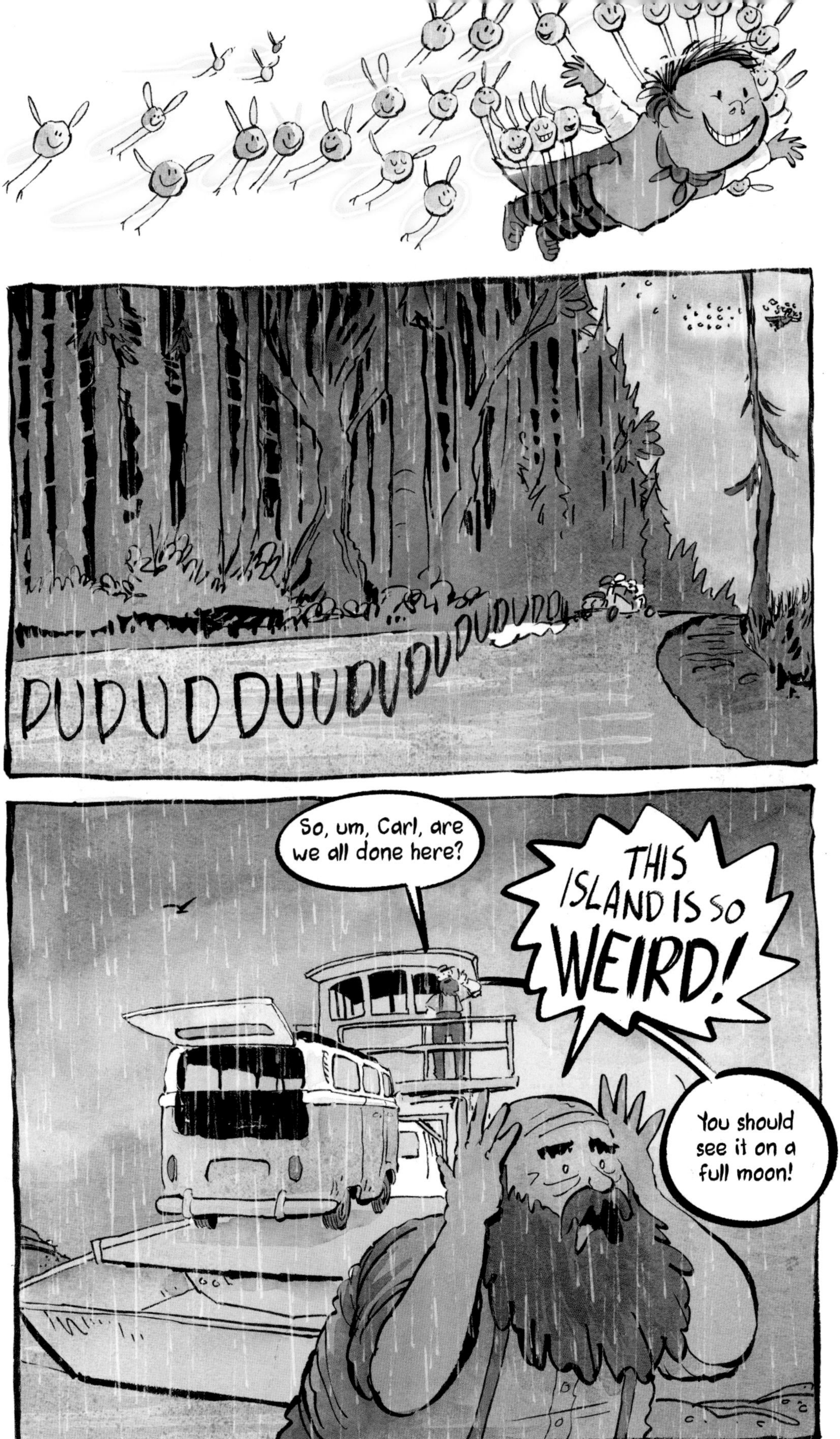
DUDUDDUUDUDUDUDUDD
So, um, Carl, are we all done here?
THIS ISLAND IS SO WEIRD!
You should see it on a full moon!

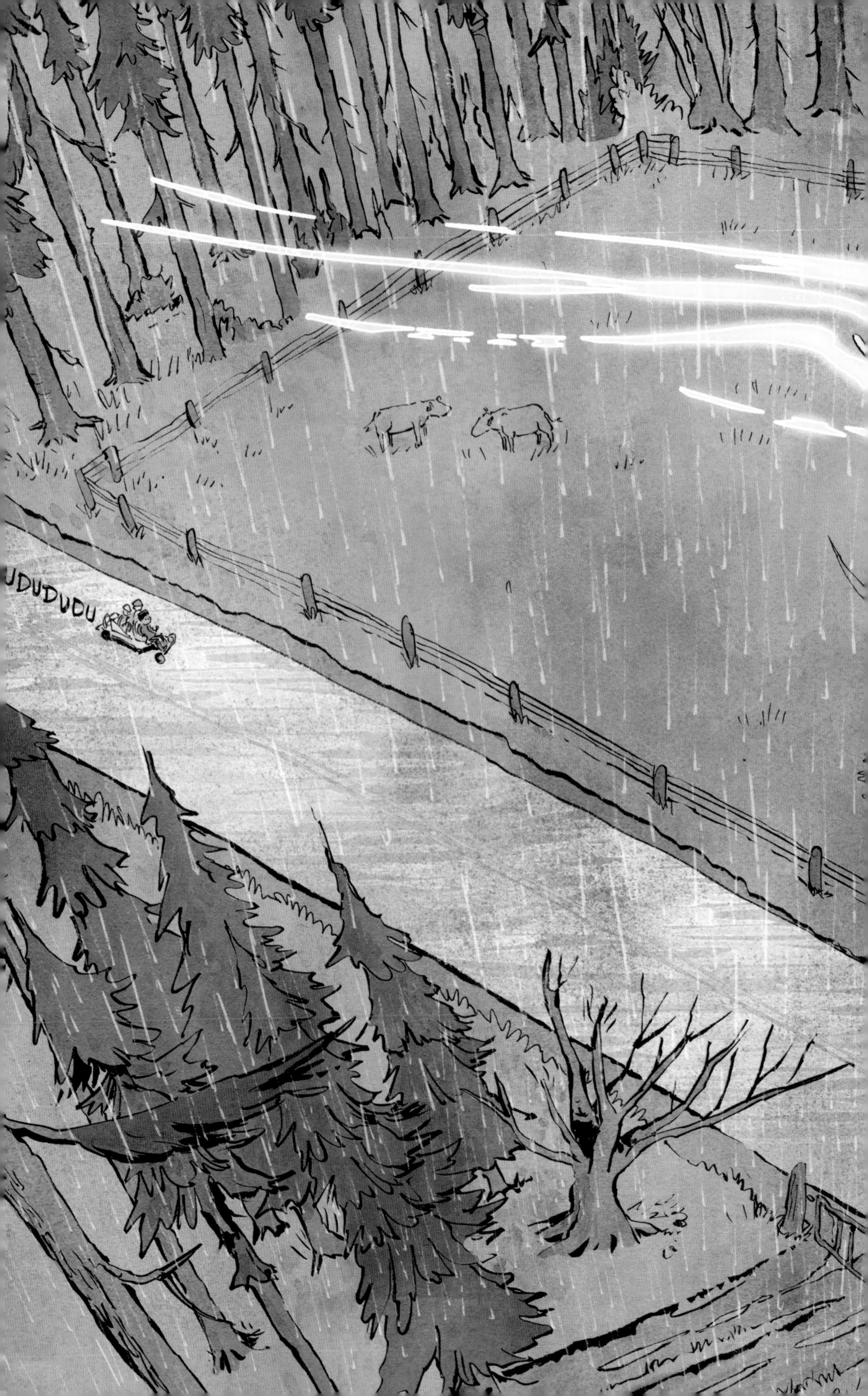
UDUDUDUDU

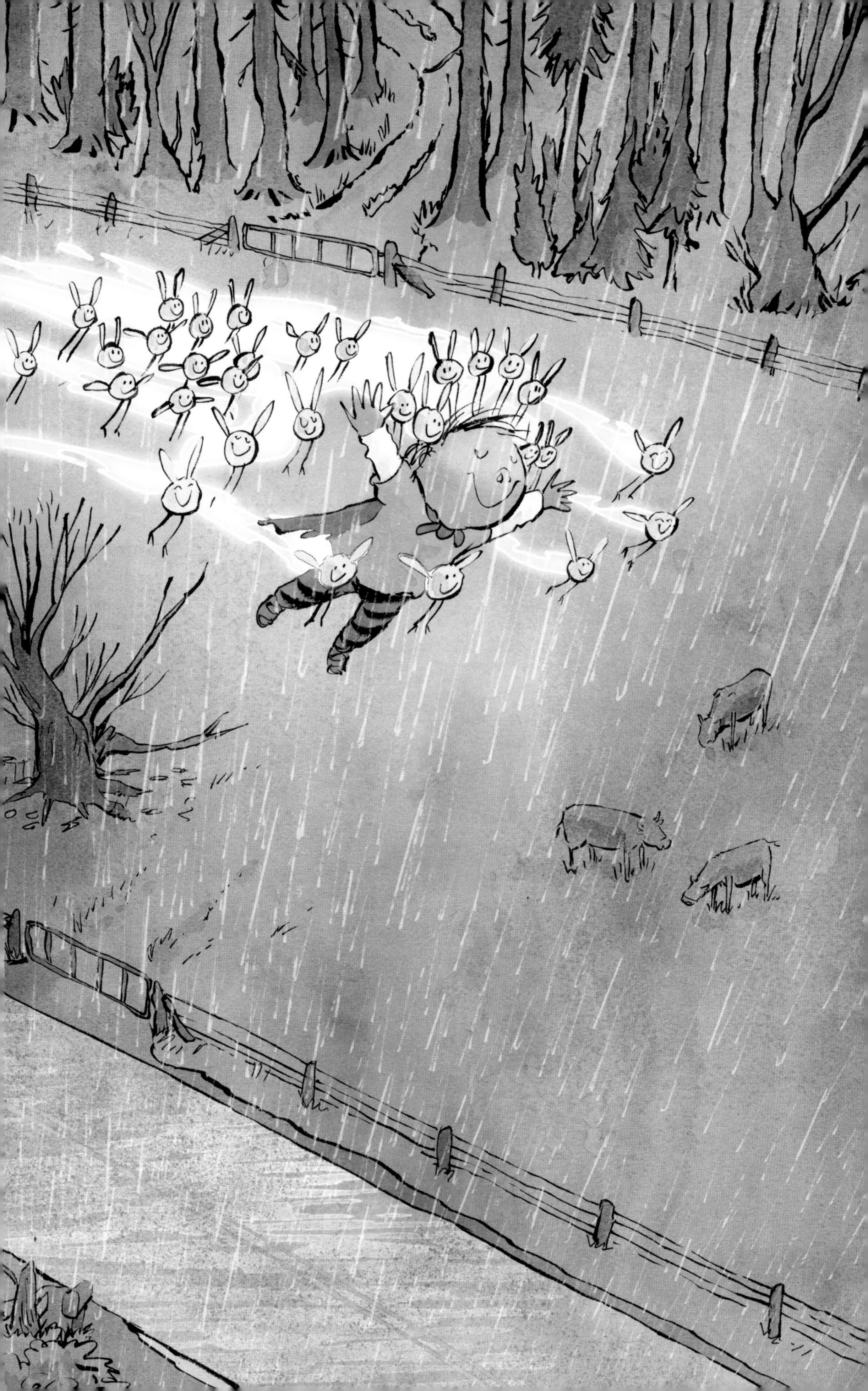

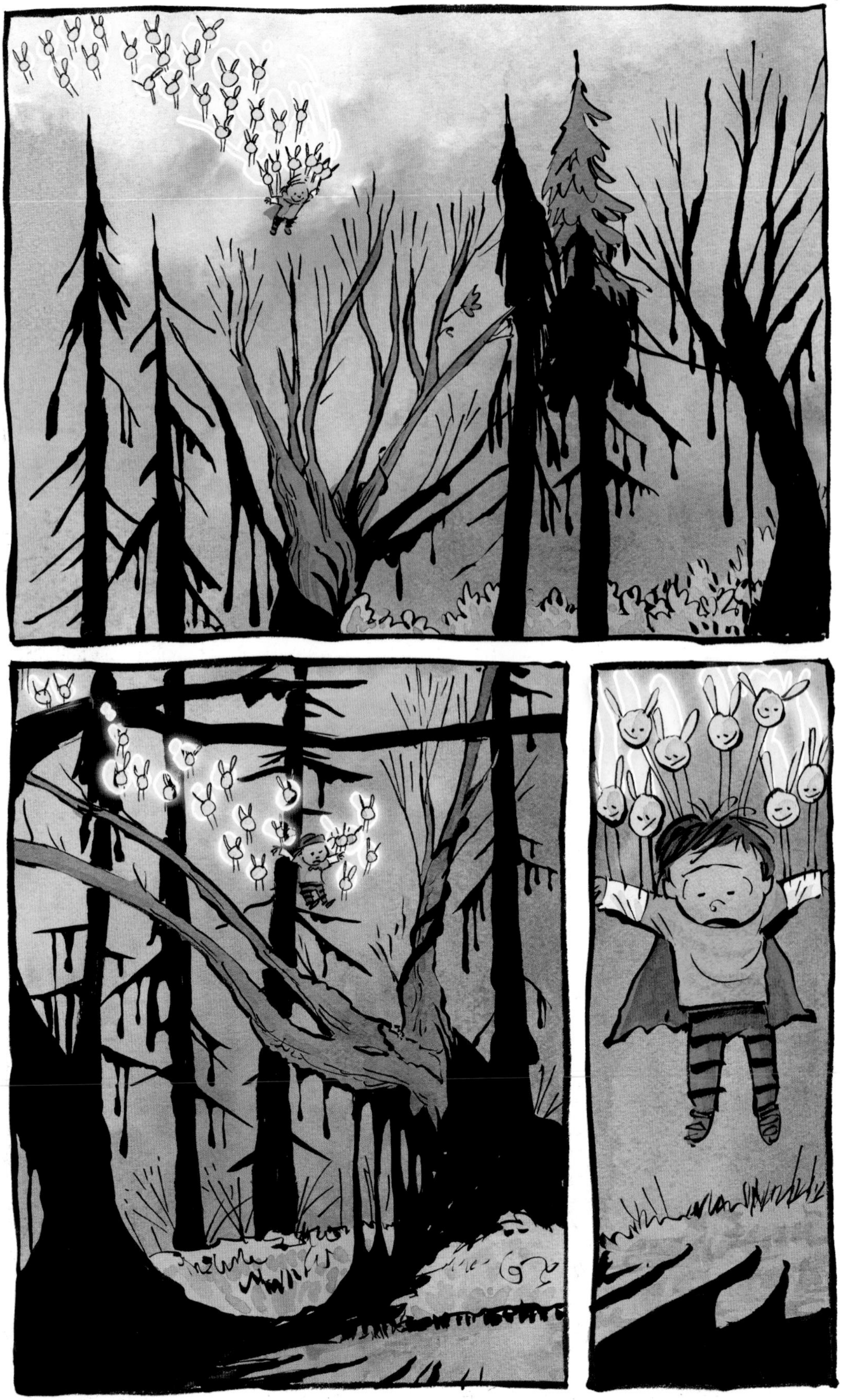

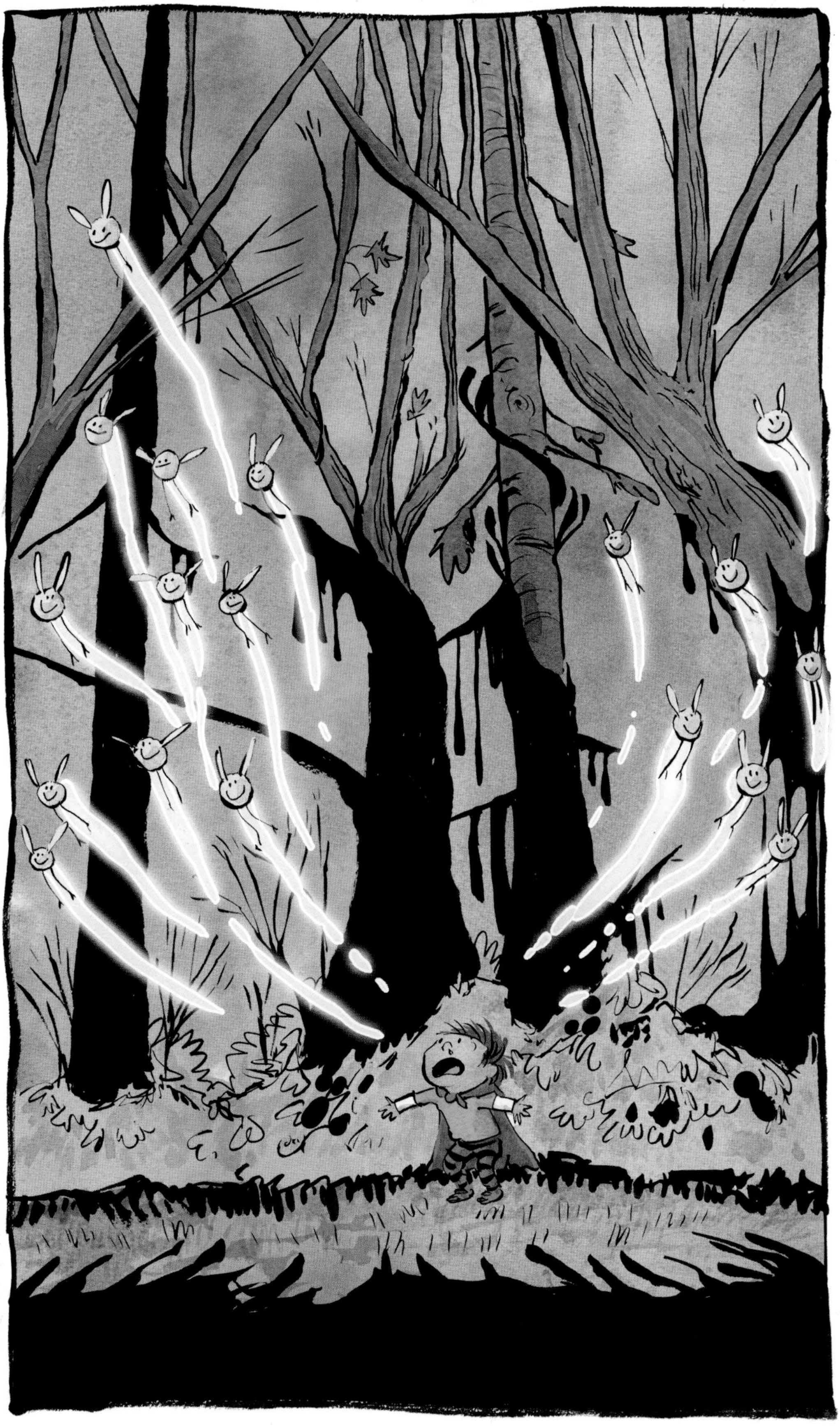

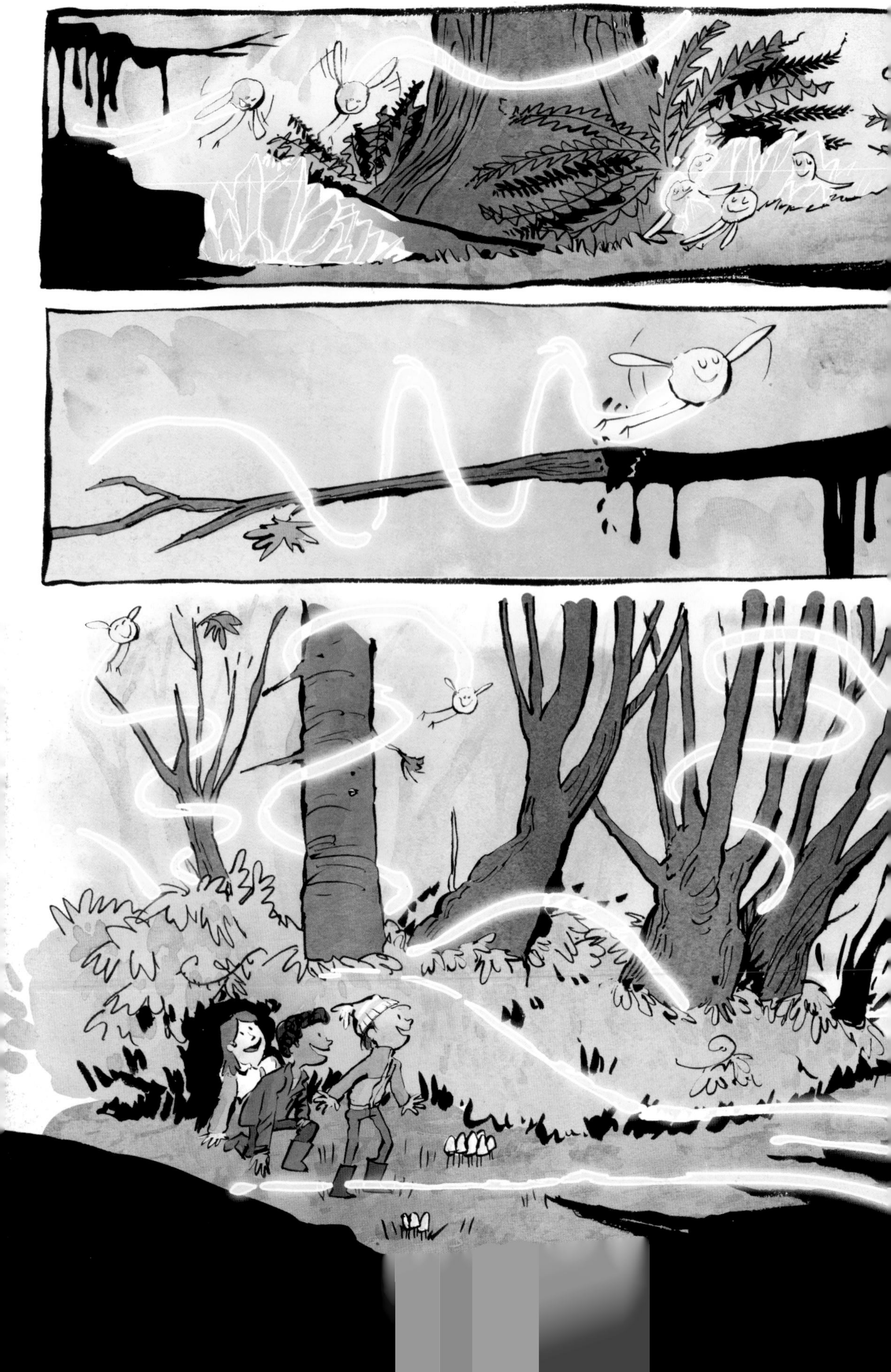

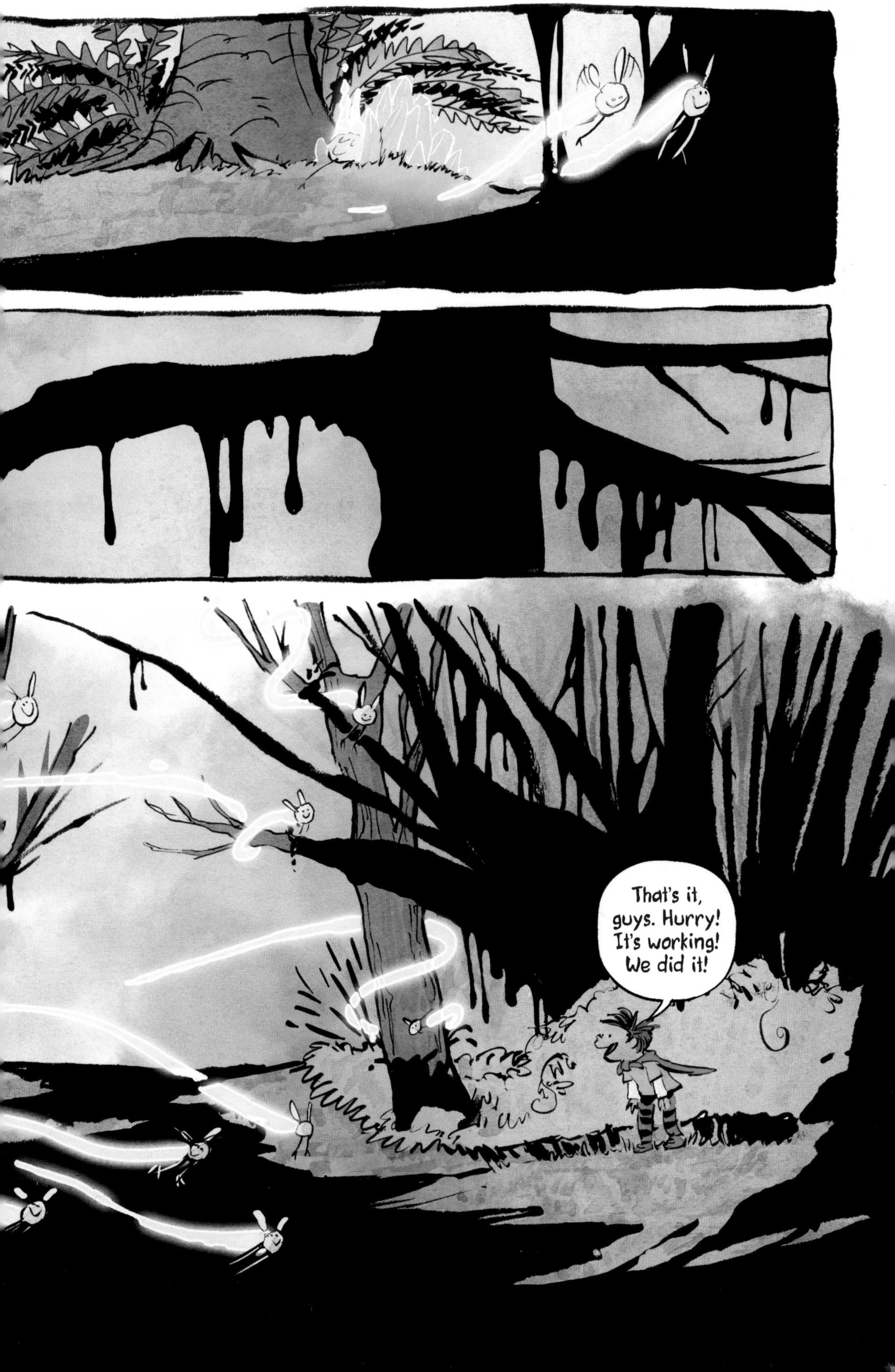
That's it, guys. Hurry! It's working! We did it!

CHAPTER SIX

All's Fair at the Fair

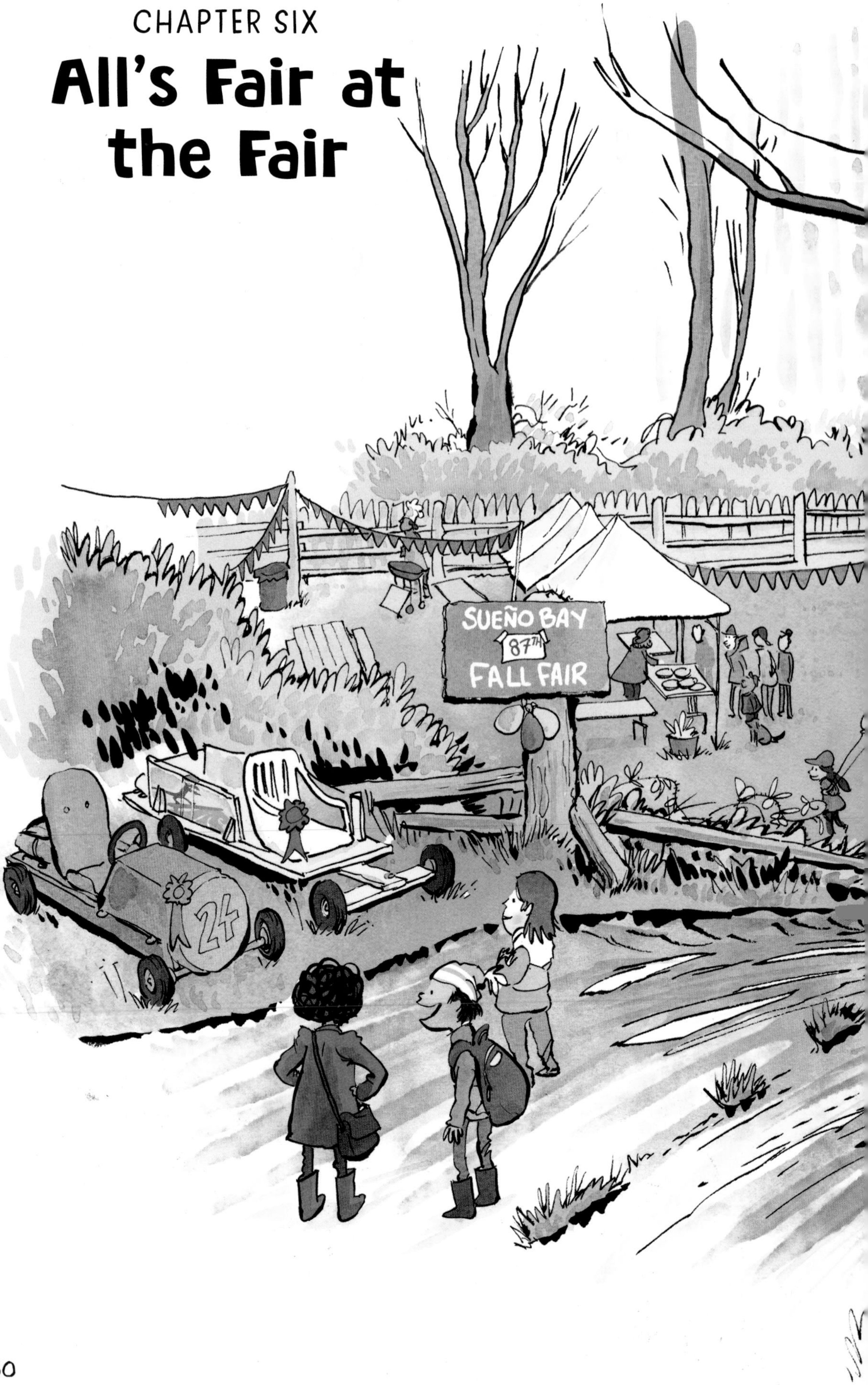
SUEÑO BAY
87TH
FALL FAIR
24

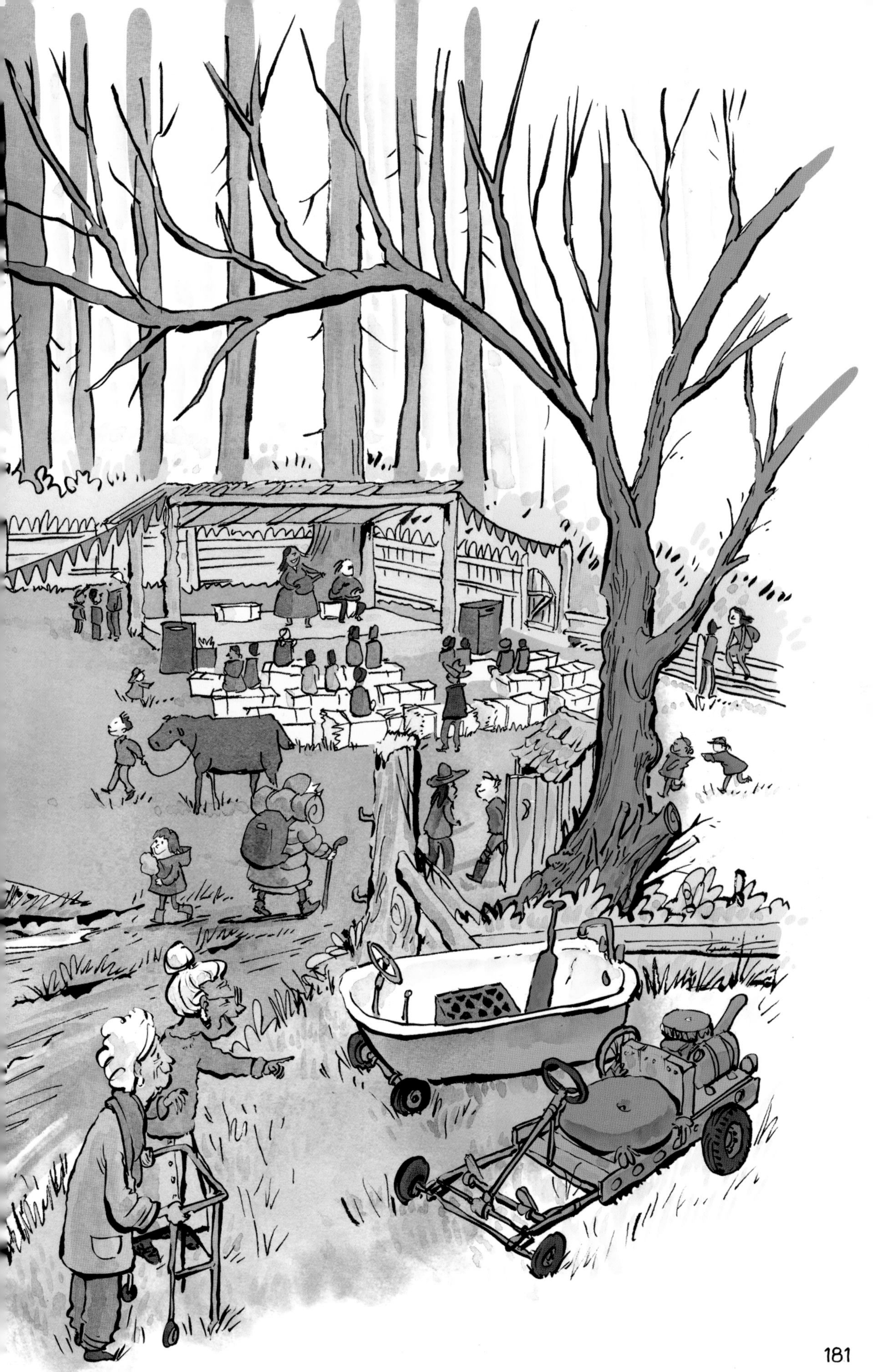

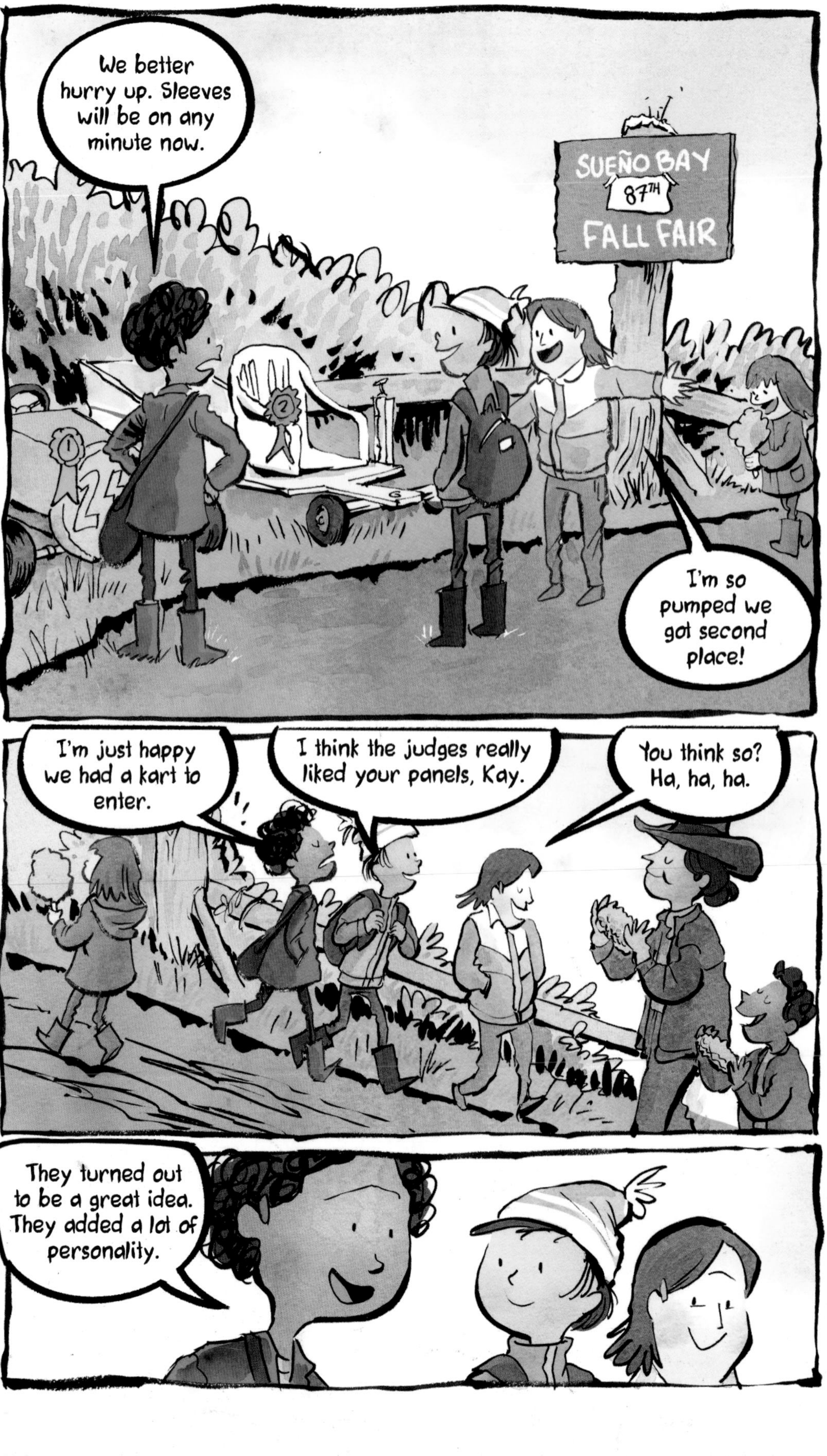
We better hurry up. Sleeves will be on any minute now.
SUEÑO BAY 87TH FALL FAIR
I'm so pumped we got second place!
I'm just happy we had a kart to enter.
I think the judges really liked your panels, Kay.
You think so? Ha, ha, ha.
They turned out to be a great idea. They added a lot of personality.

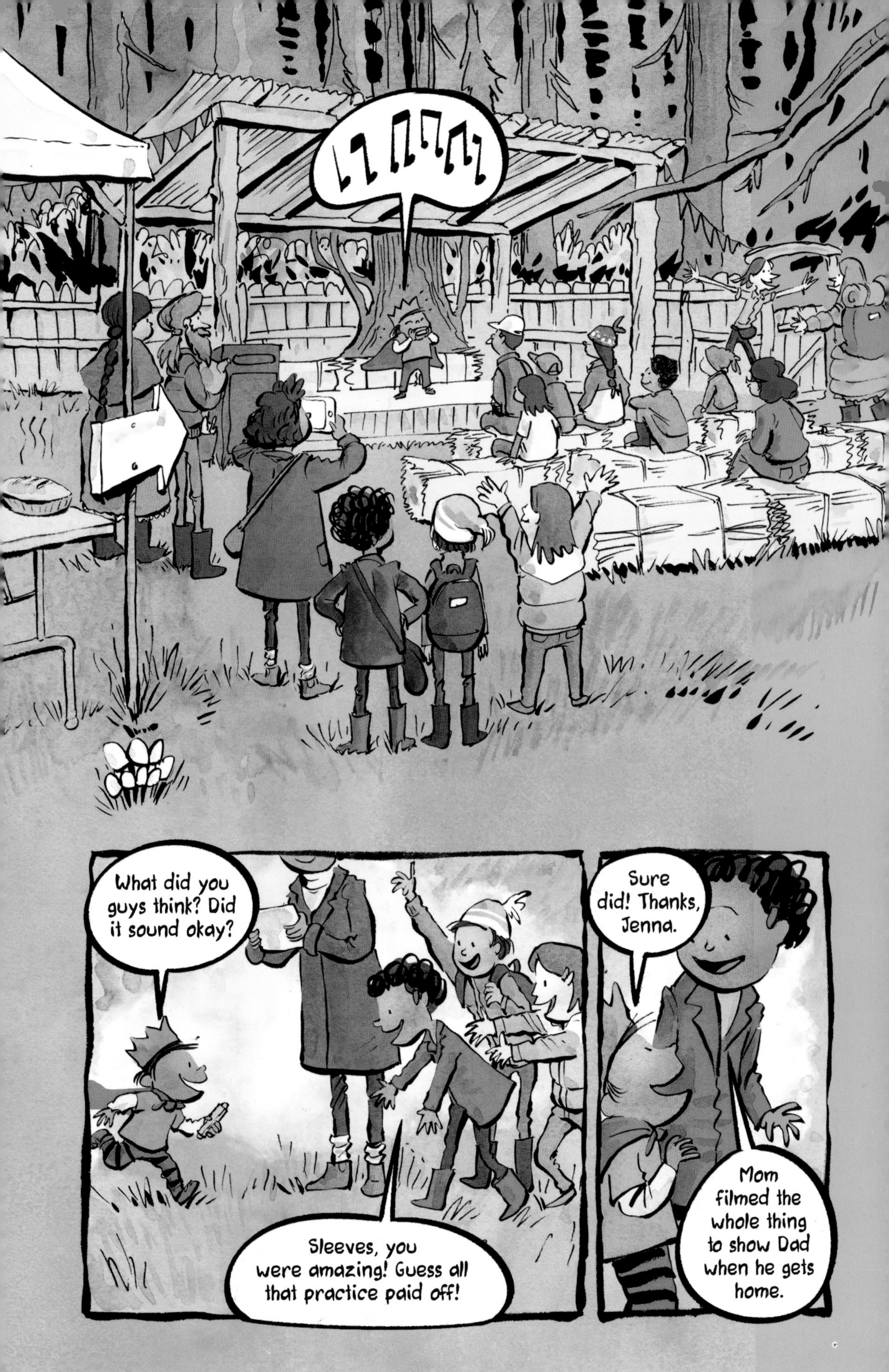
What did you guys think? Did it sound okay?
Sleeves, you were amazing! Guess all that practice paid off!
Sure did! Thanks, Jenna.
Mom filmed the whole thing to show Dad when he gets home.

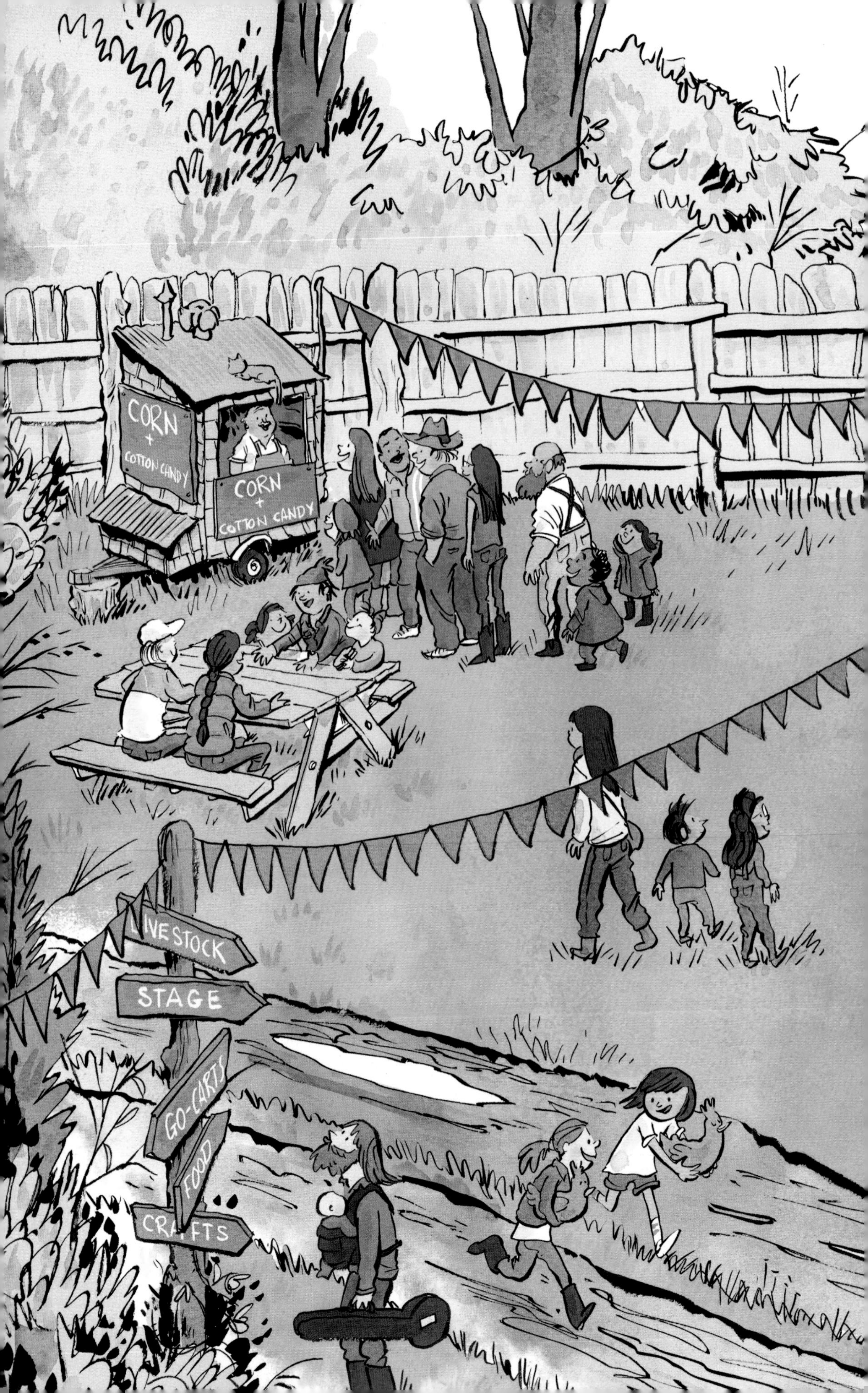
CORN
+
COTTON CANDY
CORN
+
COTTON CANDY
LIVESTOCK
STAGE
GO-CARTS
FOOD
CRAFTS

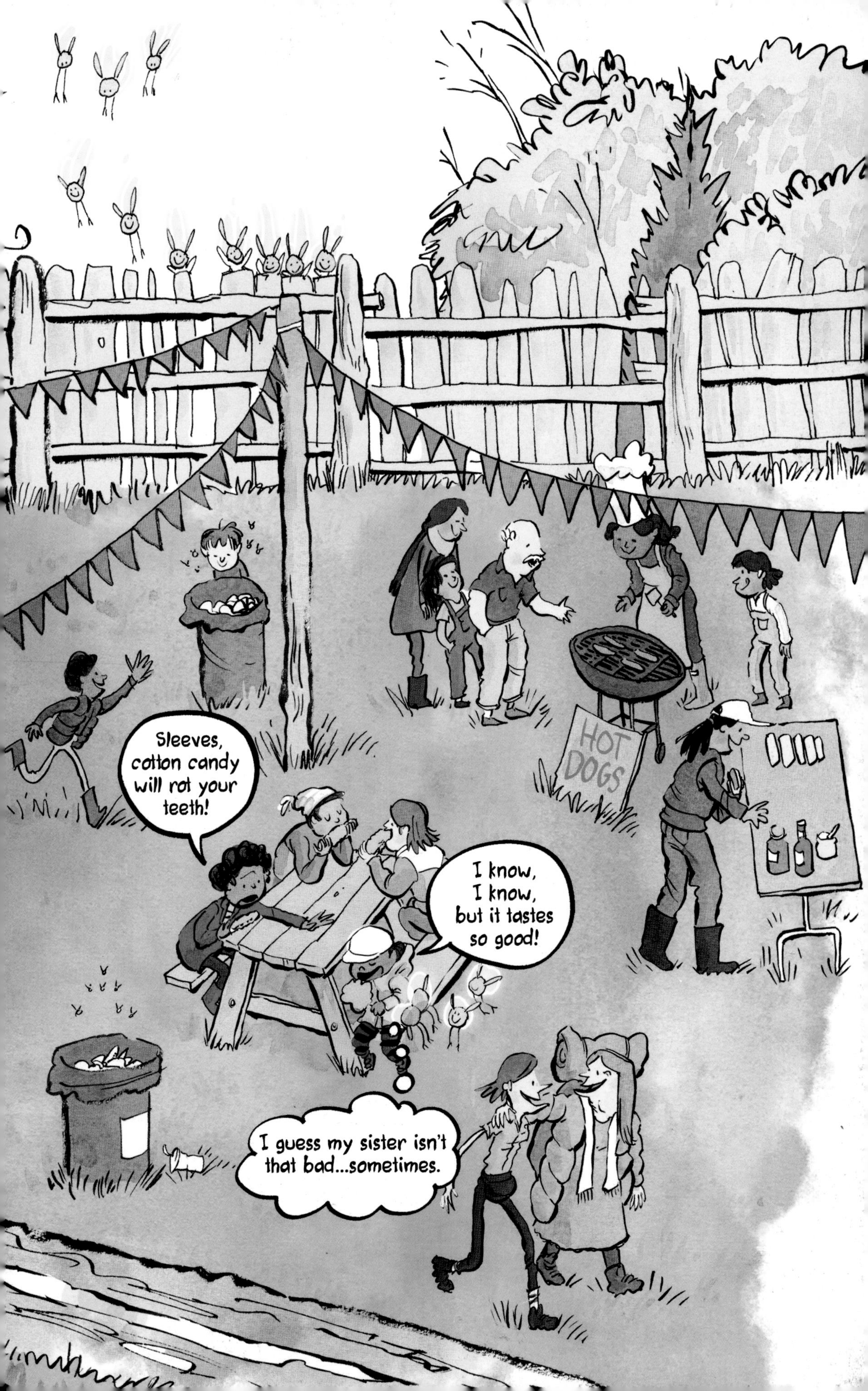
HOT DOGS
Sleeves, cotton candy will rot your teeth!
I know, I know, but it tastes so good!
I guess my sister isn't that bad...sometimes.

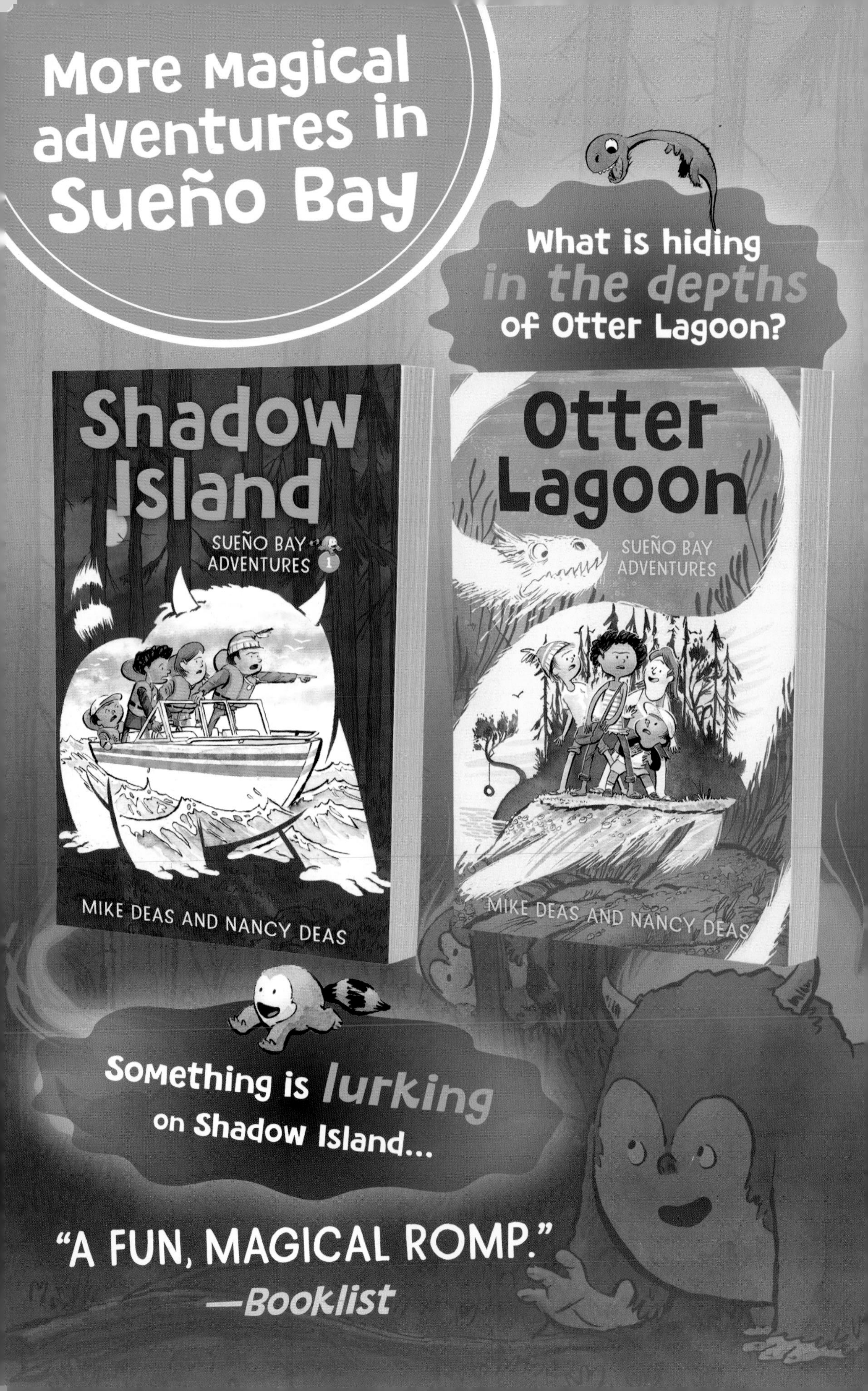
More Magical adventures in Sueño Bay
What is hiding in the depths of Otter Lagoon?
Shadow Island
SUEÑO BAY ADVENTURES 1
MIKE DEAS AND NANCY DEAS
Otter Lagoon
SUEÑO BAY ADVENTURES
MIKE DEAS AND NANCY DEAS
Something is lurking on Shadow Island...
"A FUN, MAGICAL ROMP."
—Booklist

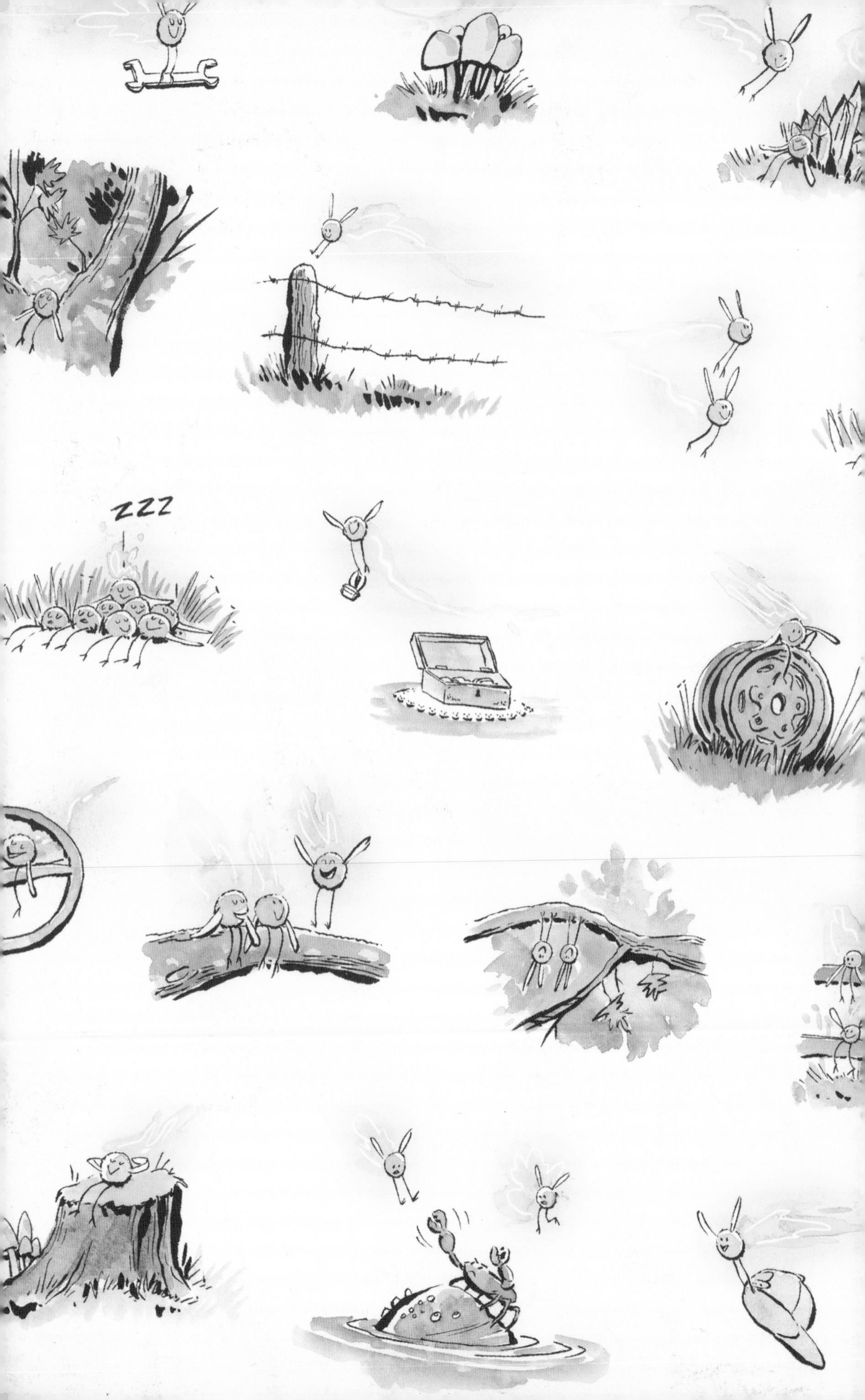
ZZZ

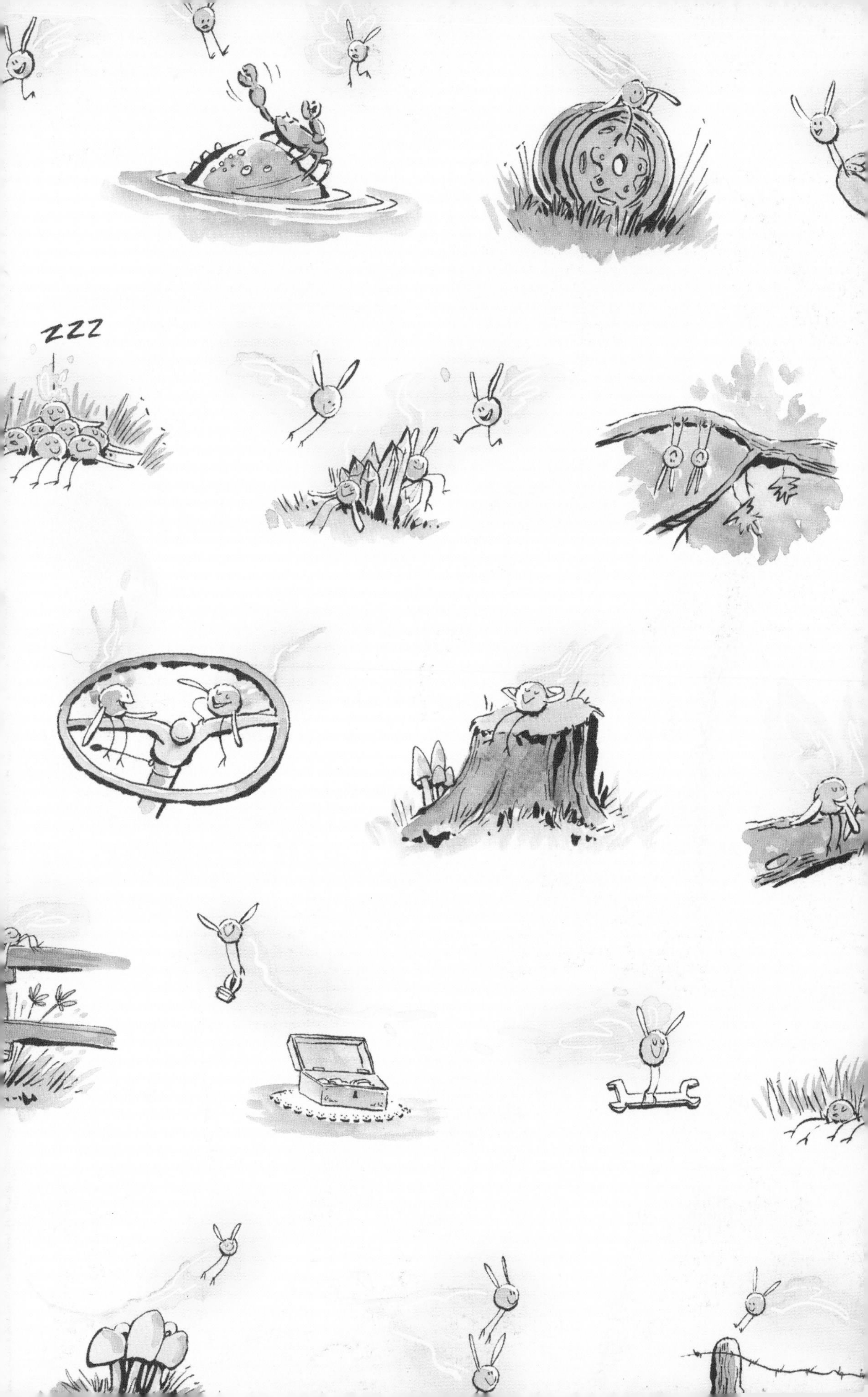
ZZZ

Husband-and-wife team **NANCY** and **MIKE DEAS** enjoyed collaborating on this project. Nancy grew up on a farm on Mayne Island, British Columbia, where she wandered the forests and beaches. She has a great love of travel and adventure. Nancy holds a bachelor of arts from the University of Victoria. Mike is an author/illustrator of graphic novels, including *Dalen and Gole* and the Graphic Guide Adventure series. While he grew up with a love of illustrative storytelling, Capilano College's Commercial Animation program helped Mike fine-tune his drawing skills and imagination. Mike, Nancy and their family live on Salt Spring Island, British Columbia, a magical and mysterious island that inspired Sueño Bay.